The Secret Girl

Book One of The Lonely Raven Trilogy

ERIKA FAIR

CLAY BRIDGES
PRESS

To Alan and Finn, for everything.

"What of the darkness? Is it very fair?"

—Richard Le Gallienne

"Deep into that darkness peering, long I stood there wondering, fearing, Doubting, dreaming dreams no mortal ever dared to dream before..."

—Edgar Allan Poe, "The Raven"

CHAPTER ONE

Fallon Quinn was sniffing a rose-lavender-wood-fire-scented candle with a preconceived notion of doubt when the premonition hit her. She gave a sharp little intake of breath as it flashed violently into her brain. No matter how often they came upon her, year after year, each premonition always took her by surprise. What should have by now been a familiar sensation, was instead forever unexpected and jarring.

As she closed her eyes and focused on inhaling slowly, the blur of colors, motion, and figures in her head gradually cleared and settled into a recognizable picture. She exhaled, squinting in surprised recognition. Most often the people she saw in her premonitions were strangers or passing acquaintances. Rarely she saw loved ones, but there were not many left of that group. Tonight, she was particularly caught off guard by the identity of the main character being shown in her mind's eye—a familiar face, though she'd never actually met him. Bret James had been a big deal twenty years ago, traveling the globe with his wildly popular hard rock band BlueStar. From what she could recall, the band had broken up after much success and hard partying, and possibly one of them had died? Alone in the candle aisle, she did some quick research on her phone. Yes, the guitarist had been killed a decade ago in a drug-fueled motorcycle accident.

But Bret, their flashy wildman of a lead singer, still had an off-and-on mildly successful solo career. He wasn't headlining stadiums anymore, but apparently, he still played clubs and mid-sized venues when he toured, and he managed to sell a healthy number of albums every few years to an aging fan base that remained loyal.

Fallon was surprised. She was a music-lover, and BlueStar had been a definite favorite of hers when she was younger, but she hadn't seen a recent photo or even thought of Bret James in years. And now here he was, in her head, and therefore apparently in some sort of imminent peril.

From her mind's view, she saw that he was sitting in a club—she didn't recognize it, but she assumed it must be nearby—casually drinking and conversing with the people around him. A VIP room, she surmised, filled with too many people. Handsome at fifty, Bret's dark blond hair was still long, and his grey eyes were bright as he flashed that trademark devilish grin she remembered from long ago. Fallon and her brother had seen BlueStar in concert more than once back in the day. She wondered what Luca, if he'd still been alive, would have thought of her current situation.

Straightening the candle on the shelf she'd returned it to, Fallon mused that it truly had smelled curiously like a rosy lavender-infused smoky wood fire. She wandered out of the organic grocery store that was currently one of her favorite haunts, back out into the warm Las Vegas night. It was after ten, and the city was alive with people, traffic, lights, and sounds. She had no affinity for Vegas. It had nothing to offer her, and she was baffled by its popularity, but it had nonetheless been her place of residence for a little over a month now, one more location to check off her list. There were a lot of people in Las Vegas, many of them making poor decisions. It had been a rough several weeks, premonition-wise. Exhausted, she was scheduled to head home in a couple of days, back to the small Texas town that she always returned to, and to her waitressing job, which her boss Diego always faithfully held for her.

On the crowded sidewalk, Fallon wandered with a slight frown, winding her long honey-blond hair up into a messy knot and shifting the strap of the black messenger bag slung across her chest. She wondered where Bret James was, and why he now populated her over-crowded mind. He didn't appear to be in any immediate danger, but her brain fairly thrummed with the warning that this night would prove fatal for him unless she acted quickly.

She tried to spot the name of the club, some hint that would help her identify it, but the room he was in was too busy. A pretty woman in a black lace bustier and barely-there skirt was making obscenely friendly overtures to him, and Fallon wished she could look away, but her mind's vision stayed firmly on him. Often her premonitions would show her other clues, but for now, a live feed of Bret's situation seemed to be all she was being offered.

To her relief, Bret suddenly stood, glancing at his phone, and left the room. She watched as he exited the club through a guarded back door, heading out into, of all places, a dim, lonely side street. Considering his status of being in her mind, this was probably not the smartest of moves. She stopped herself from rolling her eyes. At least he'd left that room. Her mind felt cleaner already. And she'd finally recognized the club, so now she knew where to go. Only a couple of blocks away.

She stopped to shake a small stone from her sandal, then began heading swiftly in Bret's general direction, watching the unalarming scene that was playing out in her head. She still had no sense of the danger, but she realized that now she could actually *feel* where he was; it was odd and unnerving, to sense a subject that strongly. It had never happened before. She tried to pay no attention to this new aspect as she concentrated on figuring out what trouble lay in wait for Mr. James.

For that was her M.O. The unique skillset that had been bestowed on her nearly from birth. When trouble went looking for someone in her vicinity, the universe often alerted Fallon Quinn, and then she had to quickly jump into action, interpret the scene, and come up with a solution. Or what? What if instead she just shrugged and walked away? It didn't matter; something always compelled her to help.

* * * * * *

Bret James took a deep breath of outside air as he stepped away from the back door of the club, noticing a small group of people standing out on the narrow sidewalk. He checked his phone again and saw that Bergen had called him about twenty minutes ago. Though it was after ten-thirty, he called her back, wondering what his seven-year-old daughter was doing up so late and why she hadn't just sent a text. She had obviously wanted to hear his voice.

As he brought the phone up to his ear, he realized one of the men in the group was waving enthusiastically at him. Bret headed towards him with a grin as he recognized one of his oldest and best friends.

Bergen's sweet, sleepy "Daddy!" was in his ear as Tayce Williams greeted him with a strong handshake and a smile. Tall, lanky Tayce was an outstanding guitarist who had been in a rock band called Dangerous Eye during BlueStar's heyday. He was hanging out with two other men, one of whom, Jack Lane, had been quite a popular singer himself back in the day and was now also a solo act like Bret. Dark-haired Jack was dressed all in black and smoking a cigarette, and with him was his current bassist, a young man named Peter. Hanging onto Jack was his assumed conquest for the night, a sharp-eyed brunette who was flirting with everyone present.

Bret motioned to Tayce that he had to finish his phone call, and with a smile, he greeted Bergen, moving several feet away from the unexpected sidewalk reunion. No one else was around, which was a bit of a relief after the high energy going on inside the club. He was tired after a long stretch of being out on the road touring, and hanging out in clubs wasn't really his thing anymore.

It turned out that Bergen had called him because she'd had a "very-bad-horrible-dream," though she wouldn't say what about. To get her mind off of it, he asked her about her day. While she was telling him about a pool party she'd been to, a second voice suddenly cut in, as if someone had crossed onto their phone line.

Go back inside the club.

Bret frowned. "Bergen?"

The child was perplexed at his sudden question, which had absolutely nothing to do with her Very Important Story. "Dad, are you listening to me?" Her voice was slightly accusatory. She was used to having to fight for his attention.

"I am, Bee," he promised.

Go in now. The voice was female and not to be questioned. Bret looked around briefly but saw no one else around. The woman hanging on Jack was busy telling a story.

"Is your mom trying to talk to you?" he asked the child.

"Dad, what are you talking about?"

"Didn't you hear that voice, Bee?"

"No, Dad! So then, when Tom pushed Grace into the pool..."

Bret, hang up with your daughter and go back in the club.

He held the phone away from his ear a moment, looking around. He could tell that no one else was hearing what he was hearing, this voice out of nowhere. And it wasn't on the phone with them. The voice was in his head.

What the hell, he thought, running his fingers through his hair.

You can hear me? There was startled realization in the voice. *Bret! Listen to me, please, I know you think this is crazy, but you have to go back in the club now. There's something bad; I can't explain it. There's a van around the corner, I've got a horrible feeling. Just get back inside.*

"Dad? Are you still there?" Across the miles, Bergen was glaring.

Hang up with her and listen to me, the voice warned, *or you will never hear her voice again.*

Bret's heart stopped for one, cold moment. Dread began welling up within him. "Baby, I have to go sort out something," he told Bergen. "I'm sorry. I'll call you first thing in the morning, alright? I love you. No more bad dreams."

He heard a small, adorable yawn. "'kay, Daddy. Be good. I love you." And she hung up.

He held his phone and pretended to be looking at it, as if possibly reading a text, giving himself a moment to understand what was happening to him. *I'm going crazy, I'm hallucinating,* he thought. *Someone drugged one of my drinks.* He again looked around and again saw nothing.

You're not hallucinating, the voice assured him. *I agree this is unusual, but you've got to listen to...*

I'm not listening to you, he replied in his head, unnerved that he could do so, *until I can see who the hell I'm talking to! Or whatever this is.* He glared at his phone, aware that Tayce had glanced at him a few times since he'd hung up with Bergen.

Step to the side a bit and look around Tayce's left shoulder, the voice instructed.

He hesitated, then took a small step to the side and looked past Tayce. Standing on the sidewalk, yards and yards away, was a young woman, probably in her mid-twenties. Her blond hair was pulled back from her face, and she was wearing ripped, dark grey jeans and a snug, black t-shirt, the strap of her messenger bag slung across her chest. She was coming towards him, but slowly, and she kept looking back over her shoulder. Even at a distance, he could see her lovely face was troubled. She did not, he thought, look like an addict, a con artist, or a party girl out for a good time. There was an intelligence in her expression. A quietness about her. A sadness.

Her voice in his head was filled with urgency, and now he had the facial expressions to go with it. *Bret, there is a blue van around the corner. I don't know what it's going to do, but you don't have a lot of time. All I know is you need to be out of here. Now. I get these feelings. They're never wrong. You're in danger. I know it's ridiculous—trust me, I know. But I'm not making this up.*

I just don't...you're in my head! He stared at her accusingly.

She stopped her approach and bit her lip. *I know. It's usually not this way. But please believe what I'm saying.*

And how did you know I was talking to my daughter?

I could hear the conversation. Her eyes widened in annoyance at the subject change. *Irrelevant! Get back inside that club. You should be able to get Tayce to come with you, but try for the others, too, if you can. Bret, I'm not joking around.* Her voice was growing more agitated. She shot a glance to her right. *The van's starting to move. Please. Just go.* She looked panicked. He saw her clench her fists helplessly.

Instinct and his love for Bergen took over. Bret walked over and nudged Tayce's arm. "Hey, come back inside with me a minute, there's this girl you've got to see. Come on," he pressed, "before she leaves." He extended his invitation to the rest of them.

Tayce, as the mystery girl had suggested, turned readily to accompany him. The other three were not as willing, busy as they were with conversation and the brunette's flirtations.

"Jack, come on, dude," Bret urged, feeling an odd nervousness in his stomach.

"I'll be right back," Jack Lane drawled, handing the woman, Cyn, his latest just-lit cigarette. "Gotta go see what Mr. James is up to."

"You'd better come back right away," Cyn ordered, as she and Peter-the-bassist fell back into their conversation.

Bret hesitated when he saw that those two weren't coming.

Go, she commanded in his head. *They won't follow you, concentrate on Jack and Tayce. You're out of time. Move.*

Without further hesitation, Bret guided Tayce inside the club, looking over his shoulder to check on Jack's lazy progress, feeling nervously ridiculous all the while. The mystery girl, he noticed, was stepping more and more into the shadows, her eyes not leaving him. He blinked as she began to disappear, almost as if she were becoming a shadow herself.

Back inside the club, amid the bright lights and music, Bret admitted to himself that he felt the brief, overwhelming sensation that he'd just dodged a bullet of some sort. He wanted desperately to peek back outside and see if anything was happening, but Tayce was heading over to one of the bars, and Jack was side-tracked talking with a loud group of people. Bret had the strong feeling he needed to stay in with them for the moment.

He joined Tayce at the bar a few minutes later. "Sorry, that girl just left," he apologized, continuing the lie.

"It's alright," said Tayce good-naturedly, raking his fingers through his long brown hair, pushing it away from his face. "I was getting tired of listening to Jack, if you can believe that, and I could use another drink. Haven't seen you in a while, man, how've you been?"

They sat at the bar talking for some time. They hadn't seen each other face-to-face in well over six months due to touring and such, and each had long-considered the other to be one of their best friends. As they talked and laughed out loud, Bret's relief was slowly replaced with a sense of foolishness. What in the hell had he been thinking? Where had that girl gone? If she was so concerned, if there was so much danger lurking, then why hadn't she come in with them? He'd tried to talk to her again—in his head, Lord help him—and there had been only silence. What kind of a fool was he? Drugs in his drink, surely. Damn.

Nearly an hour had passed when Jack finally joined them, frowning at his phone, not entirely steady on his feet. "You believe this? My effing bass player left with that chick." He shook his black hair back from his face and ordered another drink.

"Yeah?" Tayce raised an eyebrow, feeding the drama.

Jack shrugged. He was fairly drunk and somewhat stoned, but he was aware enough to know that his chosen woman for the evening was no longer around. "I don't know. I went out just now, and they're gone. It's strange, though, when I was standing out there calling his phone, I swear I heard it ringing over by the dumpsters down the alley." He drank from his glass. "I did not investigate."

Tayce chuckled, while Jack's dark eyes scanned the room.

Bret felt the strangeness return to his stomach. "Let's go look," he offered, downing the rest of his drink and getting to his feet. "We can give him hell." He had, truly, no desire to ferret out the whereabouts of Jack Lane's wayward bassist and latest hook-up, but alarm bells were going off in his head.

He followed Tayce and Jack back outside, and as he looked around, he saw no van, no mystery girl. No sign of Peter and Cyn. The street was empty.

Jack tried Peter's phone again, and they all heard the definite answering ringtone from the area of the dumpsters. They drew closer, calling for Peter and throwing out joking comments. But they found no one, and eventually, they stood still and just listened.

"It's coming from inside the dumpster," deduced Tayce with a puzzled frown.

"Peter wouldn't throw away his phone," said Jack dismissively. "He never lets that thing out of his sight."

"Maybe your chick got mad at him and threw it in," Tayce suggested.

Jack shook his head. "I'm telling you that he'd be in there right now digging for it if she had."

There was a long, awkward moment of not knowing quite what to do. A knot was forming in Bret's stomach.

Finally, Jack turned to leave, swaying a bit, but expertly righting himself. "Well, he obviously knows it's there. Or not. I'm not fishing it out for him, either way, and I can't hang around all night babysitting his ass. If he did lose it, at least I can tell him where to look."

They headed back into the club, and Jack turned towards the VIP room with a replacement woman in his sights, but Tayce and Bret returned to the bar.

"You look like you saw a ghost out there," Tayce observed, as they sat down and ordered fresh drinks. "You alright?" His brown eyes watched Bret with genuine concern.

Bret was staring into space. He was shaken, and he had to say something. "It's the weirdest thing. I'll be honest with you. When we were standing out there earlier, before I asked you to come in with me, I just suddenly got this horrible feeling. Like something bad was about to happen. Don't ask—it's never happened before. But it came on real strong, and I had this singular thought that we all needed to be back inside the club." He shrugged and sipped his drink. "So, I made it up about that woman you needed to see." He shook his head. "Crazier by the minute, that's me, man. I'm sorry. The tour is taking its toll on my mind."

Tayce laughed easily. "Well, whatever. I told you I was tired of listening to Jack. It was a win-win situation for me." He drank some of his whiskey. "Strange about Peter's phone though."

CHAPTER TWO

Two days later, Bret was standing in the southern California sun in his long, curving driveway, watching his daughter ride the BMX bike she'd both requested and received as an early birthday present. He couldn't believe Bergen was going to be eight next month. The years were flying by, just as everyone had warned. He was happy to be home from the tour with her for a few days, but he was distracted with continuing thoughts of the mystery girl from Vegas. Now, in broad daylight and with a clearer mind, he was having a hard time believing the conversation in his head had actually happened, but what other explanation was there? And, strangely, the absence of her voice was almost uncomfortable, like something was now missing that he hadn't missed before. At times he wondered if he had imagined the whole thing, but regardless, he couldn't stop thinking about her.

As he was standing there absently watching Bergen, his phone rang with a call from Tayce, and after some initial small talk, Tayce finally mentioned what he'd called for.

"Hey, remember the other night in Vegas?"

"Yeah?" Bret grinned at Bergen as she topped a hill and hit air for a second, after which she flashed him the two-fingered rock-and-roll sign and stuck out her tongue in a devilish fashion. Her mother, Lisbeth, shook her head but smiled, pleased she'd insisted on a helmet. And elbow pads. The neighbor's dog was chasing after Bergen with enthusiasm.

"I didn't know if you'd heard," Tayce went on, "that Peter and that woman went missing that night?"

"Missing?"

"Yeah, man. Peter still hasn't turned up."

Bret frowned. "Peter hasn't? You mean the woman did turn up?"

Tayce hesitated uncomfortably. "Her name was Cynthia Woodard. They found her body yesterday morning in the desert. Some guy walking his dog near a rest stop found her. She'd been shot once in the head."

Everything went out of focus for a moment. Bergen, Lisbeth, the dog, the sunshine and the driveway.

"What?!"

"No one saw them after we left them on the sidewalk, man. No one. The next morning Jack finally had to call the cops, because they were scheduled to head to Denver for a show, and it apparently isn't like Peter to go MIA like this. That, coupled with his cell-phone being in the dumpster—the woman's phone was in there, too. And apparently, the cops found a burned-out van abandoned in the desert, they think it's connected, it was seen in the area or something. From what I read, there aren't any prints or anything, and the guy it's registered to is out of the country and didn't know it had been stolen. But there's zero sign of Peter. He's just gone."

The cold, hard knot returned to Bret's stomach and the earth seemed to drop out from under him. He sat down heavily on a large rock as Lisbeth eyed him curiously from a distance.

He thought about everything from the night in Vegas. The blond girl saying he would never hear Bergen again if he remained outside. Cyn clinging to Jack, ordering him to return, while Peter laughed with her. He watched now as his beautiful child, who shared his long dark blond hair and grey eyes, shrieked with laughter as the dog tried to tackle her.

"Hey, man."

Bret came back to himself. "Tayce. Sorry."

"No, look, it's obviously freaked me out some, too. I haven't said anything, about what you told me about having a bad feeling and needing to go back inside the club. And I won't, I mean, that's your deal. Jack was too stoned to remember why the three of us went back in. But, umm...thanks. Thanks for getting me to go back in with you. I don't know what the hell happened, or anything. But I get the feeling that if I'd been out there... I don't know. Just thanks."

"Let me know if you hear anything else."

Tayce promised he would, and they hung up.

Lisbeth joined Bret on the rock, the smooth surface warm from the sun, the mingling scents of jasmine and plumeria wafting around her on the gentle breeze. "What's up?" she asked.

Bret stared at her a moment, taking in her long, willowy body, golden brown hair, big dark eyes. He still loved her after all this time, but he loved most that she was such a good mother to Bergen. Things hadn't worked out between them as lovers, due mostly to his lifestyle at the time, but they were excellent together as friends and parents.

"Did you hear about Jack Lane's bassist, Peter Stillson, being missing?" he asked. A former model, she'd been a part of his life for long enough that his friends and acquaintances in the rock world were often a part of her world as well.

She nodded. "My girlfriend was telling me about it earlier. Strangest thing. And they found that woman's body. Well, there's no way anyone who knows Peter thinks he did it, right? I wonder where he is and what happened."

"I was there with him that night, outside the club. Just before he vanished, apparently."

Her gaze upon him sharpened, her body leaning forward.

He told her the same thing he'd told Tayce, that he'd gotten a bad feeling and convinced Tayce and Jack to go back inside. Again, he left out the bit about the girl talking to him in his head.

Lisbeth slid an arm loosely around him. "Oh, hon, that's strange." She squeezed him gently. "Thank goodness for you and your feelings."

He smiled weakly.

* * * * * * *

Just after eleven that night, Fallon zipped up her dark grey travel backpack and surveyed the tiny apartment. It was now bare but for the furniture it had come with. All that was left out was her laptop on the coffee table and her messenger bag on the couch. She sat down cross-legged on the floor and opened the laptop. Sipping a cup of hot jasmine tea, she let her hair loose from its ponytail and reviewed the searches she'd been making while she packed.

The young bassist, Peter Stillson, was still missing. He was dead, she was sure of it, or else he would be soon. The evil she'd felt coming from the van, plus Cyn's body being discovered... Peter would not be found alive.

With a small sigh, she closed that page and focused on the other pages she'd had open: Bret James' official website and a general search for his name. She wasn't sure why she was doing this. Whenever she was able to steer someone away from danger, she never looked back. Never so much as gave herself a mental high-five. Whether she succeeded or failed in her attempt, when the gig was over, she always turned away, and her "subject" faded from her mind and her memory. It was a necessary trick.

But Bret and everything about that night, even secondary characters Tayce Williams and Jack Lane, were sticking defiantly in her head, demanding attention. Especially Bret—what was going on there? The only other person she'd ever shared a telepathic connection with had been dead for nine years. Such a link had never existed with anyone else. Why Bret James, of all the unlikely people?

She was surprised to see how much of a career he still had going, and again wondered why she hadn't known this. She still listened to old BlueStar music, but for whatever reason the solo doings of Bret James had not been on her radar for the past decade. She could see from his website that he was almost done with a lengthy tour. There was a recent photo of him with his pretty daughter, as well as some pictures of Bret with various fellow musicians and a few non-music celebrities. He really had gotten more handsome with age, she mused.

Before she knew it, two hours had gone by, her tea had grown cold, her neck had developed a painful crick, and she had read every magazine article and news posting having to do with Bret James for the past five years. She'd even watched some video interviews and performances on YouTube. She was very nearly ashamed of herself.

Her accidental research showed her he was much changed from his days of raising hell as a young man. He seemed like a nice enough guy, not at all pretentious, someone you could sit in a bar and drink a beer with. A present father. Happy. Down-to-earth. Quite a healthy ego, but then, it was often impossible to make it big in the artistic world without an ego. He seemed to be into running, which she approved of, being a regular runner herself.

She pulled herself to a screeching halt. This man, this stranger, needed to be out of her head, and that wasn't going to be accomplished through intensive fangirl research. With a growl, she snapped the laptop shut. Time for bed. Her flight home was in nine hours.

In the tiny apartment's single bathroom, she viciously brushed her teeth, then turned out the lights and crawled into bed. But her mind would not be still, and she felt unusually lonely. Out of habit, she turned the brass ring she always wore, round and round on her left ring finger, rubbing her thumb against the raw labradorite stone.

She thought briefly of reaching out to Bret's mind, just for the company. After so long, it had been nice to be able to talk to someone in her head again. But what would she say to him? "Hi, remember me?" He would probably be driving somewhere and be so startled, he'd run off the road.

She closed her eyes tight and willed herself to sleep.

CHAPTER THREE

(Eighteen Months Later)

Bret leaned back in his chair and laughed out loud at something that had just been said. Their waitress, a cute, giggly young woman named Casi, was taking their dessert orders. Tayce Williams grinned as he studied the menu, rubbing his goatee thoughtfully.

Tayce and Bret were dining that evening with Paul and Katrine Crist in a tiny town about an hour or so outside of Dallas, Texas. The quaint little restaurant, Solu, operated out of the downstairs of an old two-story Victorian house.

Paul Crist had been the lead singer of Dangerous Eye, Tayce's old band. He and Tayce still got together now and then to reminisce, reconnect, and write new material. When they were ready to record, the other two members of Dangerous Eye were dug up out of happy obscurity and dragged into the studio. Afterwards, Dangerous Eye would hit the road for a brief but enjoyable tour.

Paul and Katrine owned a picturesque farm just outside of town, and Tayce was currently staying with them for several weeks so that he and Paul could write and record in Paul's fully-equipped on-site studio. Bret had been in Dallas for a couple of days to perform at a music festival with his solo band, so when Tayce called and invited him out for dinner with old friends, he'd readily accepted.

The restaurant, Solu, was enchanting. Most of the tables were inside in several downstairs rooms, but there were a few tables out on a large, screened-in back porch, replete with paper lanterns fluttering in the breeze, tiny lights strung here and there, candles on the tables, and flowering vines wafting their sweet scents through the screens. It was early spring, and the Texas weather was still pleasant in the evenings. Music reminiscent of an old French café streamed from speakers in the wall. Paul and Katrine came to Solu quite often, and whenever they had guests along, Solu's owner, Diego Sanchez, usually let them have the back porch to themselves for privacy. Tonight was no different.

After she'd finished taking their orders and cleared away a few empty wine bottles, spunky Casi reappeared, empty-handed and bright-eyed in a short black skirt and tight orange t-shirt. Tayce eyed her approvingly and wondered how old she was.

"I'm leaving early tonight, guys," she announced. "Fallon will bring your desserts out. She'll take care of you for the rest of the night; I'm sorry it won't be me." She looked reluctant, for she was quite smitten with Bret and Tayce, and was cursing her luck that she had to turn them over to Fallon.

The guys all made a big show of not wanting to let her go, which pleased her to no end, and Tayce got a kiss on the cheek, but finally she was gone.

Bret had thought about asking her for a cup of coffee before she left, but hadn't wanted to delay her when she was clearly on her way out. He turned his attention back to his friends. "The food here is excellent," he commented, glancing around, and feeling both relaxed and happy, his stomach pleasantly full, his head mildly buzzy with the wine they'd been enjoying. "I admit, I'm a little surprised." The town they were in, Gray, was quite small. Though sometimes on the road he'd discovered a gem or two here and there, for the most part, through the years, he'd found small town dining to be extremely lacking.

"We like it a lot; it's definitely our favorite in the area," Katrine told him, tucking a long lock of wavy chestnut hair behind her ear. Probably somewhere in her mid-forties, from Bret's best guess, Katrine was a flower-child/mother earth-type who wore little makeup and exuded a warm, peaceful energy. Bret had met her only once before that he could recall. He hadn't seen Paul in years, and couldn't remember when he and Katrine had gotten married. They seemed to have a close, loving relationship, and Bret was enjoying their company.

"There's also a Mexican place here in town that's alright," she continued, "not great, we mostly go there for the salsa and the drinks. But those are the only two restaurants here in Gray. Well, there is a café on the edge of town, but..." she shook her head in distaste. "For anything else, you have to go north to Dutton or all the way to the Dallas suburbs. In a town as small as Gray, we're lucky we have any choices at all. When Tayce is here, we usually go to the Mexican place, Madrigal, for drinks, but we do love coming here and having the porch all to ourselves, like royalty. Diego is very good to us. Solu always seems to have a magical atmosphere."

Her husband smiled fondly at her.

When the new waitress came out with their tray of desserts, Bret caught a glimpse of blond and black out of the corner of his eye, but he did not immediately look up.

And then, as she set Katrine's cheesecake in front of her and said, "Here you are, Kat. I had them add extra raspberry drizzle for you," Bret stiffened, feeling something like a vise close around his heart. He could not breathe.

"That's my girl," praised Katrine happily.

Paul was smiling up at her as his chocolate torte was set before him. "Nice to see you tonight, Fallon. How are you?"

Bret raised his eyes unwillingly to watch her as she moved over to Tayce and set a slice of lightly-iced lemon-strawberry pound cake in front of him. Long, honey-blond hair. Green eyes that were now staring serenely back at him as she moved closer to him. He struggled to breathe.

"Oh, I'm lovely," Fallon replied. "A distinct lack of idiots in the house tonight." Her voice held a touch of sarcasm, and the Crists laughed as if at a private joke. "I brought you some coffee and a few of Mariana's sugar cookies," Fallon said to Bret, "since you ordered no dessert." She smiled a crooked little smile. "On the house."

He couldn't find his voice, and he couldn't look away from her.

The other two men focused on their desserts. It was only Katrine who noticed the sudden change in Bret. His silence.

Fallon set the coffee and a small plate of three simple cookies in front of him. "Would you like me to bring cream and sugar?"

Bret nodded. It was all he could do. He usually drank his coffee black, but he wanted an immediate reason for her to return.

Fallon glanced at everyone else. "Anyone need anything? No?" She looked at Bret. "I'll be right back."

Paul and Tayce continued to tear happily into their desserts. Katrine was thoughtfully savoring her cheesecake, casting a glance now and again at Bret.

He sat with his steaming cup of coffee and stared into space. Though he appeared calm, deep inside he was staggering from the shock of seeing her—this ghost from his past he'd thought to never meet again. Who he'd half-imagined had never been real to begin with.

Fallon returned with a little blue and white ceramic pitcher of milk and a bowl of sugar packets, and this time he was watching for her when she came through the wooden screen door onto the porch. She was light on her feet, smiling, confident in a short black skirt and snug, long-sleeved black shirt. Athletic-looking, her skin was lightly tanned and her bare legs toned. She was quite pretty, and just as in Vegas, he saw the intelligence in her face, the otherworldliness.

After she'd set the milk and sugar near him, she stood there at the table between him and Katrine, inches away, and looked around at everyone. There was, for Bret, a brief electric moment where his senses all seemed heightened. The breeze was blowing pleasantly, ruffling his hair. From the hidden speakers, Madeleine Peyroux duskily crooned an old tune. Fallon was so close; he could detect a faint citrus scent. She was holding her small, round tray on its side, her left hand hidden from view of everyone but him. Without thinking, he reached out and touched her fingers, as if to check that she was not an apparition. *I'm real.*

That voice, the one he hadn't heard in a year and a half, was back in his mind, and it felt so familiar, so like a homecoming, that he caught his breath and blinked back tears. As if he'd been waiting for that voice for all his life.

She looked down at him, holding his gaze, and touched a hand lightly to his shoulder for the briefest of moments. A wave of calm washed over him, his nerves immediately settling back down. "You guys let me know if you need anything. I'll be back to check on you." And then she was gone.

"She's gorgeous," commented Tayce, who despite his seemingly full attention to the cake was never one to miss a pretty face. "Why haven't I seen her here before? Is she new? I need her in my life."

Paul shook his head. "Fallon has been here since Solu opened six or so years ago. I would say she's Diego's most-trusted employee, by far. She works fairly regularly. Though sometimes a whole month or two will go by when we don't see her. When we ask, she says she travels. She says, 'But then, like a ladybug, I always fly away home.' She's always used that phrase, it's sweet. She's extremely private, but never anything less than friendly."

"All the staff are usually nice, but she's definitely our favorite," added Katrine, still eyeing Bret surreptitiously. "We like to consider her something of a friend. I even have her number in my phone, which felt like a major coup when it happened. She's been out to the farm a couple of times to go running on the trails with her dog. We often request her when we're bringing people here for the first time because she's such a gem. I requested her for tonight, Bret, since you had never been here before, but she hadn't begun her shift yet when we arrived. Tayce, I honestly don't know how you've missed her, as often as you've eaten at Solu over the years. Odd. I suppose she's always been away."

Bret was quietly in misery. Fallon. There was so much he wanted to ask her. The fact he could not sit her down and talk to her openly right now was killing him. It was unbelievable that all this time he'd been wondering about her, wishing for some idea as to her whereabouts, she'd been right here in this magical restaurant, serving wine and desserts to Paul and Katrine Crist. Visiting their farm. He felt strangely cheated they'd been able to enjoy her all this time, and he had not.

But he didn't know this girl, knew nothing, in fact, about her beyond that she was apparently a waitress at Solu and could talk to him in his head. And really, wasn't that enough?

When they were done with their desserts, Fallon reappeared to gather up their plates. Paul touched her arm as she came near him. "Fallon, forgive me for not doing so earlier. Let me introduce you to our good friends, Tayce Williams and Bret James. Though, as I know where your music appreciation lies, I suspect you may have already known who they are."

Fallon smiled at Tayce and Bret in turn. "Of course. I could go home right now and dig out my Dangerous Eye and BlueStar door posters from decades ago and embarrass everyone present."

Everyone but Bret laughed. He watched her, still taking her in, the realness of her.

"She's threatened the door poster thing before," Paul reassured them. "So far she's never delivered."

"Nice to meet you, Fallon," greeted Tayce. "I understand I've missed you over the years." He cocked an eyebrow. "We must make up for lost time."

"Oh, we must," Fallon agreed, winking at him. Then she glanced from Tayce to Paul. "So, more wine, or are we seriously drinking tonight?"

It was a good night. They were all enjoying themselves, the atmosphere and the company, despite Bret's inner chaos.

Tayce slapped the table. "I don't know what it means, but I think we're seriously drinking."

Paul nodded agreement, meeting Fallon's eyes for confirmation.

Fallon pointed at Tayce. "That one's trouble," she told Paul.

"Don't I know it," he acknowledged with a long-suffering sigh.

She looked questioningly at Katrine. "Vodka tonic?"

Katrine nodded. "Extra lime slices, please."

"Of course." Fallon turned to Bret.

"More coffee," he requested wryly, and she suppressed what he was sure was a grin. With the whirlwind his mind was in now, he couldn't imagine drinking any more alcohol tonight.

"Hey, wait, beautiful," Tayce stopped her as she turned to go. She paused, amused. "Yes?"

Tayce leaned back in his chair and graced her with a cocky grin and a mischievous glint in his brown eyes. "Why don't you join us?" he invited. "As you can see, our numbers are clearly skewed. One to three."

She tilted her head. "I do have other tables besides yours. Contrary to what you may believe. And table eight is waiting for drinks."

Paul looked up at her. "Send Diego back here. Please."

She rolled her eyes, smiling, and went away with a nod.

Diego Sanchez was in his early thirties, a devoted family man and shrewd businessman. He was grinning when he joined the group on the porch. "Paul, Katrine, everything is good tonight?"

"Excellent, as always," Paul assured him. "We'd like to acquire Fallon as our exclusive waitress for the rest of the evening. What's it going to take?"

"Have you taken Miss Fallon's wishes into consideration?" Diego asked, chuckling. "Shouldn't be a problem. Tonight is not the busiest of nights. I'll see what I can do."

Back inside near the cash register, Diego pulled Fallon and another waitress, Tessa, into a huddle. "Fal, how many tables do you have inside?"

"Just eight and four."

He looked at Tessa. "You can take them?"

Tessa popped her gum in resignation, flipping aside her long brunette ponytail. "You mean the aging rockstars want her to themselves?"

Fallon winked at her. "You can have my tips."

"Done." Tessa gave her a smile that lit her pretty eyes.

Diego pointed at Tessa. "Gum. Out." Then he patted their shoulders and left them to sort it out.

After updating Tessa on the status of her two indoor tables, Fallon grabbed an unopened bottle of Jack Daniels and two glasses in one hand, and placed the vodka tonic, coffee and a bottle of sparkling water on a tray, then returned to the porch. "I'm all yours."

There were cheers and more laughter, and Tayce pulled up a chair for her between Bret and himself.

"You know, you remind me of someone," Tayce told her, as she distributed the drinks and handed Bret his coffee.

"Your wife, perhaps?" she asked, setting aside her tray and dropping lightly into the chair with her bottle of sparkling water.

Everyone laughed at that, even Bret. Even Tayce, who shook his head with a sigh. "No," he said, "definitely not my wife."

"I'm sorry," Fallon said soothingly, shaking her head as he offered her his glass of whiskey to share. "You would have had far better luck with Casi. I'm highly allergic to married men." She squeezed a lemon slice into her water bottle, then shook it up a little.

"How did you know I was married?" he asked, examining his hands and confirming that he wasn't wearing his ring.

She leaned back in her chair and considered him. "I have a sixth sense for that kind of thing."

"You have a sixth sense for anything else?" Bret asked mildly.

She turned her head and stared at him. "Maybe you'll find out," she murmured. Then she took a sip of the water and leaned forward to ask Katrine how things were going at the farm.

An hour passed quickly, the camaraderie of the group running high. With effort, Bret was able to set aside his mixed-up feelings and appear sociable, but he remained tense. He and Fallon did not say another word to each other, though they exchanged a number of glances.

Fallon was at ease with all of them, flirting teasingly with Tayce and joking around with Paul and Katrine. Bret saw, as Paul had pointed out, that she could say a lot without revealing anything real about herself. He tried several times to talk to her in her head, but each time she gave a slight shake of her head, as if warning him off. His level of frustration increased.

"Why aren't you drinking anything stronger than water?" Tayce asked Fallon accusingly.

She laughed. "I am still technically on the clock. Diego is the coolest boss ever, but he's not that cool."

"I heard that, *mija*," Diego called from the other side of the screened door. He came out, carrying a replacement vodka tonic for Katrine. She thanked him, and he was gone again.

At midnight, Diego leaned out the door. "We're closing, but you guys can stay out here as long as you want. Fallon needs to settle your bill, though."

"We'll be out of here soon," Paul promised him. "Thank you, as always."

Diego nodded and then disappeared.

Fallon had gotten to her feet. "Katrine, coffee?"

Katrine nodded, and Fallon went back inside the restaurant.

About a minute after she'd left, Bret headed inside to the restroom, his head swimming with a blur of thoughts. As he was coming back out, he saw Fallon alone at the computer, printing out the tab, and he joined her.

"I'll get it." He held out his credit card.

She glanced at him. "Are you sure?"

"Of course. I knew I'd have to beat Paul to it." He waited while she ran the charges through, and then he signed for it on an electronic pad. She put it away, and then turned towards him, not meeting his eyes. He thought she was showing the first signs of being nervous. They were standing in a hall near a roped-off wooden staircase that led to the second floor. "What's up there?" he asked, weighted down by the general awkwardness of the situation.

"Diego lives up there. With his wife, Mariana, and their three little kids." Still, she would not look at him.

He was like an explosive about to detonate; the pressure had built to a point he could no longer stand. He grabbed her arm and pulled her close, lowering his voice. "What the hell is going on? Who are you? Why am I seeing you again? What happened to Peter and that woman? Why can I hear you in my head? What in the hell happened that night in Vegas?"

She pulled her arm out of his tight grasp, rubbing the reddened flesh. "Bret, this isn't the place..."

"Do you know what happened to them?" he asked in a fierce whisper.

"No!"

"You could be lying. Why should I believe you? You could have been involved."

"If I had been involved," she countered gravely, "why did I fight to get you out of harm's way? And Jack and Tayce?"

He shook his head. "I don't know. But what are the chances of you and I running into each other again? In another state? In a ridiculously out-of-the-way place when I just happen to also have Tayce along with me? Can you tell the future? What are you?"

There had been so many questions he'd wanted to ask her. He'd been thinking of them for a year and a half, making a long mental list, imagining that one day they might sit down and discuss it over tea or coffee. This was not going at all how he'd planned. He was so scared of losing her, of her slipping away like she'd done in Vegas, that it all came pouring out, including his frustration and fear. He was bullying her; he knew it. And she was getting angry.

She pulled away from him again, after he'd unconsciously grabbed her arm a second time. "I'm going to leave now." Her tone was cold and steady. "Tell them I'm sorry I didn't say goodbye, but there is an emergency I must attend to." She turned and started walking away.

Panic rose up in him. "No, Fallon, wait..."

But she was fast, and knew her way through the old house. She slipped into the kitchen and out a side door, and by the time he'd caught up, she was in a black car speeding away into the night. He momentarily considered jumping into his own car and following her, but he stopped himself. Everyone in the kitchen was staring at him.

Bret could barely make himself return to the back porch. "I'm going to call it a night, guys. I truly had a wonderful evening, thank you."

Paul and Katrine voiced their concern at his sudden departure, and despite his assurances to the contrary, they both thought to themselves that he looked out of sorts. Paul shook hands with him and Katrine gave him a big hug.

"You and Fallon leaving together?" Tayce teased.

Bret smiled faintly. "No. She had to leave, she said she's sorry she didn't get to say goodbye." Then with one last wave, he was gone.

Katrine turned and frowned at her husband.

Paul frowned back, humoring her. "What?"

"Something's going on."

"And what would that be, Kit-Kat?" Tayce asked. "He didn't look like a man who was about to take that lovely girl back to his hotel with him."

"No, I agree with you. But there's something... something there." She shook her head. "I don't know."

CHAPTER FOUR

Bret was weary and defeated as he returned to his Dallas hotel room after midnight. Disappearing into a long, hot shower, he let the water wash the tension from his body. Once out of the shower, he pulled on a pair of loose black shorts and crawled into bed with a yawn. He turned on the TV, opening a cold bottle of water from the mini-fridge. Lazily, he responded to some texts and scrolled through social media. In the old days, it would have been a beer in his hand, no question, but he'd had quite a bit to drink at Solu before Fallon's appearance on the scene, and he did try to limit his alcohol intake, especially on days when he had not been able to work out. Bergen's birth had instilled in him a penchant for healthy living, and he had maintained it more or less successfully for nearly a decade now.

Not too many minutes later, he faintly heard something like a knock on his hotel room door. He muted the television, not sure what he'd heard. The knock came again, and he swung his legs over the edge of the bed and went to check. He peered out the peephole, and then immediately threw open the door.

Fallon was standing there before him, looking beautiful and miserable, still in her work clothes. A familiar black messenger bag hung from a strap across her chest.

I'm ready to talk. Her voice rang sweetly in his head as she met his eyes.

He stepped back to let her in, closing and locking the door behind her with the vague feeling he had just captured a rare creature. Fallon paused a moment to survey the room, dimly lit by only one lamp and the silent television, and then she went over and perched on the edge of the firm sofa. She set her bag on the floor near her feet and clasped her hands as if they needed to be steadied.

Bret was pulling on a grey t-shirt. "You want something to drink?" he asked, wondering how this was going to go. He turned off the TV.

She nodded. "Water?"

When he'd handed her a bottle of cold water, he dropped down into a chair directly across from her. Despite his uncertainty, he was overwhelmed with something like happy relief to have her sitting here before him, no one to interrupt them. A great weight had been lifted from his heart, which now fluttered with anticipation. "I'm sorry about how I acted tonight," he apologized, ashamed.

But she was kind. "Coming face-to-face with each other in that way wasn't something either of us could have anticipated, and you're completely in the dark about what's going on. Understandably, there was going to be some frustration, especially seeing me and not being able to discuss things with me right away. But I couldn't let you talk to me in front of them at Solu, in our minds." She tilted her head. "Do you understand?

You aren't used to it, so you don't know how to keep your facial expressions from accidentally revealing that there is an entire conversation going on in your head. You aren't familiar with it. They all would have noticed. I didn't want to draw anyone's attention. Do you see? I wasn't trying to be cruel."

He admitted that her words made sense. "I see. I didn't at the time, but I can see that now. I was a little overwhelmed," he added dryly.

She nodded as she sipped her water, and then took a deep breath, setting the bottle aside. "I know you have hundreds of questions," she acknowledged, "so I think I'll just dive right in and see how many of them I can answer simply by telling you a little of my backstory. Then afterwards..." She lifted her shoulders in a slight shrug, and he nodded agreement.

"I get premonitions. I've had this gift, curse, ability— whatever you want to call it—since I was born, though I didn't recognize it for what it was until I was six years old. It's sometimes called 'second sight.' I involuntarily receive visions of the future that show me a person and the danger that they're about to be in. Sometimes that person is about to die. Sometimes there is only injury—it could be physical, mental or emotional. At times, it's a very simple problem; other times, it's complex and devastating. It varies. What I see in my head can be specific—I'll know exactly what's going to happen to someone. Other times it's just a strong feeling, like with you in Vegas: I knew you were in danger, that you were going to die. Eventually I figured out that something was wrong about the van, and about you being out on the street. It could have been that the van was going to run you down by accident, I didn't know. I still don't for sure.

"Clearly we know now the people in the van kidnapped Peter and Cyn, and I assume they would have taken and/or killed the rest of you as well, but I don't know." She was frowning. "It sounds a little far-fetched, doesn't it? And it's just my own private speculation. Why would anyone do such a thing to you guys? To you? You were the only one I saw in my vision, but Peter and Cyn are gone, there's no denying that. Something horrible did happen to them. My visions are never incorrect, they just don't always cover all the necessary parties." She retrieved the bottle and took another sip of water. Her hand was shaking.

The dull buzz of the air-conditioner and the occasional slam of a door down the hall were secondary to Bret as he listened to her, leaning forward with his arms resting on his knees, not wanting to miss a single word.

"When I was little," she went on, "it was scary to have these visions and bad feelings. It took a long time for me to see what they were, to learn how to handle them, how to use them. I got better at it as I got older, and I had my brother Luca to help me. At this point in my life, it's second nature, though that doesn't mean it's easy for me. Sometimes I'm able to steer people to safety without them knowing that I did it. Sometimes I try to appeal to their better judgement. Often people think I'm crazy or simply don't believe me. That's why it's always a relief when I can change the course of events without letting the person know I did anything at all."

She looked into his grey eyes. "Never has anyone I'm trying to help heard me in their mind like you did. Like you do. The only person who ever talked to me in my head was my brother, and he died nine years ago. There's been no one's voice in my mind for so long; it was an enormous shock to me when I realized you could hear me, and that you could talk back to me. I don't know why it's happened this way, with you and me. I don't have any answers for you there. I could tell by your reaction that you had no experience with telepathy."

"Telepathy?" he repeated. "Can you read my mind?"

She shook her head. "That's difficult to answer. I can hear everything you send me, either directly or indirectly, because you don't even realize you're doing it. Like tonight at Solu, your wish for a cup of coffee after dinner. Of course you weren't sending it to me; you didn't even know I was there. Yet I picked up on it while I was still inside the house, I could read that you wanted coffee. When we were in Vegas, I could hear your conversation on the phone with Bergen because I was concentrating every ounce of mental strength I had to get through to you. I do that sometimes when I'm trying to help someone—I try to impose my will on them telepathically. It never works, but it helps me focus on the problem at hand. Because you and I seem to be connected mentally, it allowed me to hear that phone call. You can learn how to block me. It's not difficult once you figure it out. It becomes as natural as breathing. At least that's how it was for Luca and me."

There was a heavy silence between them as he thought things through, and she waited patiently. He shifted in his chair, bringing his hands together and holding them to his lips. He didn't want to think about what she'd said earlier, that he had been about to die. She had sounded so certain; the words had spilled from her lips as smoothly as if she'd been discussing the weather.

"Your brother, could he..."

"Yes, he had the same ability as me. Premonitions, second sight."

"Anyone else in your family, can they do this?"

She sat back. "Our parents died when I was seven. Our grandparents were already dead. No aunts and uncles to speak of. No family that we know of. I have no history, no way of knowing where this ability came from. Luca said our parents were oblivious to it; he had to figure it all out on his own. We kept it, him and me, as our secret. He's been gone for years now, and it's been my secret alone."

The corners of Bret's eyes crinkled in pain at her words, but her matter-of-fact tone did not invite him to feel sympathy for her, so he looked down and tried to think of his next question. He feared the allowed number of questions might be limited, but he had no idea.

"You hadn't met Tayce before?" he asked, suddenly curious, though he felt like he was wasting a question. He'd been a little jealous at their easy, flirty repartee that evening, however, so he had to know. "Tayce has been around a lot over the years, I imagine, because of Paul living out there, but he said he didn't know you."

She shook her head. "No, I'd never met him, but I've known that he's sometimes around. He's developed a bit of a reputation with some of the girls at work," she twisted her lips together to hide a grin, "but I usually steer clear of their gossip, so I don't know all the details. I think I've seen him once or twice at the restaurant, but I didn't have their table that night. If I'm available, Diego will usually give me their table, but not always. It's quite odd that he and I had never met, considering the proximity, but it's true."

"Did you do it on purpose tonight? Switch with our waitress so you could get to our table?"

"No. I could sense you as soon as I got to work tonight, and it threw my mind into a tailspin. I guessed you were there with Paul and Katrine. Who else? But I didn't know what to do. I hadn't thought I'd ever see you again. I wasn't prepared."

"Nor was I."

"When I realized Casi was leaving early, I knew Diego would give me your table. I had time to compose myself. I didn't know what would happen; I half-believed you wouldn't recognize me at all."

"I just thought that maybe you knew Tayce," he explained, "because of the way you specifically wanted me to get him to come in with me that night in Vegas."

"You were my main concern in Vegas, like I said." She leaned forward. "You were the one that showed up in my head as being in danger, but I hoped to get all of you off the sidewalk, just in case. Someone not being in my head never means they're necessarily safe, it just means I'm not seeing them, for whatever unknown reason. With the amount of darkness, of evil, coming from that van, I assumed everyone would be better off going back inside the club. But I didn't want you to stall too long and further endanger yourself while trying to convince everyone to follow you. That's why I hurried you along when I saw you had at least Jack and Tayce. It wasn't that I valued Cyn and Peter any less, it was just that as far as I knew, they weren't specifically in danger, but you were. First and foremost, I had to save you. It's risky, making judgement calls like that. Maybe if I'd pushed, had risked your safety more, I could have saved them, too. Or maybe if Tayce and Jack had stayed out there with them, everyone would have been fine. Though I doubt it.

"I can read Tayce clearly. That's something else I can do. Not read his mind, but just him, a general feeling. That night in Vegas, I could immediately tell that he would go with you easily. I thought Jack might, too, though he would be more difficult, drunk as he was. Peter was a toss-up as to whether he would follow Jack, but when Cyn stubbornly remained out there to smoke, I knew he would stay with her."

"You knew who we all were?"

"I didn't know who Cyn was, and I didn't know Peter's name, though I guessed he was associated with Jack somehow. I knew who you, Tayce, and Jack were by sight. I wasn't lying about the door posters. I grew up loving your music; I was totally a child of that era. I saw Dangerous Eye, and BlueStar, and even Jack's band in concert with my brother more than once. You know," she smiled, "when I was eleven."

He rolled his eyes. "Yeah, yeah. I know I'm old. What are you now?" He got up to get more water for himself, wanting to drink something stronger but also wanting his mind to stay clear.

"Twenty-eight."

Fairly close to his estimation. "Paul said you leave town a lot," he mentioned as he returned, and this time he sat down beside her on the couch, close enough that his knee touched hers as he turned towards her. Some kind of warm vibration passed through his body, but he didn't move his knee away, and neither did she, though he saw her glance flick away for a second, as if she were making a decision.

"Mmm, not 'a lot,' but I do leave now and then, for a month or so here and there. There are several reasons. I get restless. I go away to clear my head, I guess. Come back fresh, if you will. Of course, wherever I go, I find more trouble." She set the water aside again and leaned back. "That little town is like a hiding place for me. I'm safe there. Not many people in the world know about me, about what I can do. It's not something I ever share. If you think about it, you can imagine that it would cause problems. If someone I know loses their mother in a car accident, they might blame me. Why didn't I see it? Why didn't I stop it? The problem is that I don't see everything. I have no control over what gets shown to me. I can't save everyone."

She turned her head and looked at him as he leaned back as well. "It's just easier to be alone. I'm definitely not always easy to be around. Visions, heartache, trouble, and so many secrets. It's tricky. I can be difficult to like, let alone love." She smiled. "That's my story, though. I knew I owed you that much. It's not a tale I relay to anyone, ever. But no one else can talk to me in my head, so..."

"It's unbelievable." Bret felt as if a whole new world had been laid bare in front of him, and he wasn't sure what to do about it. In his head, he knew he should be cautious, should hold her at a careful distance, but his heart was not behaving accordingly. Impulsively, he placed his hand on top of hers, encouraged when she did not pull away, though the touch of her skin sent lightning sparks through his body.

"You believe me, I can tell," she observed, looking at him thoughtfully. "Lots of people might not."

"Yes, well they don't have your voice in their heads." He looked uncomfortable. "Maybe I'll regret telling you this, but for a year and a half, I've been hoping I'd find you again. The questions that arose because of that night in Vegas left me troubled, and the connection I felt to you was obviously unlike anything I've experienced before. I've thought about you pretty much daily since then," he confessed. "Give or take."

She smiled, somewhat shyly. "Me, too."

"I even went back to Vegas a few times, and the whole time I was there I was looking around, watching for you, hoping to spot you in a crowd of people."

She contemplated the slightly embarrassed singer beside her, crooked smile returning to her lips. She turned her hand over and laced her fingers through his. "I was only in Vegas temporarily, a few weeks. As it turned out, I left a few days after that particular night."

He squeezed her hand. "Thank you for telling me all of this; I realize it wasn't easy for you. And you're right, I do believe everything you've said, as crazy as it all sounds. I'm sure once it sinks in, I'll remember the other hundred questions I had." He looked in her eyes. "So why has this happened? It's an insane coincidence that we've run into each other like this."

She nodded. "I agree, and I have no idea, but I don't think it's an accident. Most of what happens in my life is definitely not without meaning. That night in Vegas changed me, because it presented me with a subject—you—whom I could not forget, and that has never happened to me before. You've stayed in my mind. I've been troubled." She sighed. "And the 'news' section of your website is not updated regularly enough."

He laughed out loud. "You've kept track of me?" He couldn't help sounding enormously pleased.

She felt herself blushing against her will. "I stopped myself just short of subscribing to the text updates, but yes, I have kept up."

He was grinning at her, looking completely at ease. Now that the allegedly difficult part, telling him about her second sight ability, was past them, a whole new range of feelings were bubbling up between them. Fallon was struggling to think around the strength of his presence there beside her, the feelings she felt emanating from him, feelings twisting up inside her as well, fast catching fire. She couldn't let this get out of hand. Much as she'd like it to. Surely it would not end well. Something this powerful could not be safe. She had to find a way to distract him, to stop him from looking at her so intently with those clear grey eyes.

"Eighteen months is a long time to be thinking about someone," he admitted. "I did write a couple of songs about you."

This was not the way.

"You didn't." She tried not to feel delighted. Fail.

"I did," he confirmed, "last year. I think I was trying to purge you from my mind." He squeezed her hand again. "It didn't work, but one of them is pretty good. One day I'll play it for you."

Her heart was doing somersaults. She was certain it had never had acrobatic tendencies before. *You are so grounded*, she thought fiercely to that traitorous internal organ. Bret was still smiling that devilish smile at her. She felt herself losing complete control, and that was not something she was familiar, or pleased, with. She wanted more than anything to lean forward and kiss him.

Instead, she gently took her hand from his, rising and crossing the room to the window. She pulled aside the heavy drapes and stared out at the lights of Dallas, trying to focus. Now that his skin was no longer touching hers, she found she could breathe again. She knew she should say goodbye, goodnight, should be quickly on her way. But she had never felt a connection and attraction to anyone like she did to him right now, and she was unwilling to turn completely away from him. She had just spilled out to him so many of the truths she always kept hidden, which meant to some degree that she trusted him, and in her world, she trusted next to no one. And the telepathy, it had to mean something. Saying "goodbye" to Bret James was not currently an option. She glanced at him over her shoulder, and saw that his grin had faltered, uncertainty in his face.

"Tell me about your daughter. She's so beautiful."

Despite the obvious subject change, his face lit up. "Bergen May. She's nine years old. Very independent. Artistic. Driving her mother and me for a loop. She's so sweet. She's a daredevil with an angel face. A tomboy. I got her her first dirt bike last Christmas. Her mom and I couldn't get enough safety gear on her; we finally had to stop ourselves. I've got a track on my property, and she and I ride it together. She loves it. I miss her so much when I'm on the road. We talk every morning and every night, sometimes during the day if we've got something to share. She's had a cell phone since she was four so she and I could stay in touch, so she could reach me anytime of the day or night."

"Her mother is beautiful as well," Fallon observed. It was the truth and had to be said.

"Lisbeth, yes, she is. We've known each other for something like twenty-five years. We were always together off and on. She was the one I always came back to. Bergen was planned, if you can believe it, even though my relationship with Lisbeth had never been perfect. I was in my early forties and some difficult stuff had been going on. I had absolutely no long-term relationship in my sights with anyone, and I was imagining that any chance for a family might be slipping away from me. Lis and I talked about it at length, knowing that even if we might not be together in a relationship, at the end of the day, we could still be parents together. It was a risk. I can't imagine if Lisbeth and I didn't get along, how that would affect my time with Bergen. But you know, somehow, we're even better parents together than we ever were lovers. All my priorities changed when Bergen was born. Lisbeth and I are best friends, but we stopped being lovers when we became parents. Like we knew that the only reason we'd ever been together was to create that perfect little girl." There was a light in his eyes, a fondness in his face. "Bergen is who I live for, who I work to bring happiness to. She consumes my heart. I've only been involved casually with other women since she was born, because my heart's been too busy loving her."

But I think that it could love you.

That single thought, raw and unfiltered, left his mind unbidden, and her eyes went to his face when she heard it. His chest tightened when he realized the slip. There was a long, tense moment where neither of them spoke.

Bret finally got up and joined her at the window, and after only a moment of hesitation, he reached for her and pulled her close, his lips softly finding hers.

CHAPTER FIVE

When Fallon awoke later on in the morning, she felt peace, her mind momentarily quiet. She was also exhausted. They had been awake till six a.m., talking, and laughing, and making out. She hadn't let it go any further, though it had been incredibly difficult to maintain control. It was now only just past ten. She turned over carefully and looked at Bret, who was deeply asleep. Her body tingled when she saw him, her heart pounding happily in her chest. She glared in regard to the latter. What was she doing?

She was about to begin considering what had happened, what it all meant. But she was given no time.

The premonition slammed violently into her head, taking her breath away with its force. She closed her eyes and tried to breathe while image after image poured in relentlessly, suffocating her. She was out of the bed before she knew it, struggling to get air into her aching lungs, when the mental pictures finally became clear enough to make out.

"No!" She collapsed to her knees, clutching her head in her hands. Images of Bret James flashed through her mind with utter brutality, none of them entirely clear, the feelings of dread and doom overwhelming her. She tried to slow it down, this cruel barrage; she tried all her usual tricks, but it wouldn't cease. "No," she murmured desperately. "What is it? What? What? What?!" She strained to get a read on it, a reason, but there was nothing. A single tear ran down her cheek, her resolve being undone by the pain and pressure and fear.

The images wouldn't stop, the feelings of a distantly impending nightmare gripping her tightly. Though nothing like this had ever happened to her before, she knew with certainty that if she didn't do something about it, it would begin to destroy her mind. She crawled over to her bag and dug through it, but she already knew she'd forgotten what she needed back at home in Gray. When she was sure she was correct, she stumbled into her shoes, only half-aware of the room and of Bret still sleeping in the bed. Her hands were shaking as she fumbled for her car keys. Maybe if she got away from him. Maybe it was her proximity. Because of the connection in their minds. She had to get home.

Another tear followed the first as she looked at him, wanting to kiss him goodbye, wanting to wake him and see his grin. But he would delay her, with questions, with not understanding, with wanting to help. She grabbed her bag and fled out the door.

The danger to Bret, whatever it was, was not imminent. She could tell that much. The only reason she was allowing herself to leave him was her belief that he was safe for now. Regardless, she was no good to him in her current state.

By the time she returned home to her garage apartment in Gray, the images and feelings were still going strong, and she had a blinding headache. Glass was being shattered repeatedly in her skull, cutting her with sharp edges, deafening her with noise. She had no idea how she'd made it all the way home, at least an hour's drive.

A black dog of medium size was immediately at her side as she got out of the car, and he accompanied her around to the back of the garage and up the wooden stairs to her little apartment. With difficulty she unlocked the door and tripped inside, landing on her knees. The dog, Azul, whined at her, solicitously licking her face in concern. Fallon got to her feet and found her way to the bathroom. There she dug around in a little red bag and pulled out a plastic injector, loading it with trembling, clumsy fingers. She held it against her bare thigh and pressed the trigger button, the needle puncturing her skin. The pain of the drugs entering her body steadied her with its promise, and she went out and fell onto her bed, quickly losing consciousness.

Azul pushed the door she'd left open shut with his nose and paw, then leapt up onto the bed and curled up against his mistress. His worried black eyes shone in the sunlight as he guarded her.

* * * * * * *

When Bret finally woke up, he knew by the sunlight and his internal clock that it was probably close to noon. His flight to L.A. wasn't until six, and he wondered what he and Fallon would do in the hours they had left. He wasn't ready to say good-bye to her. Truthfully, he wanted to take her home with him and introduce her to his world; his feelings about her were that strong. But he didn't want to scare her away.

They'd talked for the rest of the night about a thousand different things. She'd been so sweet. The feelings she stirred up in him were unreal. The mental communication, telepathy, he was still trying to wrap his mind around that.

He realized he was alone in the bed, and raised up a little to look around. And he knew from the quiet and the stillness that she was gone. He sat all the way up and looked around again. There was no note that he could see. Nothing. Her bag was gone, her shoes, her keys. He felt like he'd been punched in the stomach. Something wasn't right. She wasn't the type that would run out on him. And he'd been run out on his fair share of times over the years, so he figured he should know. Never before when it happened, had he been surprised.

This surprised him.

He was numb as he showered, dressing quickly in jeans and an old red t-shirt, drying his hair with a towel and pulling on a baseball cap. Her continued absence was proving that she had not, as he'd faintly hoped, gone out to get them breakfast. Packing up his things, he texted back and forth with various associates, then he called Bergen and discussed what time he'd be home, and if she and Lisbeth were picking him up from the airport. He promised they would ride their dirt bikes together in the morning.

"Dad, what's wrong?" she asked at the end. The child could always read him. Her father was usually laughing, smiling, happy-go-lucky.

"I'm just tired, Bee. Wanting to be home with you. I love you. I'll see you tonight."

Grabbing complimentary coffee and a blueberry muffin from the downstairs restaurant, he went out to his rental car and threw his bags and guitar case in the trunk. He climbed behind the wheel to think and eat. He would not allow himself to believe she had just left him like any other hit and run. But he only had four or five hours, maybe less, to figure this one out. And at least two hours of that would be spent on the road. Crushing his napkin and tossing it aside, he started the car, getting on the interstate and heading back towards the small town she called home. There was someone he wanted to talk to.

Diego Sanchez was sitting on the front steps of his house/ restaurant, reading the local paper while his three kids played in the yard, when he saw Bret James pulling to a stop out on the street. Curious, he folded the paper and set it aside, waiting. Bret waved as he got out of the car and approached him.

"You know, sadly, we are not open for lunch," Diego called out to him amiably.

Bret smiled. "I was wondering if we could talk for a minute or two."

Diego rose, and the two men shook hands. "About Fallon, I presume?" He had heard from his staff about Fallon fleeing Solu the night before, Bret too slow to catch her. He had wondered about that. Fallon called him from her car to apologize profusely for running off early, claiming an emergency. He doubted the truth of that, though he would never hold it against her. She was by far his favorite and most reliable employee. He would forgive Fallon anything.

Bret nodded. "Yes, about Fallon."

Diego sat once more and patted the step beside him, and Bret joined him. "Sophie, don't let your brother climb on that! Luis! Down!" He lowered his voice. "Fallon is a dear friend. Precious to my family. I do not talk about her with strangers, though you seem like a good guy, and are friends with the wonderful Paul and Katrine. I'm sorry."

Bret had his hands loosely clasped and his arms on his knees, staring into space. "Do you know her well?" he asked softly. "You know what she can do?"

Diego looked him a moment. Then he nodded soberly. "Of course. Better than most."

Bret swallowed hard, his mouth dry. "Nearly two years ago, in Las Vegas one night, I believe she saved my life. Mine as well as two of my friends. She and I, there was a connection I can't explain, but she disappeared before we could talk. Seeing each other last night was a surprise for both of us. And then later, she tracked me down at my hotel in Dallas. We were finally able to talk about everything in depth."

Diego's face was unreadable as Bret went on.

"She ended up staying the night, but when I woke up this morning she was gone. I don't think she intended to leave. Maybe that's just my ego talking. But I'm trying to find her, to make sure. I'm worried about her. It doesn't make sense that she would just disappear. I wasn't ready to say goodbye." He was staring at the ground now, the awkwardness of confessing these things to a stranger more difficult than he'd imagined. "Look, I don't know how to explain this to anyone. But Fallon is not a normal woman."

Diego was nodding slowly. Finally, he spoke. "Six years ago, my wife and I moved to this little town to open a restaurant. We only had the two kids then, the one just a baby. We'd leased an old building with an apartment upstairs, a few miles from here. We'd done some remodeling in the restaurant in preparation for opening, and I'd begun the hiring process. Fallon was one of the last to be interviewed. The interview went well—a friendly, well-spoken, pretty girl—but as she was about to leave, she suddenly froze and closed her eyes. She remained that way for a moment, and I thought she might have some kind of medical condition. Then she looked at me and told me my family could not stay upstairs that night."

Bret looked at him.

"I thought she was crazy. She repeated this to me a couple of times, and I finally asked her to leave, and when she was gone, I tore up her resume. I would not be having such a kooky girl on my staff!" He chuckled to himself.

"Two hours later she was back, and this time my wife was there in the restaurant with me. Fallon repeated her warning to us, and my wife took her seriously. I was adamant that this girl was psychotic. My wife, Mariana, who has always been more superstitious than I, was afraid. That evening she packed up the kids and went to stay in the hotel in Dutton, which we'd first stayed at when we came here. I wanted to stay at the restaurant, to prove them wrong, but I couldn't stay a night without my babies, and it had made me uneasy, anyway. So, I went to the hotel with them."

When he looked at Bret, Diego's dark eyes were damp. "At two in the morning, a gas line ruptured. It had been nicked by a construction crew earlier that week. The restaurant and the buildings on either side of it exploded with flames and burned to the ground. Fortunately, no one was injured, and insurance allowed us enough money to buy this house, to begin again. Mariana had Fallon come along with us when we looked at this property, just to reassure herself, despite that Fallon told her she couldn't predict the future at will. I owe that girl my family. She has been family to us ever since. We protect her secret, and try as best we can to protect her. She is a vulnerable creature, tough as she is. A lonely girl. She does not easily let people near her. So often, Fallon is alone." He was thoughtful. "I could see, last night, that there was something different with her, as soon as she came on shift, long before she went out to your table. I didn't know what it was: she seemed distressed, confused. After an hour or so, that was gone, and she looked her old self again. But I looked out once last night, when she was sitting out there with you all, and I saw her watching you. And there was a look in her eyes that I have never seen before."

Diego slid a pen from his pocket and scribbled something on the edge of the newspaper, tearing the piece off and handing it to Bret. "Her number. Knowing that she drove to Dallas last night to find you, I do not take that lightly. It means something. As for her departure this morning, maybe she had a premonition. Maybe she had to leave." He got to his feet, and Bret did the same. "And if she doesn't answer when you call, know that she gets very bad headaches. She takes powerful drugs that knock her out, for hours at a time. That could be the case. If your intentions are good, my friend, then do not give up on her. As you said, she is not a normal woman."

"Can you tell me where to find her? Where she lives?"

Diego shook his head. "I do not trust many people when it comes to her. There are those out there who I think would use her, exploit her abilities. Think of it, how useful she could be. She is always seeing the danger facing others, yet she is always in danger herself. I believe everything you told me, and I believe you mean her no harm. But her location I cannot give away; I promised her once I would not. It is her sanctuary. Please respect that of me."

Bret appreciated the other man's loyalty, even though it did not help him in his quest. He shook Diego's hand, complimented him on his restaurant, and hoped to see him again soon. Then returned to his car.

Fallon did not answer his call, and he drove slowly, aimlessly through the little town, his heart heavy. This was a cruel twist he hadn't seen coming. After obsessing about a beautiful stranger for a year and a half, he got to share one perfect night with her, only to lose her immediately afterwards? As Tayce might say, what lame movie-of-the-week plot was this? And here he was like a complete fool, driving through her little town as if she might look out the window, spot him, and come running out to be joyously reunited with him. That probably wasn't going to happen considering her disappearing act and the lack of a note explaining such.

He didn't even know what kind of car she drove, so unless she happened to be strolling along the side of the road or hanging out in her yard, his drive was going to prove fruitless. He needed to leave, get away from here, back to California and Bergen.

A shiver went through him then, as of someone walking over his grave, and an image popped into his mind of the tattoo on the back of Fallon's left arm. She also had tattoos on the inside of each wrist, but he hadn't paid much attention to them last night.

On the back of her upper left arm, though, were two lines of black script that read: *I see, but not in the light.*

He'd run his fingers over the words thoughtfully. "When did you get this?"

"Five years ago."

He'd started to ask what the phrase meant, but then felt something like a hand touching his mind, stilling him. He wondered about the phrase now. There was an "otherness" about Fallon, a darkness. He thought about her lifetime of premonitions, of loss.

With a sigh, he turned his car in the direction of the interstate, simultaneously calling Tayce.

"Hey, man, what's going on?" Tayce greeted him. "Too bad you and Fallon had to cut out early last night. And without each other, at that."

"Actually, she found me later at the hotel," Bret revealed. "You guys give her my room number or something?"

"Really? No, I... oh, dang it, that sneaky Katrine. Fallon must have texted Kat last night, because on the way back to the farm Kat was innocently asking for the name of your hotel, and a few minutes later she was texting someone. Not the room number, though. None of us knew that. Paul made a joke about why she was asking, but nothing came of it. Ah ha! Fallon!"

He never used his real name at hotels, so once she got to the hotel, she must have trailed him, sensed him, till she came to the right room. Was that even possible? Apparently.

"So that all worked out, huh?" Tayce asked with a big smile. "I could tell she liked you, that there was something between you guys, even if you barely said two words to each other. Dude, I am astoundingly jealous! What a girl! Have a nice night, did you?"

"I did," Bret admitted, stopping to let two boys on bicycles cross the street.

Tayce gave the laughter equivalent of a high-five. "You should come out to the farm, man, it's great out here. Recharges your soul."

"Love to, but I've got a flight to L.A. in a few hours. My daughter's waiting for me." Fleetingly, he wondered if Katrine and Paul would know where Fallon lived, but then he stopped that train of thought. She'd left him no means to contact her, and she wasn't answering his call. All indications that she wanted to be left alone.

"Want some company for a while?" Tayce offered. "There's some folks I could visit in Dallas later tonight, if you want to go have a drink or something."

"That actually sounds good. I'm supposed to meet up with Travis at some point; we're on the same flight. I'll let him know where to find us."

They made plans to meet in a few hours, and Bret got back on the interstate. Swallowing still more pride, he sent a text to Fallon's phone, though he did not expect her to respond. Short and simple, the text hoped she was well and asked her to call.

At an austere little bar not far from DFW, Tayce and Bret drank a few beers together before the Bret's flight. Tayce playfully prodded him for more information about Fallon—would he be seeing her again, or was she just a one-night thing? But Bret was evasive. And when his guitarist, Travis, finally appeared, Tayce watched Bret's strange mood slip away entirely, as if into a hiding place, and he knew Bret would confide nothing about Fallon now.

Back in Los Angeles at last, Bret's heart melted as Bergen greeted him enthusiastically at the airport, flinging herself up into his arms.

"Hey, sweetheart." He kissed her tanned cheek, then smiled at Lisbeth as she fell in step beside him. She looked at him closely, frowned a little, then shook it off and laughed at something Bergen was saying.

Later that night at home, after they'd had ice-cream and put Bergen to bed, Bret retired to his room to shower and change. Lisbeth soon appeared at his door.

"You look tired," she noted.

Shirtless, in long dark blue shorts, he was rubbing a towel over his damp head. "It was a long week. I'm glad to be home for a while."

She took a step into the room. "Liar. What's wrong?"

He sat down on the bed. He and Lisbeth had separate bedrooms at opposite ends of the house. When he'd told Fallon that he and Lis hadn't slept together since Bergen's birth, it had been the truth. They dated other people freely, though they usually didn't bring them home unless they knew the other person wasn't going to be there. He knew this arrangement couldn't go on forever. Surely one day either he or Lisbeth, maybe both, would meet someone they wanted to share their lives with, and that would necessitate shaking up the current living arrangements. He worried some days about how Bergen would take it. Lisbeth had dated several men, a couple seriously, but none seriously enough. The one she'd been seeing lately, though, an architect named Leo…Bret thought there was something there. A future, maybe. But as a rule, they never discussed their love lives with each other.

Which was why he was both desperate and reluctant to tell her all about Fallon. Lisbeth was his best friend. There was no one he trusted more. Whatever he told her, he knew, would never be leaked to anyone else, not even to Leo. She would lock it away in her heart if he asked. She had always been steadfast in that way.

He indicated she should join him on the bed. "I do have something to tell you. A story. But I'll warn you now, it's complex."

"I can handle it." She came in, shutting the door, and sat cross-legged on the end of the bed, hugging a pillow on her lap.

And he told her, beginning with Las Vegas, the true version this time, followed by the eighteen months of dreaming of the unknown girl and the answers she held. He described all that had happened the previous night and day, including Diego's tale. When he was finished, Lisbeth said nothing for a while. "I know it sounds a little crazy," he added, perhaps inadequately.

"More than a little," she agreed, looking at him. "And yet, I believe it, I do. You couldn't make something like this up if you tried, clever though you may be. You aren't easily fooled, either.

I remember the afternoon you told me about being there when Peter and that woman disappeared. I could tell you were shaken up. Second sight. Premonitions. Wow. And you sound," she narrowed her eyes, "like you really, really like this girl, Fallon."

He lay back on the rest of his pillows. "That's because I do. So, until I hear from her, if I hear from her, I may or may not be something of a mess."

She leaned forward and patted his ankle before getting to her feet. "She'll come around. You have a way about you."

"Do I?"

Her laughter trailed behind her as she left his room. "Oh, you do."

CHAPTER SIX

LUCA

Nine-year-old Luca heard the child crying and instinctively went running to her. Even if he hadn't been able to hear her sobs, he'd have known she was upset and been able to find her. Though she'd only been with them since last Friday, he could sense her. He could feel—know—where and how she was. What a weird thing, it had never happened before, and his young mind could barely comprehend it. And it got even weirder than that. But first he had to go to her.

She was outside in the backyard. Fallon's small face was a window of fear. His mother was trying to comfort the little girl to no avail. Fallon, not quite four-years-old, wanted nothing to do with her. When she saw Luca, though, she ran towards him, panicked, and he did what he'd learned would calm her: he held her close. Immediately she was quiet and still. His mother placed a hand on his head, briefly, and then returned to the house with the smallest of sighs.

Luca, it's dark.

Ah, and here was the weirder part. He and Fallon could talk to each other in their minds. It was called "telepathy." He'd looked it up.

It's not dark at all, Fallon. You're safe. It's alright.

She looked at him. *I feel bad.*

He nodded. *I know. But you'll feel better soon. It'll go away. It's just for a moment.* He looked at the kitchen window, where his mother was watching them curiously. Well, he'd always believed she was his mother. Until last Friday night, when The Stranger had brought Fallon to their house.

"She's been kept a secret so far," the unknown man was telling Luca's parents, "but we don't know how long that will continue. Her last situation was not a good one. We thought she should be with her brother, finally."

Luca was listening and watching curiously from his bedroom doorway. "Her brother?" He couldn't see either the man's or the girl's face. She was in his strong arms, holding onto him tightly, her face hidden against his neck, his long hair. The conversation with the adults seemed to have reached an end point, and as Luca watched, the man squeezed the child close in a hug, his lips touching the side of her head with a kiss as he handed her to Luca's mother.

Then the man left.

As soon as he was gone, Fallon began to scream in absolute grief-stricken horror, fighting to run after him, calling the man's name over and over as she sobbed. Luca felt her fear and sadness twist inside him like someone was painfully squeezing his heart. Before he knew what he was doing, he was running down the hall towards her. She was so little. When she saw him, she quieted and stopped fighting. And ran to him.

They put her to bed in his room, just for the one night, because she was still so upset. After she'd finally fallen asleep, holding onto his hand, his mother took him out to the living room and sat with him on the green couch. She'd told him then that he was adopted, that this tiny changeling was, as far as they knew, his sister. They had no idea who his real parents were; he had been brought to them as a one-month-old baby by the same man who had just shown up unexpectedly with Fallon. Neither did they know where Fallon had been for the first few years of her life.

He had many questions, but she was vague then, and wouldn't tell him anything more. She held him close and promised that she loved him like her own flesh and blood, his father, too. But he'd immediately somewhat doubted that, though it hadn't bothered him as much as he'd thought it should.

Because now he had Fallon.

In the beginning, his sister was a shy, nervous little creature who always seemed haunted. She looked like she had endured some sort of trauma. He knew that she deeply missed the man, though she never spoke of him.

"Was that your father, who brought you here?" he asked once.

She shook her head, whispered, "No," and turned away.

She took great comfort in their shared telepathy, which was something they discovered within their first twenty-four hours together. For a long time, Luca didn't tell her that the times when she was so afraid and felt bad and saw darkness, that those were premonitions. He couldn't imagine explaining it to anyone, let alone someone so young. There would be time for that later, when she was older. His job now was to keep her safe. And to teach her to be happy. She'd smiled at him just once, since arriving, and it had been an amazing sight. He wanted to see that smile again.

Where in the world had she been that she seemed so traumatized?

CHAPTER SEVEN

Fallon's eyes fluttered open, then quickly shut against the bright sunlight. Her head ached and her mouth was dry; her throat crackled with pain. Someone in the apartment moved around, and she could hear the shades being drawn. She tried again, opening her eyes slowly. A beautiful, dark-skinned face hovered over her.

"Are you going to be sick, or can we move on to feeding you?"

Fallon groaned, her body shuddering.

"A drink, then." The face faded, then soon returned. A glass of cold orange juice was held to her lips, a hand supporting the back of her head, and she drank thirstily. Then she lay back on the pillow, and her friend's face came into focus.

"Selah." Fallon licked her chapped lips. "How long have you been here?"

"Not long, love. How long have you been unconscious?"

Fallon shrugged, her eyes still not staying completely focused. Azul nosed her hand, and she weakly petted her loyal dog.

"What day did you give yourself the shot?" Selah pressed.

Fallon swallowed more of the juice as Selah offered it to her. "Friday. Noon-ish."

Selah nodded, her long turquoise-beaded earrings swinging back and forth. "Today's only Saturday. Mid-afternoon. Not bad. But we need to get some food and water into you."

Fallon's eyes widened, and she raised up a little, wincing at the pain in her head. "Saturday, I..." She looked around for her phone.

"I already called Diego. Tessa's covering your shift tonight. Like the martyr that she is." Selah handed her the phone when she noticed Fallon continued to reach for it. "Though I see that obviously that's not what was concerning you. Diego will be disappointed to find your loyalties lie elsewhere."

Fallon checked her phone and saw the missed call and text message from a California number. She exhaled slowly. She would deal with that later.

She turned her attention back to Selah. "Thank you for coming for me. Where's Indio?"

"At home with Michael. He did want to come, but I didn't know what I'd find, or how long it would take to bring you around. You know I rarely bring him to these events."

"And how did you know I was in need of your assistance? The same?"

"The same." Selah eyed the black dog that lay beside Fallon on the bed. "I heard barking in my backyard. At my back door, specifically. But no dog was there." She narrowed her eyes at Azul, who panted happily and looked at nothing in particular.

"Have you given him cheese?" Fallon asked. "You know he loves cheese."

"I am long-aware of his cheese passion. I gave him a few cubes of Colby-Jack when I arrived. He was most appreciative. You're lucky he knows how to open the door with his nose and paw, to allow himself access to the yard when you are incapacitated in this way."

"He is special." Fallon raised up gingerly to a sitting position. She looked around in her mind, fearfully, and with care. But there were no images. All was still and silent. The pain was beginning to subside with the sweetness of the juice hitting her bloodstream. Her eyes met Selah's dark ones. "Have you seen any news lately?"

Selah sat back and raised an eyebrow. "As a matter of fact, I have, Miss More-Cryptic-Than-Usual-As-If-That-Were-Even-Possible. What interests you?"

"Bret James, you know, the singer? From BlueStar? He didn't die yesterday, or today, did he?" She tried without success to keep the faint quavering from her voice. If she reached out to sense him, then she would be able to tell if he was alive or dead. She was afraid to try.

Selah tilted her head slightly. "I've seen nothing which would indicate that. I assume it would at least briefly make headlines. If there was nothing else going on." She had never shared Fallon's taste in music. "Why him, love?"

Fallon sighed. "I have so much to tell you."

Selah rose to her feet, rubbing a hand over her sleekly-styled hair. She was lovely, as always, in a turquoise and deep blue shirt and long narrow skirt. "Go and take a shower to clear your muddled head while I make us a late lunch, and we'll eat in the backyard. Then we can talk."

Fallon obeyed without another word.

Thirty minutes later, they were seated at a grey cafe-style metal table with matching chairs; Azul lay at their feet chewing on a treat stick. Fallon, clad in black leggings and a white tank top, her long hair damp, stared at her lunch. There was chicken salad on a flaky croissant and a small bowl of fruit, as well as a glass of freshly-brewed, sweet iced tea. She looked across the table at Selah, who had the same. "You are too good to me."

Selah sipped her tea serenely. "I know this. Now tell me your long, sordid tale."

Selah and Fallon had been best friends since the second grade, when Fallon, coming down the sidewalk one day, came across Selah, who was out in front of her house playing hopscotch, and ordered her to call her dog back into the yard. Selah had seen Fallon at school, but they'd never spoken. Now she looked out at where her beloved brown and white puppy, Kib, was playing in the street, and then she looked at Fallon as if she were crazy.

"Why?" she demanded, hands on her hips.

Fallon, her long blond hair in two braids, looked out nervously at the dog, twisting one of the braids around her fingers. "There's a car coming. It's going to hit him. I think."

Selah listened, but heard nothing. She looked up and down the quiet street, and saw nothing. "You might be crazy," she determined.

"What's his name?" Fallon asked quickly, releasing the braid. "Kib."

Fallon began calling for the dog. Kib hopped around, wanting to play, but as desperation grew in Fallon's voice, Selah joined her in calling him. Kib ran to them immediately. Without warning, a car full of teenagers came weaving down the middle of the street at high speed and was gone in a flash. It had just missed the dog.

Selah looked down at the warm, wiggling puppy in her arms. Then she met Fallon's eyes. At that moment something unspoken and eternal passed between them, binding them. Selah didn't tell anyone about what had happened that afternoon. The two girls became each other's protector, and were inseparable from that day forward.

Through the years, they had been apart at times. Selah had gone to the University of Texas in their hometown of Austin, where she'd eventually met and married Michael Lowe, a future doctor. Fallon had tried to continue her education, but a college campus had proven not to be the best place for her. Too many people getting themselves into too many regrettable situations. And so, she had traveled the world while Selah studied.

After graduation, Selah and Michael settled immediately in the tiny town of Gray while Michael finished his medical studies and residency in Dallas. Fallon, the world traveler, had not found what she was looking for. She was restless and lost, and needed to be back in Selah's world.

So, she followed them to Gray, renting the garage apartment from a widow and getting the job at Solu. A few years later, Michael opened his own practice in Dutton, the slightly larger town to their north, which also had the closest hospital. Michael and Selah's only child, a boy named Indio Luca Lowe, had been born five years ago; Fallon was his godmother. The Lowes lived in a pretty, Queen Anne-style house on the edge of town, and

Selah, a former ballerina who had taken up painting when she was a teenager, taught art classes to kids during the summer.

Michael knew all about Fallon's abilities, but he was more interested in the physiology behind it, as well as the physical side effects, like her headaches. He had performed several MRIs on her out of curiosity, and was the one who prescribed the strong drugs for her, a special combination high-strength sleeping-pill-and-pain-pill-in-one, which Fallon could inject quickly for instant relief and unconsciousness. Because, as she had explained to him once, she didn't just need to stop the pain. She needed to stop her mind as well.

Selah hated the drugs, and thought that sometimes Fallon leaned too heavily on them, but Fallon and Michael had gone behind her back more than once to keep Fallon supplied, and Selah had given up the fight.

After she had finished most of her lunch, Fallon felt fully revived, and she told Selah all about Bret James, beginning with the night in Vegas eighteen months earlier and leaving out nothing.

When she was done with the story, Selah admitted silently to herself that she was astonished. The night in the hotel room was definitely not Fallon's usual cup of tea, though Selah inwardly cheered her on. But she also felt protective. Fallon sounded almost as if she could fall in love with this man. Selah had not really thought that was even possible. But where was this Bret James person, if he truly had similar feelings for her Fallon? And the family, that was troubling. A daughter, and the child's mother living with him. Tricky, at best. The shared telepathy—just like with Luca who had been gone so many years now. What could that mean? Fallon and Bret were destined to be in each other's lives for some reason; that was obvious to her. The incident in Vegas—bizarre. The images Fallon had been besieged with in the hotel room yesterday morning—those were of course most troubling.

"Obviously you must see him again. Have you called him? Of course not, I've been with you since you woke up. Call him. Now."

Fallon crossed her arms over her chest. "Anything else?"

Selah smiled, and Fallon instantly felt warmer. When Selah smiled, it was like the sun coming out from behind clouds. "I suppose I'm being slightly bossy," Selah allowed. "But this is the most interesting thing that has happened in a while, which is saying a lot, considering, and I'm wanting all the answers immediately." She leaned forward. "What's also noteworthy to me is that the guitarist, Tayce, happened to be with him again when you came across him. Just like in Las Vegas. If you'd told me, what was his name? Jack Lane? Was also at the table that night, I might be doubly concerned."

"Jack was in Dallas that night, if you'd like your concern fueled. He had performed at the same festival Bret played at. Tayce invited him to dinner as well, but he had a prior engagement. Yes, I felt the same way when Bret told me that. The three of them in the same area again. And then the images of Bret, the sense of him being in danger, just like last time, only much worse. As if what happened in Vegas was meant for those three. And now there is unfinished business. And I caused it."

Selah shivered. "A goose just walked over my grave. Let's talk about something else. Like the sex."

"There was no actual sex."

"Exactly my point."

Fallon laughed, and Selah grinned as she rose and started picking up the dishes. Selah glanced at her watch. "I do have to go, love."

Getting to her feet, Fallon gave her friend a tight hug. "Leave these, I'll get them. Thank you so much for coming to take care of me."

"Call him."

"Yes." Fallon rolled her eyes and waved her away, and Selah disappeared around the garage, laughing merrily to herself. A minute later, Fallon heard the sound of the Volvo starting up and driving away.

She carried the dishes inside and set them in the sink, then glanced around the apartment. It was decorated simply in neutral tones of whites and greys, with splashes of brighter colors here and there. The layout was open, each area flowing into the other. The kitchen and living area were all one, and her bed was off in a corner, hidden behind a black curtain embroidered with beads and ribbon. Only the tiny bathroom had a door, and it was antique, made of heavy wood, with three small squares of wavy glass near the top. Vintage concert posters and framed color photographs that she'd taken during her travels covered the walls, offering most of the bright spots of color. The apartment was small, but cozy and private. Here, more than anywhere else, she felt secure.

Fallon picked up her cellphone and curled up in her desk chair, turning on her laptop as she finally read the message Bret had left. She sighed. It was brief and gave her no hint of anything. Well, she had run out on him without a word after a wonderful night together. She supposed she was lucky he had tried to contact her at all.

Chewing on her lip, she wondered what he'd thought when he realized she was gone. She wished she'd had time to leave a note. Who had given him her number? The odds were on Diego, though she supposed Kat was also a possibility. Bret was back in California now with Bergen and Lisbeth. Did he really care if she got in touch with him? He hadn't called since returning to L.A.

She set the phone back on the desk. Then, after a second, she slid it out of her line of sight with the tip of her index finger as she checked the weather online. Sunny, seventy-five degrees, unusually low humidity. She would go for a run with Azul. Maybe then her brain would sort itself out.

For a moment, she rested her forearms against her knees and stared at the tattoos on the inside of each wrist. Done only in black ink, the right wrist held a beautiful eye surrounded by flames. The left wrist held a majestic black raven in flight, its visible left eye a faceted prism. The raven eye was always unsettling to her, though that tattoo was her favorite of the two. She felt like it was forever watching her. The tattoos were intricate and exquisitely done. Over the years countless people had commented on them. Unfortunately, when people asked where she'd gotten them done, she truthfully had no answer for them.

CHAPTER EIGHT

As she ate her lunch, nine-year-old Bergen James was bubbling over with exuberance. "Dad, did you see that last time around the corner, when I leaned it? Mom, it was so cool, you should have seen me!" She was sweaty and dirty, her long, dark blond hair streaked with mud, her cheeks flushed with excitement.

Bret was standing several feet away from them at the island in the large, sunny kitchen, eating a sandwich and talking on the phone to someone in his management team. He was also sweaty and dirty, wearing only a pair of long, black swim trunks. His tanned body was fit and toned, his reward for a full decade of following a steady work-out regime and eating mostly healthy fare. He was in far better physical shape now in his early fifties than when he'd been partying hard in his twenties and thirties. He winked at his daughter to acknowledge that he'd heard her.

Lisbeth was at the table with Bergen, eating a salad as she listened to her daughter give a detailed play-by-play of her morning motocross ride with her father. "When you're done eating you need to take a shower, and then you need to pack," she instructed Bergen. They were going to spend a few days at her boyfriend Leo's beach house with him and his two sons. The boys, twins, were around Bergen's age, and got along with her fairly well. Lisbeth picked up her phone to call her sister.

Bret hung up and finished his sandwich, swigging a bottle of cold, tart lemonade.

"You're going to be gone again, right?" Bergen asked him, to verify. She didn't like to leave for long if he was going to be home.

"I'll be around, Bee, but I'll be in and out. Meetings, studio, and one show. I'll still be here when you guys get back."

"Okay." She hopped up, put her dish in the sink, and disappeared from the kitchen.

Lisbeth soon followed her, and Bret looked down at an incoming text on his phone.

From Tayce: "Kat & Paul are inviting you to come stay at the farm for a week or so. I highly recommend it. Be cool to jam together at night, the three of us. Plus, Kat can COOK. Think of it as an artistic retreat. Look at your schedule & let me know what you think. Kat said Fallon's also invited. Whatever that means."

Bret leaned against the island and thought about this. It sounded beyond enticing, the proximity to Fallon aside. He'd been so busy wrapping up the new album. And he had really enjoyed spending time with those guys the other night at Solu. Looking briefly through his calendar, he saw that he had a block of free time coming up before tour rehearsals started. Interviews could all be done via zoom or phone. There didn't seem to be anything involving Bergen that necessitated his presence, no theater performance, no dance recital—Lisbeth always updated his calendar with Bergen-related information, and if not Lisbeth, his assistant Kara always knew Bergen's schedule. There was a theatre show she was rehearsing for, but it would still be going on when he came back. Softball was on-going, but she never expected him to be at every game. She was easy with him that way. He texted Kara to be sure he was free, and she texted back immediately, confirming that all he was committed to were some phone interviews that could be handled from anywhere.

He called Tayce back. "Hey, man, that sounds nice. I'm free in about two weeks. You'll still be around?"

"Hell, I just got here. I may be here for months. I'll let Kat know you're coming. What about that pretty girl?" he drawled.

"I'll get back with you on that." He hung up and stared out the window at the pool. He wanted to call her, but his pride refused.

* * * * * * *

Fallon's three-mile run took her throughout the majority of her little town. Gray was no more than a smudge on the map, an old farming community that was a little too far from Dallas to have been sucked in as a suburb. There was no defined town square, just a centralized smattering of old neighborhoods. Some houses had been expensively remodeled by people looking to turn a profit. Some houses were falling down but still inhabited. There were not a lot of job opportunities. Most of the people who lived in Gray were either retired, self-employed, unemployed, or worked in Dutton, which was also the location of the nearest full-sized grocery store and a community college. There was a small primary school in Gray, which was where Indio currently attended kindergarten, but after fifth grade the kids went to school in Dutton. There was a handful of churches, a tiny post office, a general store that sold basic groceries and household goods as well as feed and light farm equipment. There were three restaurants: Solu, Madrigal—the Mexican dive that was run by Mariana's uncle—and the Gray Cafe. All three restaurants depended on both local Gray-ites and customers from out of town to turn a profit.

Gray was home to families with kids, a high number of older, retired folks, and a smaller number of young singles who were still there because of family connections. Despite its small size, it was a good place to remain mostly anonymous if that's what you wanted. People kept to themselves.

Fallon's landlady, Ms. Landrum, was a nice enough woman in her eighties who'd lost her husband a decade prior. Every now and then she and Fallon would stand together in the yard and exchange pleasantries, but for the most part Ms. Landrum left Fallon alone. She appreciated what a good, steady, quiet renter she had in Fallon, and so wasn't one for the gossip regarding her reportedly strange young tenant.

Though most people in the town knew Fallon by sight, few knew anything about her besides that she was a waitress at Solu and a close friend of the handsome doctor and his family. She had steered several townspeople from peril or simple trouble, and of those that told their family and friends about her, less than half were believed. Some kids called her a witch, which always made her smile, unconcerned. She faintly believed that her close friendship with such a highly-respected local family protected her a little from the adults.

Slowing to an easy jog and catching her breath, Fallon hit ahead to a different song on her phone. Azul trotted along happily at her side, sniffing the air. She'd had no great revelations along the way, but she'd determined one painful and obvious thing: if she did nothing, she would probably never see Bret again. He had too much self-respect to come hunting for her after how she'd acted.

She slowed to a walk. The very thought of it—of never seeing him, speaking to him, touching him again—made her feel ill and weak, made her heart feel strangely bruised. She blinked in surprise. She never had to deal with these kinds of emotions. She never put herself in situations where her heart could be touched in such a way. She was meant to be alone in this life, she'd always felt that. Casual flings here and there— never local—were all she could handle. Falling for Bret James would only bring grief later, surely. Maybe that one night had gotten her out of his system, now that he knew the what, the how, and the why of her. Maybe he felt like now that his search was over, he could get on with his life.

Well, she would at least text him to let him know she was sorry about running out without a goodbye. She would do that much. She'd be able to tell from his response, or lack thereof, if she'd hit a dead end with him or not.

She actually groaned as she remembered: there was that whole foretelling-of-his-future-doom that she was going to have to tend to. She'd been so selfishly caught up in the strange new feelings welling up in her heart regarding this man that she'd pushed aside all thoughts of what really mattered: his life and death.

Whether he liked it or not, she wasn't going anywhere till that was sorted. With a renewed sense of ferocity as she returned to Ms. Landrum's driveway, she dropped to the ground and did twenty pushups. Azul crouched in front of her and playfully tried to lick her face.

* * * * * * *

Bret was floating around alone in the pool after lunch when his phone beeped with another text. He swam to the edge and glanced at the screen.

From Fallon. Finally. He held his breath as he read it: "Sorry about the other morning, it wasn't what you may think. I had no intention of leaving without saying goodbye. But my mind made other plans without consulting me. I miss you."

His lips curved into a smile as he texted her back: "I miss you, too. P & K invited me to stay at the farm a while, since T is there. I'll be there in less than two weeks, depending on what you think about it. If you want to see me again or not. They've invited you as well."

He hit send and waited, tapping his fingers in a nervous rhythm on the side of the pool. He was so intent on listening for the beep of an incoming text that he jumped a little when the phone rang with a call. His smile grew. "Hello, Fallon."

On the other end, she smiled back. "Hello, handsome. You forgive me?"

"I'll let you explain it to me later, but yes. Not that I haven't been a little troubled, wondering what happened. After that night, I must confess, I did not expect to wake up alone."

She grinned, letting herself into the backyard and locating the garden hose to fill Azul's water bowl. "I am sorry. I had to leave, suddenly, and then when I got home, I gave myself a shot for a headache. I didn't wake up till today after lunch."

"Are those drugs legal?"

"Mmm. They're custom."

"You have much to tell me. Again."

She sighed. "Yes."

"So, you'll see me when I come to town?"

"Of course I will! I'll have to bake a cake for Paul and Katrine right now to thank them for getting you back here so soon. And Tayce was involved, too, I'm sure."

"Are you okay?" he asked. He was wondering about her need for such a powerful shot.

"I'm fine now." But she sounded uncertain. "Look, I've got to go. Tessa's covering for me tonight at work, so I'm going to take the opportunity to get some things done around here."

He stared at the shimmering water all around him. "Can I call you later tonight?"

She smiled and thought she might be blushing a little. "I was hoping you would."

She hadn't been lying. She spent the next two hours baking and icing a vanilla-almond cake, which she carefully boxed up in cardboard. Then she changed into jeans, a black t-shirt, and sandals. She pulled her long hair back into a loose ponytail, then grabbed the cake and her car keys.

Her car was parked out in the driveway, though Ms. Landrum allowed her to park in the garage. She hadn't been able to fathom maneuvering into the garage when she'd gotten home yesterday from Dallas.

Fallon's car was a classic, black 1966 Dodge Dart GT convertible. Her brother had bought it when he graduated from high school and spent the next three years and much money fixing it up. He'd died not long after. The car had come to her in his will—what twenty-two-year-old has a will? She wasn't one for materialism and possessions, but she did deeply love this car—with its reliably non-functioning odometer and fuel gauge—as much for its physical beauty as for its memory of Luca. She sometimes thought he'd spent so much care fixing it up because he'd known his little sister would be the one driving it.

Luca also had second sight, but his ability had varied from hers. He could purposefully seek things out—answers, visions. He wielded his power, while she shied away from hers. When she was little, his use of their ability had scared her. She didn't want the visions she got without asking. Why would she seek out additional ones? He'd told her it made her gift more useful, but she didn't believe him.

Then when she was eleven, her secret training began, training even Luca did not know about. Powers she could barely comprehend swirled around her and through her. Six years later, Luca was dead. Murdered. He hadn't seen it coming, she assumed. And she'd seen it too late. The visions had failed them both, stealing from her the only family she'd had left. She'd turned her back on all of it, for a while at least.

But she wasn't thinking about any of that now. Fallon set the cake on the backseat, made sure it wouldn't slide around, then got in and whistled for Azul, who came running and quickly took his place in the passenger seat. She backed out of the long driveway with care, and then headed out of town.

Star Fall Farm lay about five miles east of Gray, one hundred and twenty acres, reachable only by a dusty, gravel road lined on either side by wooden fencing. The main house and its associated buildings were located in the general center of the property. Paul and Katrine resided in a beautiful, quaint, old farmhouse with a wraparound porch. There was an ivy-covered cottage-style guesthouse out back, as well as a more modern-looking silver metal building that housed a recording studio along with an upstairs apartment.

The property included an old wooden barn that was still in use, and a greenhouse where Katrine grew herbs, strawberries, and flowers year-round. Several roads and trails led to fields of vegetables, rows of berry bushes, fruit orchards, and a pasture full of angora goats, plus a couple of donkeys. Chickens, guineas, and geese wandered around freely with three dogs and a number of cats. A pond full of fish lay hidden in one far corner of the property. It was all divinely picturesque, and the few times Fallon had been out there previously, she had been in love with it all.

Parking her car in the shade of a leafy oak tree, though the sun was already low in the sky, Fallon got the cake out of the back and headed up to the main house. Azul trotted off to reacquaint himself with the canines he'd met on his two prior visits.

Katrine came out on the porch to meet her, smiling. "Well, this is a wonderful surprise. How are you, Fallon? We, well, I, was a little worried about you the other night when you seemed to abruptly disappear." Katrine was barefoot, dressed in a long, flowy red skirt and white tank top, her wavy chestnut hair falling around her shoulders. She looked earthy and pure, pretty with no make-up. Various crystals hung on chains around her neck, and she smelled of sandalwood and vanilla as she gave Fallon a gentle hug.

"I would have been worried," pointed out Paul as he joined them, "if I'd thought there was anything to worry about." He smiled at Fallon. "How are you, girl?"

"I'm fine," she assured them. She held out the box. "I made you guys a cake."

Much was made of the cake as together they urged her inside and into the large, sunny, farmhouse kitchen. Katrine got out plates and a knife as Paul removed the cake from the box and licked icing off his fingers.

Fallon sat on a wooden stool at the butcher block-topped island, admiring the touches of antique décor throughout the kitchen. A rainbow of fresh-cut flowers filled vintage mason jars and enamel canisters, scattered around on countertops and windowsills. "Where is Tayce?" she asked. "I have a feeling he wouldn't want to miss cake."

"Very astute of you," Katrine acknowledged, adjusting an errant sunflower. "He's gone for a walk; he should be back soon. He always loves spending time alone down by the pond. It's his favorite spot. He takes his guitar with him and sits beneath a sycamore for hours sometimes."

"I talked to Bret," Fallon mentioned. "He told me he'll be here in about two weeks."

Katrine watched her with bright, amber eyes, while Paul took a large bite of cake and murmured his appreciation. "Yes, we had such a nice time with him the other night, and we thought it would be fun to have him around a while, especially since we're currently housing one of his partners in crime."

"Hadn't seen Bret in years," Paul mentioned between bites. "Always loved that guy."

"And I thought," Katrine looked down at her slice of cake, "for some reason, about you. Oh, Fallon, this is delicious."

Fallon smiled briefly and looked out a window.

Paul and Katrine were both watching her curiously. Through the years, they'd become a bit enamored with her, charmed by her despite her elusive nature, and they'd regretted that she seemed to keep so much to herself. That she had appeared at their door for an unplanned social visit bearing a delicious homemade cake was almost too much to have hoped for.

Still staring out the window, Fallon said, "My friend Selah, her little boy would love it out here."

"Bring him," Katrine instructed. "Bring them both, we would love to meet Selah. Selah Lowe, do you mean? The doctor's wife? Don't they have that pretty blue and white Queen Anne over on Oak Street?"

Fallon returned her attention to them. "Yes, that's her. Selah has done wonders to that old house. She's solicited my help for most of the remodeling, though my skills are questionable." She laughed softly. "She and I have been best friends since we were kids. Their son, Indio, is my godchild. He's five. Could I really bring him?"

"We'll even let him ride Archimedes, our Shetland pony," promised Paul.

"Well, hey now, who started this party without me?" called Tayce as he ambled in the side kitchen door looking like a handsome, carefree hippy in ragged jeans, sandals and a grey t-shirt, his long, straight hair loose. His face was handsomely flushed with good health and the great outdoors—Fallon thought the farm agreed with him. He eyed the cake happily and then came over and gave her a big hug as if they were old friends, kissing her cheek. "Hello, beautiful. Did you bring this culinary treasure for me? It looks homemade."

"Partly for you," she confirmed, as he reached for a plate and accepted the large slice Katrine had cut for him.

He settled down onto a stool beside Fallon. "I wondered when I'd see you again. Talked to Bret since he got back home?"

Katrine thought Fallon would shrink from Tayce's up-front nature, but Fallon simply looked amused and calm beside him. She had to remind herself Fallon wasn't shy, she simply kept to herself. When she visited with them at Solu, she was always fun and talkative. Maybe it was the quiet of her soul that made one think at first that she was shy. But it was just the quietness, the stillness of her. There was something about Fallon that Katrine hadn't figured out yet, couldn't quite put her finger on, but she had a feeling it was something important.

"I talked to him earlier today," Fallon relayed. "He's looking forward to coming out here for a visit. And I'm looking forward to hearing you guys play and sing together. It will be total nostalgia immersion for me. I will be thrilled down to my toes."

Tayce pointed a fork at her. "I can make sure that happens," he promised. "The thrilled-down-to-your toes part." He wiggled an eyebrow suggestively.

She winked at him and squeezed his arm. "Such a shame. All this charm, wasted."

Paul laughed.

CHAPTER NINE

LUCA

Their parents had been dead for three months. Neither child missed them, because they had always been held at somewhat of an emotional distance, especially after Fallon made her appearance a little over three years ago. The children did not miss the love and affection they'd never had. And besides, life had since become extremely interesting.

Twelve-year-old Luca thought their previously-unknown cousin Jacob Roth—their court-assigned legal guardian—had been an okay guy so far. He didn't ask them too many questions, didn't seem to have unrealistic expectations of them, and was in no way trying to become their new father. Luca wondered why he'd never heard of Jacob before their parents' deaths. He'd always been told there were no living relatives nearby, only distant cousins scattered here and there. But to discover they'd had a cousin in the same city all this time? He couldn't believe it. And there was something about Jacob that nagged at him, something familiar.

A few times he brought it up, the question of why he'd never known of Jacob before, but their guardian always shrugged it off.

"Your parents and I, we were planets on different celestial courses," Jacob offered by way of cryptic explanation. "We had no reason to come into each other's universes."

"I just can't understand why they never even mentioned you," Luca said somewhat stubbornly. He wondered if there had been some kind of rift.

"You don't like kids." Fallon's accusation came out of the blue. She was standing in the middle of the kitchen as Jacob cooked dinner, staring up at the man with the faintest hint of a crooked little smile on her lips despite her assertion.

From across the room Luca stared hard at his seven-year-old sister, but she ignored him. She was always doing things like that. She had no filter. She didn't know yet that she shouldn't respond out loud to the things her ability to read people showed her, without first thinking it through.

Jacob paused a moment before settling his striking gaze upon her, and when he did, the gaze was not unkind, nor kind, it simply was. "For the most part, I've had no use for children in my life," he admitted.

Fallon looked at him, unwavering, with those penetrating green eyes.

After another moment, Jacob's face softened with a grin. "But you and your brother are not children, little one. It appears to me that I have been tasked with the care-taking of two very young-looking adults, that is all."

Her smile grew just a bit before she turned away.

Jacob's age was indeterminate, but Luca, who spent much time observing him, had guessed early fifties. He was tall and fit, his body lean and strong; all of his movements were purposeful and full of a rough grace. His thick, wavy brown hair hung just past his shoulders, and his handsome face was set off with a goatee, and was marked with the lines of a life lived fully and possibly lived hard. There were tattoos up and down his arms and onto his hands, mostly strange words and symbols that Luca had not been able to study closely, but most notably, on the inside of his left forearm, was a large, beautiful black raven with one faceted prism eye. On the same arm, he always wore a silver chain, dark as iron, double-wrapped around his wrist, and from which hung a square, darkly-tarnished locket.

Jacob shared no details of his life with them, and he disappeared frequently, his schedule without pattern. He always seemed to be around, however, when they needed something. They weren't even sure where or if he worked. He had a car, but it was never gone when he was, leaving them to wonder how he got around. Truly the car was only ever used when he had to take one of them somewhere, such as to a doctor or dental appointment.

The only thing he did regularly, besides disappear, was cook. He clearly loved being in a kitchen, and had shelves and shelves of cookbooks at his disposal. Everything he prepared for them was delicious, and he opened up their palates to a much wider variety and quality than they had been used to. Even when he was not around at mealtime, there were always leftovers waiting for them in the fridge.

Jacob's voice was rich and rough, with an indeterminable accent, and Fallon loved listening to him talk. Talking was not something Jacob did a lot of around them, but she eventually found a way to ensure the sound of his voice filled her world: she persuaded him to read to her at night.

Luca had felt pity for his sister while he observed Jacob's initial refusals to her request, but then one night, unexpectedly, she broke him, and Luca was surprised to hear Jacob's voice rolling down the hall from Fallon's bedroom as he read a few chapters of *To Kill a Mockingbird* to her. From that night forward, Jacob read to her at least three nights a week, and Luca watched as a bond began to form between them. A bond she had not had with their parents.

This troubled Luca. Despite that he was nothing less than kind to them, Jacob seemed like a bit of a dark, mysterious figure. The connection that was forming between Jacob and his little sister made Luca keenly aware t there was still much darkness in her; she was different from him in that way. He even wondered, during the most sleepless of nights, what the darkness in her meant, and if it meant she had a capacity—and here was his unforgivable thought—for evil? She was definitely a different creature from himself; she was difficult for him to interpret.

Before their deaths, the Quinns had lived a fairly modest existence: a rented house, only one car, no trips to the movies or restaurants. Luca still wondered why their parents had been going out to eat the night of their murders. Where had that money come from?

Money was not an object for Jacob Roth, and he was immensely generous with the siblings. Anything they wanted was theirs for the asking, though they were not greedy children, and did not abuse his generosity. More than anything, they embraced the freedom he allowed them. As they grew older, they spent a lot of time away from the house, exploring Austin, swimming in Barton Springs, lingering in bookstores, discovering new music, and learning about the world as you only can when you're young, and unfettered, and without much of a care.

CHAPTER TEN

With the directions she'd given him, Bret easily located Fallon's garage apartment on a sunny Wednesday afternoon. Since that first phone call two weeks ago, they'd called and texted each other every day, sometimes talking for hours at a time as their budding friendship strengthened and grew. While she could still sense him when they were states apart, they could not talk in their heads, and she told him it was probably the physical distance between them. Maybe if they were in the same state or general area—she wasn't sure—the communication would be present again.

"Luca and I, for sure, we were never out of state without each other. We were never that far from each other at all, really." Except once.

They couldn't speak in each other's heads until his plane touched down in Dallas.

Interesting, she mused, as his plane taxied down the runway. Around him, there was a flurry of activity as people started gathering up their belongings, but he sat calmly in his seat, listening happily to her voice in his mind. *I'd never even thought of it before,* she continued, *that there might be a complication to the communication, a limit.*

A few hours later, Bret parked his rented SUV in Ms. Landrum's simple, long dirt driveway. As he got out, he spotted an elderly woman in a big straw sunhat working in a flowerbed up by the house, which was about two hundred feet away from the garage and closer to the street. She was watching him closely. He smiled and waved, and she lifted a hesitant gloved hand and waved back. Then she returned to her roses.

Following a stepping-stone path through a gate and around to the back of the garage, he found the wooden stairs to Fallon's apartment. He was greeted with a single bark by a scruffy black dog who ran up to him, sniffed him enthusiastically, and then stood aside as if agreeing to let him pass. Bret climbed the stairs and knocked on the weathered blue door, which Fallon opened with a smile.

Barefoot in black t-shirt and gray running shorts, her hair down, she looked sunny and beautiful. "Hey!" She was absolutely giddy about seeing him again, and was beyond any attempts to keep those feelings at bay. They could not be contained.

He was grinning as he hugged her close, burying his face in her hair, breathing her in. "I missed you," he murmured.

"Me, too."

Then, unable to stand it, he kissed her deeply, and she returned the kiss, wrapping her arms tightly around him. After a few minutes, Bret pulled away, breathless, and looked around. "Do we need to leave, to get out to the farm?"

She shook her head, pulling him back to her. "We have plenty of time."

Just before seven that night, Bret stopped Fallon's black Dart, with which he was thoroughly in love, beneath the oak tree at Star Fall Farm, and as he got out, he looked around appreciatively. Tayce had been right. It was gorgeous out here. Little white lights were strung through the trees, and everything had a magical feel.

Azul leapt out of the backseat and raced off into the shadows, barking a greeting, tumbling around with the other dogs. Bret looked over to Fallon as she came around to join him, and he slid an arm around her waist, smiling down at her. She was wearing a vintage, knee-length, sleeveless blue and gray floral print dress, and she looked lovely.

A welcoming shout brought their attention to the front porch, where Tayce was coming down the steps, casual in jeans and a button-up cotton shirt. "You're just in time for dinner. Kat has been in the kitchen most of the afternoon, and I've been banned. Not even a nibble. Fallon, hello again, sweetheart." He hugged her tight, then he and Bret greeted each other enthusiastically. "How was the trip, man? A few days here and I'm telling you, you aren't going to want to leave."

"I already don't want to leave." Bret purposefully did not look at Fallon.

Tayce shook his head, feigning jealousy as he observed them. "I see she even let you drive this fine machine." He indicated the convertible.

"When I saw how he handled himself in other areas, I felt sure he could manage it," she teased. "Tayce, why doesn't your wife come along?" she asked, as he went around to help Bret with his luggage, which consisted of a large duffle bag, a back-pack, and a guitar in its case.

"She'd get bored," he answered easily. "She's a city girl, through and through. She has no use for..." he gestured around them, "...this."

But you're usually not lonely out here without her, Fallon mused to herself, reading it off him and recalling the scraps of rumors she'd heard.

"Where am I staying?" Bret asked.

"We did some rearranging. By the way, Katrine is, obviously, still busy in the kitchen, and Paul had to run to the store, so that's why they handed the greeting duties over to me, and they apologize profusely for the inadequacy. Anyway, there's an apartment up above the studio, they moved me in there. So, you have the cottage to yourself."

"Sweet. Sorry you got booted, dude."

Tayce shrugged and laughed. "I'll get it back when you're gone. Nothing will be going on in the studio unless I'm down there in the middle of it, so it won't be like it'll disturb me."

They walked through the beautifully-landscaped backyard down a stone path and entered the cottage, which was comfortably appointed with a living area, a bedroom, a bath with big claw-footed cast iron tub, and a tiny laundry room. There was an adequate kitchen area with a sink, small fridge, even smaller stove, and a table and two chairs. It was all decorated with mildly rustic, antique charm. Old, blue glass bottles filled with fragrant, freshly cut sweet peas lined the front windowsill.

Bret put his bags away in the bedroom, and Tayce turned to Fallon. "Where's your stuff, princess?"

"Mmm, I don't know if I'm staying."

He laughed. "Whatever. You kids are so cute."

She punched him gently in the ribs. "I'm going to go see if Katrine needs any help," she told them.

"Alright, I'll show Bret the studio."

Fallon headed up to the farmhouse, and in the kitchen, she was greeted with the aroma of a roast just out of the oven. There were all sorts of vegetables fresh from the garden, butternut squash soup, a caprese salad, a loaf of just-baked wheat bread, and a dewberry pie for dessert.

Katrine laughed to see Fallon's amazement at the bounty before her. Drying her hands on a dish towel, she came around the island and gave the younger woman a hug. "Yes, I do love to cook. Nice to see you again. Don't you look sweet? I'm so glad you and Bret are here! I was surprised we got him back as quickly as we did, but I believe we can blame it completely on you."

"This all looks amazing. What did Paul possibly have to run to the store for?"

Katrine shook her head. "The exactly right bottle of wine." She swept her arm aside to indicate the wine rack filled with about twenty wines. "And there are more in the cellar. He's very particular about his wine choices. How did Bret like the cottage? Is it going to be alright for him?"

"Of course, it's perfect, so pretty the way it's decorated. Can I set the table?"

"Already done. You can put ice in some glasses for water if anyone wants some. And you can pour yourself some of the chardonnay that I'm drinking, if you'd like. No need to wait for Paul!"

Paul finally returned, coming into the kitchen with Tayce and Bret, who had finished the tour of the studio. "Tomorrow you can get the full tour of the farm," Paul promised their new guest.

"What is this?" Bret was eyeing the food. "Katrine, I can see you're going to spoil me."

"Why do you think I stay for such long stretches at a time?" asked Tayce. "No one cooks like Kat."

Bret caught Fallon's eye from across the kitchen, and he grinned at her like a devil. She felt herself involuntarily begin to swoon, and inwardly berated herself. As she watched him standing there looking relaxed in jeans and a black t-shirt, laughing with Tayce and Katrine, Fallon felt defeated. How was she supposed to resist him? That smiling, bright-eyed, gentle man was sweeping her off her feet. He was leading her into all the places she had always resisted. Getting close to people was practically illegal in her book, and yet here she was, glowing in his company, not to mention having dinner with an entire group of people who were already beginning to feel a little like family. This would not end well. She should leave them, say goodnight, and vanish out into the darkness.

But instead, she smiled and went to Bret's side when he held out an arm and called her over. She leaned against him as he held her close and kissed the side of her head.

Beautiful girl, he said to her in her mind, and she looked up at him. *I could fall in love with lovely you.*

Her heart fairly trembled. And she knew he could see it in her face. Dammit.

The raven tattoo on her left wrist began to tingle uncomfortably, but as she frowned curiously down at it, Tayce called out to them.

"Break it up, lovebirds, dinner is served." He handed Fallon a hunk of the still-warm bread he'd broken off. "Try this, it makes me melt inside, it's so good. And check it out, she makes her own honey-apple-butter."

"How do you not gain a ridiculous amount of weight here?" Fallon asked him, nibbling on the bread as she walked by his side to the heavy wooden dining table. The raven tattoo had settled back down, and she pushed it out of her mind. She and Bret sat down directly across from each other, and Tayce sat on her right, Paul and Katrine at each end.

Tayce patted his mid-section. Though he was tall and lanky, she could tell that exercise was not on his usual to-do list. "You mean, how do I maintain this stunning physique?"

She pressed her lips together.

He leaned close. "Maybe one night I'll show you, huh?" He raised a teasing eyebrow, but then laughed and sat back before she could even roll her eyes.

The evening was pleasant, the food delectable, the wine perfect. The mood was light, and there was much laughter. Katrine could see the difference in Bret, that he was no longer as tense and strange as he had been at Solu once Fallon entered the scene.

"I keep thinking you two knew each other before," Katrine said to them at one point. "I mean before that night at Solu. Am I wrong?"

Fallon and Bret both froze, the latter looking a little surprised. Tayce noticed their reactions, and was curious, watching them with interest.

Katrine covered her mouth with her hand. "I'm sorry. Sometimes I do that. I spoke out of turn. It's none of my business."

Fallon glanced briefly at Bret. "No, it's fine. You're actually correct. About a year and a half ago we saw each other for the first time, one night in Vegas. We spoke briefly, and then we went our separate ways. That night in Solu a few weeks ago, when we recognized each other, it took us both by surprise. We were overwhelmed at the coincidence."

"Vegas? A year and a half ago?" Tayce was on the alert. "You don't mean that night those two went missing?" He was staring at Bret.

Fallon also looked purposefully at Bret. *I shouldn't know who he's talking about,* she reminded him.

"Yes," he said firmly, taking over, though not smoothly. "Yes, it was that night. So much went on that night. I met Fallon, and then we parted ways, but I never forgot her. She stayed in my mind so strongly, then when I saw her at Solu that evening I felt like I was losing my mind."

Katrine was thrilled. "But that's a wonderful story! How strange and beautiful. Destiny." She looked misty-eyed. Paul smiled at her across the table. Bret and Fallon stared at each other without expression. Tayce looked thoughtful.

Then Paul asked about that night in Vegas, what they knew, and Tayce launched into a complete re-telling of that evening and the aftermath. There had still been no sign of Peter Stillson, no clue to his whereabouts. Jack Lane faithfully made sure posters with Peter's photo and pertinent information were posted in every city his tour stopped in. When Katrine first saw one of the posters, she had joked lightly that the physical description perfectly matched Tayce Williams but for the difference in age.

"All rockers start to look alike after a while," Paul commented with a chuckle.

It was after midnight when the party broke up; Katrine and Paul refused everyone's polite offers to help clean up. Yawning, Tayce said goodnight and headed out into the starry darkness towards the studio. Bret and Fallon went to her car without a word, and he got her bag out of the trunk.

"I guess I'm staying," she said unnecessarily, as they wandered back towards the cottage in the faint moonlight, arms around each other.

"If you didn't, I'd follow you home," he confessed. "It's nicer this way, and less with the stalker element."

Azul was waiting faithfully for them at the cottage door, and Fallon knelt and greeted him with a hug before letting him inside.

CHAPTER ELEVEN

JACOB

The clock in the hall was striking midnight as Jacob made his way from the kitchen towards his bedroom. A shadow of movement caught his eye, and he stopped. Fallon was curled up in a leather chair in the faint moonlight, watching him, and he turned to face the small girl. She was smiling at him, clad in blue and white pajamas, twirling her long hair around one finger.

"What is it, little one?" he asked softly.

She let go of her hair and leaned forward. "Will you stay forever, this time?"

Everything in him stilled, at her emphasis on the last two words. "This time," he repeated. "What other time was there?" Surely, she had been too young?

She looked like she was thinking hard, and after a long moment she just shrugged, as if she couldn't quite remember. "Jacob," she said softly, as if to herself, as if she were speaking a memory. Then she hopped off the chair and scampered down the hall to her own room.

He rested a hand on the back of the chair and watched her go.

CHAPTER TWELVE

The next several days were so pleasant, Fallon could almost forget Bret was in some sort of unknown mortal danger. And could almost not feel guilty for not telling him the truth about said danger. Now and then, with faint hope in her heart, she imagined that the premonition had been wrong. But they had never been wrong before. She had never been sent a false premonition.

The two of them were mostly inseparable, either locked away in the cottage or wandering around the farm together. Most days they went running on the various trails and roads throughout the farm. Paul and Tayce were frequently in the studio, but Tayce broke away fairly often to hang out with them, and the three went swimming together in the pond a few times as well as venturing to Dutton to eat Chinese food on more than one occasion, giving Paul and Katrine a break from having guests.

On the nights she didn't work, Fallon would sit in the kitchen and chat while Katrine cooked dinner. After the meal, Paul, Tayce, and Bret would get out their guitars and gather on the patio, sitting around the fire pit to drink, play, and sing to Fallon's never-ending, giddy delight.

"You're doing irreparable damage to their egos, all three of them, you do realize this?" Katrine admonished her playfully, squeezing in beside her on the chaise Fallon was perched on. The flames from the fire pit sent shadows and light dancing across their faces

Fallon laughed. "I know I'm being such a groupie. But I love this. I always loved their music. It brings me joy; it runs through my veins. And I have always been a sucker for a guy with a guitar."

Katrine glanced across the flames where Bret sat playing his guitar, singing along with Paul. Every now and then his eyes strayed to Fallon. "I don't think we have to wonder if he's also a sucker for you," Kat noted. "He's a goner." And he's not the only one, she observed in amusement, as she watched Tayce watch Fallon as well. But Fallon seems to only have eyes for Bret, Kat mused to herself.

All three men had excellent voices, but Tayce's talent with a guitar easily blew the other two away. Technically, he was an absolute genius, enormously respected by his peers, and he liked to show off. When he wasn't playing with Dangerous Eye, Tayce was in demand in other bands, always on the road, touring with whoever would have him. After each Dangerous Eye tour, Paul could happily return to the farm to his other hobbies and artistic pursuits for a space of time. Bret, though he loved being on the road, sought an even balance in his life. But for Tayce, playing his guitar was all he had ever wanted to do, all he had ever asked for. It came ahead of everything else, and his passion showed through fully.

Fallon was thoroughly entranced with his skill. "Tayce Williams, did you sell your ever-lasting soul to the devil, to be able to play like that?" she teased.

He grinned wickedly back at her. "I'll never tell."

"I signed a non-disclosure agreement years ago," commented Paul, "or I'd tell you all about it."

On the nights that Fallon worked, Bret drove her to Solu, and then picked her up at the end of her shift, often with Tayce in tow. Sometimes the two men arrived early enough to have a drink with Diego, who was curious about these new friends in Fallon's life. Tayce and Bret's regular appearances were fueling the gossip fires among the staff. No one said anything to Fallon directly, but Tessa kept her updated: "You're sleeping with both of them, and the details are quite scintillating. Casi is madly jealous."

One night Bret and Fallon had dinner with Selah and Michael at their home, and the evening left Bret feeling glad that Fallon had two such friends so near her, who so obviously cared about her.

"I love them," he told her, as they were getting into the car that night to head back to the farm.

"I've had Selah all my life," she explained, "and when Michael came along, he just fit in perfectly to the way she and I are together. He accepted me, strangeness and all, without hesitation, and quickly became like a protective big brother. We were all lucky. I don't know what would have happened if Selah had met someone who wanted her to choose between him and me, or who couldn't accept what I am."

"I think I know who she'd have chosen." He squeezed her knee. "I'd like you to come to California soon."

Fallon looked over at him. She was quiet for a moment, speculative, and he wondered briefly if he'd said the wrong thing. But then she smiled. "I can't wait to meet Bergen. Let me know when, so I can talk to Diego and Mariana about my schedule."

"I'll look at my schedule tomorrow." He handed her his phone. "Or you can check it right now. Look at the calendar."

She maneuvered to a calendar that looked to her to be quite full. She squinted. "Who's KI?"

"Kara Inger. My assistant."

"You have an assistant?"

"Don't sound so surprised. It's part-time. Honestly, would you trust me to keep track of everything? Every person, place, time, event, flight, bus, car, hotel, appointment and appearance?"

"Well, not when you put it like that. No."

"Kara's been with me for about seven years. She also coordinates with Lisbeth, makes sure I have everything on my calendar that Bergen's doing, too. She handles my website maintenance and updates, all the social media stuff that I would never remember to do. She's invaluable, really, especially when you begin to realize how scattered my brain is."

"Sounds full-time to me."

CHAPTER THIRTEEN

LUCA

They'd been living with Jacob for seven months when something clicked in Luca's subconscious, and he realized an important fact. It unsettled him, and for a while he debated telling Fallon. What he had realized was that Jacob really was familiar to him. He was without a doubt the same man who had delivered Fallon to his house four years earlier. And therefore, if what his "mother" had told him was true, it was Jacob who had also presented baby Luca to the Quinns twelve years ago. This meant Jacob must know their history, who their real parents were. And maybe even how and why they had these strange abilities.

Despite this exciting epiphany, Luca found himself unable to confront Jacob about it. To him, Jacob was still intimidating. How Fallon had wrangled the man into reading to her at night still stumped her brother. Though once he realized who Jacob was, he remembered how three-year-old Fallon had held onto him so tightly, how Jacob had hugged and kissed her goodbye, her overwhelming grief when he left her with the Quinns. Fallon might not remember him clearly, Luca reasoned, but Jacob knew exactly who Fallon was, and any fondness he'd had for her four years ago must still be in his heart. Of course, he would give in and read to her.

Luca decided in the end not to tell Fallon about Jacob. He had never told her that their parents were not really their parents—he'd always thought that was an unnecessary fragment of their lives that she was better off not knowing. To inform her of Jacob's role in their past, he would necessarily have to let her know that they had been adopted. She didn't seem to remember that her brother had not always been in her life. She was only eight years old, and though far spunkier and seemingly tougher than she'd been just a few years ago, he knew her mind was still fragile in places. He worked hard daily trying to make her strong. Dropping this new information on her now would only undermine his quest to heal and strengthen her.

In these months with Jacob, she had improved in leaps and bounds, becoming more comfortable with herself and her abilities. This environment was much more to her liking than their old life with the Quinns, that much was clear.

CHAPTER FOURTEEN

A fter a light lunch in the cottage one afternoon, as Fallon was clearing the table, Bret suddenly caught both her hands in his and turned them over, exposing her bare wrists and the two tattoos.

"What do these mean?" He'd been wondering about them for days, but for some reason hadn't wanted to bring them up. They were as unsettling to him as the phrase on the back of her arm.

She gently pulled her hands from his and turned away. "Stories for another time." She went over to the sink and began washing the dishes.

Somewhat surprised, he sat back in his chair and watched her, sipping his unsweetened iced tea. "You aren't going to tell me?"

"Not today, no." She rinsed the soap off the dishes, and then began drying the plates and silverware. Her hair was pulled up in a knot at the back of her head, and she was wearing short, cut-off denim shorts with a green tank top.

He admired the flash of muscle in her arms and shoulders as she moved. "I've been meaning to ask you about those tattoos." He set his glass back on the table. "I guess that first night in Dallas I was too distracted by the rest of you to pay them much attention."

She threw a grin at him over her shoulder, and he smiled back, but she still refused to offer any information. His own arms had their fair share of tattoos, garnered during his younger days as the singer in a struggling, then wildly successful, rock band. Nothing horribly regrettable, really. No names of past lovers or images he was uncomfortable with Bergen seeing, nothing like that. His favorite tattoo was the bee between the thumb and forefinger of his left hand, if only because of what it symbolized.

Fallon put away the last dish and came over to him, leaning down to kiss him. She saw that he was thoughtfully rubbing the bee, and she pointed to it questioningly.

"For Bergen," he explained. "Since she was a baby, I often call her 'Bee.' So, this is for her. My busy little bee."

Fallon sighed dramatically as he pulled her down onto his lap. "Now, if that cute sentiment doesn't get the women to go home with you, I don't know what will."

He laughed. "I usually don't give the details. I usually just say, 'It's for my daughter.'"

"Mmm-hmm."

"Well, on a really off night, I do whip out my phone with all her baby pictures and choke up when I'm talking about her."

"Of course you do." She kissed him again, then paused with her nose touching his. "I'm a little crazy about you."

He kissed her back. "I'm glad. I wouldn't want to be crazy all by myself."

"No danger there." She grabbed his hand and hopped up. "Let's go for a walk."

They had been wandering around the farm a while when suddenly she stopped, closed her eyes, and let out a breath.

Bret stopped, too, watching her closely. This was it, he supposed. She was having a premonition. He'd wondered how long it would be before she had one around him. He'd been relieved to find out she didn't seem to have them every day.

When she opened her eyes, she had a funny look on her face. "I didn't bring my phone. Please call Tayce and let me talk to him."

He did as she asked, handing her the phone as Tayce answered. The latter laughed when he realized it was Fallon on the line. "What are you, doing administrative work for him now? Placing his calls?"

"Listen to me—call your wife and tell her she just left her wallet in the dressing room at Nordstrom."

"What? You know she's not here, Fal, she's in California. Have you guys been getting into those funny weeds down by the pond?"

"I know she's in California. She's at The Grove, shopping. I'm not joking around. Call her and tell her. Say you were napping and had a dream that she lost the wallet, and that you can't shake it as being true." Her voice was firm. "If it turns out she's at home watching TV and hasn't been to Nordstrom today, I'll bake you another cake."

"Too easy!" Tayce crowed. "That's all I have to do? Piece of cake, as they say. Call you right back."

She folded her arms and looked at Bret, who raised an eyebrow. "Yes, sometimes it's as simple as that," she confirmed. "Now, the whole monetary and identity theft that they would have had to deal with was not going to be so simple. Plus, now I'll have to decide what to tell him about myself, since he is a recurring character in my life."

A couple of minutes later the phone rang, and she placed him on speaker so Bret could hear how it went. "Yes?"

"Now she's pissed at me," Tayce complained, "and thinks I'm spying on her."

"But..."

"But yes, she's at The Grove and had just left Nordstrom and the wallet isn't in her purse. She's going back to look for it right now. I think she's more worked up over how I would know this than about losing her wallet. She's not so much buying the 'I had a dream' thing. You and I are going to talk later, little girl. This is not over. She's mad at me, and now I don't even get cake? What kind of not-working-out-for-Tayce deal was this? We're talking later." He hung up.

She handed the phone back to Bret, who had struggled not to laugh. "What are you going to tell him?" he asked.

"The truth, I think."

"He's a really good guy, despite his big talk and his antics. I trust him."

She nodded with certainty. "So do I."

"Oh, yeah," he slapped a hand to his thigh with faint sarcasm, "you can read him, right? Is that why you know you can trust him?"

She lifted a shoulder. "More or less. I don't rely on it one hundred percent, but everything I get off of him tells me that he would be absolutely loyal to you and to me." She laughed a little. "More so than to his wife, anyway."

"Mmm. Too true. Can you read everyone?"

"Very nearly, yes. If I can't read someone, I get suspicious. And everyone is different. Tayce is an open book; I can read lots off him, and in detail. For instance, Diego and Jack Lane are ones where I get only a general feeling. Of course, I've only seen Jack the one time, and he was under the influence."

"Paul?"

"He's in-between. So are you."

"Selah?"

She shook her head. "I don't read Selah."

He looked surprised.

"She asked me not to, long ago. She doesn't like it. So I don't."

"What about Katrine?"

"Oh, with her it's vague."

In truth, she could not read Katrine at all, and she wasn't sure why. She didn't know if she should be troubled by that or not. Paul's wife seemed like such a benign figure.

She tugged on Bret's hand, wanting to change the subject. "Come on, I want to go look at the fainting goats. They make me giggly."

As they strolled, Azul ran here and there, sometimes following along with them, other times darting off into the trees or fields after a rabbit, always returning after some time. Bret loved most dogs, and he was quickly growing fond of Azul, who seemed to be a loyal, well-behaved, good-humored animal who was devoted to Fallon.

"He's a great dog," he mentioned. "How long have you had him?"

Fallon smiled a far-off smile. "Azul has just always been around. He showed up as a stray and stole my heart."

They walked hand-in-hand down a shaded dirt trail. They were far from the house, all alone but for Azul's continued company and a mockingbird that was singing to them from the top of a pear tree. The heat and humidity were not something he was enjoying, but aside from that Bret was enjoying his time at the farm. And he was curious after listening to her conversation with Tayce.

"So, you can't choose who you see things about?" he asked.

She hesitated for more than a few seconds. "The Gaelic for 'second sight' is '*darna shealladh*'—the involuntary ability to see the future. The visions are just sent to me at random. If I'm around someone all the time, chances are, you know, that I might see something about them, if something is about to happen. You see, I've been around Tayce for a week now, and I get a premonition about his wife. But it's not necessarily always that way. I do only get visions regarding a person I have a good chance of reaching before whatever happens, though."

There was a calculating look on his face.

"No, you cannot attach me to Bergen's side for the rest of her life," she warned.

"It's crossed my mind."

"It's a common side effect of knowing me. People want me to be a lucky charm, a talisman. The protector of their loved ones. But that's not what I am. Every image I'm given is by chance, and there's always the possibility that I won't be able to interpret it in time even if I do get one. Never forget what I'm telling you: I cannot save everyone."

"What about Selah? She's been closest to you forever. You've had premonitions about her?"

Fallon gritted her teeth. "Oh, yes."

He eyed her. "And don't you think she wants you to watch over Indio every second of the day?"

"Of course, but Selah is realistic about it. Because she knows me so well. She knows I'd do anything for that child, to keep him safe. But she also knows I have no real choice in the matter." She shrugged. "But nothing bad has ever happened to Indio, so who knows for sure? A mother's heart, I imagine, is less forgiving, no matter the circumstances, when harm comes to their child. Perhaps she would blame me, after all, in spite of herself."

"So, it's mostly strangers whom you get visions of."

"Mostly. As I've told you, I don't have a lot of people who I'm close to. I don't want bad things to happen to the people I love. I'm not strong in that way. It's easier for me to love fewer people, to be a loner. That way when things happen, there is at least an emotional distance for me. Because I don't always succeed." She sighed. "For people who don't know the truth, I get the reputation for being a good person to go to for advice. For instance, with one of the girls at work, I cautioned her not to date a particular guy. And it turned out to be a supremely smart decision. Only she didn't know I had a premonition of her getting beaten black and blue by said guy. Or I tell someone not to go through with a business deal, and they do anyway, and it tanks. Suddenly I am Fallon-of-All-Knowledge. Then they think they can just come get advice. Not knowing that there was a premonition behind it the last time. My non-premonitory advice is as hit-and-miss as anyone's. They eventually lose faith in me, which is fine, until the next time I have a premonition and need them to believe me."

"How does it work? What information do you get? How do you find them, especially if they're strangers?"

She thought a moment. "It's difficult to explain."

"Have you explained it to many people?"

"No. Only one, actually."

"Selah?"

"Yes, she's the one."

He kissed her temple. "You don't have to tell me."

"I think I'd like to." She glanced at him. "So you'll know."

They were still in the pear orchard. They stopped and sat down in the shade of a tree, on the lush green grass that had not yet been singed by months of summer. He sat with his back against the trunk of the tree, and her between his legs, so that she could lean back comfortably against his chest.

She told him as best she could about how the images slammed into her head in a blur, how she had to close her eyes and breathe to get them to settle. Then how the bad feelings would hit, how she could usually tell by the degree how bad the danger was. She'd gotten only a twinge of unhappiness from the vision of Tayce's wife. On the other side of the coin, there was the night in Vegas when she'd gotten the vision of him. The strong feelings of danger and death had worked themselves slowly into a frenzy inside her, making her feel weak and sick and frightened.

If the person was unknown to her, she usually looked for either landmarks in the vision to tell her where they were, or for other people they were with. It was like a puzzle every time, with varying degrees of difficulty. Sometimes she knew the person, their location, and exactly what danger they were in within seconds. Sometimes she spent hours working it out. A few times, by the time she'd figured it out, it was too late. Sometimes people didn't listen to her. People had died because they didn't listen, or because she didn't get to them in time. She'd learned long ago that she couldn't carry all of that with her, inside herself, the guilt over the deaths, and damage, and sadness she hadn't been able to prevent. That it would eat her alive.

"I told you I leave this town at times because my head fills with the people, their problems and difficulties, and that's true. But really, for such a small population, not that many bad things happen all the time. I leave and go away, in part, because I feel like I should. Because I don't know why I have this ability, but I feel like I'm supposed to go out in the world and help people if I can. After about two months in one location, I'm usually drained physically and emotionally, and I come back here to recharge." She shrugged. "I don't know. I've spent a lifetime trying to figure it out."

She took his hand. "One last thing you do need to know about me, in case you see me doing it and start to doubt everything that I am, is that I can lie like the devil. All my life I've had to lie, about who I am, what I can do, where I live. And to save people, I lie all the time, because rarely is the average person going to believe me if I say I've just had a premonition of this or that, please do this now to avoid certain disaster. So, I get extremely creative."

"Do you lie to me?"

She looked back at him and smiled her crooked little smile. "All the time."

He pulled her hair aside and kissed her neck, holding her closer. She relaxed against him, and they both sank into a dreamlike state, the heat buzzing around them, making them tired.

The images flew unbidden into her head, breaking her mind with their intensity. And she saw, with fear wrapping around her heart, that it was the same as the morning in the hotel room—images of Bret, one after the other. She braced herself, but still the severity of feelings that crashed into her made her lean over at the waist. If she hadn't already been sitting, she would have fallen. She held her hands to her head, moaning, shaking her head as if to deny them.

Bret was immediately on his knees beside her. Fallon curled up into a ball in the grass. How was she supposed to help him, if the visions were so crippling? Had Luca ever endured anything like this? Could she just wait for them to pass? She caught a glimpse of Bret, there beside her; he had his hands on her, speaking to her, but she couldn't hear him. What danger was he in? She closed her eyes tight and strained to focus. Had she left her shots at home? If only she could fight against it. What was causing this? She'd never had visions of this magnitude.

She heard Azul barking in the distance. She grabbed Bret's hand and held it tightly to her chest, focusing on it, concentrating. She dove inside herself, swimming through the darkness and the pain, looking, looking for something to tell her. Then she saw something, a shadow, no, it was coming into focus. A large black bird. A raven. It looked at her with one gleaming black eye, the other eye a prism. It opened its razor-sharp beak, and she jerked away. Then everything went black.

Fallon woke up in the cottage on the bed, a cool, damp rag smelling of clary sage on her forehead, the ceiling fan spinning lazily above her. Bret immediately came into her view at the foot of the bed as she tried to sit up, and she fell back on the pillows with a sigh. Her head ached viciously, but at least he was safe.

Katrine came to her side and patted her hand. "How are you feeling? That heat can sneak up on you. You two should have taken along something to drink, since you were going to be out so long." She held a glass of cool water to Fallon's lips, and she tasted the mint from the crushed leaves Katrine had mixed into it.

"Thank you, Kat. I'm fine." She looked to Bret, who was eyeing her soberly. He didn't say anything.

Katrine set the water back on the bedside table next to a half-full carafe. "Just let me know if you need anything, or if you think you might need a doctor? But you're young and strong, I think you just need to rest. You can't fool around with heat sickness, though. If you start to feel nauseous or get a headache, you let me know."

When she was gone, Bret came closer. Tears came to Fallon's eyes as she looked up at him. "I'm sorry."

He looked curious at her apology.

She turned her head away. "Can you bring me my bag? I need to take something for this headache."

"Not a shot?" He got up and retrieved the messenger bag for her.

She reached into the bag blindly, fishing around, and came out with a dark blue glass vial with a black lid which she unscrewed, tapping two white capsules out into her palm. When she'd swallowed them with some water, Bret lay down beside her on the bed.

"I didn't realize that some of your visions were that brutal," he said softly.

She breathed in slowly. She had thought about this a thousand times. "They never have been before. Close, but not this bad. This was like the one I had in the hotel, when I had to gracelessly run out on you. In fact, it was the exact same vision. Same person, same feelings. Last time I went home and gave myself a shot. This time I met it head on, tried to work it out by force. It was too much for me, obviously."

"You scared me," he admitted. He rested his head on her pillow, staring into her eyes. "Who was it about? How could you have another one, weeks later? Wouldn't the thing have happened to them already?"

She blinked rapidly to keep the tears at bay. "Apparently not."

"Who?" he whispered.

The tears tumbled onto her face. "You."

He lay there beside her quietly for what seemed like a long time before he spoke again.

"Me?"

She nodded.

He shook his head, puzzled. "I don't understand."

"Neither do I."

He looked confused. "Well, what do you think it means? It means I'm going to die?" His voice was soft and cautious.

She pressed her forehead against his, clutching his arm. "No. I'm not going to let you die. I think it's telling me about something in the future. That's why it's so different. I think it's the connection of our minds that's causing the crazy intensity. Like it's an entirely different ability than what I usually have. Bret, as connected as we are, I won't believe I'm getting these visions only to lose you in the end. I think I'm getting them so that I'll be ready. I don't think it's anytime soon. I'm so sorry." She slid her arms around him.

CHAPTER FIFTEEN

Exhausted and emotionally drained, Bret and Fallon didn't leave the cottage for the rest of the day, so Tayce had to wait to have his talk.

Fallon sought him out first thing the following morning, locating him alone in the studio with his guitar. When he saw her come in, he slid the headphones he'd been wearing down to his neck.

"Come to tell me my fortune?" he asked dryly.

She sat down in a chair near him, folding her legs up into a cross-legged position. "I'm not as useful as that."

"Hmm. I wonder." He played a few chords on the guitar. "Want to tell me what's going on?"

"I see things. Visions. Of trouble that people are about to be in. It's all random. Chance. I've always been this way, since I was a child. I'd appreciate it if you didn't share this new knowledge with anyone. Paul and Katrine don't know."

"Bret does, obviously." He was paying close attention to her, his joking manner set aside.

She nodded. "Bret knows all about it. He's known for a year and a half." She took a deep breath. "That night in Las Vegas, Bret went back inside the club because I told him to. It wasn't a bad feeling he had. It was a feeling I had, about him being in danger. I got him to take you and Jack in with him just in case, though I didn't think either of you were in trouble. There was no time to try to convince the other two. I had no feelings of doom about you, Jack, Peter, or Cyn, but look what happened to those two. If you and Jack had remained outside, I don't think we'd be sitting here together right now."

"Whoa." Now he looked genuinely startled. He set the guitar and the headphones aside and leaned towards her. "You're saying you knew something bad was going to happen on that street."

"Yes. I was able to figure out that it was something to do with the blue van, I just didn't know what. And it was going to happen for sure to Bret, that's all I knew. But that didn't mean everyone else wasn't in trouble as well."

His eyes had widened. "It really was the van? I remember reading about it. Are you playing with my mind?"

"I kind of wish I was, but I'm not. It's all true. This is my life."

He let out a long breath. "Does Jack know about this?"

She nearly snorted, trying to hold in her laughter. "Jack Lane is probably one of the last people I'd confess my abilities to."

He nodded sagely. "True, true." He sat back, looking a little shaken. "So here we are, huh? Still waters. Wait, did you just say 'abilities' plural?"

She bit her tongue at the slip, and shook her head.

But he was grinning now. "Mind if I ask Bret more about it later?"

"Ask him whatever you want. Just please, for my sake, tell no one. Ever."

"No, beautiful, don't worry. I can keep your secrets. I can do that much."

"I know you can. That's why I told you." She got up, impulsively leaned over and kissed his cheek, and then left him alone in the studio.

He sat and stared into space for a long while after she was gone.

Fortuitously for a curious Tayce, that night Paul and Katrine were out of town, leaving their guests to their own devices. Fallon fetched take-out for them from Solu. For a long time after they ate, Bret and Tayce sat outside by the blazing fire pit, drinking and looking up at the big sky full of stars and talking while Tayce strummed an acoustic guitar.

His tongue loosened by the alcohol, and relieved to be able to talk about everything with someone other than Fallon, Bret ended up telling Tayce a lot more about Fallon and her abilities than she'd revealed in the studio, but she didn't try to stop him when she overheard the conversation in his head. She smiled to herself—when he drank, she could hear absolutely everything.

As she finally joined them later, bottle of wine in hand, Tayce couldn't help staring at her in wonder. "I can see why you don't usually tell anyone all of this," he commented.

"Yeah, no kidding," she agreed, sitting down between them. "Would you like to see a card trick next?"

He raised his glass to her. "You don't have to impress me, sweetheart. I'm already a big fan."

Did I say too much? Bret asked, as she pulled her knees up and leaned comfortably against him.

She looked at him and shook her head, smiling. *He's a secret-keeper.*

Tayce was glancing back and forth between them. "Are you doing it now? 'Talking' to each other? This is totally wicked cool."

"'Wicked cool?'" She squinted at him. "Too much alcohol and you start breaking out the cutesy adjectives?"

"It's my single weakness. And I've got daughters. Give me a break."

She laughed. "I believe you have other weaknesses. And I work with one of them."

He grinned. "I've only seen Casi once. Maybe, well, a few times. I don't know." He toasted her with his glass. "Diego does always hire the prettiest girls around. I will never understand how I've missed you all these years."

She nudged his knee with her foot. "We weren't supposed to meet yet. Obviously. Butterfly wings, and dust, and all that."

CHAPTER SIXTEEN

When Bret returned to the west coast Saturday night, his house was dark and empty. Bergen was performing in a show with a local theatre group, and she and Lisbeth wouldn't be home for another few hours. The lonely house made him miss Fallon, and as he passed from room to room, he tried to imagine her in each of them, but it was difficult. She seemed somehow temporary, ethereal, and he kept having the recurring fear that she would slip through his fingers.

He was unusually nervous about introducing her to Bergen. His daughter often saw the women he dated, but rarely in a situation where he was bringing them together specifically for that purpose. Most, he freely admitted, weren't Meeting-Bergen quality.

He'd already spoken on the phone to Lisbeth about Fallon's impending arrival.

"Should I not be here?" she had asked. Women were often intimidated by her, by her presence in Bret's house, her role as his beloved daughter's mother.

Bret shook his head, knowing what she was thinking. "No, you can be there. Fallon is in no way alarmed by the idea of you. I think she's looking forward to meeting you, actually."

"Likewise. You sound really happy."

"I am really happy."

Lisbeth smiled, her heart genuinely glad for him. "Of course, you had to find the girl who's magic. Does she have premonitions on a regular basis?"

"It doesn't seem so. She only had two, that I know of, when I was with her for, what? Eleven days? I don't know what a 'regular basis' would be for premonitions."

"Neither would I. I suppose we'll find out."

He did not tell Lisbeth about Fallon's dark premonition regarding himself. It wasn't something he wanted to think about, to speak out loud.

* * * * * * *

Selah let herself into Fallon's apartment Sunday after church and found her friend in the midst of giving the place a thorough spring cleaning. Often Fallon accompanied the Lowes to the small local Baptist church, but this morning she had been absent. Selah went straight to the kitchen and poured herself a glass of sweet tea, before settling on the couch, crossing one leg over the other and delicately kicking off her shoes. The two women had been unable to chat since Bret's departure, and Selah was foregoing a church luncheon to visit with her friend.

Fallon turned off the vacuum cleaner and came over to join her, snagging her own glass of iced tea off the table on the way.

Selah smiled at her. Sun out of clouds. "Well, love. Do you have much to tell me?"

"I missed church. I'm sorry."

"No apology necessary to little ol' me. We'll catch you next week."

"Or not." Fallon sipped her tea. "I'm going to California on Thursday. I'm going to meet his daughter. What did you think of him?"

Selah pointed and flexed her bare foot with the precision of a ballerina, a memory from years ago. Her red and gold earrings jingled with the movement. It felt so odd to be having this conversation with Fallon, so unexpected. "I will not be downloading any of his music anytime soon. However, he pleases me." Selah nodded to herself. "He is a charmer, no doubt. But he is not a liar. I like him."

Fallon smiled. From Selah, this was extraordinary praise.

"I'm glad he came to stay, that the two of you had just a perfect time together, away from his world, and even somewhat from yours. It brings me joy to see you open yourself up to him, to see you so happy with him, laughing together like conspirators, thick as thieves. I've been thinking he might be the one to take you away from me finally. Surely you are safer with him than with me."

Fallon twisted the ring on her left ring finger, the ring which Selah remembered as showing up when they were about twelve years old. When Jacob and Luca were still in their world.

"I had that bad vision again. Just like at the hotel." Fallon told her about it in detail, including the raven, as well as her theory about it being a future event, a warning, and the mental connection being the cause.

"You've never done that before, have you?" Selah asked. "Jumped inside your own mind in the midst of such turmoil? I'm thinking you could have died."

"Doing nothing was killing me. Just enduring it was killing me. I had to do something."

Selah fiddled with one of the many jangly bracelets on her left wrist as she thought about this. Then she stopped and looked up. "This raven, was it anything like..."

Fallon held up her left wrist, palm towards her friend. "Yes." She nodded. "It was undeniably this raven. Complete with prism eye." She put her hand back down on her lap.

Selah uncrossed her legs and leaned forward. She was not smiling. "All of this troubles me."

Fallon met her eyes. "I know."

* * * * * * *

Sunday night, Bret was walking down the hall past Bergen's room when he heard her singing. This was not unusual in itself; Bergen was always singing. But he stopped to listen, surprised, because it was one of his own songs. Specifically, it was "Blur," one of the songs he'd written a year or so ago about Fallon, when he was in complete despair over her, not knowing who she was, where to find her. Most songs that found their way onto his albums were various variations on the well-loved, tried-and-true hard rock numbers he'd done all his life, but he wrote a considerable number of ballads as well; they simply didn't see the light of day as often, and "Blur" was one of them.

Was it simply my imagination?
A dream my faded heart wants to believe?
The stars shine down,
Their pale illumination
Upon me as I—I begin to grieve.

How can just one glimpse,
one shadow to another,
Dispel all other thoughts, my heart betrays...
And you, you're gone
a spark within my soul
If I could only hold you, make me whole.

My mind recalls you
though my eyes deceive me.
I hear your voice
it carries me from here.
Till all the world I knew is just a blur
And I am yours for always evermore.

When the song ended, he was leaning against her doorframe, his arms folded over his chest. She had such a pretty voice. He never tired of hearing it.

"Bergen."

She spun around, a guilty thing surprised. "Hey, Dad."

"You know that entire song by heart? It's not even on an album yet."

She wrinkled her forehead. "It's only like the best song you've ever written."

He raised an amused eyebrow. "I didn't realize you were familiar with my entire catalogue. I am hoping you are not familiar with my entire catalogue."

Her hands were on her narrow little hips. "Well, it is the best. I don't know why you aren't putting it on the new album."

He rubbed his chin. "You think I should?"

She nodded emphatically.

"I actually did, at the last minute."

She clapped and smiled.

"It's about someone, you know," he told her.

"I thought it might be. It sounded…specific." She chewed her lip. "Did you ever find her?"

He nodded.

"Is that where you were last week?" She'd thought he'd sounded evasive every time they'd spoken on the phone while he was at 'the farm,' whatever that was. And she could tell that he was hiding something from her.

"Yes," he confirmed. "Would you like to meet her?"

She crossed her arms, mirroring him. "Are you in love with her?"

He smiled softly. "I believe I am."

That declaration surprised her, and her nerves began to hum. "Will I like her?"

"I think so. I hope so."

"When?"

"Soon. Next week."

"What's her name?"

"Fallon." He came into the room and folded her into his arms. "You're still my one true love," he said against her hair.

She held onto him tightly. "You're mine, too, Daddy."

CHAPTER SEVENTEEN

LUCA

Jacob was sitting alone at the dining room table. It was just past ten, and he had finished his usual candlelit dinner. His hair was pulled back from his face, and he was drinking some amber liquid Luca could not identify, staring into space, looking as relaxed as he ever did.

Eleven-year-old Fallon was spending the night with her best friend Selah at her house. Luca seized his opportunity. He joined Jacob at the table, sitting down across from him.

"I have a question."

Jacob looked at him, considered the sixteen-year-old boy a moment, and then nodded for him to continue.

"Where was Fallon for the first three years of her life? Before you brought her to me?" It was the first time he had verbalized his knowledge of Jacob's involvement in their early life, but Jacob did not flinch. Luca doubted anything in history had ever made Jacob Roth flinch.

Taking another a sip of his drink, Jacob looked away, as if rolling Luca's question around in his mind a moment. Then he said, "She was with her mother."

Luca frowned. "Her mother? Our mothers are not the same?"

Jacob shook his head. "Your mother, Lea," he let out a short breath, as if the words troubled him, "was killed when you were about a month old, necessitating your move to the home of the Quinns. Fallon's mother lives still."

Luca was startled by this, but quickly pressed on, lest he lose his nerve or his opportunity. "What happened to my sister while she was with her mother? She was not well, emotionally or mentally, when you brought her to me. It took years to fix her."

Jacob wet his lips with the tip of his tongue. "Fallon's mother was slowly going mad. She was unstable. Damaged. She held onto Fallon fiercely, but she was not fit to be that child's mother. Fallon needed much more than Carolina could give."

There was something, some note in Jacob's voice that caught Luca's attention. "You were there, too. Weren't you? With them."

There was a brief pause, and then Jacob nodded. "I was around now and then. I tried to protect Fallon from her mother's dark turn of mind, but eventually it became clear to me that she would need to be removed from the situation entirely before serious harm was done. Your father agreed to it. And so, one night, I tricked Caro and stole her only child away." He leveled his sharp gaze at Luca.

Luca knew his own eyes were probably wide, his heart beating fast in his chest. Jacob's openness was unprecedented, the territory unfamiliar. Though since entering his teenage years

Luca was usually overflowing with confidence and a carefree air, tonight he was tense, afraid of taking a wrong step. "If you were around her for the first three and a half years of her life, you're familiar to her, in her deepest subconscious. That must be it. That must be why she has become a different person since we moved in with you. Healthier, happier, calmer. Unbelievably, you have been a balm to her soul, and she has no idea."

His eyes twinkling in the candlelight, Jacob raised an eyebrow at this new idea, something he had never before considered or realized. And Luca could tell that, in spite of himself, the knowledge pleased Jacob.

"What about her father?" Luca continued. "My father? Where has he been this whole time?"

But Jacob shook his head dismissively.

"You're not our father, are you?" Luca ventured.

The lines around Jacob's eyes actually crinkled with a smile that did not quite materialize on his lips. "No. Not I."

"Is our father alive?"

"He is."

Luca leaned forward. "Her mother, Carolina, you said she's alive, as well?"

Jacob nodded.

"Is she angry? That you stole her daughter? Does she want Fallon back?"

"Of course. Desperately. She orchestrated the murders of your adoptive parents quite well. She never considered that Fallon would be placed with me for safe-keeping."

Luca's heart was in his throat at this revelation; he choked a little and continued. "What will we do? If she tries to take her back?"

"She's already tried, several times. As long as I am here, she will fail. While I am around, nothing can touch Fallon."

"Does Carolina love her?"

Jacob's eyes went far away, as they frequently tended to do. Then he got to his feet and began gathering up his dinner things. "Yes. But not in a good way. She is afraid of her daughter, as well as jealous. She would destroy her, if given the chance. But we will not give her the chance, no?" And then he disappeared into the kitchen, and Luca knew their moment of disclosure was done.

It was the only time Jacob spoke openly to him. And three years later, Jacob Roth was gone from them.

CHAPTER EIGHTEEN

On Monday morning, Fallon awoke with a start to an image of her landlady in her head and a mild sense of alarm flooding through her. She focused for a second. Ms. Landrum had forgotten to take her heart medication. She looked at her phone. Nine-fifteen.

Suddenly she heard a car starting up in the garage below, and four more images—these of little children—flashed into her head, and a wave of nausea swept over her. She leapt out of bed and streaked barefoot out the door and down the back stairs, pain radiating from her heart and wrapping around her unforgivingly. Beatrice Landrum was going to suffer some sort of cardiac episode while driving home from her Monday morning coffee klatch and unintentionally steer her car into a group of school kids on their way to a library field trip, killing four of them.

The shiny white Mercury Grand Marquis was rolling down the long driveway, already halfway to the street. Fallon screamed and waved her arms, running as fast as she could, Azul racing along barking at her side. Fortunately, the neighbors were all already at work.

Ms. Landrum squinted through the windshield, saw her tenant racing after her, and slowed hesitantly to a stop just as she reached the street. Fallon collapsed, breathless, against the side of the car, and Ms. Landrum rolled down her window. "Dear, what is it?"

"Did...did you," Fallon was shaking so badly she could hardly catch her breath, "forget to take your pills this morning?"

Ms. Landrum's damp blue eyes widened, and she brought a trembling hand to her lips. "Oh!" She patted Fallon's hand. "Good girl. Oh my. I wouldn't have remembered till it was too late. Help me inside, would you, dear?" She sounded flustered, her wrinkled face white with fear. "I never forget. Never. But this morning...my nephew called from Montana. Oh my. I can't imagine..." Her voice trailed off as she leaned on Fallon's arm.

After helping her inside, supervising the pill-taking, and then calling a friend of Ms. Landrum's to give her a ride (just in case), Fallon returned to her apartment. She was trembling uncontrollably. One of the children's faces in her mind had been Indio's. She sat down on her couch, hid her face in her hands, and wept. Azul crawled up beside her and lay his head on his lap.

Bret called a little while later, just as she was splashing her face with cold water and regaining her composure, and she picked up her phone.

"Hello, handsome."

"Good morning." He was smiling. "How are you today?"

She breathed in deeply. "Not the best. I had a vision of several people. One of them was Indio." She stopped a moment as her voice cracked. "I stopped it. But it's still not easy. He was going to die. I stopped it," she repeated softly, as if to reassure herself.

He closed his eyes. "That's my girl. I'm so sorry."

"I'll be there in three days," she reminded him, trying to smile, not wanting him to hear her sadness. "I'll call you later today, alright? I need to hop in the shower."

Later that morning, Fallon stepped around a chalk drawing of a fire-breathing dragon on the sidewalk, and headed up onto the porch of Selah and Michael's pretty house, letting herself in the front screened door.

"Selah?"

Wearing dark grey leggings with a black tank top, Fallon was on her way to Dutton to run some errands, but she'd needed to make this stop first. She had a feeling, darkly, that this visit would not take long.

Selah appeared in a red and pink floral dress. "I notice the dragon on the walk did not so much as singe you. Indio will be pleased. He told the dragon to let only pre-approved individuals pass unscathed."

"I'm so happy I made the list."

Selah didn't notice at first how colorless Fallon's voice was. "We were afraid," she continued, "that by leaving you off the list, we might offend you and lose your handy premonition skills that would tell us whether or not our latest grill purchase will in fact catch fire to the back porch like the last one, or not."

But Fallon did not smile, and as Selah saw her quickly turn away, she felt as if all the blood had drained out of her heart. "Fallon?" She came closer and touched her friend's wrist. "What is it?"

Fallon shook her head.

Selah could see she was fighting back tears. She clasped her hands together and brought them up to her mouth, pressing them against her lips. "You saw Indio?" she whispered hoarsely. The moment she had dreaded for five years, and now it was upon them. Fallon nodded that her guess was correct. "But he's alright?"

"Yes." Fallon turned to her. "I even went by the school just now to make sure. He's safe."

Selah dropped her hands and looked around distractedly. Fallon led her into the kitchen and poured them both a glass of water, which they drank together in silence.

"You always promised me you would tell me," Selah said. "And so I can assume this is the first time you've ever seen him in your head?"

Fallon looked at her. "Of course it's the first time."

"Will you tell me what..."

Fallon shook her head sharply. "No. What was going to happen didn't happen. I stopped it. Leave it at that. Please. I only came here to tell you because I promised you long ago that I would. I think it would have been better if I hadn't told you. Now you will wonder, and worry. But I promised you that I would. You were always adamant on that point, that I tell you if it happened."

Selah nodded, setting her glass on the counter. "Yes, you're right." She looked tense, worlds away.

Fallon knew that now their friendship would end. In her heart, she already mourned it. She didn't say anything. Selah was staring into space. Slowly Fallon began heading towards the door. Selah did not stop her. In the doorway, Fallon paused and looked back.

"It was an accident. A car. A driver with a medical condition. All chance. I stopped it in time." Then she was gone.

When she was finished with her errands in Dutton, Fallon made a stop she usually loved making, but her current frame of mind was busily sapping her capacity for enjoyment. She parked in the white gravel lot beside Sunny Girl Bakery, a small, stand-alone shop painted a cheerful red and yellow, and headed inside with an inward sigh. The smell of warm sweetness and fresh bread hit her immediately, but she did not inhale deeply or take any particular notice as she usually did.

The tall, red-headed college girl behind the counter saw her and grinned. "Hi, Fallon! Sunny's in back."

"That's alright, Rae. I'm just going to pick up a box of kolaches and get going."

Rae's smile faded slightly as she sensed Fallon's dark mood, and she quickly assumed a more business-like attitude, fetching a box and heading to the case that held a selection of kolaches. "Lemon and peach, like always?"

Fallon nodded. Ms. Landrum never strayed from those two flavors. It had been a year or so ago that Ms. Landrum mentioned to Fallon that she'd tasted a kolache from a new bakery in Dutton, that she'd never tasted anything so heavenly, and how sad she was that she was unable to make the drive to Dutton to visit the bakery herself. Since that day, about once a month, Fallon stopped by Sunny Girl Bakery and got a box of kolaches for Ms. Landrum as a gift. She often picked up something for herself as well, and sometimes a treat for Indio. She had gotten Michael firmly hooked on the sugar cookies, and his office staff were now all regular customers.

In doing all this, she had somewhat befriended the bakery's proprietress and namesake. Sunny Lewis had a personality that definitely fit her name. She was somewhere in her early to mid-twenties, and had apparently gone to college in the Northeast, but Fallon knew little else about her.

Rae was closing up the cash drawer and handing Fallon her receipt when Sunny came bounding out from the back room, her long black hair in a neat ponytail. "Felicitous Fallon! How are you, my friend?"

Despite her mood, Fallon couldn't help but flash her crooked smile. "I've definitely been better. But I've also been worse."

Sunny laughed. "Let me make you some tea! You look like you could use some girl talk." She was wearing a black tank top and jeans. Both of her arms were an artist's sketchbook of tattoos, but with her hair in the ponytail and the perky look on her face, she was a confusing mix of edgy girl-next-door. She was also full of secrets, and Fallon read things off of her that didn't always make sense, and so Sunny remained a mystery that she didn't entirely trust. And then, there was the game they always played.

"Can't stay today. Thanks, though. I'm packing for a trip."

"Good for you!" Sunny enthused. "You could use some sun."

Fallon regarded her a moment, smile still in place. "Did I say I was going somewhere where there was a lot of sun?"

Sunny, undaunted, shrugged. "I just assumed. You always take the best trips. Can't believe you've never been to California before. You're going to love it."

Fallon was silent a moment. Then she held out her hand, and Sunny lay her own hand palm-down on Fallon's. They held each other's gaze.

"Don't accept the catering job for the Chamber of Commerce," Fallon warned after a moment. "They'll go totally over budget and won't pay you; to get out of it one of the members will claim food poisoning."

Sunny grinned and took back her hand. "Duly noted. Have fun in California."

Rae watched them silently, round-eyed, waving as Fallon finally left the store with the box of a dozen fresh kolaches under her arm.

In her car, Fallon reflected, as she usually did after leaving the bakery, about this unusual girl. Sunny could obviously read her mind, but only fragments, pieces of it. General things, just like Fallon could do with people. There had never been any sign that she could do much more than that—no premonitions, no telepathy. They'd never stopped and talked about it, they just continued their playful verbal sparring, each trying to apparently startle the other with their knowledge-gathering techniques, and Fallon usually winning. Both enjoyed the game too much to ruin it with a discussion and confession. Sunny was the only person in the world that Fallon tried to seek out premonitions for, an unforeseen competitive streak rearing its head every time Sunny cheerfully said something to Fallon that she could not have possibly known.

* * * * * * *

Fallon was busy for the next couple of days as she prepared for her trip, and so she was able to push painful thoughts of Selah from her mind. Selah did not call. She did not stop by. Michael texted Fallon once to ask how she was and how long she might be away, and she texted him back. But that was it, and she could tell from his words that Selah had not yet told him about her premonition.

She had not been gone from Gray in a while, and it truthfully felt good to be leaving, if only for a week or so, especially with the Selah-issue hanging over her. Azul, as he always did when not invited along, was going to stay at Solu with the Sanchez family.

CHAPTER NINETEEN

At the airport in southern California, Fallon and Bret found each other by talking in their minds. "This is the coolest thing ever," he declared out loud, wrapping his arms around her tightly and kissing her.

"We are the future," she quipped.

"We could go back to Vegas and make a fortune cheating at cards."

She shook her head. "There's probably a karma thing we'd have to worry about. Like the idea that if you're a witch and use your magic to do harm, it comes back to you times three."

"Are there really witches?" He slung her bag over his shoulder. "I mean true wicked ones, not the Wiccans."

She shrugged. "Anything's possible, I guess. Who knew there was a Fallon?"

He grinned.

"But don't get me started on vampires and werewolves and the Fae," she warned playfully.

"And ghosts," he added with a laugh.

But her smile slid away.

Bret lived about an hour and a half south of Los Angeles, in a pretty, hip, beachside town. They stopped briefly at a farmers' market where she purchased fruit and a fresh loaf of sour dough bread, then they headed towards his house. Fallon thought he seemed the slightest bit nervous, and she read off of him that it was due to her impending meeting with his daughter.

"Does Bergen usually meet the women you date?" she asked, realizing that she was anxious about the meeting herself. Bergen was the apple of her father's eye. She ruled his world.

Bret glanced at her and shook his head. "Pretty much never, these days. Or if she does, it's just casually. She's been out on tour with me her whole life, though, so you can imagine what she's seen. Look, there's Daisy, the cafe Lisbeth and her sister own." He was pointing, and she looked out and saw a café with bright blue clapboard walls painted tastefully with a few white daisies, and an intricate mass of umbrella-covered outdoor tables and strings of lights. "Marcella is more of the chef, the cook, while Lisbeth handles admin, publicity, the staff and such."

"Cute. So obviously her sister lives here in town, too."

"Marcella and her husband have lived here since they got married about fifteen years ago. I had been out here with Lisbeth many times to visit them, and I loved the attitude and peacefulness, being away from L.A., but close enough. When Lis was pregnant with Bergen, some property I could afford came up for sale, and I bought it and remodeled the house, and I added the dirt bike track. I wanted Bergen to grow up in a place with a smalltown feel, yet with all kinds of opportunities. The schools are great, there's lots of artists living here, cool old bookshops, an active local theatre group, just lots of stuff for kids and young people to be involved in creatively. Plus, it's healthier for me not to be in close proximity to all my old friends and a bunch of familiar bars and clubs," he added with a shrug. "It keeps me home."

Bret's house and property had obviously not been cheap, but it was all understated and simple, nothing ostentatious or overly-pretentious about it. Bergen had been at a friend's house after school, and had just gotten home twenty minutes before Bret walked in with Fallon. When she heard them, she came running into the front entryway, a vivacious little blond lightning bolt of energy.

"Daddy!" She leapt into his arms, and he held her tight. Her arms and legs were tanned from hours at the beach playing volleyball, swimming, and surfing. She was every bit a California girl.

"Bee," he let her feet touch the ground again, "I'd like you to meet my friend, Fallon."

The child extended her hand, which Fallon accepted. "Nice to meet you," Bergen said politely.

"You, too, beautiful girl." Fallon was smiling. "Your dad can't stop talking about you."

Bergen smiled back, sweet but non-committal.

Leaving Fallon's bags in the hall by the foot of the stairs, the three made their way into the kitchen together, making small talk as they went. Fallon and Bergen remained acutely aware of each other, slightly cautious.

"Where's your mom?" Bret asked his daughter.

"Taking a shower. She was working out in the flowerbeds... you know she likes doing that, I guess. I think she's going in to Daisy tonight."

Bret glanced through the mail that lay on the island, pointing out the blender to Fallon, who intended to make a smoothie. She went to the sink and began washing the fruit. Moments later she frowned as she recognized the rare sensation of someone trying to read her. Her mind was blocked firmly against such things, but it had been over a decade since anyone had tried, and that had been her brother. She glanced casually over her shoulder. Bret was still looking through the mail. Bergen was on her way to the fridge, but slowly, a curious look on her face.

Returning her attention to the fruit in her hands, Fallon was surprised. What was going on? Was that *child* trying to read her?

Bergen had retrieved a Tupperware bowl from the fridge. "I haven't eaten anything since lunch, I'm starving."

"I'm going to make a smoothie. Would you like one?" Fallon offered.

"No, thank you. Mrs. Reeves, my friend's mom, sent home some of her chicken and sausage gumbo, my favorite," Bergen raved, happily getting out a bowl and spoon.

Fallon, almond milk in hand, stopped what she was doing and took a slow breath, then looked from Bergen to the gumbo. She pointed at the latter. "Don't eat that."

Bergen looked at her as if she'd lost her mind. She threw a glance back at her father.

Fallon turned fully towards her. "I mean it, Bergen. It sat out too long. You'll be horribly sick. I know it's weird for you to hear me say this, but please trust me."

Bret watched the exchange silently and didn't move.

Bergen pressed her lips together tightly, her ingrained need to be polite challenged by her fury at being told what to do by her father's new girlfriend who hadn't even been in the house ten minutes. "It didn't sit out," she argued, as nicely as she could. "We brought it right home. I saw Mrs. Reeves get it out of the fridge."

Fallon nodded. "It sat out before it went into the fridge," she explained gently. "Please. You'll be so sick you'll miss the final performance of your play Friday night."

Bret looked at his daughter. "I thought Saturday was the final performance."

Bergen was now glaring, unable to maintain her composure. "It was Saturday, but they texted me ten minutes before you guys got here and told me Saturday night's been cancelled all of a sudden, so tomorrow, Friday, night is the final night. How did you know that?" she demanded of Fallon with barely concealed indignation. "I just found out."

Fallon turned her attentions to the blender, at a loss for how to deal with the girl. "Don't eat the gumbo."

Bergen gazed at her father with wide, incredulous grey eyes. He shrugged and tried to look neutral, knowing full well that if she made a move to actually go for the gumbo, he would strike it from her hand.

"Why don't you eat something else, Bee? Fallon is usually right about these feelings she gets."

Bergen set her bowl and spoon down loudly on the counter. "I'm not hungry." She left the kitchen in an angry flourish of nine-year-old frustration.

Bret sighed as he joined Fallon at the blender, where she was finally adding the almond milk, and placed his hand on the small of her back. "I'm sorry. That didn't go quite like I expected."

"Who knew I would have a vision about her a minute after we walked in the door? I'm more than used to having people react to me the way she did, but it does hurt because it's her, and because we just met." She looked at him. "Throw it out before someone accidentally eats it. It would have landed her in the hospital for one, maybe two nights."

Only five minutes later, Bergen, stomach growling, wandered back into the kitchen and eyed the smoothie Fallon was pouring into a glass. "I'm still hungry," she mentioned frostily.

Fallon acknowledged her with a nod. "I made enough that you can have some, if you'd like."

Instead of answering, Bergen went over to Bret and wrapped her arms around him possessively, resting her head against his chest. He rubbed her back for a moment, then picked her up and set her on the island, giving her a look that told her to behave and be nice.

She accepted the glass Fallon handed her, and cautiously took a sip through the straw. And though she tried, she couldn't hide the pleasure in her face. "This is good. Mom makes smoothies, too, but she puts, like, all this green stuff in hers. This is really good."

Fallon topped Bergen's glass off with what remained in the blender, and then moved away from the girl to give her some space.

Bergen sat cross-legged on the island and contentedly sipped the drink, watching carefully while pretending not to watch as her father interacted with Fallon. He kept casually touching her, as if he didn't want to not be touching her at any moment. His eyes were bright. Every now and then they smiled at each other as if they were sharing some silent communication. They spoke out loud about this and that, and Fallon commented on the pool she saw through the windows; they agreed they would go swimming. Her father looked remarkably happy. He was usually happy, but Bergen thought this was different.

She was confused. She could always easily tell if someone's intentions regarding her father were good or bad. It was just something she could do; she'd never told anyone, and she'd never questioned it. Never before had she been unable to figure out someone's real feelings. But Fallon was unreadable.

In spite of this, Bergen felt as if she was falling under a spell. She thought Fallon was beautiful, from the casual but cute way that she dressed to her natural honey-gold hair and those green eyes. And Fallon wasn't fawning over Bergen in an attempt to win points with her dad. She wasn't giggly and ditzy; she wasn't inappropriately trying to make out with her dad right there in front of his daughter—it had happened before, more than once—and she wasn't wearing a lot of make-up or crazy jewelry. Growing up in her father's world, Bergen had pretty much seen it all. Fallon Quinn was not like most. Bergen liked her a lot.

Except for the thing with the gumbo. That would have to be settled eventually.

Lisbeth came in then, her hair blown dry and glossy, her long body clad in expensive jeans and a white blouse, make-up exquisitely applied. "Fallon," she came right over and gave her a perfumed hug, "I'm so glad to meet you. Bret's been over the moon about you, and I've been waiting in immense anticipation to see who you are."

Fallon smiled. "It's nice to meet you, too. I've heard so much about you and Bergen."

"Mom, now tomorrow night is the final night for the show," Bergen reported.

Lisbeth turned to the girl. "Oh, really? It's a good thing we're all going to that one, then, isn't it? That's perfect, Leo wanted me to go to that gallery opening with him Saturday night but I couldn't because of your show."

"We're going to be at Rich's Saturday night, at least for a bit," Bret mentioned pointedly.

Lisbeth tapped her manicured nails on the table. "She can probably stay at the café with Marcella until you're done. I assume you won't stay at Rich's long if you've got Fallon with you." She got out her phone and called her sister, turning away.

Bret exchanged a glance with Fallon from across the kitchen.

Was that a dig at you? she asked.

Yes. That's what that was. Me going to Rich's infamous parties was never healthy for our relationship back in the day, and she hasn't let it go completely. Fifteen years later.

Who in their right mind would have been involved with you fifteen years ago, anyway? she pointed out.

Exactly. Wait, what?

Fallon looked away, smiling.

Downing the last of her smoothie, Bergen sighed happily. "That was super good, Fallon. Thank you."

"You're welcome, my dear." Fallon was amused that Bergen's manners were still intact.

Bret took Bergen's glass and set it in the sink, then came back and snatched her off the island, throwing her over his shoulder and running through the kitchen and out the back door. Fallon ran to watch in the doorway as Bret pulled her from his shoulder and heaved her out into the middle of the pool. Bergen came up giggling and choking.

Lisbeth came out on the patio. "Marcella said Bee can hang out at the café as long as we want Saturday; she'll be there all night." She looked at Fallon. "Tell him, would you? I doubt he heard." Bret was too busy laughing with Bergen, whom he was helping out of the water. "I'll see you later, Fallon, I'm on my way to the café. I really am glad that you're here."

Lisbeth disappeared back into the house, and when Fallon looked back at the pool, Bergen had disappeared. Bret had stripped off his shirt and was skimming some bugs out of the water. The pool had a rough, asymmetrical shape and included a waterfall; the surrounding patio area was done in reddish brown stones with a Mediterranean look. The backyard was picturesque, landscaped with various plants and flowers. The high stone wall all around gave it a secluded feel. Through a locked iron gate out the back was the field where Bret had created his dirt bike track—under an agreement with the neighbors, he was limited to certain days per week and times of day that he could ride, but he reasoned it was better than having no track at all.

"Bee's getting her suit on," Bret called. "Go change if you want, and we can swim now before dinner. My bedroom's upstairs, third door on the left."

Bergen emerged from the pool house in a purple and black bikini and leapt back into the water.

Retrieving her bags from the hall, Fallon carried them upstairs to Bret's room. Spacious and simply decorated, a guitar leaning in the corner, his bedroom was comfortable. She went to one of the windows and saw that it looked down on the pool—perfection. Bergen was swimming alone and Bret had vanished, she assumed into the pool house to change clothes.

She watched the girl for a moment. When she read Bergen, it was a tangle of glitter and rainbows and emotions. And sweetness. She was a kind-hearted child.

Fallon got her black bikini out of her suitcase, shedding her clothes and putting it on. No one that she knew had a pool. It was one of her great disappointments that she had so far been unable to convince Michael and Selah to install one in their backyard, but they were worried about Indio's safety, despite Fallon's promise of free swim lessons. She winced at the accidental thought of Selah and fled back downstairs and outside to join Bergen in the water, happy that the girl seemed to have at least temporarily forgiven her.

CHAPTER TWENTY

The next morning at around nine, Bergen called her father from school to inform him that her friend Tom was in the hospital with possible food poisoning. Bret looked at the screen on his phone and saw several missed calls and voice mails waiting.

"He's going to be alright?"

"Yeah, he's fine, just super sick. Dehydrated. They think he'll probably come home tomorrow sometime."

He glanced at Fallon.

"Dad," Bergen lowered her voice, "how did she know?"

He licked his lips as Fallon nodded and disappeared back into the bathroom in search of her clothes. "We'll talk about it tonight. I promise."

They had agreed that they would tell Bergen the truth about the premonitions if/when she asked, talking it over in-depth with Lisbeth after Bergen went to bed the night before. But they had all three agreed to leave out any mention for now of the telepathy, a phenomenon Lisbeth was still having a hard time with. It would be far too much, Lisbeth told them, for the child to process, and she might always be thinking that they were talking secretly while with her.

After he'd finally hung up with his daughter, he looked at Fallon, who was slipping on a pair of cut-off denim shorts. "You're not doing much to sway me from my desire to attach you to her side permanently for the next twenty or so years. And when Lisbeth finds out about Tom, she'll be completely on my side."

"You guys don't understand yet. But you will. My fallibility." She pointed at his phone. "Call Lisbeth and assure her that the gumbo was disposed of yesterday."

* * * * * * *

That evening at the show, Bergen was a delight to watch. She had her father's easy stage presence. Afterwards Lisbeth left with Leo, and so Bret and Fallon had Bergen to themselves in the car on the way home, but she didn't say anything about the gumbo incident. Instead, she chattered on and on about the show. When they got home, she went to take a shower, but then eventually she summoned them to her bedroom.

Bergen's room was an explosion of woman/child cuteness. The decor had an edge to it, sweet little girl with a rockstar-drama-queen touch. The girl was sitting in the middle of her queen-sized bed, in black pajamas, looking innocent and sleepy amid the fluffy white comforter and white pillows. Bret sat on the bed on her right, and Fallon sat on her left.

Bergen looked closely at the latter. "Can you tell the future?"

"In little ways, yes," Fallon confirmed.

"Like a psychic?" Bergen quizzed.

"'Psychic' is a word that can mean a lot of things; I tend to not think of it that way. I have 'second sight'—I receive visions of future events. I see things about people, things that are going to happen to them. But the instances are random. You might run outside right now and get hit by a car, and I wouldn't have seen it coming. Or I might have. You just never know. A useful tool, but not reliable." She'd never imagined she might be explaining her ability to so many people, and especially not to a child, but here she was.

Bergen was thinking hard. "So, you knew I was going to get sick if I ate the gumbo?"

Fallon nodded. "First, I saw you in my head; when I saw the gumbo a few minutes later I had a bad feeling, bits of information. And I figured it out."

Bergen looked at her father, but didn't say anything. Then she took a breath. "Does mom know?"

Bret nodded. "Yes, I told her a few weeks ago, when I realized my feelings for Fallon were serious enough that I'd be bringing her here to meet you."

Bergen's eyes widened, incensed. "But if you told mom, why didn't you tell me? I'm more important to you than she is! Shouldn't I have been pre-informed?"

Fallon hid a smile.

Bret squeezed one of Bergen's toes. "I thought it would be enough for you to handle, me bringing home someone I am in love with, not casually dating but truly in love with. I didn't know how you would take that. I didn't want to throw in the extra info and have you obsess about it and hold it against her."

She was still facing her father, but eyeing Fallon. "You thought I wouldn't like her?"

"No, I thought you would. But I've never brought someone to you and told you I was in love with them, have I?"

Bergen shook her head that he hadn't, still watching Fallon, who was twisting and twisting the ring on her finger, her eyes gone far away.

"It was immensely important to me that you and Fallon got off on the right foot with each other. And yet still that almost didn't happen."

Bergen turned fully towards Fallon. "Are you a witch?" She sounded almost eager. She had been watching re-runs of the original "Charmed."

Fallon gave the child her full attention and shook her head. "I don't think so."

"How long have you been able to... do that?"

"Since I was very young. Younger than you are now."

"Wow." Bergen tried to suppress a yawn. "Okay." She looked at her father. "Can we talk more later? I'm really tired."

He laughed softly and tucked her in under the covers as she lay back, kissing her forehead. "Sweet dreams, Bee."

* * * * * *

The following evening Bret and Fallon dressed for the infamous party at Rich's, he in black pants and black shirt, she in a diaphanous black slip dress with a tighter black dress underneath. She wore sexy high-heeled black sandals, and her hair was swept up in a messy bun. She was not looking forward to the evening, but she understood that it was something he had to do. Maintaining connections with the right people throughout his life was one of the reasons he was still able to enjoy a career he loved and that provided for his daughter.

Despite her antipathy, she was smiling and confident as they got out of his car and headed into the fabulous Hollywood hills home of his friend Rich Connor, a music industry executive. The property was overflowing with fancy people drinking impressive drinks and eating exquisite food, everyone gushing to each other about this and that.

After less than an hour, Fallon was bored and drowning in a sea of superficiality. She had been introduced to countless people, but there was no one there who sparked her interest. That changed when they ran into Jack Lane, temporarily without a woman on his arm but with the requisite drink in hand. Handsome in all black, his long, wavy dark hair fell across his left eye as he approached Bret and Fallon with a smile.

"Hey, man, how's it going?" Jack greeted Bret, shaking his hand firmly. "Touring this summer, aren't you?" There was something about Jack that made him come across as sly and slightly superior, always a smirk or smug look on his face. He cast a look of over-familiarity at Fallon.

"Yeah," Bret confirmed, "you, too?" He knew Jack well; they had been acquaintances for decades, but a friendship between them had never developed. And never, as far as Bret was concerned, would it ever. He and Jack did not mix well together.

"Always on the road, man. Always." Jack took a sip from his glass, winking at Fallon with a cocky grin.

She couldn't help humoring him with a smile. With his raspy voice and casual movements, Jack played the part of the way-cool, sexy rockstar like a pro, she mused. But then, he'd been playing this part for well over thirty years.

He was looking her over appreciatively. "And who is this lovely one?" he asked.

"Fallon Quinn, Jack Lane," Bret introduced them.

She held out her hand, which Jack smoothly kissed. "New to the neighborhood?" Jack asked, though he seemed to already know the answer.

"Just visiting," she told him.

Jack and Bret made small talk about their respective tours, then they all moved on.

Bret led her outside to see the pool, which was expensive and impressive, all grottos and stones and waterfalls and lights, on a scale ten times larger than his own nice pool. There were many people swimming, most of whom were quite inebriated, which she assumed was something of a safety hazard.

"I admit to pool envy," she sighed. "Maybe I can talk Ms. Landrum into upgrading from the inflatable thing I have currently, which Azul keeps sinking his toenails into."

"Maybe you should just adopt my pool," he suggested, swallowing his drink.

She squeezed his hand. "Hey, I'm going to try to locate a restroom. Will you stay here so I can find you again?"

You just want to look at the pool some more, he accused.

Well, you're right, she agreed. *But also, all these people are giving me anxiety, and I don't want to have to search for you. Just stay put.*

I promise.

Jack joined him out by the pool shortly after Fallon went in, causing Bret to think that he'd been watching, waiting for the opportunity to do so. "She seems cool," Jack observed, hands currently empty. "Where did you meet her?"

Bret licked his lips and stared at the water as he thought about the question. Jack's friendly interest was unlike him, and he wondered where this was going to lead. "It's actually a complicated story. But the weekend of that festival in Dallas, remember when Tayce invited us to dinner with him and Paul?"

Jack nodded.

"She was there. We hit it off immediately."

"Huh." Jack looked out at the night.

Bret watched at him closely. "Why?"

Jack rubbed his nose. "Remember that night in Vegas when Peter and that woman went missing?"

Bret nodded. "Of course."

"The three of us—you, me, and Tayce—went back in the club and left Peter and Cyn outside, I can't even remember why, maybe it was something you wanted to show us? Anyway, I decided to go back out and get them, tell them I'd be in the VIP room. Why was my bass player hanging out with my chick, anyway, right?"

"You'd just met her that night, hadn't you?"

Jack looked at him. "Yeah. Anyway, I got to the door to go back outside, but someone stopped me."

No expression touched Bret's face as he waited.

"Pretty woman, young, not really dressed for a night at a club. But anyway, she grabbed my arm and smiled at me and whispered something naughty in my ear, and told me to go wait for her in the VIP room. She said—and I remember this so vividly—she said that I could text those two as easily as I could go out and get them. Well, she was right. And I was drunk, and high, and very susceptible. I liked what I'd heard, what I saw. I followed her request. Of course, I never saw her again." He glanced at Bret. "Until tonight." He looked around. "It's funny, I only saw her for a moment, but I remember that dark gold hair, the big green eyes. Those lips." He shrugged. "When she didn't show up after a while, I got pretty annoyed, and Peter wasn't answering his damn phone, so I went outside to find him, but as we know, he and Cyn were gone. I went in then and talked to you guys. Needless to say, it's been more than a little perplexing for me to find you here tonight with her of all people, a year and a half later."

Bret was still. He cast around in his mind for something to say.

What's going on? Fallon asked in his head, sensing his unease as she tracked him on her return from the bathroom.

He quickly explained the situation.

Fallon paused. She had assumed Jack was too lazy to be that observant. She growled a little in her head. *I don't know. Tell him the truth. I guess. Or don't. I don't know. Dammit.* She sounded tired and frustrated.

Bret folded his arms across his chest. "I met her for the first time that night in Vegas," he admitted finally. "Like I said, it's complicated. We only spoke briefly that night. There was undeniably a connection between us. When we met again at dinner in Texas, it was a wonderful, crazy coincidence. As far as your encounter with her in Vegas," he shrugged, "I don't know. Maybe that night she was trolling for musicians."

Nice, Fallon hissed.

Jack smiled. "Maybe so. It's just always stayed with me, the thought that if she hadn't stopped me from going back outside at that moment, maybe I would have seen what happened to those two."

"Or maybe what happened to them would have also happened to you," Bret suggested.

Jack nodded soberly. "Touche'. Maybe so." He rolled his head from left to right, relieving the pressure in his neck. "There's also always been the question of how she knew exactly what I was going back outside to do, when she stopped me." He turned on his heel and disappeared back into the house.

Bret looked back out at the pool. *Fallon?*

Later. We will talk about it later. Oh, that man. She reappeared beside him, clearly flustered. "Can't I leave you for five minutes without drama going down?"

"Apparently not."

She took his arm, and they went back inside where he visited with a group of people he knew. Fallon hung out beside him and smiled at all the appropriate times, her mind still filled with confusion at Jack's memory. Several times, various overly-friendly women approached Bret and hung on him, but he always managed to gracefully extricate himself and re-wrap an arm around Fallon.

"Should we go get Bergen," she asked finally, "or do you want to stay?" *Please let's leave.*

He looked at his phone, where five texts from Bergen asked him to please come get her and her cousin Chloe because they were Really Bored. "Let's go. We hit all the high points. As well as one low point," he added, spotting Jack, who was watching them casually from across the room.

She took his hand. "Quick, then, before yet another woman tries to wrestle you away from me."

The drive back seemed to take forever. They listened to and discussed music, not wanting to ruin the evening quite yet by addressing the new information from Jack. Finally, they arrived at Daisy and collected Bergen and ten-year-old Chloe and went back to the house, where the giggling girls scampered up to Bergen's bedroom and shut the door.

"We should maybe talk about how long I'm going to stay, don't you think?" Fallon asked, as he poured them some wine in the kitchen. "So I can let Diego know something more definite." She slipped off her shoes and wriggled her toes in relief.

"Well, I was thinking about it. And here's the deal. In one week, I start rehearsals for the tour, which kicks off June first." He handed her a glass, and they went out on the patio for a moment. Fallon stared at the illuminated pool and thought she must have been a water spirit in a former life. The water literally sang her name.

"I was wondering if you might like to come with me. On the tour. It's not glamorous, but I think we'd have fun together. I'd miss you too much, otherwise, and it will be difficult for me to get to Gray to see you. My blocks of free time are usually saved up for Bergen, who, by the way, will be on summer vacation and will want to come along for some of it."

She didn't have to think twice. "I'd love to. I haven't been gone from Gray in a while. Diego is practically expecting me to take my usual leave of absence. Yes. Count me in. And I will happily watch Bergen while she's with us. What do you usually do about her?"

"Sometimes Lisbeth comes. Sometimes we've hired a nanny, when Lis couldn't make it. Sometimes my brothers will be there." He kissed her. "I'm glad. I was wondering if you'd want to or not. Let's go make sure the girls are good, and then watch a movie or something. I feel like unwinding."

"I want to swim."

"I'm not surprised."

"You get more wine," she directed. "I'll go check on the girls; then we swim. Movie later."

"As you wish."

Later that night, when they'd showered and gone to bed, and he'd wrapped her up in his arms, he finally brought up the subject that had been bothering him for most of the night, and which she had been expecting.

"Why didn't you tell me you came into the club that night? I thought you just disappeared out on the street. Why did you come in? And what," he lowered his chin, eyes not leaving her face, "did you whisper in Jack's ear?"

She traced a pattern on his bare chest with her index finger. "Whatever I may have whispered in his ear, I don't remember."

"You're lying. Poorly."

"Does it matter, Bret? I lied to him. I can see where it would be different if I'd actually followed through with whatever I said, but Lord knows I didn't and wouldn't." Her hand dropped away, and she lay back on the pillow. "I came into the club looking for you. As soon as you three were back inside and the door closed behind you, the image of you in my head, the bad feelings, vanished. I knew you were safe. Peter and Cyn were none of my concern. As far as I was aware, they were safe. But when you were gone from my head and my sight, the emptiness it left me with was something I was unprepared for. Always when I'm done with someone, I turn and walk away and never look back. But with you, it was over too quickly. I didn't want to let you go. Plus, there was the whole deal of our mental conversation. I wanted to see you again, so I went inside. As soon as I was in the door, I saw Jack heading my way, and a feeling went through me—panic, danger—and I realized what he was about to do, and that it was going to mean his death, and so I stopped him. I used the only tool in my arsenal that I knew he would respond to: sex. When he was gone and safe, I looked around for you, and finally saw you sitting at a bar talking to Tayce. You guys looked so relaxed and happy; I wasn't about to intrude. I was suddenly shy. I watched you for a moment." She glanced at him. "But I was too scared to approach you. So, I left."

He looked shaken. "Jack was going to die, too," he said softly. "I can't even believe it." He touched her face. "I wish you'd stayed. I wish I'd at least looked around and seen you watching me, and then I would have known, I guess, that I'd mattered to you for a moment in time. That you'd been real. Sometimes I thought I'd imagined you."

She snuggled up against him. "I do wish we'd been reunited sooner. I had no idea you wanted to find me, or that when you found me, I would be more than just a curiosity to you. I might have gone looking for you."

"Yeah, it's wearing me out having to make up for lost time," he whispered, kissing her throat, and she giggled.

CHAPTER TWENTY-ONE

FALLON

"Little one."

Fallon paused on her way to her room when she heard Jacob call to her from down the hall. Turning, she headed to his room and found him sitting in a chair by the window, smoking a strangely fragrant Turkish cigarette and looking thoughtful, a tumbler of whiskey in his left hand. When she hesitated in the doorway, he gestured for her to enter. She could count on one hand the number of times she'd been in Jacob's room. She and Luca never entered without invitation, and they had never thought to snoop while he was out of the house. It was sacred.

Tonight, Luca was out with his best friend, Simon, hitting various clubs, seeing some bands. Eleven-year-old Fallon was too young to go clubbing, and so on nights like this, she was left behind, but she didn't care to be around crowds of people much, so she didn't really mind. In truth, she sometimes liked having the house to just Jacob and herself.

"How are you?" he asked, in his rich, rough voice. "Come sit. I haven't seen much of you lately." He had been away for several weeks, and Fallon and Luca had been busy with school.

She went and sat cross-legged on the leather ottoman near his feet. Usually, she couldn't stand cigarette smoke, but these that Jacob smoked were different, not as harsh to her senses, and with an unusual scent. Luca had told her that the brand of cigarettes—Ramleh—wasn't made anymore. He'd looked it up out of curiosity.

"That brand is from the early 1900s. Over a hundred years ago, Fal." He shrugged. "So of course it makes perfect sense that Jacob seems to have an endless supply of them."

Little about Jacob made sense, but they had grown used to this over the years and were unconcerned.

Jacob put out the cigarette, took a swig from his drink, and set it aside. Then he leaned forward with his forearms on his knees. "Tell me how you are."

In spite of herself, Fallon froze. Jacob had never asked her such a thing. She didn't know really what he meant, or what she should say.

He was smiling faintly now. "I have surprised my small one. I apologize." He straightened up, stretching a little, then sat back, crossing a leg. Wearing a long-sleeved, dark shirt, jeans, and loose-ly-laced biker boots, he looked like a handsome rockstar, his long hair pulled back from his face. "I want you to try something with me. Alright? I want to try to change the way you receive visions."

This was the first time he had acknowledged that either of the siblings possessed powers of any kind. Something had changed. Fallon swallowed the fear that had begun to balloon in her chest and faced him head-on. She was a fighter; he'd always thought that about her, but she hid in her brother's shadow too often.

"Let me tell you a secret, my secret girl." He leaned towards her again. "You look at your brother, and you think he is strong, yes? Unstoppable. So much more capable than yourself. This is true?"

She nodded. "Of course." Finally, she had found her voice. "Of course he is."

Jacob shook his head. "It's you. You are the force to be reckoned with. Luca could light a small flame—you could set the world on fire. You must not doubt yourself. They are all out to get you. Even the ones you would never suspect do not want to see you survive. But I will help you survive. I will never turn my back on you." He sat back again. "I want to train you. On nights like these, when Luca is out. He doesn't need to know. It would trouble him, the realization of your powers. We do not want to trouble him."

It was taking everything Fallon had within her to quickly process all he was telling her.

"Will you let me train you?" he pressed, his face full of intensity, his blue eyes like lights that looked right into her.

Adrenaline was racing through Fallon's veins, and she nodded. "Yes. But only if you continue to read to me." Her eyes sparkled with a challenge, and he laughed out loud.

"It is a deal, Fallon Rose."

CHAPTER TWENTY-TWO

That night when Fallon got out of the shower, she could hear Bret's guitar and Bergen's voice coming from the child's room. She had found that on many nights, father and daughter sang together. Bret played while Bergen sang songs ranging from rock and blues to country and pop—the girl's head was full of music. She was a fairly average singer, but what she lacked in vocal talent she made up for with enthusiasm. Bergen was taking guitar lessons, and sometimes instead of singing, they worked on what she'd learned that week in her lesson.

Around ten, Bret finally appeared in his bedroom doorway with his guitar in hand, just as his phone started ringing. He glanced at it. "My guitarist, Travis. I'll be back up in a minute, I need to go downstairs and look at something for him." He handed Fallon the guitar.

As she went to set the guitar in its stand in the corner, she realized she had quietly made a decision to approach something she'd turned her back on long ago. Jacob Roth, her teacher and her prophet, was gone, but everything he'd taught her was still in her heart and mind. And here was something that mattered more than anything. If she possessed the tools within her to keep Bret safe, to save Bergen from prematurely losing her father at a tender age, then she was going to use them.

She began immediately, sitting cross-legged in the center of the bed, closing her eyes and letting her hands rest loosely in her lap, concentrating on breathing deeply. When she was relaxed and centered, she fell back deep into her mind, where she could see a group of shimmering lines, each a different color. The main one, which glowed the brightest, was blue-green. That line was her premonition ability. She didn't know how she'd always known this, but she had, even before Jacob began instructing her on such things. She knew what a few of the others were, but most of the lines were unknown entities, and she'd ignored them for so much of her life that she barely saw them anymore. That they might be other abilities, lying untapped and secret, was an idea she purposefully avoided. Jacob had taught her many things, but the number of colored lines in her mind far surpassed the handful of abilities he'd awakened in her.

She concentrated on the blue-green line, and it hummed happily under her attention. Then, with care, she used her mind to bend it, just a little. It was not easy, and there was the fear that she would slip and hit the other lines. So, she moved it a small amount at a time, taking breaks to rest, until it had a soft angle in it. The line, the ability, had to be manipulated, changed, in order to open it up to other uses. It had already had the faintest curve to it, which she'd done a few years ago to keep ahead of Sunny, but she never used it for anyone else, the bend wasn't sharp enough. Jacob had taught her all about this, how to change the lines.

Once, when she'd casually mentioned the lines to Luca, he surprised her by knowing what she was talking about. But he'd only *seen* his lines in his mind; he hadn't thought to manipulate them in any way, and she said nothing to suggest it. Luca's premonition line had been purple, and he'd had three other lines in his mind—one silver, one orange, and one green—that he guessed must be the abilities of mental telepathy, reading people, and seeing in the dark, which were all things both siblings could effortlessly do.

When he'd asked her what color her other three lines were, and she had looked in her mind and seen an endless canvas of lines burning with a rainbow of colors, she was scared, and lied to him. She told him her other lines were red, gold, and orange. He went to his grave never knowing how full her mind was of the unknown.

She returned to herself there in Bret's bedroom and turned on the TV, flipping to a sports channel and locating a game of college baseball. This was always how she'd practiced in the past. She would watch the game, and as she watched, she would try to see in her mind what was going to happen before it did. Taking more deep breaths, she focused intently on the game. At first, she couldn't see anything, and her guesses all wrong. It had been so long since she'd tried this, and even with the angle she'd put in the blue-green line, it was something she had to ease back into. After about fifteen frustrating minutes, things finally became a little clearer.

When Bret came back in, he found her glued to the game, calling things out and then clapping softly when the things happened as she said, frowning when they did not. He came and sat beside her. After a moment, he realized what she was doing.

"I thought you couldn't do this. Purposeful premonitions. Seeing things before they happen of something you choose."

She turned the television off abruptly and tossed aside the remote. "I can. It's just been lying dormant."

He rubbed her leg. "Why are you doing it now?"

She looked at him. "I thought it might be a good idea. Until I can figure out what the visions of you mean."

He nodded. He had privately hoped that issue, his impending doom, had maybe simply gone away, but apparently not. "Oh, Bergen said I'm supposed to play a song for you."

"Is it the one you said you wrote about me?"

He nodded, reaching for his guitar. "That's the one. Apparently, it's her favorite."

Fallon lay back against the pillows and waited.

"It might sound... I was under a lot of stress," he warned her. "It's very emotional. To me."

She blew him a kiss. "Play it."

He paused. "This means your visions don't have to be random. Is that what you're saying? That you can see things about people you choose?"

She bit her lip. "I'm out of practice; I told you."

He stared at her.

She nodded with a heavy sigh. "If I work at it long enough, yes. I can predict things about anyone I choose."

He sat on the edge of the bed, and without another word he began to play and sing for her.

CHAPTER TWENTY-THREE

O n Thursday evening, Fallon borrowed Bret's second car to drive around for a while by herself. After so many days of being engaging and popular, she needed some downtime to recharge.

"I'm so used to being alone," she told him. "It's a little overwhelming to my senses. My introvert heart is tired. I'll be fine; I just need to drive for a bit with just me and some music."

When she got home around nine, Bret and Lisbeth's vehicles were both gone, and the house was silent as she came in. She smiled. The pool was all hers. She went immediately upstairs and changed into a bikini, then came down and stopped in the kitchen to pour herself a glass of sangria. The patio area was dark, the pool glowing from within as she walked over to the edge of the water.

She stopped when she saw there was someone sitting in the hot tub.

Jack Lane raised his beer to her in greeting. "Well, hello there, darling. Come to keep me company?"

She looked around. "I didn't know you were here, actually. Where's your car?"

"Friend dropped me off."

She came closer, and his dark eyes looked her over. "Where's Bret?" she asked.

Jack shrugged. "He had to go get Bergen from something."

Bret.

Yes, love?

Why is Jack Lane in your hot tub?

He's still there? He told me he was leaving, that a friend would be by in five minutes to get him. I assume he's going to try to seduce you. Should I break the speed laws getting home, or can you handle it? Bergen wants me to stop for food.

Take your time. This will be mildly amusing.

She stepped into the hot tub and sat down across from Jack, who grinned at her. "Why so standoffish?" he asked. "We're already good friends, you and I."

"Oh, yes?" She sipped her drink.

"Oh yes." He took a swig of his beer. "I have a question for you, darling."

"If you stop calling me 'darling,' you can ask it."

"Deal." He set the bottle aside. "That night in Vegas, when you stopped me from going back outside..." He squinted at her, but she watched him and waited, her expression giving away nothing. "How did you know I was going back outside to those two? To Peter and Cyn?"

She shook her head. "You must have misheard me. I didn't stop you from doing anything."

He stared at her a long moment, and she returned the stare, unblinking, but uncomfortable with her lie. Something deep in her heart told her Jack deserved the truth, but how could she possibly tell him? He seemed like such an unlikely person to confess her secrets to.

Fallon could faintly tell that he was getting angry. He moved a little closer.

"We have unfinished business, you know."

She shook her head. "I don't think we do."

He was beside her now, close enough to touch her. "You never followed through with what you promised me that night." He leaned into her, eyes burning into hers. Jack had always been fairly good-looking, but the lines in his face were more defined—he had not left his years of hard living and partying behind, as Bret had, and it showed.

"I think we both know I never had any intention of following through," she assured him calmly. She set aside her glass, not wanting to break it in Bret's hot tub in case she had to go all martial-artist on him.

"I think you should re-think that," he advised. "It's not nice to make promises you don't intend to keep." His hand was suddenly sliding up her thigh. She seized his wrist with a strength that surprised and stopped him, but he was, nonetheless, stronger. He pressed himself against her, pinning her to the wall, and kissed her hard on the lips. She tried to push him off, but he didn't move, so she wrapped her fingers around quite a bit of his long black hair and pulled as hard as she could. He yelled, backing off for a second, knocking her hand away and freeing his hair. In anger, he seized her shoulders and shoved her underwater. Surprised, she immediately grabbed his arms for leverage and kicked him hard between the legs, and then surfaced, coughing, as he fell aside with gritted teeth, leaning on the edge of the hot tub.

Fallon went under again to smooth back her hair, then settled herself in the bubbling water and picked up her glass, not taking her eyes off him. She did not feel threatened. She could tell that shoving her under had been a knee-jerk emotional reaction for him, and she was in no way afraid that he would touch her again.

In a little while, he reached for his beer, still catching his breath. "After talking to Tayce, I thought you'd be easier than that. You didn't put up a fight with him."

She rolled her eyes. He was clearly lying about Tayce, who would never imply such a thing. He was jealous that she apparently had an alliance with Tayce, and he wanted to shake it. Most of what she could read off of Jack was sex. And that he hadn't intended her any real harm. In fact, she could read that he was currently feeling fairly ashamed that he'd allowed his feelings to escalate to the point of being so rough with her. He was filled with regret, which was not a typical Jack Lane emotion.

He was also annoyed with her because he felt like she was smarter than him. That was news. Jack was actually a smart man, business-minded, the whole nine. But he was puzzled by the things that had happened in Vegas. He'd been curious about her since she slipped away from him that night, and seeing her with Bret, hearing their unified denial that anything was odd with how she'd acted the night Peter and Cyn disappeared, was making him crazy. Jack didn't like being shown-up by someone in any area of his life. He was mad, pure and simple.

"I could teach you some things about lying," she said.

He eyed her darkly. "I could teach you some things, too. If you'd let me."

She lowered her eyelashes and said nothing

He was examining his left arm. "What the hell did you do to me?" he demanded, squeezing his arm like it hurt, looking at it closely.

She looked up alertly, maintaining the distance between them, though she was curious. "What do you mean?"

"It hurts like fuck, like you burned me or something."

She went still. Then she set down her glass and came near him, kneeling beside him and peering around him at his upper arm, just above his elbow. There was a large reddened burn mark that had obviously just happened. She looked quickly around the hot tub, though she knew there was nothing there that could have caused this. His lighter and cigarettes were on a lounge chair several feet away. There were no candles, nothing nearby.

She recreated in her mind the moment when she grabbed him to fight him off. She reached towards his arm with her right hand, felt her wrist tingle as it drew near him. Turning her arm over to look at it, she saw with some shock that the lines of the eye and flames tattoo were glowing a soft red, like a dying ember. Jack grabbed her hand and looked at the tattoo, comparing it with the burn mark on his arm. Then he looked into her face, not releasing her hand, squeezing tighter. He looked wild.

"Put your arm in the pool water," she directed. "Maybe that will ease the pain." What in the hell was going on? Her tattoo had burned him?

His stare did not waver. "What are you?" he breathed.

She radiated some calmness in his direction, and nudged him gently towards the wall that separated the hot tub from the pool. He released her and cautiously lowered his elbow into the cool water. She could see from his expression that it helped immediately. Returning to her glass of sangria, she sat in the water with her knees pulled to her chest—thinking, thinking.

After a moment Jack returned to his side of the hot tub and picked up his beer, sliding down to his chin and staring at her. Then with a grimace he shifted and raised up his elbow to rest it on the side, because the temperature of the water caused him increased pain.

She eyed his arm. "Is it worse? Blistering?"

He looked at it. "No, it's smooth, just red and hurts like hell, a little swollen. Does Bret know about this, demon woman?"

She downed the remainder of her sangria in one swallow and wished for more. "Jack, trust me, this is news to me, too."

He sneered. "Yeah, right."

"I'm not lying to you this time."

"Where'd you get that tattoo? Satan's workshop? And what does the other one do? Bring rain?"

She closed her eyes. The absolute last thing she'd wanted: Jack Lane alert to her strangeness and quizzing her in-depth. And with good reason. She looked at him, and he thought she appeared tired. "Can we just call a truce, maybe talk about all this at some other time?"

"Show me the tattoo again," he ordered.

She held up her arm to him. The tattoo was no longer glowing, appearing now just like any black-line tattoo. He looked around. "You burned me with a lighter or something."

"I guess so. You were trying to drown me."

He scowled. "I wasn't trying to drown you."

She came closer to examine the burn one more time. "Jack, it is blistering." Was it getting worse as she watched it? She looked at his face and saw he was in quite a bit of pain, but was trying to hide the fact, gritting his teeth. "Close your eyes for me," she whispered.

He looked at her with full mistrust.

"Close them for me." Her voice was gentle, like a song, and against his better judgement—almost against his will—he closed his eyes. He felt her fingertips lightly touching his burn, and prepared to flinch in pain, but instead the pain began to slowly dissipate. Soon there was almost no pain at all. His eyes finally flew open, and she drew away from him as he looked at his arm.

Not only was it no longer blistering, but it was less red and swollen, and only a little sore. He looked at her, but she was staring away into the darkness, face set with determination and some kind of internal reflection. With a tightly clenched jaw, he stopped himself from saying anything more about it. But he knew two things for certain: Fallon Quinn had just burned him with a tattoo, and then healed him with her touch.

When Bret appeared several minutes later, Jack and Fallon were ignoring each other from opposite sides of the hot tub.

"Jack, you're still here," Bret observed, crouching down behind Fallon, who reached up and took his hand. He'd sent Bergen straight to bed.

"I was trying to get Fallon to give me a ride home," Jack explained with his lazy drawl.

She squeezed Bret's hand. "But I decided I shouldn't be alone with him for too long. It's far too tempting."

Jack leaned his head back and closed his eyes. "It's only a matter of time before you come around, darlin'."

Bret looked at her, seeing that she seemed quiet and unsettled. *Did he try to do something to you?*

She shook her head slightly.

Jack was climbing out of the hot tub, the sound of a horn honking from the driveway. "I believe my ride is finally here. I'll see you cats later." He stared at Fallon. "I'll see you again, for sure." He unabashedly stripped down naked, drying off and pulling on dry clothes. Lighting a cigarette, he headed out a side gate without looking back.

"That was weird," Fallon breathed. "Let's go in."

Bret stood and handed her a towel, watching her face closely, for she seemed a million miles away in her head. He wished, not for the first time, that he could read her like she could him.

She dried off, and they headed into the kitchen, where Fallon set her empty glass in the sink. "He's a serious pain in the ass. What was he doing here?"

"We were talking about a combined tour our record company wants us to do. Neither of us want to do it, not the least because we can't really stand each other for too long at a time."

"Like five minutes?"

"Maybe ten. But we agreed it would make money."

"Then you had to go get Bergen?" She slid on a long-sleeved, see-though black tunic that fell to her upper thigh.

"Yeah, and I thought he was on his way out as well, when I left. I couldn't believe it when you told me he was still here." He chewed on one of the banana nut muffins she'd made that morning.

"He was waiting for me. He had definite plans. He's angry about Vegas, about the mystery of it all. Our lies."

CHAPTER TWENTY-THREE

Bret narrowed his eyes. "Did he try to touch you?"

"Yes, but we quickly arrived at an understanding."

She hugged him as she saw him losing his temper.

"It's fine, Bret. Truly. But he's...maybe not always the greatest guy."

"That's not a revelation." Her touch was quelling his anger, sending waves of calm through him.

"I don't want to talk about him anymore."

He held her close and kissed her. "Neither do I."

CHAPTER TWENTY-FOUR

On her first morning back at home in Gray, Fallon was up inexplicably early. After breakfast and a quick shower, she began doing laundry and making a grocery list, Azul at her heels all the while. She didn't have to go in to work until the following evening. Now that she was back in town, her thoughts turned painfully to Selah, whom she had not spoken to in nearly two weeks. It was the longest they'd ever gone without communicating. The grief over their broken friendship gripped her as strongly as if Selah had died. She could no longer remember a time when her world had not included Selah. For so long now, Michael, Selah, and Indio were the only family she'd allowed herself to have. She didn't want to feel as if she were trading them for a new world with Bret and Bergen. But Selah was hard as steel, and Fallon knew this better than anyone; there was no fighting her once she'd made up her mind. Fallon could do nothing but wait.

She kept herself busy over the next few days, working extra hours at Solu and helping out at Madrigal one night for a birthday party. She and Bret talked and texted throughout every day, and Bergen texted her regularly as well.

She continued to practice purposeful vision-seeking daily, but it was not coming back easily. She half-wondered if the ability was being stubborn because she had denied it for so long. She wished she could ask Jacob or Luca for help—their absences caused her renewed pain as she now learned to navigate without Selah just as she'd learned to navigate without Jacob and Luca years ago.

That Bret James was now an enormous part of her world was taking some getting used to. She had a feeling, almost like a shadow in her mind, that this relationship wasn't the right choice for either of them. She wondered—maybe unfairly—if the ability to talk in each other's head was fueling much of the connection they felt. But she cared deeply for him; there was no denying it. She missed him when they were apart. And she felt such a strong connection with Bergen, which had been unexpected. Besides Indio, she had no real dealings with children. Even Diego's kids, whom she was around quite often, she had no attachment to. But towards Bergen, she felt an indefinable pull.

One day Fallon made a dewberry pie from berries she picked along a dirt road outside of town. She took it out to Star Fall Farm around lunchtime, where she had a lengthy visit with Paul, Katrine and Tayce. Paul and Tayce had begun recording parts of the new album, and their bassist and drummer were scheduled to arrive the following day. Fallon texted Bret's tour schedule to Tayce, and he promised/threatened that he would drop in on a show one night to jam on-stage.

Several nights, she and Tayce met at Madrigal for drinks. Being friends with the guitarist was easy, somehow intuitive. They greatly enjoyed each other's company, almost as two old souls who had known and loved each other in a previous existence, and now finally found each other again in this life, but only as friends, nothing more. They sat at the bar together sharing a basket of chips and salsa, drank a fair amount, and talked about any number of inane subjects—movies, music, taking care of long hair, favorite conditioners, etc.,—but they also had deep conversations, quite a few focused on his family and his marriage, his past and his future.

One night in particular, he seemed moody when he joined her at the bar, immediately ordering whiskey and not saying much till he had it in hand. She could read the gist of what was wrong, and so she began the conversation, knowing which direction she wanted it to go.

"How long have you lived in L.A.?" she asked.

"Ah, since I was in my early twenties. Moved there after college, immersed myself in the music scene, played in some bands, and finally found a musical soulmate in Paul. The rest is misery, I mean history."

"You've lived there a long time now; you must like it." But she already knew what he would say.

"Hate it. I've never liked L.A., but my wife won't live anywhere else. I'm on the road or otherwise away about ten months out of the year, so I can deal with it for two months. Honestly, Fallon, despite my flashy appearance," she grinned appropriately at his quip, "I am the adopted son of a Wisconsin dairy farmer. Los Angeles was never my style."

"Hence your love of Star Fall Farm!"

He shrugged. "Most likely, yes."

"What made you, of all people, choose to get married? How old were you?"

"I was thirty-four." He sighed. "I married Ella because she was pregnant with Jane, my oldest daughter. I thought it was the right thing to do, you know. That all that family stuff would just fall into place, magically, somehow." He shook his head. "It was a mistake before it even happened. After three years, I told her I wanted out. I was going to be there for Jane and take care of her, but I couldn't stay married. Ella must have known that was coming. She alerted me that I could not leave because she was pregnant with Annie." He looked at her. "I never brought up leaving again."

He drank some of his whiskey and sat back. "I love my two girls. God, I love 'em. Every time I'd say goodbye to go out on the road when they were little, their tears, their heartache, their pleas for me to stay—it shattered me. I wasn't equipped to handle the emotions they created in me. Consequently, I stayed away more, to avoid those awful goodbyes. Well, despite it all, I have great relationships with them both; they allegedly love me dearly." His face was alight. "Jane's my twin, she's a singer in a rock band called Sweet Jane; her boyfriend is the drummer. My little Annie is already seventeen. They video chat with me all the time and fly out to see me when they can. They are the great joy in my life besides my guitar."

"I'm waiting till Annie is out of the house, then I'm getting a divorce. And my wife knows it. Though Annie recently told me not to wait on her account, to just go ahead and do it. I've always been super-protective of her because, not only is she the baby, but also because I always felt she was conceived for the sole purpose of my wife being vindictive towards me. I know I was a fool to marry her simply because she was pregnant with Jane.

But I've always been a bit of a fool. And so, twenty-one years later, here I am, still married to her."

"Why would Ella want to stay with you? Knowing how you feel?"

"Power. Status. Not letting anyone else have me. I don't know. It's not for my income, I can promise you that," he laughed, "though she does try to spend what I do bring home. A divorce—it's going to be messy. Royalties to deal with, various things. Friends, relationships, family members... but I guess people manage to do it all the time."

"She knows you sleep around."

He made a face. "She's always known. I cheated on a girlfriend to sleep with her—never an auspicious start to a relationship, in my experience. I mean, I keep things fairly quiet, always someone far away. I'm not sleeping with her best friend or anything like that. But she knows, as some women tend to do. About ten years ago, she started doing the same." He shook his head. "When my girls come see me on the road they're always, 'You're so happy! So relaxed! We love you this way!' This is Annie's senior year coming up. I'm filing for divorce in January. My little Christmas gift to myself. Sad, huh? Now you know the truth—I'm not so much cool as just pathetic."

She gave him a tight smile and squeezed his hand gently, her fingers pressing against the veins in the underside of his wrist. A wave of calm swept over him. He felt his body relax, his heart lighten with sweet joy.

"Witchcraft," he murmured, but not very loudly.

She turned to order another drink.

CHAPTER TWENTY-FIVE

Fallon had been home from California for two weeks when one afternoon brought a knocking at her door. When she went to look, she saw Michael Lowe standing there. A tall, pleasant-looking man, a good and gentle soul with a serious joker streak, Michael was often caught up with his job, but he loved to laugh, and he cherished his family, and in his mind his family had long-included Fallon.

She opened the door and looked past him at Indio down in the yard, playing with Azul. When the child saw Fallon, he raced up the steps and hurtled into her arms.

"Hello, you," she greeted him, picking him up and swinging him around. She had missed him. She had not seen Indio in over a month. Since before she had saved his life.

"Fallon, Fallon, Fallon!" he shrieked happily, and then he was bouncing around her apartment, full of energy. Michael sat on the couch and watched as she played with Indio a while, talking to him and giggling with him till he was satisfied that she'd given him enough of her time. Then he was happy to play with a tub of Legos she kept in the closet for him, knowing his father had wanted to speak to Fallon in private.

Fallon turned the music she'd been listening to up a little, and then sat down on the couch next to Michael, and together they watched his son.

"She blames you," he said softly, without preamble. "She blames you for the feelings of dread she has, knowing that he was in mortal danger."

Fallon nodded. "I was afraid she might. People do, you know. Blame me."

"I don't blame you. And of course, she knows it's not your fault, that she's being irrational. And we both know that Selah is nothing if not completely rational. So not only is she upset about you, and him, but she's also upset with herself for entertaining a single irrational thought." He looked at her. "She'll come around. It may just take a little more time."

Fallon tried to smile for him, but managed only to twist her lips in a sad way. "There was always the chance that it would come to this. No one ever lasts, with me. Every relationship dies, no matter what anyone says, what they promise."

He looked pained. "I know you think that. But Selah is different. You're family. I'd swear she loves you more than she loves me."

She stared at Indio, her mind going to Bret and Bergen. She didn't want to go through the pain of losing them. She wasn't going to be able to stand it. Losing Selah was proof that she would always lose, in the end. Bret and Bergen were, therefore, impermanent. She felt as if something in her soul had been suddenly set adrift.

"Thanks for bringing him by. Does she know you're here?"

"She guessed but didn't say anything. He's been asking to see you for weeks. We told him you were still in California."

Fallon drew her knees to her chest, hugging them close. "It's amazing, isn't it? Twenty-plus years of friendship, done in by one little image in my head. And I even saved him. But it doesn't matter."

Michael blinked back what he suspected might be a tear. He couldn't stand the pain he heard in her voice. "I'll talk to her..."

"No, don't. Don't do that. We need to make a clean break." She nodded at Indio. "He needs to forget about me." But her voice was shaking, and Indio's innocent brown eyes met hers, alert to the tone of distress he heard.

All of a sudden, Michael got to his feet, the strong emotions overwhelming him. He pulled her up and held her close a moment, crushing her against him. Indio also got to his feet, watching them. When Michael finally let her go, he was wiping away tears. "I can bet she never told you this, but thank you." His voice was low, his eyes on his son. "Thank you for saving him. I could never thank you enough if I thanked you for the rest of my life. I am indebted to you forever for him. You are my girl, Fallon. For life. You are with us forever. Indio, come on; we're leaving."

Indio protested, but his father scooped him up and left the apartment. "Take care, Fallon," he said before he shut the door. "This is not the end."

When they were gone, and she'd listened to their SUV drive away, Fallon lay down on her bed and buried her face in the pillows. Selah had always been her only proof that perhaps everyone she loved would not be lost, but now that proof was shattered. Nothing and no one would be hers for as long as she needed—the universe would not allow it. It wanted her to be alone. It would not let her solve Bret's future doom; it would let him die. Bergen would be lost and Fallon would be completely and entirely alone. Bret was going to die, and Bergen would never forgive her.

Her mind would not be still, racing around with memories and thoughts of all the pain she'd known, all the pain she assumed would come. *Jacob abandoned you when you needed him most. Luca is dead. Murdered. Selah is lost. Bret will die. Jacob abandoned you.*

Azul jumped up on the bed with her and lay beside her, snuffling near her ear. She turned and buried her face against his fur.

When Bret called a few minutes later, she ignored it. When Mariana called to find out why she wasn't showing up for work, she ignored that, too. She lay there till the sun had set, the shadows in the room getting longer and longer. Then came the soft glow of twilight, then darkness. Every now and then Azul raised his head and whined, then lowered his chin back onto his paws.

The phone rang again: Bret. Again: Tessa. She kicked it off the edge of the bed and turned away, trembling. The raven tattoo was tingling painfully on her wrist, but she dug her fingernails into it in annoyance. *Jacob abandoned you. Luca is dead. Selah is lost. Bret will die. Jacob abandoned you.*

She sat up and went into the bathroom, getting out the little red bag. Loading the injector, she held it to her thigh and pressed the button. As she made it back to the bed and dropped down, her mind dissolved into sweet darkness.

Azul whimpered, and let out a long, low whine.

* * * * * * *

Mariana Sanchez pulled into the driveway in her old black Suburban and saw by the glow of the security light Ms. Landrum insisted on that Katrine had just arrived in her dusty red farm truck. It was close to eleven. When hours had gone by without being able to reach her, Bret had finally called Solu. A concerned Mariana told him Fallon had not come in that night despite being scheduled to work, and he immediately called Katrine, who was alone at the farm. In the end, Katrine and Mariana agreed to meet at Fallon's apartment.

The two women nodded in a sober greeting to each other, then climbed the back steps to Fallon's door, knocking at first, then pushing it open when they realized it was unlocked. The apartment was completely dark.

"Fallon? Fallon, honey, are you here?"

Katrine switched on a lamp. Azul appeared from behind the black curtain, whining unhappily, and the women went straight to the bed, pushing the curtain aside. Fallon was lying there, deeply asleep, and when they tried, they could not wake her.

Mariana turned on a small lamp and sat on the bed, picking up Fallon's wrist to check her pulse. "A little slow, but her breathing sounds fine."

"Bret said she sometimes takes shots, for headaches?" Katrine offered questioningly. He had mentioned it in his frantic call to her.

Mariana nodded. "Yes, and that must be what's happened here, if I had to guess. Though it is unusual that she didn't alert us that she wouldn't be coming in. She's been out for days sometimes because of those shots. Her friend Selah is always the one who takes care of her, I don't know much about it."

"Should we take her to the hospital?" Katrine wondered. Her phone began ringing, and she realized she'd forgotten to call Bret back. "Bret, she's here on her bed, unconscious, it looks like she gave herself one of those shots you were talking about. Should we call Selah, or take her to the ER?"

"Selah's not speaking to her at the moment." Bret was relieved that they'd at least located her. "Take her to the ER, Kat, please. I don't like those shots; nothing should knock her out for that long."

Diego entered the apartment as Katrine was hanging up with Bret, and she told him she wanted to take Fallon to the emergency room. He agreed reluctantly— "Fallon will not like it," he muttered—and easily lifted her limp body up in his arms.

At that moment, a dark figure appeared in the doorway, blocking their way. "You must not take her from here."

All three were startled to find Selah watching them solemnly, sternly. Looking petite in dark gray leggings and a paint-spattered white t-shirt, clutching her key fob in her left hand, she nonetheless looked like she would willingly fight all three of them before she'd let them take another step with Fallon. Azul went and sat at Selah's feet, as if to throw his lot in with her, show his support.

They immediately tried to argue their case.

"She's unconscious."

"Bret is out of his mind."

"Her breathing seems slow."

Unconcerned by their comments, Selah set down her keys and approached them as Diego obediently lay her back down on the bed. She observed Fallon a moment, then went into the bathroom and saw the injector on the countertop. After confirming that Fallon had used only one vial, she returned to the concerned citizens gathered at Fallon's side.

"She will be alright. She's taken a drug my husband prescribes for her, to deal with her unbearable headaches. She doesn't use it often, but when she does it knocks her out for hours. This...," she extended her hand out to indicate Fallon's sleeping figure, "is normal."

"I was sure she'd need a doctor." Katrine was eyeing Fallon worriedly. Marianna and Diego were familiar with Michael and Selah, however, and were quick to accept the latter's reassurances.

"My husband will be along later to check on her," Selah lied, managing a quick, close-lipped smile.

With varying degrees of relief and reluctance, Fallon's three would-be saviors took their leave, and Selah found herself alone in the garage apartment with a loyal black dog and her unconscious best friend. She looked down at Azul. "You won't tell her I was here, will you?"

Azul licked her hand and wagged his tail.

Selah texted an update to Michael, who had encouraged her to go alone to Fallon's apartment when they heard Azul barking at their back door. The barking had seemed more frantic than usual; they had both immediately been alarmed by it. Selah had not hesitated. She'd wanted Michael to come along, but Indio was already in bed.

Now she retrieved a cube of cheese from the fridge and handed it to the dog, who took it with care from her fingers and then devoured it joyfully. Crouching down, she rubbed his head. "You wanted me to come right away, because you saw they were about to take her to the hospital. You wanted me to stop them. You always alert me when she's about to wake up, but she's nowhere near waking up right now. You wanted me to stop them." She held his furry face in her hands a moment. "Good dog," she whispered, and stood up again.

Locating Fallon's phone on the floor, Selah scrolled through the texts and missed calls. Bret was apparently on his way, flying from LAX to Dallas. Katrine had obviously spoken to him to reassure him, but he was coming anyway. An overreaction on his part, mused Selah, but he was new to all this.

Copying his number to her own phone, Selah texted him detailed directions on how to care for Fallon when she woke up. She reassured him that no doctor was needed, and gave him Michael's number to call if he had any questions. Then she bid goodnight to Azul and let herself out the apartment door.

CHAPTER TWENTY-SIX

FALLON

Fallon was sitting cross-legged on the leather ottoman in Jacob's room, ready for her lesson. These special evenings had become important to her, and it seemed like Jacob had been home more than usual lately. Secure in the knowledge that she wasn't home alone, her brother went out more and more often to enjoy Austin's live music scene.

Jacob sat down in his chair and emptied a black velvet bag of objects onto the ottoman with her. Crystals, gold coins, a wooden chess piece, a rough square of iron, and a wicked-looking silver dagger. She reached instinctively to touch everything but he grabbed her wrist, stopping her.

"This you must learn," he warned. "Objects can have powers, they have a history, can be a link. You never want to touch a strange object unless you are mentally prepared. You must feel it just before you touch it—you will learn to sense if it is full of evil, of some spell that looks to drain you, see your secrets, even destroy you."

She looked a little startled, and he sighed at having to teach such things to such a young girl, but she was an excellent student; there was no question. It was all progressing more smoothly and much more quickly than he'd anticipated. The rumors of her powers, the hints of things he'd sensed about her, the episode eight years ago with the Ruen crystal...it was all true.

He nodded at the objects. "Choose one, but don't touch it yet. Hold it in your mind, then reach for it, not only with your fingers, but with your senses. Figure out its intent, if it even has one, it might not. Then, when you have it in your grasp, you will be able to read its past."

He was unsurprised when he saw her focusing immediately on the dagger, the deadliest item in the group. His girl was a dark one. In her eyes he often saw shadows passing like clouds or wayward spirits. There was a darkness in her core, despite that she could light up a room with her smile and laughter when she chose. He wondered how much she would battle the darkness as she grew up, how much she would hold onto the light. Luca kept her in the light, it seemed his life's goal. But Jacob did not assume that Luca would be with her forever. This child who sat before him was destined for loss, again and again; it made even his tough, battered old heart ache for her. They would not know what to battle against her with. And so, they would steal from her, wound her with heartache. Loss would be their weapon.

He was brought back by an anguished cry—Fallon had wrapped her fingers around the hilt of the dagger, and was shaken by what she saw in its history, the murderous, horrible deaths. She dropped it, and it clattered to the floor. Slowly she met his stare. And in her eyes, he saw that she had seen it all.

And she had seen that the hand wielding the dagger had always been his own.

Thus ended Fallon's first lesson in psychometry.

CHAPTER TWENTY-SEVEN

Fallon's eyes fluttered open, and immediately Bret popped into her hazy view. She cried out in surprise, her voice little more than a croak. Azul promptly commenced licking her arm in reassurance.

"Do you want juice? I was told to give you juice."

She was dying to ask him why he was there, but she couldn't form words. She allowed him to help her drink cold grape juice. Several minutes passed before her vision cleared and her voice found itself.

"What's going on?" she demanded hoarsely. "What's wrong? Why are you here? Is Bergen alright?"

He gave her a brief rundown on the previous night's events. "It's all my fault, because I panicked." He looked sheepish. "I had everyone I could enlist."

She rubbed her hands sleepily over her face, yawning. "Thank goodness Selah showed up and stopped them from taking me to the hospital." She shivered at the thought. She was also surprised that Selah had bothered.

"I didn't know hospitals were off limits."

"Sorry, I should have told you that early on. But who knew?" He squeezed her hand. "So, it was a bad headache yesterday?"

Her eyes stayed on something unseen; she did not speak. Finally, she looked at him. "You flew out here last night, in the middle of the night, to be with me. You've got tour rehearsals going on."

"I had to be sure you were alright. I don't trust anyone with you as much as I trust myself." He hazarded a grin. "See? Ego, still firmly in place."

She did not smile back. "Bret, my friendship with Selah, it was always the one thing in my life I could count on. Since I was a child, it was central to me. Especially after I lost Luca and others, she has been the only one in my life whom I have never had to endure the loss of. My premonition ability has taken her away from me. I realized yesterday that I can't endure the pain of losing you and Bergen. That I could not survive any more losses in my life."

He frowned at her. "Why would you lose us?"

"I lose the people I love. Every one. It's like a curse."

"But Selah came last night to make sure you were okay…"

"Out of a sense of decency only."

Can you hear me? he asked in her head.

Yes, she answered back.

Can Selah talk to you in her head?

She looked away. It was a rhetorical question.

I love you, Fallon. More than anyone beside Bergen. Do you hear me? I have never spoken truer words. I want to know that you hear me.

She nodded, tears streaming onto her cheeks.

"Tell me you hear me." There was a catch in his voice.

"I hear you," she whispered.

He wrapped his arms around her. "I will never let you go."

She went to take a much-needed shower, and he went to the kitchen to fix her a sandwich, Azul following him hopefully.

When she was finally sitting at her little dining table with the sandwich, a bag of chips, and a bowl of fruit, Bret sat down across from her and looked at her steadily. "There are some things you maybe need to tell me. Like why you can't go to hospitals. And what's in those shots you take."

She didn't answer for a moment, chewing her food thoughtfully, taking her time. She helped herself to some grapes.

"I'm going to tell you a story. I've told you that Luca had premonitions, too. It was different than with me. He had much more control over it; he could seek things out, find answers. What I'm trying to re-learn how to do? He could do it without thinking. His ability seemed to have fewer boundaries than mine. I thought I was," she searched for the right words, "so much less than him. Less brave. Less powerful." She ate a jalapeno-flavored potato chip. "But then when I was eleven, I started learning things about myself, amazing things that I could do, things Luca was completely unaware of, incapable of. It turned out I had powers that he would not have been able to fathom." She twisted the ring on her finger that she always wore, intricate brass holding a raw blue-grey gemstone Bret could not identify. "Luca and I were always very close, but even we had secrets from each other. Deep ones.

"When our parents died, I was seven, and it was the first time I realized what my visions were—that they meant something.

I'd always been too young to understand; I just knew that sometimes I felt bad. Sometimes I saw people and things in my mind, like a dream, but while I was awake. Then one night I saw my parents in my head. I must not have thought anything of it. They were my parents. They should be in my head. Then I had the horrible feeling, it always gave me a stomachache back then. I heard what sounded like fireworks popping in my mind. In reality, my parents were leaving to go out to dinner. I didn't even say goodbye to them, I just hid under the covers, wanting the bad feeling and the sounds to go away. Eventually I fell asleep. Luca woke me up later and told me our parents had been killed, shot by some men who, as far as anyone could guess, wanted to steal their car. The robbery had apparently gone wrong, and at some point, the car was set on fire. A freak occurrence for Austin at the time, but it happened all the same and was never solved.

"But then suddenly, it all fell into place for me: the fireworks sound in my mind had been gunshots. I described it all to Luca, and he finally explained that I was having premonitions, and that he got them, too. I was devastated; I took full blame, that I hadn't stopped them from leaving the house. But he just held me, and loved me, and didn't blame me at all.

"We went to stay with a… cousin who lived in an expensive old neighborhood in central Austin. Jacob Roth was our guardian for the next seven years. He was good to us in his way, and despite that early loss, we were happy kids. With Jacob, we were very much on our own, raising ourselves; we quickly became quite independent and capable. Luca wasn't troubled by his ability as I was, and I was lucky that I had him as I grew up, to listen to me and support me. He was protective of me. We'd always been able to talk to each other in our minds. I thought this was normal for the longest time, and was surprised to find out it wasn't. When Luca was nineteen and I was fourteen, Jacob died, leaving us the house and everything he'd owned, which was quite a lot of money and investments. And so, we continued to live in that house together. We were responsible for kids our age. We handled everything, and had no real problems. Somehow, we just weren't on anybody's radar; no one questioned that we lived there or who we lived there with."

She relayed that six months after Jacob's loss, Luca vanished without a trace on his twentieth birthday. No note, his car keys and cell phone left behind, nothing missing. He was simply gone. Fallon tried to talk to him in her mind, but there was no answer. When she tried to sense him, there were only shadows. The siblings had never trusted authority figures, and this included the police, so she didn't report him missing. With Selah and another friend there to support her, she went about her little life as best she could, going to school, taking care of the house. But she was numb. She had just suffered the devastating loss of Jacob a few months before; Luca's disappearance was like a sucker-punch to the heart. She couldn't understand why she hadn't seen something, had some warning. She knew for certain Luca would not have left her alone of his own accord. And she could tell that he wasn't dead, he was just... elsewhere. And so, she waited for him to come back, because that was all she could do.

"Seven weeks later to the day, he reappeared. In the backyard. He was fine, not harmed, and remembered nothing. The only thing we knew had happened were the tattoos." She held up her wrists. "Before he vanished, he had no tattoos. When he came back to me, he had some similar to these on his wrists."

A chill went down Bret's spine. "Did you have them then?"

She shook her head, and took a bite of her sandwich. "Not yet." She indicated her right wrist. "His eye didn't have flames like mine does." She held up her left. "His raven didn't look quite like mine. And see the eye of my raven is a prism? His had just a regular raven eye. Both of my tattoos were done far better, more artistically, than his, but by the time I got mine, he'd been dead several years, so there was really no comparing."

For a moment she thought about Jack, burning his arm. "Luca and I researched the hell out of them, but there were so many conflicting possibilities for what they could mean. We learned nothing definitive. We finally gave up." She gathered up her dishes and took everything into the kitchen.

"Two years later, Luca was dead." She turned to face him, folding her arms over her chest. "I had a premonition. One of the most blinding, strong ones I've ever had. He was out; he'd gone running. I was home with Selah. I screamed to him in my mind. The danger was unclear, I couldn't work it out, but I felt the death around it. I screamed and screamed for him. He never answered. When I tried to sense him, there weren't shadows, there was just darkness. The link between us was broken. I could feel that he was gone. Dead. I could feel the loneliness rise up to greet me, like a physical thing. My head was empty without his voice in it. My heart was empty. I was a ghost."

He held out his arms to her, and she went and sat on his lap. "Eventually I recovered; I continued on with life. When I was about to turn twenty, Selah and I were ready. Just in case whatever had happened to Luca when he turned twenty was going to happen to me, like a curse, we wanted to be prepared. We weren't going to let me disappear. Selah was going to the University of Texas, sharing an apartment with another girl. I had been traveling the world, but I came to her two days before my birthday and never left her side. I went to classes with her, everywhere. On the actual day of my birthday, we didn't leave the apartment. All day we stayed in and ate cake and watched TV. By eleven that night we were feeling foolish; you can imagine. I took a shower and got into her bed, and then she went to take a shower.

"When she got out of the shower, I was gone. At first, she thought I was playing a joke. We'd been so worked up about it all day. But she searched the apartment, and I wasn't there. She went outside and called for me. She called my cell, which was also gone." Fallon shook her head. "I had vanished."

Bret had the sensation of being in an elevator that had just begun to free fall.

"Unlike me, Selah called the cops. She spent weeks looking, putting up flyers, making phone calls, visiting radio stations. I received quite the publicity. Seven weeks later, on a Saturday, I realized I was sitting by a fountain on the university campus. My cellphone was lying next to me. I looked at the date, and then I called Selah. She had been expecting my call. She said, 'Seven weeks. To the day.' And then she started crying. She immediately came to get me. And as I was walking to the parking lot to meet her, I happened to look at my wrists. And there they were. The same tattoos that Luca had, though different. My first thought was that this meant I was going to die in about three years."

Chapter Twenty-Seven

He held her closer. "You didn't remember anything?"

"Nothing visually. I remembered one thing only. A man's whispered voice. A phrase: 'Do I fear you, my Rose?' That's all I remember. Over and over again in my head. That's it, after seven weeks, those six meaningless words and two tattoos, that was all."

She took a deep breath. "For the next two years we were scared, like I said, that I was going to die like Luca did. That it was a pattern we could not stop. We were nervy, especially since I was still traveling. Luca was twenty-two years, three months, and seven days old when he died. When that same day arrived for me, I was with Selah at her parents' house. Michael was with us, too. He never left my side that day; he was pretty much daring anyone to harm me. The day came and went. Nothing happened. I was still alive.

"It was still a while before we all relaxed, but finally I left again. I traveled some more, still trying to find a place that felt like home to me. But nothing did. Only Selah felt like home. She and Michael got married after she graduated, and I moved to Gray to be near them. They chose this little town in large part because of me, to give me a quiet place to live."

She turned in his arms and kissed him deeply, wanting a distraction from the heaviness she'd just waded through. As he returned her kiss and felt her body press against his, he was aware she had answered none of his original questions.

When they woke up later, Fallon hurriedly took another shower, wanting to make it to work on time. Bret ate a sandwich while she got dressed in a short black skirt and long-sleeved white t-shirt with "Solu" in black script over her left breast and across her back. She grabbed her messenger bag, and they went down to his SUV and drove to the restaurant.

At Solu, he kissed her as she got out. "I'll be by around eleven; I told Diego I'd have a drink with him."

"Okay. Stay out of trouble," she warned, and he winked before he drove away. She knew where he was headed.

CHAPTER TWENTY-EIGHT

B ret drove around for less than ten minutes before he found what he was looking for. He parked the SUV on the street in front of the blue and white Queen Anne, and headed up the sidewalk, glancing around at the peaceful, quiet neighborhood. The front screened door swung open as he reached the porch, and a grinning little boy greeted him. "Hello, Mr. Bret!"

Bret smiled. "Hey, Indio. Is your mom..."

"Yes, I'm here." Selah appeared behind her son, casual in black leggings and a long-sleeved grey t-shirt. "Hello," she greeted him coolly, looking resigned to his presence, which she'd long been expecting. He saw smudges of paint on her hands, and recalled Fallon telling him that Selah was an artist.

"I'd like to talk to you."

She nodded, and gestured at the wooden swing at one end of the porch. "Indio, go back inside and watch your show. You can watch for thirty minutes."

"Okay, Momma. See you, Mr. Bret." Indio waved and scampered back in.

Selah followed Bret to the swing and sat in it herself when he indicated that he was waiting for her. He joined her, and she tucked her legs up beside her.

"Mind if I swing?" he asked.

"Not at all."

She watched him carefully without looking directly at him as they began to sway back and forth. He was clad in old, worn jeans and a black t-shirt that couldn't hide the muscles in his tanned, tattooed arms and fit torso. There were two silver chains around his neck and various bracelets around his wrists. Bret was, she admitted freely, quite handsome—the beautiful gypsy rockstar. He was polite, and friendly, and as genuine as he could be. Now just a ghost of the bad boy he'd apparently once been, fatherhood had definitely mellowed him. She couldn't imagine a better choice for Fallon to love. She shifted as her heart ached at the thought of her friend.

"Where would you like to begin?" she asked him finally.

"Fallon is heartbroken that she's lost you," he explained. "She told me that she always loses. That no one is permanent in her life. That she knows that she couldn't take losing me and Bergen. I have some concern about the shot she gave herself the other night and the emotional state she was in when she did it. I don't think she had a headache at the time. And I believe your husband had just been to see her."

Selah's face was dark in thought at his words. "First of all, she hasn't lost me." The words were hard to say, but true.

He raised an eyebrow. "It seems like she has. As far as she knows, she has."

"And second, I don't imagine that she will lose you or your daughter," she went on.

"I don't imagine it, either, Selah. But she saved your son's life. And to show your thanks, you've slammed the door in her face."

Selah was still at the anger in his voice. She wiped away a tear as it hit her cheek. She nodded. "I was scared. I reacted badly. I haven't been myself since that day. It's as if it changed me inside. There was another time, years ago, that one of her premonitions came true and completely changed the course of my life. The bad thing happened because she was in no position to stop it, and because I was too stubborn to listen to her. I believed that I alone could make her premonition not come true. But I was wrong. And I lost something I loved. I didn't want to hear her, about Indio. I couldn't bear it."

Bret turned his head towards her. "I'm sorry. I trust that you'll make things right with her eventually. I've been wanting to say to you what I just said. But what I really came here for is information."

Selah sniffed and sat up straighter, looking at him expectantly.

"There are things going on that I don't understand..."

"Don't expect that to change," she cut in.

He narrowed his eyes at her. "One of the things I'm highly curious about is her brother's death. The details. Something she probably doesn't want to talk about, so I haven't asked. Can you tell me about that?"

Selah shifted around a little, nodding. "I remember it all as if it happened yesterday. That was a terrible time. So much had gone on that was unknown. She told you about their twentieth birthdays? How they both disappeared?"

He nodded.

"Alright." She sighed. "Luca was just a wonderful, beautiful boy, and he was growing into an amazing man. Living with Jacob Roth, I don't know what it was, but they both flourished during that time. Luca was full of life, of joy, completely carefree aside from his usual worry about his little sister. He was like a sun, and we were the planets that revolved around him. He would play his guitar and she would sing, and it was glorious. *They* were glorious together. He told me once that before she came into his life, his world was lonely and dark. Then he was graced with Fallon, with a sister who loved him completely, who completed him, and he changed for the better. And he was good for her, because she was always so much a part of the dark, all quietness and stillness and being worlds away in her mind. Time and again he brought her out of the darkness. Not unlike yourself." She looked at him thoughtfully. "You know, it troubles me beyond reason, you and she being able to talk in your heads just like they did. I try and try to think what does it mean?"

She looked away. "Anyway, I was over at their house late one evening, when she suddenly got a terribly strong vision, and she was horrified because it was an image of Luca in danger. Then the feelings hit and brought her to her knees with their power. She just stayed like that, on her knees on the ground, head bowed down, trembling. I got down and tried to talk to her, but she wouldn't respond to me. I guessed that she was trying to talk to him in her head; it was taking everything she had. Then she screamed and fell over onto her side, and she started sobbing—

that was when she'd realized he was dead. And instantly it was like the light inside of her went out." Selah used both hands to wipe tears away this time. "Not only did we lose Luca, but the Fallon I loved went away as well."

Bret was frowning. "How did he die?"

She cast a loaded gaze at him. "Suicide."

His eyes widened.

She nodded. "Oh, yes, you can imagine how that professional declaration went over with our girl. She pleaded with them all that he would never have killed himself, would never have left her. No one listened. Case open, case closed." Her gaze drifted across the porch. "He'd been out jogging along the greenbelt, just past twilight. Too late at night for jogging, said the proud policemen, but then, they didn't know what night owls the siblings were; she still is. That child can see in the dark."

"I've thought the same thing," he admitted, surprised. He'd seen her go into and then come out of a pitch-dark room once, at his house, in a room she wasn't familiar with, having retrieved exactly what she went in there for. And then once, at night in his dark garage, he'd fumbled around for the light, only to turn it on and find her waiting for him on the other side of the car, having maneuvered around bikes and toys without tripping or stumbling. "What killed him?"

"Gunshot to the head. Close range. Fingers wrapped tightly around the unregistered gun, which had no fingerprints but his own. They told her he must have tried to slit his wrists, first, as if that makes any sense. The tattoos she's got, that he had? Gone. Cut out. That was his first attempt, they said. When that didn't work, he put a gun to his head. Honestly."

Bret swallowed. "My God."

Selah shook her head. "My God doesn't work that way."

He let out a long, low breath. "What do you think?"

There was a smile that didn't fully materialize on her face. "What does it matter what I think? He's been dead eleven years. He's not coming back. She continues to live. I grew up with them. Luca was as much my big brother as he was hers. I loved him passionately." She looked into Bret's face. "He would never in a million years have left her behind. He would never have committed suicide. It was not a part of the fabric of his being. He was murdered, and cleverly. For eleven years, I've held my breath and waited for those same clever people to steal my Fallon away from me. But she's always one step ahead of them."

Bret leaned towards her, his grey eyes glowing with intensity. "What do you mean? What the hell do you mean by that?"

She unfolded her legs and got to her feet. "Let's go walk in the backyard. My roses are blooming. They make me happy."

He accompanied her around the side of the house, through a white wooden gate. All along the inside perimeter of the backyard roses of different varieties bloomed—their perfume met them and danced around them.

"I wonder if she's contacted Simon?" she mused to herself out loud as they walked.

"Who's Simon?"

"He was a guy Luca's age; they were in grade school together. He was Fallon and Luca's closest friend beside myself. He was the only other person who knew all about their visions. The four of us were a strange team. Simon was the classic computer researching wizard. He helped them with a lot of their digging into what their abilities were, and especially about the tattoos on their wrists. He was still around for a while after Luca died, but after it became apparent that Fallon was not going to be killed when she was twenty-two like her brother was, Simon took off into the world. She's stayed in touch with him, to a certain degree. He currently exists, as Fallon puts it, in Seattle. Anyway, Simon is your best information source for all things spooky and weird regarding the siblings. He has boxes of file folders of data just about them. He would be interested in you, your telepathy."

"Why is she terrified of hospitals. Is someone out to get her?"

She spread her hands out helplessly before him. "Bret, we just don't know. We don't have answers to most of the questions, even after all this time. Her entire life she's felt hunted, but she can't put her finger on it. Someone murdered her parents, her guardian disappeared without a trace, and then her brother was killed. Obviously, there are larger things afoot!"

"I thought her guardian died?"

Selah hesitated. "Umm, sure. Well, he died, and there was not much known about it. Anyway, since Luca died and Fallon left Austin, she's been living mostly under the radar, except for the big fuss I raised when she went missing at twenty. She's been particularly anonymous in this little town, traveling around under assumed names—yes, she does that—and no one's gotten to her yet, and so we wonder, is that enough? There have always been odd occurrences that let us know someone is watching her, seeking her. Michael's offices were broken into years ago, and all that was taken were his files on Fallon, though they had no real data in them, just superficial files—his real information on her is here in the house. In some of the cities she's been in, she's sensed that same evil feeling, intended for her, and has fled without looking back. Nothing ever catches up to her. And nothing ever happens to us here, in Gray. Never. Are we strangely protected here? Are they simply watching? Waiting? How could they be so inept, when their murder of her brother was carried out so seamlessly? And then, five years ago, just before Indio was born..." Looking quite tired, she shook her head and fell momentarily silent, staring at a hydrangea bush, thick with blue blossoms.

She looked up at Bret. "She doesn't ever want to be in a situation where she's not in control, and that would definitely be a hospital. She never goes to doctors, and especially not to hospitals. Michael has always treated her for anything she's needed. We often joke that I married a doctor solely for Fallon's convenience. She doesn't like a lot of information being out there about her. Simon's supplied her with everything from fake IDs and passports to encrypted email accounts and secret bank accounts. Her goal is to forever be untraceable."

Bret stuck his hands in his back pockets, struggling to process all this new information.

Pressing her fingertips together as if in prayer, Selah shook her head. "Some things are too unsettling for me to think about." She gave a short laugh. "It's all very cloak-and-dagger around here sometimes, and I often wonder if the joke is on us, if there really is nothing at all waiting in the shadows. But then things happen that let me know that, yes, something is waiting there." Her gaze was far away.

Michael was at the back door then, waving at them.

Selah took Bret's arm. "Come in and eat with us. Michael picked up a couple of pizzas on his way home. We would be glad to have you."

"No, look, I realize I barged in on you and demanded information…"

"Bret, please." She stopped him and looked up into his face again. "You love her, you want her to be well, to be safe. To do that, you need to know as much as possible about what we're dealing with. You needed to know all of what I have just told you. You should have been told before now, and I blame myself for that."

A troubled looked settled on his face.

She patted his arm. "I know about that, too. Her visions of you. Her heart's desire is to keep you and Bergen safe. She will do so with everything she has. I would not bet against her. Now come in, before Michael and Indio steal all the prime slices."

* * * * * * *

When Bret returned to Solu that night to have a drink with Diego, Selah was with him. Upon entering the restaurant, they saw Fallon right away, heading to the register to settle someone's bill. When she saw them together, she paused. Selah went right to her and folded her arms tightly around her. Fallon rested her head on Selah's shoulder and began to cry.

Diego slid by and whisked the bill out of Fallon's hand, taking it to the register himself. He waved at Bret, and motioned towards a small, empty table. "Have a seat, friend. I will join you shortly."

Bret sat down, and watched as Selah and Fallon disappeared down the hall towards the bathroom. When Fallon reappeared about ten minutes later, the only evidence of her small breakdown was slightly reddened eyes. She came over to him and leaned down for a quick kiss before heading off to one of her other tables.

Selah appeared a few minutes later. She stopped beside Bret. He noted that her eyes were also reddened. "I'm headed home to make sure my boy is in bed. I'm grateful that you came by this evening. I needed someone to shake me out of my current state of being. It had gone on much too long, but I can be a little stubborn. Though I'm sure you've noticed no such thing."

He smiled up at her. "Take care, Selah."

* * * * * * *

As they pulled into her driveway later that night, Bret frowned at his phone, and Fallon glanced at him. "What is it?"

"Jack Lane. He's been calling me for days now, never leaves a message. Who the hell knows what he wants, I guess to talk some more about the potential tour, but I really don't feel like talking to him."

She bit her lip, reflexively rubbing the eye and flames tattoo with her thumb. Then she changed the subject. "So, Selah told me that she filled you in on quite a bit about me."

They were now climbing the stairs to her door. It was just after midnight.

"I found her to be quite knowledgeable, yes. Do you mind?"

"No, of course not. As she probably told you, you needed to know. As much as you can. Before you decide you want to remain entangled with crazy me."

He stopped her in the doorway and kissed her. "But I long ago decided that I do want to. And I especially enjoy the entanglement part."

She touched his cheek, and there was a faint sadness in her face. "You may rethink it one day." Then she went past him into the kitchen to pour herself a glass of wine.

Bret wandered around the apartment. He was near her desk, and found himself looking around on it curiously, spotting a framed picture he hadn't noticed before. He picked it up. Two teenaged girls and two older boys, all in swimsuits.

"That's us at the lake, about two weeks before Luca died. That's him with the blond hair. And the other guy, that's our friend Simon."

He studied the picture closely. Selah and Fallon, seventeen years old, were sitting in the middle in bikinis, leaning in close to each other. They were laughing at something, the contrasting colors of their skin standing out. The girls were beautiful. Dark-haired Simon, on the other side of Selah, had his left arm extended around both girls, his fingers were visible on Fallon's bare arm. It was difficult to make out the features of his face. Luca was next to his sister, his blond hair shaggy. He was looking at something in the distance, smiling faintly, one hand on Fallon's arm. Sitting right behind the girls was a scruffy black dog.

"Hey," Bret smiled, "this looks just like Azul."

Fallon came over and looked at him. "It is Azul." She drank some of her wine.

He frowned. "What? No. This photo was taken..."

"Eleven years ago," she confirmed.

He nodded at where Azul lay on the rug. "He doesn't look that old."

She set down the wineglass and pulled open a desk drawer in which she dug around, then took out an envelope which she rifled through a moment before taking out another picture. She handed it to him.

A little girl with long blond hair smiled at the camera, her arms around a familiar black dog. The crooked smile was undeniable. He knew it was Fallon as a child, probably around nine or ten. He compared the dog in both pictures. He looked over at Azul, sleeping on the rug. Then he looked back at Fallon.

She sat down on the couch with her wine. "Azul showed up as a stray the week after our parents died, shortly after we'd moved in with Jacob. Twenty-one years ago. He's been with me ever since."

He sat down beside her on the couch. He was quiet for a long time. Then he sighed. "All the crazy shit you and Selah have told me, and I'm most disturbed by an immortal black dog."

Azul whined a little, but didn't lift his head. Fallon took Bret's hand.

He gestured at the dog with his free hand. "So, what is he? Shape-shifter? Malformed werewolf?"

She lay her head on his shoulder. "We think he's a kind of guardian. Or a shape-changing sorcerer. It remains to be seen."

"He stays home when you travel, though?"

"Mostly. Sometimes I take him along. Depending on where I'm headed. If I don't take him along, he usually shows up eventually."

Bret rubbed his eyes and chose to ignore that last bit. "Has he ever actually guarded you from anything?"

She shrugged. "Not to my knowledge. Then again, here I am."

"You know, I hate to state the obvious, but there is a hell of a lot you guys don't know about all of this strangeness."

"Yes. We're aware."

He nudged her gently. "So why did you give yourself the shot last night?" A topic he had not gotten to address with Selah as he'd hoped. "Did you get a headache because you were so upset?"

Despite his suspicions, he was unprepared for the look of actual guilt that slid quickly across her features as she turned from him. He saw her one hand clench tightly into a fist as she stared at something he could not see, her entire body tensed as if for flight. Azul raised his head and gazed at her. Fallon's lips parted, as if she wanted to speak, but then closed again, in silence.

Bret turned her back towards him. "Fallon." He held her shoulders, trying to get her to look at him. "This world needs you. There are people who love you immensely. Do not leave us."

She looked up, and he saw that her eyes were dark and full of anguish. She shook her head. "I won't," she whispered. "I just wanted the pain to stop. For a moment."

* * * * * * *

As they lay in bed that night, close in each other's arms, she turned her head to look at him in the moonlight. He was driving to Dallas first thing in the morning to catch a flight back to L.A. to return to tour rehearsals.

"So, from everything Selah told you this evening, you've had some time to think about it all. Is there anything you want to ask me? Don't worry about asking me things regarding Luca, you won't upset me. It was a long time ago."

"There were one or two things." He shifted a little. "I was thinking..." He looked reluctant.

"About his 'suicide'?"

He nodded. "Yes. I was picturing it, the whole scenario. And I was wondering. Wouldn't, not to be graphic about it, but wouldn't the tattoos that were cut from his wrists have been found there at the scene if it had been suicide? I mean, there was no way of proving there had been tattoos there, I guess, but surely enough skin was gone to indicate that he didn't just slice his wrists?"

"Good one! But no fear, our trusty law enforcement officers were all over it. They wrote it off by saying an animal had been near the body and probably took the skin."

"An animal? Took the skin?"

"The couple who found Luca claimed they saw a black dog sitting next to his body, but it ran off when they came closer."

"Azul?"

She eyed him. "Azul."

He licked his lips. "Was Azul always more your dog than Luca's?"

"You're thinking that apparently Azul didn't protect, or guard, Luca in his great moment of need? You're right. Azul tolerated Luca, but I was always his treasure. I'm the one he slept with, followed to and from school, played with. Azul was always my dog, from the very first. I don't think he took the tattoos. I think they were taken by the people that murdered Luca. I think Azul was there just waiting with his body till someone could find him, so that Luca wouldn't be alone, because he knew it would make me feel better."

"Selah thinks the people who killed Luca are after you—have been after you all this time."

"That's always been our belief. Only I don't know why I've been able to elude them for this long, when he was not. There've been countless times I was alone in dark, secluded places, the perfect prey, and yet here I remain."

A few hours later she shook him awake, her conscience troubled by the news of Jack's phone calls. "Bret, I'm sorry, I know you need to sleep, but I have to tell you something else. While you're here with me. In person."

He squinted and saw that she was sitting up, her hair loose around her shoulders. She looked anxious. Yawning, he shoved some pillows under his head for support and looked at her sleepily. "What's wrong?"

"It's about that night in the hot tub with Jack, at your house. I never really talked about it with you, but there's something I need to tell you. Now that you know more of my story. And before he says something to you about it. Which I can't believe he hasn't." She ran her tongue over the edge of her teeth as she hesitated. "That night he was coming on pretty strong, he was starting to get rough." She felt anger immediately coming off of Bret. "At one point he pushed me underwater, and I grabbed his arms and kicked him between the legs as hard as I could. My kick had the desired effect. But then we discovered that his arm had been burned."

He frowned. "Burned?"

She flashed him the tattoo. "It was this size, and it matched up with how I'd grabbed his arm. When we looked at it, the lines of this tattoo were glowing."

"Glowing?" He sat up. "You burned him with the tattoo?!" He sounded both impressed and horrified.

She nodded. "That's all I could figure out. He was in quite a lot of pain. It's never happened before; these tattoos have never seemed to be anything but plain old tattoos. It was a little unnerving to me. You can imagine how he felt about it. And honestly, I don't know what it would have eventually done to him, because it got worse as we watched it. I finally had to heal it. He was in agony."

He stared at her. "You..." he stumbled a little on his words, "...you healed him?"

She nodded. "Yes, that's something else that I can do." She shrugged apologetically. "I've not been hiding it from you; it's just never come up."

He took both her hands and turned them over, staring hard at the designs on her wrists. "Can you try to do it again? The burning?"

"What," she asked dryly, "you want me to set a piece of paper on fire?"

"I can start calling you 'Firestarter.'" He squeezed her hands. "Sorry."

"I didn't consciously do it. I think the emotion I was feeling at the time obviously was really strong—I wanted him off me. And the tattoo touched him at the moment my emotions were peaking...I don't know. I just don't."

"As far as I'm concerned, Jack got what was coming to him. I'm surprised that he's never said anything about it to me."

"I think it really shook him up. Both the burning and the healing. And I think it takes a lot to shake Jack."

He touched her chin. "You should have told me, called for me while it was happening. I can't believe that son-of-a-bitch came on to you and then pushed you under when you tried to stop him. I want to go kill him."

"It all evened out; I promise. He was in great pain." She stared into space a while, tears pricking at her eyes. "Bret," her voice was weak, "how can you want this? There is so much you still don't know."

He took her face in his hands. *Because I love you. I will always want this.* He kissed her fiercely, pulling her against him so tightly that it hurt. Tears fell onto her cheeks.

CHAPTER TWENTY-NINE

FALLON

Fallon's twelfth birthday had been, she reflected, the happiest of all her birthdays thus far. Luca had borrowed Jacob's car and taken her to breakfast at Magnolia Café. Selah had baked her a chocolate cake and hung streamers, lights and paper lanterns all around the backyard. That evening, out in the yard, with lights and lanterns gleaming, Luca played his guitar and sang with his sister for hours. Simon and Selah listened and laughed with them and tossed out song requests. Towards the end, Jacob had come and hung out on the periphery and watched the siblings for quite a while, the slightest of smiles on his lips. He turned down Selah's offering of cake.

Around ten, Simon departed, and Luca left to drive Selah home. Selah's parents thought Luca was a polite and respectable young man, and he grabbed every opportunity to ensure their faith in him remained, for her friendship with his sister was, he felt, extremely important. Out of necessity, Jacob had met with Selah's parents several times, impressing them and putting them at ease, thereby ensuring that Selah was able to spend much time and many nights at his house without question.

It was while everyone was gone that Jacob came looking for Fallon. She was sitting on her bed with Azul, looking through the box of old vinyl records that Selah had given her as a gift. When she saw Jacob in her doorway, she set aside the album she'd been holding. For every past birthday, he had given her a book—she assumed this one would be no different.

And so, she was surprised when he brought out a small black box from behind his back. "Happy Birthday, my secret girl."

She accepted the box and opened it immediately, lips parting when she saw a lovely ring sparkling at her. Brass was woven artfully and delicately around a raw labradorite stone. In the light, the greenish-grey stone flashed with hints of bright blue, then gold, then a faint coppery red, before going back to green and grey. She looked up at Jacob with a smile. "It's so beautiful."

He smiled back at her. "It's quite old, and holds many stories. I thought it was just the thing for you."

She slid it onto her finger, flinching as a million images flew through her mind, an overwhelming sense of protection settling around her. The ring fit perfectly, as if it had been made for her.

Jacob was watching her closely. "Good?"

She nodded. "I love it, thank you." She was thrilled with this unexpectedly sentimental gift from him. In the past year that they'd been training together, they'd formed a strong bond, but still they hid it from her brother... and she sometimes thought, it was not only from her brother. But from whom?

Now she impulsively wanted to throw her arms around him in a hug, but she thought he might reflexively strike her down if she tried it, so she just reached out a hand to him instead. He clasped her fingers briefly, and then they heard the sound of Luca's car in the driveway, and with a smile still playing on his lips, Jacob went away.

CHAPTER THIRTY

When Bret got home to California, he returned immediately to tour rehearsals with his band. He was in Los Angeles for the majority of every day and night, and when he was at home, he was either sleeping or on the phone. His assistant Kara came over frequently, her tablet full of his schedules, itineraries, phone numbers, and information. Bergen was busy with softball, gymnastics, guitar lessons, and the impending end of fourth grade. Lisbeth was working hard at Daisy when she wasn't shuttling Bergen between school and activities. Bret felt as if he passed them like ships in the night.

Lisbeth was used to this. From the moment of Bergen's birth, she'd had to be the more responsible parent, the one who could be counted on to be around no matter what. You never knew if Bret was going to be home at any given moment, or if he'd have to cancel on you, or leave at the last minute. He might suddenly go do a show, run to L.A. to change something in the studio, or make an appearance somewhere that had been planned, then canceled, then given the green light again overnight.

When he was at home, he was golden, an excellent father. Better than she'd ever imagined he would be, truth be told. With Bergen, he played games, sang, and watched movies. He rode motocross with her and lay in bed with her when she was sick. Lisbeth was equally pleased with how well he kept in touch with Bergen while he was away. And he didn't shower their daughter with material things to make up for being gone; he showered her with his precious time. All of this Lisbeth knew and appreciated. She'd known when they planned the pregnancy how things would be; he'd made no empty promises to her. He'd not painted a rosy picture of a future in which he would stop touring in order to stay home full-time. She knew Bret James would be on the road forever, a music man until he died. But because she knew it and accepted it, didn't mean it was always easy.

She had high hopes for Fallon. Not that Fallon would keep Bret home more; if anything, she was going to draw him away. But childless Fallon had taken to Bergen with surprising ease, and vice versa. Lisbeth was filled with something she couldn't quite define regarding Fallon. She recognized that Bret had fallen for someone whom Lisbeth felt entirely positive about in regards to Bergen's health and well-being, happiness, and safety. More so, even, because of the weird premonition ability. It all made Lisbeth hopeful about the future—one major new part of which she was about to drop on Mr. James this very night.

She met him in the kitchen after he got home and was getting out a sparkling water from the fridge. It was nearly midnight, and he was tired after a long day, his mind full of preparations for being on the road for the next six to nine months. England and Germany were a definite, but the rest of the international leg of the tour was still not a sure thing. Touring internationally was no longer a guarantee for performers at his level; touring domestically was much more easily done.

When he saw Lisbeth, he could see immediately that she wanted something. He sipped the water. "What's up?"

"Can you sit down for a minute and talk?"

Worry slammed into him. Rarely did Lisbeth want to sit and talk. "Is Bee okay?"

"She's fine. This is something else."

He motioned to the patio, and they went out. Staring at the pool water reminded him of Fallon. She'd said something about being a water spirit in another life. He half-believed her.

In the moonlight, they sat on side-by-side loungers. He kicked off his boots and stretched out, leaning back and looking up at the stars. Lisbeth remained seated with her wrists on her knees, facing him. The scent of jasmine came to them on the breeze.

"Leo and I are getting married."

He paused with the bottle to his lips, then took a long swig, perhaps longer than necessary, then looked at her. "Yeah?"

She nodded. "June seventh. We told Bergen this evening. She's fine with it. I told her living arrangements would be changing, and she shrugged and looked a little moody, so I don't know how it's going to go."

He sat up, cross-legged, and looked at her. "Lis, that's great." He smiled. "I thought there was something with him, something serious." He toasted her with his water. "Congratulations."

She smiled, and leaned over and hugged him, and he hugged her back tightly. When she sat back, there was a tear in her eye.

"I really like Fallon," she told him. "I like her a lot. I love how she is with Bergen. I hope that she sticks around for a while."

Bret nodded. "So do I." Then he laughed. "Tell me the truth. You didn't feel that you could safely get married and move out until I'd found a decent woman who may turn out to be entirely capable of taking care of me and Bergen both."

She shrugged. "Could be."

He stared off into the night. "Married. Wow." He looked at her. "Kind of quick. Anything I need to know?" He eyed her flat stomach suggestively.

She gave him a look. "No, nothing you need to know. I'm about to become the step-mother to two wild child boys. The last thing I need is a new baby at forty-four. We've been talking about it for a long time. Marcella and I have been talking speculatively about the actual wedding day for months. Daisy is going to cater, and we're going to get married on the beach with just a few friends and family."

"So, you don't want me to be there."

"Actually, I do. I wasn't sure Leo would, but he brought it up. He said that since we were such equally-involved parents, Bergen's father should be there on what will be an important day for her."

Now he was frowning. "You couldn't have squeezed it in before the tour started?"

She bit her lip. "I tried; I did. But Daisy's catering schedule is booked till then."

"We're at the mercy of the cafe's schedule?"

"So, do you think you can fly back, or not? And Leo did say he'd like Fallon there, if only to let everyone know that you're happily involved with someone."

He sighed. "It'll be tough, Lis. Really tough." He was looking at the schedule on his phone. "What will you do if I can't make it? Will that be alright?"

"No. You were flying back to pick up Bee on the eighth anyway, weren't you?"

"I was going to send Fallon, actually, to make things easier. But if you can somehow switch the wedding to the eighth, I'll be there."

She nodded. "Let me talk to Marcella. And I'll have to tell Leo it's a scheduling conflict with Daisy, not that I'm postponing the wedding so my ex-lover, father-of-my-child can attend."

He grinned. "So, where's the honeymoon?"

"Italy. For four weeks in July and August, while Bergen is out on the road with you."

He whistled. "You know how to pick them."

"Yes," she agreed wryly, "I do."

* * * * * * *

"Guess what? Lisbeth's marrying Leo."

Fallon was surprised at Bret's news. "How long have they been dating?"

"Well, I tried to remember, and honestly, I'm embarrassed that I'm not entirely sure. I didn't want to expose my insensitivity and disinterest by asking her. I didn't think for a whole year yet, but I could be wrong. I'd ask Bergen, but I can't be completely sure she wouldn't bust me with her mom at some later date."

"Well, good for her; I'm glad she's happy. But how is Bergen going to handle this?"

"I don't know. She's not wanting to talk about it, telling us it's no big deal, but I know it is. It's almost like Lis and I are getting divorced, you know? But this summer is going to be really crazy for her, schedule-wise, anyway, so by the time she's finally living in Leo's house for good, school will be starting up to distract her."

A deep sadness filled Fallon's chest. "The biggest heartbreak for her is going to be not living full-time in your house anymore. It's always been her home."

"I know." He rubbed a hand over his face. "It was inevitable that this would happen one day, but it's always been easy to ignore. Maybe we should have prepared her better from the beginning, but then you'd think that would have just instilled a sense of insecurity

"She'll be fine, I'm not trying to make you feel bad about it. How do you feel about it? Lisbeth getting married?"

"Oh, I'm cool with that. Why would I mind?"

But his answer came too quickly, and Fallon knew the road ahead was going to get a little rough at some point. But that would come later. He filled her in on the wedding date and plans, and she added a beach wedding-appropriate outfit to her list of things to pack.

In the days before she was to join Bret on his tour, Fallon wrapped up various odds and ends. She worked her last shift at Solu. She had tea with Ms. Landrum, bringing her a dozen kolaches, plus an extra dozen to put in the freezer. She also paid her several months ahead in rent. She and Selah joined Katrine for a girls-only-plus-Indio picnic at the farm. And she set Azul up at the Sanchezes with plenty of kibble and a warning to stay put because he wasn't welcome on the tour bus. Azul licked her face and panted happily. She could only assume that the message had gotten through.

CHAPTER THIRTY-ONE

FALLON & LUCA

They were lying on his bed one night watching a movie. Twelve-year-old Fallon was sprawled on her stomach, and Luca was propped against pillows. Fallon thought that at seventeen, he was suddenly looking more and more like a man.

She was only half-watching, humoring her brother, who loved movies. She preferred music. Besides going running, which she'd just recently started doing, music was the best mood-alterer she'd found. She was drawing lazily in a red sketchbook, trying to pay attention to the onscreen storyline in case he wanted to dissect the plot afterwards.

Her brother nudged her with his foot. "I saw that you finished my cereal. That was going to be my snack later."

She shrugged off his words. "I'm not the best roommate."

"That's true." He smiled fondly at the back of her head. Then he tried to sound nonchalant. "So, I saw you coming out of Jacob's room when I was getting home late the other night."

She threw a look back at him over her shoulder. "Why wait till now to bring that up? Have you been simmering on a bunch of suppositions this whole time?"

He narrowed his eyes at her sass. Sometimes she acted far older than twelve. Most of the time, actually. "I was just surprised. We never go in Jacob's room."

She returned her attention to her sketchbook. "Well, I do. He reads to me in there now. I thought you'd realized that."

He could tell there were secrets there, so much she wasn't telling him, but he didn't know how to approach it without angering her. She was so old for her years, yet so vulnerable. And such a pretty girl. "Hey, Fal...Jacob isn't...bothering you, is he?"

She took the time to sit up completely and turn to face him, looking simultaneously puzzled and outraged. "Do you honestly think that man is 'bothering' me?"

He shook his head, brushing his blond hair out of his eyes. He'd never read anything off Jacob, good or bad. But he was pretty sure he'd know if Jacob had any ill intent towards his sister. "No. I just had to say it. To be sure."

"Or that, if he was 'bothering' me, I would be ill-equipped to kick his ass or at least raise some hell about it?"

He looked sheepish.

She shook her head. "Idiot."

"Blond."

"Blonder."

He thumped her forehead with his thumb and middle finger, and she kicked him in the side.

CHAPTER THIRTY-TWO

Fallon joined Bret and his band in time for the fifth show of their tour, at a music hall in Santa Fe. She was given a whirlwind tour of the bus she'd be traveling on before being whisked off to the evening's venue, where the band was already backstage and the opening act was about to take the stage. There were no decent seats left, so she was allowed to sit behind the soundboard with the technician, where she quietly observed all the pre-concert energy—the fans, the crew, the venue employees. The last concert she'd been to had been long ago with Luca, so she was excited to see what Bret and the guys could do.

Her left wrist had been tingling all day, and now she took a moment to stare at it, the dark, beautiful raven with its prism eye. Once when she'd had too much to drink years ago, and had been lying somewhere—she couldn't remember where—staring at this tattoo, she had been startled when it began to look like it was in motion, flying, soaring, wings flapping. But, of course, it had been the alcohol in her veins, she reasoned. Nothing more.

Still, every time her left wrist tingled, she looked at the bird expecting to see it actively in flight. Had Luca's wrist ever tingled? This had only started happening after Bret entered her life. And why was her eye tattoo ringed with flames, while his had not been, and why was her raven so different? What was the significance? Why were her tattoos so much more well-done? She didn't know. She felt at times that she didn't know much of anything.

She knew with stone certainty that Jacob Roth could have told her what the tattoos were. Why had he left her when he'd promised he would always be there to help her survive? Why make empty promises to a child? The raven tattoo reminded her so strongly of him. There had been a much larger raven tattooed on Jacob's left forearm; she'd stared at it with interest for seven years. She knew it was the same as the bird tattooed on her wrist. The exact same, down to the prism eye. What did that mean? Did this tattoo tie her somehow to Jacob, and if so, what did that signify? Or had their tattoos merely been symbolic of something she was unaware of? So many questions.

Jacob would have been disappointed with the way she fell completely apart when Luca was murdered. He'd thought she was so strong, but he'd been mistaken.

Are you ready to be amazed? Bret asked her from where he waited in the backstage area, shaking her from her tattoo reverie.

That at your age you can still rock? Sure. Amaze me.

You're in trouble, he informed her, and she laughed out loud. The sound tech glanced at her.

Do I get a Bret James t-shirt? she asked.

Only if I get to autograph a body part.

Oh, is that how it goes?

Usually. We can negotiate that later.

Fallon thoroughly enjoyed the concert. Bret had always been an excellent showman, and the years had taken none of that away. On stage, he was confident, funny, and full of boundless energy, and he knew just how to interact with a crowd, the ages of which, from what Fallon could see, ran from twenties to sixties.

Most of the songs were loud and lively hard rock numbers, but at one point he did pick up an acoustic guitar, sit on a stool and play "Blur," saying softly beforehand, "This is for you, my girl," and looking out at Fallon. She smiled, and he grinned back.

People were looking around wildly trying to see who he was talking to. Women screamed, "I love you, Bret!"

It was, Fallon admitted to herself, a little surreal to witness the blind waves of love, lust, devotion, and worshipfulness that washed over Bret from the crowd. And Fallon, who had spent so much of her life trying to avoid attention, wondered how a person could take all that in—as she watched Bret soak it up like sunlight—and still maintain a shred of humility.

Back on the bus later, driving off into the night, Fallon sat on Bret's bed with him and lazily texted back and forth with Selah while he spoke on the phone to Bergen. When they'd finally put their phones away, he lay back against the pillows and grinned at her.

"Welcome to the glamorous life. Did you like the show?"

"I was twelve all over again," she confirmed.

He laughed. "I honestly don't know how I feel about that. Bergen says 'hello' and to please keep me out of trouble."

"I would try, but apparently I'm not allowed near you very often," she countered.

He tackled her, crawling on top of her and kissing her. "You're near me now. And you're always in my head. Even when I'm on stage, which is kind of crazy, and I thought it might mess me up, but it didn't. You know, I'd never be able to cheat on you or anything, because you'd know it as it was happening."

"I'm touched by those sweet words, I really am."

He snuggled against her. "You know what I mean."

"I may never teach you how to keep me out of your head now."

"Mmm." He pressed his face to hers and closed his eyes. "That's okay with me," he said sleepily. "By the way, I've kind of been researching immortal black dogs."

"Death."

He nodded. "Yeah, pretty much in myths and legends they're associated with death."

She shrugged. "Azul doesn't care what Wikipedia says. He just is who he is."

"A shape-changing sorcerer who gets to cuddle with you and watch you undress."

"You'd better be nice to him."

CHAPTER THIRTY-THREE

FALLON

Blood dripped as the dagger drew a long line into Jacob's forearm, the same wicked-looking dagger whose history Fallon had seen during her first psychometry lesson. Setting the dagger aside, Jacob looked at her steadily, a challenge in his blue eyes.

But twelve-year-old Fallon, her long hair pulled into two braids, looked calm and confident. She reached out and carefully dragged her three middle fingers down the length of the cut, her skin tingling as it touched his blood. The wound healed immediately in her wake. When she sat back there was nothing on his forearm to suggest injury besides a slight line of reddened skin, and that began to fade as they stared at it.

When she looked at him, she couldn't conceal her excitement. She'd been working on healing for six full months, and finally her hard work had paid off. It was definitely one of the most difficult things he'd taught her.

Learning to guard her mind permanently so that no one could see her thoughts or read her intentions—that had been rather easy. Fading into the shadows at night to avoid detection— "becoming a shadow" Jacob called it—had also been achieved without much difficulty. But becoming a healer had taken all of her mental fortitude. Deliberately seeking out visions had not been easy, but the biggest trick there had been learning to carefully bend the line in her mind.

"Little one, you have impressed me." Jacob sat back with something like a proud smile on his face.

In that moment, she felt a deep kinship with him. This led to bravery. "Why are you with us?" she asked. "I know you aren't really our cousin. Where did you come from? And why do you train me, but not Luca?"

He looked away as he sighed. "Ah, me, I'm just an old gypsy without a home. Staying with the two of you, I'm doing a favor for someone. And I keep telling you, Fallon, Luca doesn't have the things inside that you have. You and he are two different entities entirely. There is no comparison. I train you because you are important and interesting to many people, and not in a good way. You were being kept untrained for reasons that are unfair to you. With a lack of training, you remain vulnerable, and I, who have been with you in one way or another for longer than you realize, do not like to see you vulnerable. You must be strong always. You will be tested again and again. You will suffer; I wish I could shield you from it, but I cannot. But you must promise me that you will be strong."

Her face looked dark with worry. She nodded. "I'll be strong." But her voice shook slightly, and he wondered at her promise.

"Love is a great weakness," he murmured.

"No," she whispered back.

He nodded, and his expression was kind. "You'll see."

Her eyes went to the locket that hung from the chain on his wrist.

CHAPTER THIRTY-FOUR

On the eighth of June, Bret and Fallon flew to California to attend Lisbeth and Leo's beach wedding and retrieve Bergen. All went smoothly with the ceremony—Bret and Fallon both thought Bergen looked far too pretty and grown up, barefoot in her blue and white maid of honor dress with a wreath of yellow and white daisies in her hair. Late that night, the trio flew back to meet up with the tour in Wyoming.

Having the child along changed things up, as Fallon had expected it would, but she adored Bergen beyond reason and didn't mind the responsibility of being entirely in charge of her. Bret was constantly being pulled in too many different directions to be responsible for his daughter at all. Bergen could attend concerts held at venues other than clubs, but when the show was at a club where there was an age limit, she had to stay on the bus, the door faithfully guarded by a burly bodyguard named Seth, whose loyalty and friendship to Bret dated back to BlueStar days. Fallon would sometimes go to the show long enough to hear "Blur," and then return to the bus where she and Bergen played board games, read aloud to each other, and talked. Fallon ordered her a rather extensive bracelet-making kit, and this began to occupy her more and more. Soon everyone on the bus was sporting a custom bracelet.

Summer rain was pouring down when the tour bus rolled into Seattle just after midnight. Everyone disembarked and gathered their bags, looking forward to three nights in a hotel. Bergen was asleep in Bret's arms, and Fallon was yawning, carrying Bergen's bags as well as her own.

Bret and Fallon had gotten two adjoining rooms, and while Bret put Bergen to bed in one, Fallon unpacked and took a quick shower in the other. They were meeting Eric Carson, BlueStar's former drummer, for brunch, then going to sound check at one-thirty, playing a show that night, and then the next day they were going to call on her old friend Simon Keaton.

When she learned they were headed to Seattle, Fallon accepted it as inevitable that they would see Simon, and informed Bret of such. Bret was interested in meeting someone who had been in Fallon's life nearly as long as Selah—who knew all about her secrets. Fallon told him not to expect much. And added that Simon definitely didn't know them all.

"Does anyone know all your secrets?" he asked.

She shook her head. "No one." She gave a short, soft laugh. "Not even me." And, not unexpectedly, the raven tattoo tingled.

The alarm went off at nine-thirty that morning, and Fallon groaned at too little time to sleep, turning it off and squinting. "What time are we meeting Eric?" she asked, nudging Bret to semi-wakefulness.

"Mmm. Ten-thirty." He burrowed deeper into his pillow.

She sat up. "We need to get going, then. You go shower, I'll get Bergen up."

When Bret and Bergen were both adequately awake and showering in their rooms, Fallon brushed her hair and applied a little mascara. From her suitcase she chose a loose black above-knee skirt and long-sleeved indigo shirt. She had just gotten the clothes on when the first image shattered her mind, and she fell to the floor.

Bret got out of the shower and dried off, towel-drying his hair. He put on the jeans Fallon had laid on a chair in the bathroom for him. *If you want, you and Bee can go roam around while I'm at sound check,* he told her. *Eric can tell you some places to go. Unless you already know some places, because of Simon living here? I don't know how familiar you are with Seattle.*

There was no answer.

Frowning, he pulled a faded red t-shirt over his head. "Fallon?"

A dog whimpered in response.

Bret dashed out of the bathroom, stopping short to see Azul blinking balefully up at him.

"Fallon?!"

Azul trotted around the side of the bed, and Bret followed. He dropped to his knees beside where Fallon was curled up in a trembling ball. Placing his hands on her, he willed her to be alright. "Can you hear me? Fallon, please come back, don't try anything crazy like last time," he whispered. "Come back."

"Dad?" Bergen called from her room. "When are we leaving? I'm so hungry. I think I want waffles. They won't be as good as Fallon's, though."

"In a minute, Bee. Stay in there."

"What?" She came in the room, saw her father on the other side of the bed on the floor, and ran to join him. She stopped short when she saw Fallon. "Omigod, what's wrong with her?" Then she noticed the black dog. "Is that Azul?!"

Azul came up to her and licked her hand in affirmative greeting.

Bergen knelt beside her father, keeping one eye on the dog. "Is she having a vision?"

"Yes," he confirmed.

"Is something wrong, though? Is she supposed to be on the floor?"

Fallon, her eyes shut tight, winced and jerked her hand, startling them, and a few seconds later Bergen pointed.

"Her hand is bleeding! Is this normal?!"

Bret leaned in closer. "Fallon, talk to me. Please come back."

Following her father's lead, Bergen placed a hand on Fallon's cheek, and leaned down and whispered in her ear, "It's alright, Fallon. You can come back to us now."

Fallon sat up with a cry, and she looked immediately at her left palm, which was slashed diagonally all the way across. Bret gave Bergen a sharp look that caused her to close her mouth against the torrent of questions she'd been about to unleash. He snatched up a black bandana and pressed it into Fallon's palm, closing her hand into a fist.

"Are you alright?" he asked, touching her chin to lift her face so he could see her better.

She nodded.

"Stitches?"

She shook her head. She was breathing unevenly, as if she'd been running very fast.

"Bergen," he directed, "call room service and ask for a first-aid kit."

The child ran to comply. She knew her way around a hotel room.

Bret got Fallon to her feet and led her into the bathroom, where she sat on the countertop, holding her injured hand over the sink and gritting her teeth against the searing pain. Bret turned on the tap and proceeded to wash the wound with soap and warm water.

She reached out with her right hand, holding her index and middle finger to one end of the slash and closing her eyes—Bret paused to watch her curiously—but with a soft cry she immediately dropped her hand and shook her head.

"What was that?" he demanded.

I tried to heal it. She met his eyes. *But my mind is weak from the vision, and right now I can't.*

He looked for a moment like he wanted to say much more, but instead he went back to washing her palm.

When the first-aid kit arrived, Bergen brought it to her father and then perched up on the countertop opposite the sink from Fallon to watch the proceedings. Bret dried the slash and applied an antibiotic ointment before bandaging it up quite expertly with gauze and tape.

"I've had lots of experience with Danger Girl over here," he explained dryly, nodding at Bergen.

Fallon was staring at herself strangely in the mirror, and simply nodded.

"How did you cut yourself?" Bergen finally asked, unable to resist any longer.

Fallon looked away from the mirror. "A raven talon."

Bergen was quiet a long moment as she thought about this, processing the words. She looked briefly at the raven tattoo on Fallon's wrist. "It was in your vision?"

"Yes."

"Do your visions always hurt you like that?"

"Never."

"What was it a vision of?"

Fallon shook her head. "I can't tell you right now. Some secrets I have to keep."

Bergen hugged her knees to her chest.

Bret closed the first-aid kit. "Alright. How do you feel? It looks like it really hurts. Do you still want to go?" *Is the danger still at a distance?*

Still somewhere in the future. Nothing new to report. "Yes, I'm hungry. Food will make me feel better. I'll take some ibuprofen; that might help the pain." But she doubted it. Her hand was burning.

"What are we going to do with Azul?" Bergen asked.

Fallon looked questioningly at Bret. He moved aside so that she could see where Azul sat, panting happily, in the doorway. He looked so proud of himself. Fallon touched her forehead wearily with her good hand.

"How did he get here?" Bergen asked, leaping down from the counter and going to hug the dog. Azul nuzzled her appreciatively.

Fallon gazed at Bret. *Allow me.*

He held out his arm. *You are the professional liar.*

Fallon slipped down from the counter and knelt by where Bergen was loving on the dog. "Azul hates to be away from me, and at first your dad told me no dogs were allowed on the bus, but I finally convinced him otherwise, and Selah sent him on a plane in a crate. Early this morning, not too many hours after we checked in, the airport delivered him to the hotel. We wanted to surprise you. It's only for a little while, though."

Bergen's eyes were alight. "Wow, he flew by himself?" Azul woofed, and she hugged the dog again.

"I'll have to thank Selah for her effort," Fallon mentioned, eyeing Bret. "Don't let me forget."

He smiled and nodded. *Well done. So, what's the black beast doing here?*

I told you he usually shows up.

Yeah, but how does he show up?

He's never told me. And I've never asked.

Well, I might ask him later, he threatened lightly. *You just watch me.*

Though still shaken from the morning's brutal vision, brunch was pleasant—Fallon enjoyed watching Bret and Eric share stories and laugh together like brothers. Bergen was a little bit bored, a little bit distracted, every now and then casting a glance at Fallon's bandaged hand, which they'd explained away to Eric as being an unfortunate episode with a broken glass at the hotel. Despite that it wasn't yet noon, Fallon was drinking quite a bit of wine, hoping the alcohol would dull the pain, which her mind was still too weak to deal with.

Later that night after the concert, Bergen awoke crying in her room around four, and Fallon, who was already lying awake with the throbbing in her hand, went to the girl's side. She sat on the bed and gently trying to soothe her.

"Daddy?" Bergen's wet eyes shone at her in the moonlight.

"Your dad's in bed, honey; he's asleep. You want me to get him?"

Bergen nodded miserably. Azul crawled up into the bed with her and curled up against her.

Fallon went and shook Bret awake. "Nightmare," she reported softly, and he sat up groggily. "Sorry."

He shook his head and stumbled to Bergen's room. When he came back a few minutes later and crawled back into bed, Fallon curled up against him.

What was it about? she asked.

She never says. He kissed her, sliding his arms around her. *But now that I'm awake...*

She laughed softly, but then frowned. *You don't think it was what happened this morning, with my hand, do you?*

He shook his head. *She gets nightmares all the time; you know that by now.* He kissed her again. *How's the hand?*

Still letting me know it's there. Maybe you could distract me.

Gladly.

CHAPTER THIRTY-FIVE

The next day after Bergen and Azul had been dropped off at Eric's home as planned, to spend the morning with his four kids, Fallon texted Simon. When a return text came back almost immediately, she glanced at Bret. Her expression was indecipherable.

"I guess let's go."

He thought she sounded oddly reluctant.

She gave directions to the cab driver and settled back in her seat, fidgeting. Bret was surprised to see her looking anxious.

"I haven't seen him in a while," she explained.

He squeezed her uninjured hand.

"And then there's you," she added.

He frowned.

The cab stopped in front of a tall apartment building. Fallon paid the driver, and they took an elevator up to the ninth floor where Bret followed her down the hall, looking around curiously. The old building had been remodeled in a sleek, modern design, and was probably not cheap to live in, he surmised. Not that anywhere in Seattle was affordable, he reasoned.

"What does Simon do for a living?" he asked.

Fallon, who had stopped in front of the last door, made a sound—he couldn't tell if she was choking or laughing—but she waved away his concerned look. "He's a researcher. People hire him. He's excellent." She glanced up and down the hall once, then took Bret's hand tightly in hers before she knocked.

When the door opened, Bret was surprised. He'd expected a standard computer nerd, but Simon looked more teen idol than geek. His face was youthful and quite beautiful. His tall, slender body was clad in pricey jeans and a black t-shirt. He was barefoot, dark hair hanging in his face, no smile on his full lips.

"Hello, Lucky Charm," he greeted Fallon. He cast a dark look at Bret. "You failed to mention you were bringing along arm candy."

Fallon's expression remained neutral. "I have reasons."

He stepped back and held out an arm. "Then by all means. Enter."

As soon as they were over the threshold and the door shut behind them, Fallon released Bret's hand. She went into Simon's arms for a brief hug, and then she returned to Bret's side, showing no sign of intending to introduce the men.

The apartment was ice-cold and dimly lit, smelling musty and stale. Fallon retrieved a black hoodie from her bag and slid it on as they passed darkened rooms that looked unused. Emerging into a brightly lit area, Bret saw that it was Simon's office. Two desks were covered with notebooks and computers; boxes crowded the floor; printers and books filled the shelves. Fallon perched on top of a short metal filing cabinet, while Bret sank down into a cushioned, dusty chair near her.

Simon sat on the edge of a desk and folded his arms across his chest, eyeing Fallon closely. "You look well, as usual. Things must be agreeing with you." He looked briefly and pointedly at Bret.

"I am well," she confirmed. "Not a lot has changed."

"Not a lot has changed here, either, if you can believe that. Azul still spunky as ever?"

"Still the same Azul."

"Interesting. And how is our Selah?"

Bret saw that Fallon was different before her old friend. There was a strange tension in her that he couldn't immediately figure out.

"Selah is fine."

"Still best friends to the end, are you? You haven't cast her off?"

Fallon said nothing.

Simon clapped his hands together loudly, and Bret flinched in spite of himself. "So. Is the danger imminent? Have things grown dark and scary?"

"Were they ever not?" asked Fallon softly.

Simon looked at Bret. "Tell me the truth. Don't you just sometimes want to shake her up like a Magic 8 Ball and get some answers? She's so reluctant. She has more abilities than she knows what to do with, and she lays them to waste. This girl frustrated the hell out of me for years. Luca was so much more fun about it. He and I landed plenty of girls just because we would go out to a club and use his ability like a magic trick, like we could read their minds, or predict things that were going to happen." He chuckled at the memory.

Bret listened without a word. Fallon was staring hard at Simon. Bret had the idea that she was allowing Simon to perform, that it was necessary payment for what would come next.

"So." Simon sat back. "Fallon and The Rockstar. A little above-radar for you, isn't he, Lucky?" He looked at Bret. "But the sex with her," he raised an eyebrow, "pretty amazing, eh?"

Bret glanced at Fallon, but her expression remained unchanged.

"You did know, right?" Simon pressed. "About me and Fallon? So long ago, but you never really forget something like that."

Fallon pulled a knee to her chest. "But not as great as it was with Luca, right?"

Simon looked physically stunned, and then his eyes turned to dark slashes of pain. He was suddenly like a wounded animal, a dog that had been repeatedly kicked.

Bret had felt his own jaw drop at Fallon's words, but he tried quickly to compose himself.

Fallon got up and turned her back on them both, her face turned heavenward, breathing deeply and evenly; Bret thought that possibly she was trying to hold back tears. When she turned back around, she looked calm.

"Bret and I can communicate telepathically just like Luca and I did," she announced.

After a few seconds, Simon tilted his head alertly, face clearing. "Say that again?"

"You heard me."

He touched a finger to his lips. "Prove it."

"I don't need to prove it to you. I just told you." But she nodded at his overflowing bookcase. "Choose a book, give it to me."

He looked around a moment, then handed her an illustrated book of North American birds. She flipped to a random page. Then she came over to Simon's chair, kneeling beside him with her back to Bret, holding the book so that only Simon and herself could see it.

"Point to a bird," she instructed.

He pointed to a black cormorant.

"Black cormorant," said Bret, as she told him in his head.

Simon went to another page and pointed.

"Pomarine Jaeger."

Simon threw the book aside, leaned forward with his elbows on his knees, and looked at Bret speculatively, showing true interest for the first time. "When did you discover this?"

"About two years ago," Fallon explained, "the first time we saw each other. I'd gotten a vision of him in danger, and as I was coming to find him, we started talking in our heads, it just happened. And I can sense him, where he is, how he is. Before that, he never had any inkling of being a telepath. It seems like it's just with me. Like Luca and me."

Simon was deep in thought for a moment. Then he leaned towards her, and in an instant the last bit of animosity was gone, and they looked like comrades, conspirators. "What else? Something else must have happened for you to come looking for me."

To Bret's surprise, she began speaking without restraint. She told Simon fully about the incident in Las Vegas and reported in vivid detail her horrible visions regarding Bret. Simon grabbed a nearby notebook, flipped around for an empty page, and started to scribble rapidly as she spoke.

She showed him her left wrist. "This is the raven in my visions of Bret. The exact one—its left eye is a prism. It wasn't in the first vision. The first time it showed up it just opened its beak at me in a threatening way, like it was trying to force me back, and that's when I passed out. This last time..." She indicated her bandaged hand.

Simon's eyes were alight, his pen still writing. "This is the first time you've sustained a real injury from something you saw in your mind, isn't it?"

She nodded. "Yes. It scared me. I thought for a moment that I was truly losing my mind. Such as it is."

I didn't know you felt that way. Bret was looking at her reproachfully.

I didn't want to worry you in front of Bergen any more than you already were, she pointed out.

"Stop chatting in front of me; it's rude," Simon snapped. "It's you and Luca all over again." He stood up. "I'll see what I can come up with. This is all quite interesting. I'll have to look over some notes..." He turned and rustled around in a dusty box. He seemed more energized than when they had arrived.

Fallon seemed to recognize the dismissal, and went and took Bret's arm, directing him towards the door. After a minute, Simon followed, and when they looked back at him to say goodbye, they saw that he was staring at Fallon, his eyes like pools of midnight. She leaned forward and kissed his cheek. "Thank you," she whispered.

And then she pushed Bret out the door and hurried him down the stairs.

Out on the sidewalk, she linked her arm with his and squeezed him close. "I'm sorry about all that. Selah didn't tell you about me and Simon."

Bret had never been so relieved to be back outside in the fresh air. He'd felt suffocated in Simon's apartment. He shook his head. "Only that he was the closest friend to you and Luca besides herself."

"That's true, he was. The four of us were like a secret society. He moved in when Luca died. It was not a good time. I had managed to survive Jacob's loss and Luca being missing, but Luca's murder drove me over the edge. I drew away from everyone. I dropped out of school. I stopped eating and started drinking. I cut myself. I read about black magic. I wanted to drown in darkness. And I started sleeping with Simon."

"But he and... Luca?"

"Yes. They had been lovers for years. And so what happened between Simon and me was completely unhealthy. It was purely physical. We were both in so much pain. I often think we were using each other to try to destroy ourselves.

"It was Selah, of course, who brought me back from the hell I was in, though it took nearly a year, and every last bit of her patience. And as I came back to myself, I began pulling away from Simon, to the point that I asked him to move out."

Simon had seemed almost relieved, that she was breaking the poisonous cycle they'd been trapped in, and he left soon after to study in London. He hadn't even known about Fallon disappearing like Luca when she turned twenty until she had been safely returned for a while and Selah finally thought to contact him. Soon after that, he came home to Austin, though Fallon was no longer living there permanently. He was set to dive back into the research; he still had all his files on Fallon and Luca, all his books on symbology, mythology, precognition. But Fallon was sick and tired of it all. None of their research and endless theorizing was going to bring Luca back to her or find his murderer. She wanted to live her anonymous life, stay out of trouble, and do the best she could. For a while, Simon pushed her and pushed her, calling her at all hours with a new idea, a new path to explore, and every time she shut him down.

"Finally, I told him that I was getting on with my life, and he needed to get on with his. He left again, and this time he didn't come back. We kept in touch, though. And I knew he was still working on theories, ideas, in his spare time. He keeps me supplied with fake IDs and such. But I don't see him in person much anymore. My showing up with you was too much for him to take without acting out a little. He's always had a touch of drama queen in him."

He wrapped his arm around her. "I admit he wasn't what I expected. I wasn't expecting someone so..."

"Rude?"

"Cold, preening, difficult, attractive... So now we wait and see what he comes up with?"

"Not at all. He may come up with nothing. But I always feel better when Simon has all the latest information from me. He has some pretty unique sources."

"Have you guys ever found other people with an ability like yours?"

"No, but I'm sure they're out there. We never wanted to alert anyone to our own knowledge by digging too deep too often. For all I know, he has a stack of index cards somewhere with names and addresses of a hundred people he's located with the same ability. But these days he only shares what I specifically ask for."

"You didn't mention the tattoo."

"Burning Jack. No." She fell silent then, and he pulled her close.

That night on the bus, most everyone but Seth was playing video games in the back lounge area, and Bergen was asleep in a bed, Azul curled up with her. Everyone had seemed fine with the canine addition to the bus. Fallon had never before encountered such an easy-going group of people, but still she promised to get rid of him as soon as she got the chance.

She and Bret were lying in the bed across the aisle from Bergen's. Fallon was staring into space while Bret watched motocross on the plasma screen that every bunk contained, their curtain drawn tightly closed. Her hand did not hurt much anymore, and was beginning to heal on its own. She was careful to keep it bandaged so that Bergen didn't notice how quickly it was healing.

Long before Jacob had taught her how to heal, her body had healed on its own with unnatural speed. As a child, she had taken it for granted, but when Luca, of all people, began to regard her strangely because of it, the uniqueness of the fast healing was brought to her attention. She remembered the first time Luca had realized there was something truly odd about it. She was nine years old, and she'd broken her arm badly by falling out of a tree in Jacob's backyard. She'd been crying, in terrible pain, the arm undoubtably broken, but Jacob had taken immediate control of the situation. He gave her a sip of whiskey, put her arm in a make-shift sling, and rocked her in his arms till she fell asleep. Luca had assumed they would take her immediately to a doctor, but Jacob asked him to be patient.

When Fallon awoke a few hours later in her bed, Luca was sitting next to her watching her anxiously. Her arm didn't hurt, only felt uncomfortable, and all the purple bruising was already beginning to fade. She never went to the doctor. In a few days, her arm was as good as new.

It was to be the first of many occasions when Luca was faced with the idea that Fallon was quite a different creature from himself.

With Bret's attention firmly on motocross, Fallon wrapped her fingers around both of his wrists, held on tight, and closed her eyes. *Ignore me*, she directed, when she sensed he was about to question her, and his attention returned to the screen. She relaxed and fell into deep concentration. She'd been working on her visions for weeks, but it was a mentally exhausting task. While with Jacob, she had spent months and months perfecting this particular ability, bending the line with such care, now she felt she was under the gun, not knowing how much time Bret had left.

After surviving the stressful visit with Simon and no longer having that weighing on her conscience, she was able to focus fully. And she was immediately rewarded for her hard work. In her mind's eye Bret's fate had manifested itself into the form of a rolling thunderstorm, all black clouds and internal lightning, heading slowly towards her. It was at a great distance, but the enormity of it was troubling. She was pleased that it had at least somewhat worked like she'd hoped, but she was shaken nonetheless, and disappointed that she could see no hint of what the danger was.

The next morning, she asked him for a piece of jewelry. "I can see your fate now; I can keep an eye on its progress. But if you give me some item of yours that's really personal, I can possibly use it to see things even when you're not with me. I think it's important that I be able to do that."

He immediately unhooked a leather cord from around his neck, from which was suspended a small silver bee charm. "My Bergen necklace. She got me the charm when she was six, and I've never taken it off since. This is without a doubt the most sentimental thing I own aside from certain guitars."

"Perfect." She hooked it around her own neck. "I promise I'll take care of it."

She tried using the necklace later that morning when she was alone in bed and Bret had taken Bergen out for a late breakfast. Wrapping the little silver bee inside her closed fist, she simply closed her eyes, imagined Bret, and immediately she saw what she was seeking: the storm.

She could also, with her psychometry ability, see the necklace's past—she grinned as she watched adorable Bergen at age six excitedly picking out the bee in the store, holding it for the first time, insisting to her mother that it was perfect, and they had to get it for Bret's birthday. "Because I'm his bee, Mommy!"

Every day after that, when she checked, the storm had drawn closer. It alarmed her, for it looked so large and ominous. Sometimes she could feel the strong wind against her face, in her mind. Once she leaned forward and reached out towards the storm. The black raven sliced through the sky from out of nowhere and snapped at her finger with its beak.

She sat up on the bed where she'd been laying, crying out and holding her hand, blood trickling from a new cut on her index finger. Azul appeared and leapt up onto the bed and began licking the wound. She stared at the dog. "I've got this, buddy. Thanks, though." She placed her index and middle finger on the cut for a moment. When she removed them, the cut was healed, no evidence remaining. Azul was watching her closely. She winked at him. He put his chin back down between his paws.

The tour rolled onward. Bergen went home to stay a few weeks with Lisbeth before her departure on her honeymoon to Italy, during which the child would rejoin the tour. Fallon had visions at every other concert or so, and occasionally about a crew member. She was hoping not to have any about any of the band members. She didn't want to have to sway someone from trouble, and then be stuck on the bus with them for the next few months while they stared at her curiously or asked difficult questions.

When Bergen returned to them two weeks later, she was slightly moody after spending more time than usual with Leo and his boys. Lisbeth still hadn't made the complete move over to Leo's house. Because the wedding had been sprung on Bergen so suddenly, Lisbeth, Bret and Leo had agreed that they would ease into it. Lisbeth would move in for good when they returned from the honeymoon, giving Bergen more time to prepare herself and get used to the idea.

CHAPTER THIRTY-SIX

FALLON

A woman with long, white hair pulled back in a loose braid was standing outside their front door. There was a necklace of smooth, translucent blue stones around her neck. She didn't look as old as the color of her hair suggested, and fourteen-year-old Fallon thought she had the nicest blue eyes, which seemed to match the color of the stones in the necklace. Fallon felt nothing but goodness radiating from this stranger, and found herself smiling almost involuntarily.

When she saw that Fallon was hesitating to open the screened door, the woman smiled back gently. "Is Luca home, sweet Fallon?"

Fallon's eyes widened for a half second at the woman's knowledge of their names, her use of an endearment. Her heart began to beat a little faster. Something was wrong. Her hands clenched into fists. "No. He's not." In fact, she was all alone this afternoon, save Azul. Jacob was out, which wasn't unusual, and Luca was at his part-time job.

"I'm Colette. Would you like to come outside with me?" the woman invited. "I have something to tell you, and it's such a pretty day."

Fallon cast a quick glance all around, but saw and sensed no one else in the yard. The entire neighborhood was quiet. She looked over her shoulder, but Azul was already trotting to join her.

Colette smiled in delight when she saw the dog, leaning down to pet him as he headed out the door. "Hello, you," she greeted him. "Handsome boy."

"That's Azul," Fallon explained.

Colette nodded, still smiling. "Yes."

Yes? Fallon stepped out onto the front porch with some uncertainty.

"You're safe," Colette assured her. "But I have news. Jacob Roth will not be coming back."

Fallon held her breath and waited, but no more information seemed to be forthcoming. "What do you mean 'not coming back?'" she pressed.

"I mean that he has gone elsewhere. He will not be here with you any longer."

Everything became unsteady for a minute, Fallon's breath tearing raggedly around in her chest. "Is he dead?! What's happened?!"

Colette did not reply, but smiled her soft, gentle smile.

Fallon's chest was on fire with pain, tension wrapping around her head. "What do you mean? IS HE DEAD? Where is he?!" she demanded. "He can't be gone!"

Showing the first signs of concern regarding Fallon's reaction, Colette rubbed her hands together. "You and Luca have each other; it will all be fine. And Jacob has left you everything: this house, possessions, and his money and investments. It is already transferred into your name."

"My name? What about Luca?"

"We felt certain that you would take care of your brother. It was easier to transfer everything to one name."

"Who is 'we?' What's going on? How are you involved in all of this? Where is Jacob?!" Tears burned Fallon's eyes and splashed onto her cheeks. "You have to tell me where he is! He would not leave me! You don't understand!"

Colette's brow furrowed as she observed Fallon's obvious grief. "He is gone from you, Fallon. I am sorry for your pain. I never imagined... well, but that is that, my girl. Please take care. You are well loved." She turned and walked away.

Fallon wanted to follow her, to grab her, and shake her, and demand answers, but she felt compelled to stay where she was, as if by a physical force. She watched helplessly as the woman headed up the road, finally disappearing around a corner. More tears fell onto her cheeks as she took out her phone and looked for Jacob's number to call him, to prove this was all a lie, a strange, stupid joke. Azul was licking her knees and trying to nuzzle up against her.

Her face grew pale as she looked, then looked a second time, then a third. Jacob's number, which she'd called a thousand times, was no longer in her phone. She tried to remember it, but could only come up with the first three digits.

Luca!

Fal?

Do you know where Jacob is?

Luca frowned at the panic in her tone. *What's wrong? Are you crying?*

Please come home. Her voice was dissolving into ragged sobs.

I'll be right there, he promised. *I'll call Jacob on my way.*

She shook her head and hid her face in her hand.

Simon came over later that evening and sat at their dining table with two laptops, performing extensive on-line searches. He confirmed that Fallon Rose Quinn was now listed as the property owner for the house. "The previous property owner is listed as 'unknown,'" he reported to them. The same went for countless investments and bank accounts, all now in Fallon's name, and all with an unknown previous owner.

"Also, Fallon is now super rich," he added, not looking up from the screen, letting out a low whistle. "You're going to need a tax advisor."

While he worked, Fallon sat on the floor with Azul, a bundle of warm, furry comfort on her lap, though he was too large for actual lap-dog status. Her face was expressionless; she did not speak. Tears had dried on her face.

Fourteen-year-old Selah, sweaty and tired after dance class, was curled up in a cushy chair drinking a smoothie, keeping one watchful eye on Fallon and one on her watch—it was a school night, and she had a curfew. Luca would have to drive her home in an hour or so. Fortunately, they still had Jacob's car.

Luca was sprawled on his back on the couch in jeans and a grey t-shirt, listening to Simon's reports, throwing a baseball into the air and catching it, again and again. He was puzzled by Jacob's disappearance, but he was not in despair like his sister. He knew she felt abandoned; he himself did not feel that.

He and Jacob had not been close. But there was one nagging thought that concerned him.

"I cannot find anything on Jacob Roth. Nothing. No birth, no death, no property ownership... no existence." Simon shook his dark head. "It's like he was never here."

Luca and Selah saw Fallon flinch at those last words, and they exchanged a private glance. They had already searched Jacob's room, as well as the entire house, and found absolutely nothing that could be tied to him. His clothing and all personal effects were gone. His room appeared now to be an anonymous, seldom-used guest room, though it still smelled faintly of Ramleh cigarettes. The only thing that remained in the house which screamed "Jacob" to them were his cookbooks, but even those were simply items that might be found in any home, none had even any scribbling by his hand in the margin. This had hurt Fallon—not only was he gone, but every possible physical memento that could be tied to him was gone, too. Except for the labradorite ring on her finger. She held that hand in a tight fist, as if to guard against losing the ring.

Selah set her empty cup aside. "Since Luca is nineteen, and you have no needs financially, as well as no known living relatives, I'd like to think no one will give you a hard time about this."

Fallon looked quizzically at her, as if not quite understanding her words.

"At continuing to live here together," Selah explained. "Since no one knows your guardian was ever here or is now gone, I don't think anyone will notice that things have changed. I mean, you're only fourteen."

Seeing the panic rise up in his sister's face, Luca was off the couch and across the room in seconds, kneeling in front of Fallon and grabbing her shoulders.

"We'll be okay. I miss him, too, Fal, but I always felt there was something temporary about him."

She nodded. "I felt it, too, but I didn't think it would be this soon." She trembled with pain.

He loved you, Fallon. I could always tell it. He didn't want to, but he couldn't help himself. He loved you so much.

I loved him, too. Tears glistened in her eyes. "What do we do now?"

"We keep on, like always. Nothing's changed. There's still us. And Selah's right, I'm nineteen. I'm your legal guardian now."

But Luca was afraid inside, though he fought to hide it from his sister. Hadn't Jacob told him that he—Jacob—alone, stood between Fallon and her mother? Had something happened to Carolina, making their need for Jacob no longer necessary? Was Carolina truly Fallon's only threat? And if she was still alive, how could Jacob have left Fallon vulnerable?

Fallon bent her head in sadness while Luca returned to the couch, Simon continued his searches, and Selah spoke reassuringly to her mother on the phone.

Azul licked Fallon's face. She tried to remember every detail of the last time she'd spoken to Jacob. It had been the night before. She'd been curled up in a chair in the living room with a book. He came into the house just after midnight. Had he looked different? Anxious? No. But serious, as if he were concentrating hard on something.

He stopped by her chair and rested a hand on her shoulder. "Get some rest, Fallon."

She reached up and touched his hand absent-mindedly, barely taking her eyes from her book, but cherishing the rare sensation of his touch.

And then he leaned down and kissed her on the head. "Be well, my secret girl," he whispered. Then he was gone, heading down the hall to his room. She'd looked up and watched him walk away, stunned by what from him was a showing of great affection.

She thought about it now. Had he been saying goodbye to her? Yes. She was certain. She just hadn't realized it at that moment, because she hadn't thought he would leave them, not for years more. He hadn't finished training her. What would she do without him? There was much, so much, that she didn't know. He'd said he would keep her safe, had those words been a lie?

She looked through tears at her brother's worried face. Her mind felt like it was beginning to shut down.

CHAPTER THIRTY-SEVEN

"So, I was thinking..." began Fallon.

Bret feigned alarm.

Fallon rolled her eyes. "My house in Austin..."

"You still have your cousin's house?"

She nodded. "It's been a rental since I left. My latest renters just moved out, and I was thinking I might sell it. There are still some things there—all the furniture, plus some boxes locked in the attic. I never got rid of anything or brought much of anything with me. I just kind of left it as-is. I've had the same renters for the past six years, so it's been a good situation, but I don't know that I want to deal with it anymore. What do you think about going there with Bergen during your next break? We could stay at the house, and I could go through a few things and see about getting it ready to sell. Austin's not a bad place to hang out for a few days."

"You're right about that, and I'd love to see the house where you grew up."

"I'll call a realtor, a friend of Selah's. I can meet with her while we're down there, see what she thinks."

On the first of August, the trio flew in to Dallas. They rented a car and drove to Gray, to Fallon's garage apartment, which Bergen was immediately charmed by. They did multiple loads of laundry and slept late in the morning. There was not enough time to go to Star Fall Farm, but they promised Bergen they would go there the next time they were in town.

They had a brief, but pleasant, lunch at Selah's house, and afterwards, Fallon took Bergen and Indio out into the backyard to play and act silly for a little bit. She had missed her little man. Azul happily joined in.

Bret sat at Selah's kitchen table and watched them out the window while Selah finished cleaning up the kitchen. Finally, she came over and joined him, sitting across from him with a glass of sweet iced tea.

"I love that you love her," she told him softly, with warmth.

He smiled, pleased with her words.

"How is the tour going?" she asked. "Well, I suppose? Especially having the prettiest groupie in the world traveling along with you."

He laughed. "It is, it is. She definitely enhances the entire experience. I love touring. It's been a lot of fun having her along this time, and now that Bergen is with us, it's been nice. Oh, we saw Simon when we were in Seattle," he added. "I don't know if she told you?"

Selah frowned. "Really?"

He wondered at her reaction. "You told me yourself that you thought he would be interested in everything that's going on."

"And was he? Interested?"

"Sure, I guess." He shrugged. "If you could get past the bad attitude."

Selah touched her face with both hands, as if mildly flustered. "Yes. That's expected. So, you saw him? You went along to the apartment?"

Now he was on the alert. "Selah. What's wrong?"

She held up one finger, got up and left the room. His gaze strayed back to the trio in the backyard. There was much shrieking and laughter going on out there. He was glad to see the free joy on his daughter's face, and on Fallon's as well. His head swung around when he heard Selah's light footsteps returning. She was holding out a newspaper clipping, and he took it from her.

It was an obituary from five years before. Announcing the death of Simon Keaton, age twenty-nine, of Seattle, Washington, originally of Austin, Texas.

Bret's eyes met Selah's. "What is this?" His voice was low.

She sat down on a chair beside him. She looked like she wanted to hug him, but that impulse went against her nature, and so she was holding back. "A little over five years ago, Simon was murdered in his apartment. Fallon saw it in her mind, but too late. By the time she called him, they were already torturing him, and when the police got there, he was dead. It was a horrible death." She breathed in and out, evenly.

"For the three months prior, just on a whim, he and she had been in touch frequently, revisiting some of the old questions, exploring new avenues. He'd been extending himself in all kinds of directions to all kinds of people, searching for information. Then without warning, he was killed. The police did not investigate it fully. I was very nearly expecting them to declare it had been suicide," she added dryly, "but a robbery attempt by addicts or some such nonsense was what they came up with in the end. The funeral was held in Austin, because his family is still there. He'd left everything to Fallon—as people seem to do—including the apartment lease, and so after the funeral, she and I went out to Seattle to look things over. Thinking, of course, that we would cancel the lease.

When they got to the apartment and Fallon touched the door, it burned her hand with cold, and she'd jumped back. The air around them began to feel odd, and the girls grabbed each other's hand. Then the door flew open, and Simon was standing there.

"Finally," he sighed, and gestured them inside.

"We were shell-shocked," she told Bret, "and just stood there dumbly staring at him. You understand, we had just buried him the day before." She took another deep breath.

"Fallon and I let go of each other at some point, while we were still standing out there in the hall, and as soon as we did, I couldn't see him anymore. He apparently reached out and grabbed her hand, and then tried to grab mine. But his hand slid right through me, that's what she says. Fallon quickly took my hand again, maybe afraid she would lose me. Then he could touch me, and I could see him again."

"He's a ghost?" Bret was gripping the table so tightly his knuckles were white.

Selah was nodding. "A ghost, yes. And she is his link to this world, the only one who can see him without assistance. He is trapped in that apartment, because that was the location of his death, as far as we can guess. If anyone enters the apartment without holding onto Fallon, they will not see or hear him. We experimented. Once inside the apartment, you can let go of her and still see and touch him. But outside the apartment, you have to be touching her to see him. You have to be touching her as you enter the apartment..." She shook her head at the complexity.

"He can touch objects, and he operates with his computers. That's how he interacts with the outside world. He befriends people online who don't know he's dead; he still has sources, performs extensive research, pays the lease on his apartment." She sat back in her chair. "We don't know why he's still there. He's trapped, and he half blames her, and half craves her company. It is driving him slowly insane." She glanced at him. "Hence his unpleasant mood. And his jealousy, I'm sure, when she showed up with you... before he realized that you are now part of the grand puzzle."

Bret closed his eyes for a long moment. Selah did not say anything. Finally, "Does he know who killed him?" he asked.

She shook her head. "They were anonymous, offered no explanation, but wanted him to suffer. But then, as he was dying..." She squeezed her eyes shut for a second. "One of them whispered in his ear, 'She never sees the important ones in time, does she?' Well, of course, when Simon told her this detail, it crippled Fallon emotionally for months—that he had been so horrifically killed because of her, and that it might have been the same people who murdered Luca. Things were dark for a while, again. That's when she got the tattoo on the back of her arm. I gave birth to Indio during that time, and I believe that helped her not lose herself completely all over again like after Luca. The guilt weighed on her. But she poured herself into loving my son instead of letting it sink her."

He rubbed his hands over his face, took a long, deep breath, and then let it out in a low *whoosh* as he again looked out the window at the three in the back.

"Selah," he said finally.

"Yes?"

"You." He shook his head. "You seem like the last person who would be involved in a world like this. Fallon's world."

Selah graced him with a full smile, and he was reminded of the sun. "I wouldn't, Bret. But I love her. She is my girl. So, I open my arms to all of it and trust God."

Left unspoken was the thought that people who were closest to Fallon tended to die or otherwise disappear. When he looked into Selah's wise brown eyes, he saw that she knew this. Of course she did. But she would not waver. She was Fallon's soldier to the end.

He got to his feet. "Thanks for continuing to educate me. I really hope, though, that we're nearing the end of the revelations stage."

She looked away. "Mmm."

He was not heartened by this response. He left her and went out to join the hooligans.

When he got out into the yard, Indio and Bergen were kneeling in one corner, looking in the bushes for a wayward box turtle. Fallon came towards him, but slowed when she saw his face. They came to stand a few inches from each other and stopped, and she looked up at him.

I found out about your tattoo, he informed her.

She unconsciously grabbed her upper left arm and looked away.

You could have told me he was a ghost, he continued. *Don't you think that's maybe some information I'd have liked to have beforehand?*

She looked uncomfortable. *I'm not used to explaining things to people. It's habit, to keep secrets.* Her eyes flew back to his. *I didn't lie!*

You just withheld extremely pertinent details.

She rubbed her arm as if it hurt.

He watched as his daughter interacted sweetly with Indio. All of it troubled him. Ghosts, visions, murder, death, and the damned immortal black dog. He wondered if he was endangering Bergen by inviting her into this world of Fallon's. If his selfish need to be with Fallon was not in the best interest of his daughter. Though when he saw how much Bergen and Fallon loved each other, he couldn't believe that could be true.

Bret seemed a little moody and quiet, so Fallon took the opportunity to go in alone to see Selah, who was still sitting at the table. Grabbing a bottle of water from the fridge, Fallon sat down across from her and glanced at the obituary that rested between them.

"You took him to see a ghost without warning him of such?"

Fallon shrugged, glancing away in irritation. "It's kind of a tricky topic, wouldn't you agree?"

"I suppose so. But then, many of your topics are tricky. Simon didn't try to flaunt his 'history' with you in front of Bret, did he?" she asked, trying to lighten the mood.

Fallon looked at her and smiled her crooked smile. "Oh, he did. But I shut him down."

Selah massaged her temples. "And so now Bret knows that you embarked on a physical relationship with a man who had been involved with your brother."

Fallon toasted her with the water bottle. "Twisted, I agree. You always assumed it was the comfort of the physical relationship that I sought, but actually it was the wickedness of it that I wanted. I was done with life. Jacob and Luca were both gone. I wanted to destroy myself from within. I tried everything." She sighed. "But I was tied to life. Through you. And damn you, here I still am." Her tone was light, but Selah wondered at her choice of words.

"There's something I've always wondered about," Selah mentioned, wanting to change the subject. "I figure that I might as well ask you, since we're talking so openly. The night Luca was murdered, you didn't go running with him as you usually did, you stayed at the house with me. Why?"

Fallon ran the tip of her tongue over her lips. "I found something. Late that afternoon when I went into my bedroom, my old copy of *To Kill a Mockingbird* was laying in the middle of my bed. That was the first book Jacob and I ever read together, and for that reason it had always been special to me, and Jacob had known it was special. I hadn't put it there on the bed, and there was no reason Luca would have been in my room, so I was immediately on the alert. I opened it up, and there was a piece of paper stuck inside." Fallon reached into her messenger bag and pulled out a well-worn paperback edition of the book, opened it, and pulled out a folded scrap of paper, which she opened and handed to Selah.

Handwritten on the paper was a quote by Bertolt Brecht: "One weakness is enough, and love is the deadliest."

Selah read it and then looked at Fallon curiously.

"Jacob always told me I must be strong. And he reminded me often that love is a great weakness—it was one of his mantras. This exact quote was one of his mantras." Fallon looked at the piece of paper. "He had been gone for years, but finding this, in a book that had meant something to him and me, it shook me horribly. I didn't know if he had left it for me, somehow, or if some-one was playing a really cruel trick. I was as devastated as if he had just abandoned me all over again. And so, when Luca wanted to go running that evening, I just wanted to stay in the house in my cocoon. Not realizing it meant I would lose him as well."

"Did Jacob give you that ring?"

Fallon smiled slightly at Selah's new bravery regarding Things Jacob. She looked down at the labradorite ring on her left ring finger. "He did."

Selah said nothing more, and Fallon did not offer.

Early the next morning they threw some things into the Dart and hit the road to Austin, dropping off the rental car on the way. It was about a four-and-a-half-hour drive, including stopping for coffee and lunch. Bergen happily snuggled with Azul in the backseat the entire way.

When they got to Austin and finally reached the old neighborhood and Fallon's house, it was mid-afternoon on a beautiful but scorching hot day. As soon as Fallon unlocked the front door, Bergen was off and running from room to room. Fallon immediately went to adjust the air-conditioning, and Azul headed out to explore the backyard.

"Wow, this place is cool!" Bergen was ecstatic as she rejoined them following her whirlwind tour. "Why do you want to sell it? We could just live here. Like a vacation home."

"She has a point," acknowledged Bret, who also liked the house.

The architecture was 1930s Tudor Revival, the exterior a subtle leaf green with brown trim. Inside the layout was a mix of traditional with modern convenience. There were three bedrooms and two baths, but the kitchen and living area were not very large, and the laundry room was a tiny affair at the back of the house.

"Don't gang up on me with her," Fallon warned him. "There's no reason for me to keep this place. Bergen, come here; let me show you something."

Bret and Bergen both followed Fallon into a bedroom.

"Hey, there's a fireplace in here!" Bergen noted. "This is my favorite room!"

"There are two fireplaces in the house," Fallon told her. "The one in the living area, and this one. This was my bedroom." She sat on the edge of the stone hearth and beckoned Bergen over. Then she turned on a light on her phone and shone it up inside the chimney. "See?"

Bergen looked. "Stairs?"

Bret came over to see. Up inside the spacious chimney were metal rungs sunk deep into the stone.

"Not sure of their purpose, but I used to crawl up in here and hide when my brother and I were younger."

"That's cool! I can't believe you had a fireplace in your bedroom and no one else did."

"I was always the spoiled one. Azul used to..."

Bret broke into a sudden fit of coughing. Bergen was looking at her funny.

Fallon quickly corrected herself. "When I came to check on this place, once, Azul would lie here and stare up into the chimney, like he was looking for something."

Bret touched a finger to his lips.

They spent the afternoon looking everything over and making lists of things that might need to be attended to. Fallon ran several loads of laundry so they could put sheets on the beds and have towels in the bathrooms, since they would be spending several nights. Later, they went out to eat and wandered around downtown, stopping at a deli for cheesecake and coffee.

The next morning, they went out for breakfast tacos, then returned to the house to begin going through things. Anything that Fallon didn't want to save, she was going to give away or throw away. She didn't anticipate saving much.

With Bergen busy going through some boxes of books in her old bedroom, Fallon led Bret upstairs and unlocked the door to the attic. It was full of dust and boxes.

"I don't want any of it." She seemed distracted. He touched her arm, and she abruptly turned to him and hugged him tightly. When she'd last checked on the storm with the necklace, a stray drop of rain had hit her face. "It's so close. Any day now." She looked up at him, and her face was full of sadness and misery. "It's so close, and I still can't figure it out. What good am I? What's the point of the premonitions if I can't save the people who matter the most? I can save all the rest, but not the ones most important to me, the ones most loved? What cruelty is that?" A tear slid down her cheek.

He pressed her head against his chest, tension filling his body. "You'll get it."

A little later, after they'd made a cursory check of some of the boxes, she called Simon. "Hey, I'm going through a bunch of stuff at the house in Austin. In the attic, I found several boxes of papers, files, and whatnot from my parents. I hate to throw any of it out, in case there's something there, but I don't have time to go through it piece-by-piece at the moment."

"Too busy hanging with rockstars," he observed. "You're getting soft. Have them all shipped to me. I'll sift it when I've got the time."

"Thanks."

After posting several boxes to Seattle, they took the afternoon off. It was again unbearably hot outside, and Fallon took them swimming at Barton Springs, a popular natural spring that held steady at a bracing sixty-eight degrees. Bret posed for pictures with several people who recognized him.

They got snow cones afterwards, and walked around down by the lake together. Bergen, who talked to Lisbeth every few days, was reporting back to them some of the things Lisbeth was loving about Italy.

"When you go back to California, your mom won't be living at the house anymore. She'll be living at Leo's house full-time. When I'm out of town, you'll be living there, too."

Bergen stared at some ducks, her lips bright red from her snow cone. "What about my dirt bike?"

"You can't ride it when I'm not there, anyway," he pointed out.

"What about when I'm older, when I can?"

"If I'm not in town, then your mom will take you to the house, and you can ride. It's ten minutes away. Nothing's changing, except that now you have two houses to be 'Queen B' of instead of just the one."

"But..." she dropped off.

He put his hand on her shoulder, and she leaned against him. "But what, Honeybee?"

"When you're gone," her voice was a whisper, he had to lean down to hear her, "I really, really miss you. But it makes it easier, because everywhere in the house there's something about you. Your shoes, or your guitar, or just a memory of you. Or I can go in your room and lie on your bed and watch TV. So, I still miss you, but it makes it better."

Fallon watched Bret. She could practically feel the aching of his heart.

"When I'm at Leo's house, and I'm missing you..." There were tears on Bergen's cheeks. "It's just Leo's house. Not yours."

He picked her up and hugged her close. "When you miss me, call me. And you'll be able to take anything you want to your new room at Leo's. You can even take one of my guitars for your room if that's what you want. And when I am in town, you'll be staying with me. OK?"

She nodded vigorously.

He kissed her, then set her down as she wiped her face.

Fallon put a hand on Bergen's back. "Come on, I told you we'd rent a canoe. You still want to do it?"

Bergen perked up a little. "Yes."

"Alright. This way."

* * * * * * *

That night after Bergen had gone to bed with Azul in Fallon's old room, Bret and Fallon lay on the queen bed in the master bedroom and talked while she sipped a glass of wine. At one point, Bret indicated the messenger bag that lay on a nearby chair. "I remember this from that night in Vegas when I first saw you. Does it go everywhere with you?"

She drank some of her wine and nodded. "I am almost never without it."

He grinned mischievously. "What's inside?"

She narrowed her eyes. "My collection of daggers and shurikens, obviously."

He made a face. "The fact that I don't know what a 'shuriken' is doesn't help me."

"A throwing star."

"Oh. Of course. And you were joking?"

"Of course." She saw that he looked quietly disappointed, and she sighed. Setting aside her wine, she pulled herself to an upright position and moved the bag onto her lap. "Alright." She opened the flap. "Close your eyes. You may reach in and remove one item. Whatever it is, and should it interest you, we will discuss it to your heart's content."

He sat up eagerly and moved closer.

"Eyes closed," she directed.

He shut them obediently, reaching out with his hand, which she guided into the bag. He rustled around a little, then pulled out a book. He opened his eyes. "*The Collected Poems of Theodore Roethke.* Can't say that I'm familiar with him." He looked at her, and saw a strangely fond look on her face.

"Jacob got me into him when I was twelve. We read a lot together, Jacob and I," she explained. "This book was a special thing between us. When he introduced these poems to me, it was as if he opened up spaces in my heart and mind that had been locked tight." She shook herself, as if shedding the reverie. "Anyway. This book goes everywhere with me. When I'm feeling lonely or sad or overwhelmed, I get it out and read some of it. And Jacob comes back to me."

Bret was surprised, and cautious. "I've heard so much about Luca, I guess I never realized how much of an impact your guardian was in your life."

Her eyes still hadn't lost their faraway glaze. "He was with me for longer than my parents were. He was an enigma, a powerful force. So much about him was a mystery. I loved him immensely. And he knew it."

"He died when you were how old?"

"Fourteen." She ducked her head, as if dodging something. "I'm going to take a shower."

He sensed her desire to be alone, and lay back on the bed. "I'm going to read some Roethke."

She smiled, and brushed his lips with hers before she headed out of the room.

"Hey, favorite poem?" he asked.

She paused. "One of his most famous: 'In A Dark Time.'"

Bret flipped through the book till he came to the correct poem, and as she disappeared into the bathroom, he began to read.

CHAPTER THIRTY-EIGHT

The next morning Fallon met with the realtor to get her opinion and advice. While she was thus engaged, Bret went out into the backyard with Bergen and Azul, and called Selah, who was surprised to hear from him.

"Is everything alright with our magical creature?" she asked.

"Yes, she's fine. Meeting with your friend right now, actually, about the house. But while I had the chance, I wanted to ask you something, since you're so well-versed in Matters of Fallon."

Selah smiled. "This must be something truly bothering you. I don't imagine you'd be calling me just for tidbits of information so you can stay ahead of the game."

He ignored her slight jab. "I want to know about Jacob Roth."

She made some noise he couldn't interpret. "Don't get me started on Jacob," she warned, shaking her head despite knowing that he couldn't see her. "Don't get me lying."

"Have you ever read any of her Roethke poems?" he pressed.

"She let you read 'In A Dark Time,' didn't she?"

He eyed the back of the house. "Yes." Bergen was busy exploring the yard, ignoring, he hoped, his call.

"And much as you didn't want to, you saw her in it, and she began to feel intangible to you, as if she was becoming something you could no longer hold onto?"

"How do you do that?" he demanded.

"I felt the same way when I read it once, back in college."

"It's just that all this time I've been imagining Luca as this larger-than-life figure from her past, the ghost that I thought was haunting her. But then I saw her face when she was talking about Jacob..."

"Yes, Jacob haunts her, much more so than Luca does. Being back in the Austin house, I knew it would be complicated, since there are so many memories of him there. And then there's the whole matter of her not believing that he's dead."

He looked up. "What?"

"Oops."

"He isn't dead?"

Bergen stole a glance at him.

"Officially, he never existed. So, he couldn't die. There was no death that we knew of; he simply disappeared, along with every bit of evidence of his existence. Not a death so much as a total vanishing." There was noise in the background. "Bret, I'm sorry, I've got to go. Indio has friends over..."

"Yeah, alright. Thanks, Selah. Thanks." He hung up and pressed a fist to his forehead for a moment.

After lunch, he cornered Fallon alone. "I thought Jacob was dead?"

She pulled her hair back and began twisting it into a knot. "No. He is not. As far as I know. It was just easier, early on, to tell you he was dead, when the truth was so much more complicated."

"What is the complicated truth? Who was he? Who is he?"
She shook her head. "No one really knows."

He stared at her. "'No one really knows?'" He tried to steady
himself. "What do you mean, 'no one really knows?' Wasn't he
your cousin? A guide for you and Luca? Showing you all the ins
and outs of your abilities?"

She was quiet for a while, looking for all the world like
she was trying to come to a decision. Then she turned away,
beckoning for him to follow. She took him to the master
bedroom, and stood there looking around, as if seeing it for the
first time though they'd just slept there the night before.

"He was not our cousin, not any relation of ours, though
that story was sold for a while. He was always such a mystery
to us. He revealed next to nothing. He was difficult to reach.
When I was seven, I had taken on the challenge of winning him
over, and I believe that by the time he left us, I had gotten as
far as anyone could have. As I mentioned before, Jacob would
sometimes read to me in the evenings; he had a great voice. Luca
never quite got over how I'd managed that; he was in awe of
my skills," she chuckled softly. "Nevertheless, it was surprising
to me—and, Bret, I've never told this to anyone, not Luca,
not Selah, not Simon—when one evening, when I was eleven
years old, Jacob asked if he could train me." Her gaze traveled
unseeing around the room. "Luca wasn't home. It became our
secret thing."

Bret watched her closely, hanging on every word, sensing the
importance of what was being relayed to him.

"We trained in this room. Azul was our only audience. I
became skilled in many areas; he was an incredible teacher.

He's the one who taught me how to heal, and how to become a shadow."

He was aware that sparks of jealousy were flaring up within himself. "He was never inappropriate with you, was he?"

She shook her head. "Everyone has wanted to suggest that, but he never was." She thought about the dagger. "He was not an angel, but he never harmed me." Her eyes looked almost silver in the light. "Until he left me."

Bret worked her words through his brain, knowing he needed to be careful. "You really loved him." There was an emptiness in his chest that hadn't been there before, the sensation that the path they were walking together had suddenly grown rocky and narrow.

She was nodding. "I did." Her eyes flicked away. "And then, like everyone else, he vanished from me." Her voice was hard. And, he realized, accusatory. So, this, he mused, was the cause for her strong emotion. Luca had been murdered, had left her against his will. Simon as well. But Jacob, whom she loved, had abandoned her, possibly by choice.

That afternoon Fallon was restless and agitated, having faced the specter of Jacob Roth twice in twenty-four hours. She left Bret and Bergen napping at the house while she and Azul drove around Austin running errands and just looking around. The city had changed so much since her childhood, some good, some bad. The traffic, the number of people, was definitely worse. But she loved it here, loved visiting, at least. It had retained much of its quirky charm, despite the current level of over-development. Should she sell the house, or just rent it out again? Bergen seemed tremendously attached to it, but if it was a rental they wouldn't be able to use it anyway. And without rent, the taxes would eat her alive. She knew she'd have no trouble selling it—the realtor had confirmed as much.

After a couple of hours, she headed into a coffee shop where she ordered an iced mocha and ensconced herself in an overstuffed, red chair with earbuds firmly in place. Azul stayed happily snoozing in the backseat of the Dart.

Fallon tried to relax her mind. She hadn't had a premonition of any sort in days. Though she'd been working on her active premonitions, it had not been progressing as she'd hoped. She knew that being able to see the storm was an amazing thing, but if she couldn't recognize the danger before it hit, what was the use? She couldn't figure anything out about the danger at all, and the helplessness was nearly overwhelming her.

The previous night, something odd had happened as she watched the storm. A phoenix had appeared out of the dark clouds and come directly towards her. Just before it reached her, the raven dove down from nowhere and attacked the phoenix, and the two birds battled it out a while before disappearing in a burst of flames.

It had unsettled her. The phoenix, she thought, should be a good symbol, only she hadn't felt any good coming from it; its approach had been menacing. And the raven... her feelings about the raven were changing. Instead of a threatening presence, she was beginning to believe that the raven was not so different from Azul. Like it was guarding, protecting, her. Again and again, she was reminded of Jacob, of the raven tattoo on his arm, on her wrist.

As she sipped her mocha and listened to her music, an image of Bret's latest CD flashed in her head—*what?*—and she dug around in her messenger bag and pulled it out. On the case, Bret had written all kinds of things to her in permanent marker to satisfy her inner-groupie, and inside the booklet he'd added sweet notes near the lyrics to "Blur." She set aside her drink and read the entire booklet: lyrics, liner notes, acknowledgments, and all. There was nothing unusual or telling about any of it. What was she looking for?

As she was sliding the booklet back in the case, she glanced at the CD itself. The record label was Red Racer Records, and the symbol...

The symbol for Red Racer Records was a phoenix.

Bret?

Where are you? He sounded sleepy.

Drinking coffee. I'll be home after I stop at the grocery store. Tell me, how long have you been with your current record label?

Eight years too long. Why?

She chewed on her lower lip. *They're no good?*

Just some business things we disagree on. Again, why?

We can talk about it when I get home.

She stopped at Central Market and bought a few things for dinner, including fresh strawberries for Bergen. When she got back in the car it was just starting to get dark, and she was surprised at how long she'd been away from them that day. Before she pulled out of the parking lot, she grabbed the bee necklace and shut her eyes to check on things.

She flinched at a deafening crash of thunder, rain hitting her full in the face. She saw a premonitory image of Bret and Bergen both in a flash of lightning. Lying dead in the wet grass.

Her eyes flew open, fire roaring through her veins in alarm. The storm was upon them, and they were both in danger, Bret *and* his daughter.

BRET!

Her voice was a scream through his head.

What's wrong? He sat up alertly on the couch.

Hide Bergen! Hide her now!

He got to his feet. *What's going on?!*

No time—hide her. They're coming for you; they know you're both in the house. No time to run. Hide her!

He could hear the terror in her voice, and his heart stuck in his throat as he blindly grabbed Bergen's arm and propelled her into another room.

I love you, Fallon told him desperately. *I'll get you...*

Her voice disappeared as he heard something outside and his focus shifted.

"Bergen, hide, go. Now," he hissed at her.

His tone of voice scared her, and she clung to him. "Daddy..."

"Go! Don't make a sound; don't come out till Fallon gets here. No matter what happens, no matter what you hear, you wait for Fallon. Promise me."

The look on his face was intense, and she was terrified, but she nodded and fled. He ran back to the center of the house and looked around for a weapon. He heard another noise behind him, and swung around. Then he felt something on his neck, and his world went black.

Fallon ran into the house fifteen minutes later, screaming for Bergen, Azul at her heels. She knew Bret was gone, she could sense that he was nowhere nearby, and he wasn't answering her, so she assumed he was unconscious. But Bergen remained in the house.

Azul seemed to know this as well, for he did not pause as he raced towards her old bedroom, and she followed him, still crying out for Bergen. There was a noise from up inside the fireplace as Bergen crawled down. Tears streaming down her dusty cheeks, she threw herself into Fallon's arms.

"*Dad!*" she shrieked, and started to run to look for him, but Fallon held her back.

"He's gone, Bee. He's gone."

"No!" Bergen was sobbing. "No! What do you mean? Where is he?!" She was like a wild thing, and Fallon held her tight.

"I don't know, but we'll find him."

"They were looking for me, calling for me! I never heard my dad; I didn't know where he was. Then they left, just a minute ago." She clung to Fallon fiercely, weeping uncontrollably, choking out her words. "I was so scared. Where's my dad?!"

She was shaking so violently that Fallon, in her own numb state, was alarmed. She sank weakly to the ground for a moment with the child on her lap. "I don't know. But I will get him back." Or die trying. "I promise you, I will get him back."

With Bergen clinging to her, Fallon made a quick search of the house. Bret's phone was laying in the middle of the floor in the living area, but she did not touch it and warned Bergen not to either. Azul's sharp bark led her to the back door, where she found that the lock was broken. She fished her own cell out of her back pocket, dialing 911. This was not a time to be wishy-washy about authority figures. Bergen needed everyone in the world to be looking for her father.

While they waited for the police to arrive, Fallon sat on the couch and called Lisbeth, quickly telling her what had happened and what she needed to do. Leo walked in to find his pretty wife sitting by the window with tears running down her face, and he quickly knelt beside her. When Lisbeth finally got off the phone, after having a brief, tearful conversation with her daughter, Leo was already on his phone arranging a flight out as soon as possible. She gave him a grateful look.

Back at the house in Austin, Fallon held Bergen's shoulders and looked her in the eye. "Quickly. We have to talk about what we're going to say."

Bergen looked at her with reddened eyes. "What?"

"To the police when they come. If they find out that your dad told you to hide, they're going to look in all the wrong places for the answers to find him; they'll think he knew who was coming for him, but he didn't."

"Why did he tell me to hide?" Bergen looked like she was thinking hard.

"He didn't tell you. You heard something that scared you, and you ran and hid."

"But..."

"Repeat it to me." Fallon's voice was hard. "You have to say it this way, to help your dad. You heard something that scared you, and you ran and hid."

"I heard something that scared me, and I ran and hid in the fireplace."

"Good girl." Fallon nodded. "What did you hear?"

"What did I hear?"

"You don't know. It scared you. You can be vague. You're nine."

"How did he know to tell me to hide? We were just sitting there watching a show on my tablet. I didn't hear anything. All of a sudden, he jumped up, and freaked out, and told me to hide."

Fallon didn't miss a beat. "At that moment when he jumped up, I had just told him you two were in danger. I told him to hide you."

"He never looked at his phone. Did you text?" Bergen was staring at her stubbornly.

Fallon licked her lips. "I didn't text." She touched her temple. "I told him. Here. It's a thing he and I can do, that we hadn't told you about yet because it's so strange. Telepathy. Do you see the trouble this would cause? The police would think I was crazy and concentrate too much on me, not believe anything we say."

Bergen was wide-eyed. "Can't we say you called on the phone?"

"No call would show up on the phone records. They would check."

"Omigod, you can talk to my dad in his mind?! Can you talk to him now?!"

"Shh, baby. No. He's too far out of reach."

Bergen leaned against her. "Can we talk more about this later?"

"Yes. Just remember what you need to say."

The police arrived and stayed for several hours, interviewing Fallon and Bergen both at length, going over the entire house. When they were gone, it was well after midnight, and Fallon had decided they should try to get some sleep before driving back to Gray. For Bret was not in Austin; she knew that much. He was not, as far as she could tell, even in Texas any longer. There was no need to remain in the city to wait for news.

In bed, she held Bergen in her arms and sang to her until finally the crying child fell asleep. Then she buried her face in her own pillow and silently wept.

CHAPTER THIRTY-NINE

Fallon and Bergen slept restlessly during what remained of the night, and the latter awoke crying several times. Each time Azul quickly licked away her tears and snuggled up beside her, which calmed her and sent her back to sleep.

At six, Fallon gave up on sleep. She showered and dressed in jeans and an old, black concert t-shirt. It took her an hour to pack up the car and make sure the house was closed up, the thermostat appropriately set, the shades drawn, and the doors locked. She was having a difficult time focusing on everything that needed to be done. She was in disbelief that Bret wasn't with her. That she'd failed. Again.

Bergen drank chocolate milk and then fell asleep in the backseat with the dog as soon as they hit the highway.

As she drove, Fallon called Selah to tell her what had happened, managing not to break down in tears. Selah was calm and cool on the other end of the line and instructed Fallon to come straight to her house.

"Can Indio go stay with Tallie for a while?" Fallon asked, referring to Selah's older sister in Dallas.

"I was just thinking that. I'll have Michael take him tonight. You and Bergen can sleep here if you want."

"Thanks, but I think I'll be better at my place. I'd like to use your house as a kind of command central during the day, if that's alright. I have some plans in my head."

"Of course. Anything. Drive safely."

Lisbeth called her a few minutes later. She sounded breathless. "I just got off the phone with a girlfriend in L.A. She said Jack Lane disappeared last night from a hotel in Houston."

Fallon's heart skipped a beat, and a deep pain began to throb in her temple. "What?"

"That's what she said. She didn't know about Bret, yet. But her sister used to date Jack, and she's still friends with his guitarist, and he called her early this morning to tell her. The police are waiting twenty-four hours to declare it a missing person situation, since no one actually saw anything occur. But his band and crew know something's wrong—that he was actually sober and would not have just unexpectedly left. He went down the hall to get ice, barefoot, and never came back."

Fallon concentrated on inhaling and exhaling slowly, calming herself. "Okay, Lis, thanks for calling me. That definitely adds an angle to this." A dark, horrible angle, but an angle nonetheless.

"Do you think you can find him?" Lisbeth's voice cracked with emotion.

"I'll find him." Her voice sounded certain, though her brain was zinging with doubts and even fear. "Let me know when your flight's getting in. I'll see if someone can pick you up at the airport. Remember not to tell anyone where you'll be. The anonymity of my town is key to my existence."

"I'm not even telling my sister, which is huge," Lisbeth assured her. "Just that I'm somewhere in Dallas with friends."

As she hung up, Fallon thought immediately of Tayce, and deep inside she began to panic even further. Had he disappeared as well last night? Had she lost them all? She knew that he and Paul were in tour rehearsals with the band somewhere around Dallas.

She was looking in her phone for his number when it rang again, and with relief she saw that it was him.

"Hey, trouble," she greeted him soberly. "You're alright, then?"

"Sure, I am, beautiful. Is Bret really gone? I just heard the news."

"He's missing, yes. I'll tell you more about it later." She glanced at the backseat, but Bergen was sleeping soundly, curled up under a red blanket. "I hear Jack Lane is missing as well."

"Yeah, I just heard that, too. I'm still here, though." Silence. "Where are you now?"

"I've got Bergen; we're on our way back to Gray."

"I'll meet you there."

"Tayce..."

"Dammit, you aren't going to do this alone! I won't let this story go on endlessly like with Peter. I'm connected to it somehow. I want to help any way I can. And if I know anything, it's that you're going to be working your ass off trying to find them."

"We're headed to Selah's. That blue and white house on Oak Street."

294

CHAPTER FORTY

When Bret woke up, he was lying on his stomach, the side of his face pressed against cold metal. His mouth and throat were painfully dry, his head heavy. At first, he couldn't see anything, but he could tell he was in the back of a moving vehicle. No light shone in from anywhere, so he thought he must be in a van or a box truck. His arms were tied behind him, tingling uncomfortably, and his left shoulder was shrieking in pain from being lain on at a bad angle. He shifted around some, trying to rise up to a sitting position, but he was feeling a little dizzy, and not being able to see was making it worse.

Fallon?

There was no answer. Then a horrible thought struck him, and he called out, "Bergen? Bee?" a few times. He used his legs to stretch and feel around in the back of the van, coming up against all four sides and feeling assured that his daughter was not tied up with him. He smiled grimly. Fallon had saved her; Fallon most likely had her right now. There was that at least, thank God.

He finally succeeded in working himself to a sitting position. His eyes were adjusting to the tiny amount of light that filtered in through pinprick holes in the material that covered the windows. What in the hell was going on?

Sometime later, the van started bouncing down a rough road. Eventually it pulled to a stop, and he heard doors slamming up front. His body grew tense as he wondered what would happen now. Was this how it had been for Peter? For Cyn?

CHAPTER FORTY-ONE

It was just past noon when Fallon and Bergen arrived in Gray and entered the Lowes' house. Selah descended upon them. "Bergen, thank goodness you're here! I could really use your help."

Bergen looked up politely, her grey eyes still reddened from crying.

"I've been in a rush getting things done, and Indio needs his lunch. Just simple ham and cheese on that fresh wheat bread. Could you do that for me?"

"Sure, Miss Selah." The girl's voice was just above a whisper and hoarse with sorrow.

"Thank you, angel. And one glass of chocolate milk, not two; don't let him tell you differently."

"Yes, ma'am."

Selah placed a hand on Bergen's shoulder. "Baby, I'm so sorry about your daddy. We're going to do everything we can."

Bergen blinked away tears and hugged Selah. Then she entered the kitchen, where Indio greeted her happily. She began getting out the things to fix his sandwich, though she stood where she could see Fallon through the doorway.

Selah turned to Fallon and took her hands. "Love, you need to breathe."

Fallon shook her head. She looked fine, but in her eyes, Selah could see that she was shattering slowly. "I failed him," she whispered, her voice barely a breath as she watched Bergen. "I failed him just like I failed Luca, and Simon, even my parents."

"No." Selah squeezed her hands. "No. Look." She gestured at the kitchen. "Look in there at who you saved. They were going to take that little girl, or worse. You saved her. Bret will never be able to thank you enough."

Fallon closed her eyes. "No. He won't."

Selah's eyes burned furiously. "Don't give up on him."

Fallon glared. "I will never give up on him. But I don't know what to do. And I keep feeling like I should."

A few minutes later, when Selah went back into the kitchen to check on things, Fallon faded away and disappeared. Bergen realized she was gone but threw on a brave face in front of Selah and pretended not to care.

Fallon climbed the painted grey stairs to the second floor, which held only Selah's art studio through a door to the right and a small guest room through the door to the left. Entering the latter, she shut the door behind herself, sinking to the floor and leaning back against the wall.

Her body was on fire with pain and guilt. She stared blindly at the green and white quilt on the bed and rubbed the silver bee between her thumb and forefinger until they felt bruised. Until this moment she had been so focused on Bergen, on keeping her safe and getting her away from the media and assuring her that somehow all would be well, she hadn't had time to stop and examine what was happening. Her feelings of failure were crushing, despite Selah's point that she had saved Bergen. She'd had months of dramatic warnings, and for what? In the end, it had done nothing for Bret but save his broken-hearted daughter. She had tried so hard. Her ability, her mind, had deceived her, let her down. As it always did when it mattered most.

She would do everything she could to find him. She would dive into the areas of her mind she'd always known were dangerous, experiment with powers she'd only glimpsed in herself before. Even if it killed her, at least she'd know she'd tried with everything she had.

She closed her eyes and leaned her head back against the wall. First, she would need to organize the ground troops. Put Selah in charge of Bergen until Lisbeth arrived. Send Indio temporarily out of harm's way. Pull Simon in, if he was willing. She would send Tayce to the airport to pick up Lisbeth; she'd asked Lisbeth not to bring Leo along, and fortunately she'd agreed.

There was a soft knocking on the door. She reached out with her mind and touched Bergen, standing there sadly, alone, all the rainbows and glitter shaded and muted with grey.

"Come in," she called, and the child came in and crawled onto her lap, hiding her face in Fallon's hair.

CHAPTER FORTY-TWO

They pulled a cloth sack over Bret's head as soon as the van doors flew open. He felt sunlight and dry, cooler air flooding in. Then they—he counted two masked men—led him roughly over dusty, uneven ground till they stopped to open a door. He was forced down a few steps, then across a level floor, where another door was opened. He was shoved inside, the sack pulled from his head at the last second as the door slammed shut behind him.

Bret found himself in a small, bare room, and he saw, to his surprise, a disheveled Jack Lane sitting with his back against the brick wall, his hands also tied behind him. Clad in jeans and a long-sleeved black shirt, Jack was barefoot and had a nasty black eye. He was staring at a clear glass mason jar that sat on the ground near his feet. He gave a nasty bark of laughter at Bret's arrival, then his eyes strayed back to the jar.

Bret came closer, peering at the jar. It was filled with a variety of black leather and silver: a man's watch, a cuff bracelet, a couple of rings, a necklace. "What's going on? What's that?"

"What does it look like?" Jack's voice was cold and low. Unnatural. Bret waited tensely, and finally Jack looked up. "It's Peter's. I recognize the watch and the necklaces. I'm pretty sure the rest of it's his, too." There was a catch in his voice, and he looked away.

Bret sat down heavily on the cement floor, his legs unable to hold him, his mind running wild with the implications. "Peter...my God," he breathed. "How long have you been here?"

"About a half hour. More or less." Jack shifted around. "There's a knife in my right front pocket. Can't believe they left it with me. If you can get it out, we can cut ourselves free."

Bret moved over to Jack, who got up on his knees and stayed still while Bret fished around awkwardly in the pocket.

"Easy with those fingers, cowboy," Jack drawled. "We haven't been locked up together that long, yet."

Bret hissed something ugly at him. Finally, he had the knife, but cutting Jack free with his own arms tied behind him proved to be time-consuming and exhausting, and Jack cursed as he suffered more than a few cuts whenever the knife slipped. Eventually Bret succeeded, however, and with his hands free, Jack worked much more quickly. When they were both cut loose, Bret lifted his arms over his head, stretching his entire aching body.

"I'm blaming this whole thing on your effing girlfriend," Jack told him, returning the knife to his pocket and trying the locked door just for the hell of it. He eyed the single bulb that dimly lit the windowless room of brick walls. There was a vent in the ceiling, which he hoped was bringing in fresh air.

"Yeah, Fallon's behind this whole thing," Bret agreed bitterly. Had his captors realized the extra degree of torture they were dealing him by locking him in a room with Jack?

"Deny away. She's no good. There's something evil about her. Black magic or some shit. Have you seen this?" He displayed his elbow to Bret, who reluctantly looked at it. There was a scar from a burn. If you knew what you were looking for, you could tell the lines of the scar were in the shape of a flame-surrounded eye. Even though she'd told him about it, it still seemed unreal to see it.

"I don't know what to tell you, man. Maybe next time you'll think before you try to drown her."

"She was wrestling me like a wildcat in heat," Jack countered. "I can't tell you exactly what occurred."

"I know you're angry because she rejected you, but there was always the chance that you'd run into a woman with good taste."

Jack smiled, sinking down and resting his arms on his knees. "Are you sure she rejected me?"

Bret sat down against the opposite wall and closed his eyes. He was too tired, too traumatized, to be angry at Jack. The incident with Fallon in the hot tub seemed a lifetime ago at this point. When he finally looked around again, he saw that Jack was staring soberly at the mason jar, which seemed to be especially bothering him.

"What the hell is all this, man?" Jack tucked his black hair behind his ears. "I mean, seriously, what does anyone have to gain by snatching us off the street? Unless it's some sick, twisted fan of ours. But that doesn't sound like anything in reality." He tentatively touched his blackened eye.

Bret shook his head. "I have no idea what's going on. But I think they meant to take us that night in Vegas." He recounted the whole story from that fateful night, telling Jack the truth this time, including the telepathy. "Fallon got us back inside the club, out of the way, so they took Peter and Cyn instead. Maybe the guys who took them didn't even know who they were taking, they'd just been told, you know, to take who was on the sidewalk. But you and I went in at the last second." He glanced around. "I keep waiting for Tayce to show up in here."

"It sounds fucked up."

"What else is there, Jack?"

"So, they killed the woman, but they kept Peter."

"Peter's probably dead, too," Bret reasoned. "I mean, the jar full of his personal effects kind of alludes to that. Like it was put here as a warning to us."

Jack looked exasperated. "So now they're going to kill us? For what?"

"I don't know." Bret closed his eyes again.

"So, where's your psychic girlfriend now, huh? Why didn't she see this one coming?"

"She did. She's seen it coming for months. She just couldn't tell what, when, or where."

"Not very handy to have around."

"She saved Bergen from this. That's enough for me."

Jack cocked his head to one side alertly.

"Bergen was with me when they came," Bret explained. "Fallon wasn't with us, but she could sense they were coming. She contacted me telepathically and told me to hide Bergen. It's all I had time to do before they were there. God knows what they would have done with Bee if she'd been right there with me." His voice was rough with emotion.

Jack rubbed the scar on his elbow. "That telepathy, man, that just sounds utterly ridiculous to me. But a lot about her seems impossible. I mean, she burned me with a goddamn tattoo." He sat cross-legged and leaned forward a little. "Can you talk to her now? Do you think she can find us? Before it's...da-dum-dum... too late?"

Bret rubbed his hands over his face. "I haven't been able to talk to her since I was taken. I was unconscious immediately, and then when I woke up...nothing. She'll find us, yes. I feel certain. 'Before it's too late' kind of depends on whoever took us, I think."

"Why can you all of a sudden not talk to her?" Jack asked suspiciously.

"Distance has been the only cause that we can find. When I'm in California and she's in Texas, we can't talk. When we're closer, in the same state at least, then yes, we can."

"Where were you when they took you?"

"Austin, at her house there. Where were you?"

"Houston. At a hotel. I went out for ice, and that's the last thing I remember."

"So, I would think we must be out of Texas," Bret reasoned.

"Not close to Fallon, apparently, wherever we are," Jack noted.

"No." Bret bent his head, resting it on his knees. "Apparently not. Which makes me wonder, where the hell are we?"

CHAPTER FORTY-THREE

B y the evening of the following day, the team had been assembled and updated. Indio had been ferried off to stay with his Aunt Tallie in Dallas. Bergen had displayed much stubbornness by refusing to accompany Tayce to the airport that morning to collect Lisbeth. She would not leave Fallon.

Lisbeth and Bergen were going to stay at the garage apartment with Fallon, who didn't want Selah imposed upon any more than she already would be. Tayce was staying at the farm with Katrine and Paul. Dangerous Eye had temporarily postponed their tour rehearsals, though Fallon knew Paul's patience would be tested, that he was not fully understanding of why Tayce felt he had to involve himself in this situation, surprising and tragic though it was. Katrine had called both Fallon and Selah, offering any assistance they might need, including food.

At his Seattle apartment, Simon was fully looking into the disappearances, including those of Peter and Cyn. As soon as Fallon had called to tell him about Bret and Jack, and he heard the muted hysterical sorrow in her voice, he set aside everything he was working on to dive fully into the investigation. He, and Fallon, and Selah slipped seamlessly back into their old roles as the three remaining players from a close-knit secret team, with Fallon and Simon doing all the talking while Selah listened, breaking in here and there to pass judgement.

Tour dates for Bret's and Jack's bands were being cancelled slowly. There was still the chance they had wandered off in a drug-fueled stupor and would resurface, ready to rock and roll, though no one who knew them believed that.

Bret's friend and security guard Seth had gotten in touch with Fallon and gruffly begged her to update him if she happened to learn anything new. Travis, catching a flight back to L.A. to wait in limbo, also contacted her frequently by text, quizzing her on what she knew. He was unable to understand how someone could have broken into a house and kidnapped Bret James, of all people, with any degree of success.

"Bret's such a badass," one text read. "In my mind, he would never have allowed this to happen, especially with Bergen there with him."

Fallon didn't know how to respond to Travis, and kept her answers vague and succinct.

At the Lowes' home, where everyone congregated each day, Fallon spent hours out in the backyard alone with the bee necklace, trying to use it as a link to show her where Bret was. Selah watched her with silent worry.

Lisbeth and Tayce devoted hours to calling and texting people they knew in California, people from Bret's past and present. They questioned and quizzed them, asking them to call with any information.

Selah concentrated on Bergen, taking her into her art studio and setting her up with paint and canvas, showing her little techniques, letting her paint what she wanted. She also frequently took her outside and enlisted her in garden-related activities, such as deadheading the roses and watering various plants.

When Fallon wasn't outside, she was texting Simon and looking at the news online. For the first couple of days, the news stories were fairly small. They mentioned only that the two singers had gone missing on the same night in different Texas cities. That the police were currently investigating, looking for a connection between Jack's and Bret's disappearances.

Then Peter Stillson's remains were found in the Nevada desert just off a main highway. He had been dead for a long while, but his body had been deposited in this final resting place quite recently. Within hours of the discovery, the FBI joined the investigation, and the news exploded with the headlines:

"Rockstar Mystery: Popular Hard Rock Singers Bret James and Jack Lane Vanish Without a Trace in Texas.

Body of Lane's Bassist, Missing for Two Years, Located in Nevada Desert. Foul Play Suspected. Disappearances Connected?"

Sweet photos of Bret and Bergen were shown to add an extra emotional punch. Old, alleged girlfriends of both men surfaced to offer their personal take on the disappearances and to sob openly for anyone who would film them. Conspiracy theorists flooded social media with their take. Fallon's throat was tight, her heart beating distantly, as she scanned the articles.

Lisbeth, Bret's and Jack's families, and Bret's old BlueStar bandmates were declining to be interviewed. But the president of Red Racer Records, Rylan Thomas, consented to every interview, expressing his grief, horror, and shock, as well as his prayerfulness that Bret and Jack would be recovered.

Fallon watched as Bret's just-released album soared from number sixty-eight, close to where it had debuted, to number three on the charts. Briefly, but it peaked there all the same. Jack had released no albums in years, but his old work was experiencing a sudden resurgence. When she checked, she saw that none of Jack's releases were on Red Racer Records. That was odd. She frowned in remembrance. Hadn't Bret said that Jack stopped by that one night to discuss the tour "their" record label wanted to send them out on? And Rylan Thomas was certainly emphasizing his distress over both Bret's *and* Jack's absences.

Sitting on the couch alone in Selah's living room with her laptop, Fallon went to Jack's personal website and began scanning the news updates. The most recent posts promised a new album "soon." She scanned further back, then she stopped. More than three years ago, Jack had signed with Red Racer Records. From that point on he had recorded various new songs here and there. She bit the end of her pen. The album had not yet been released, but Red Racer Records currently possessed something valuable: at least a double-album's-worth of previously-unreleased material by the mysteriously missing Jack Lane.

She called Lisbeth into the room. "Who profits most from Bret's album sales?"

Lisbeth considered. "Well, his record label was really jerking him around in recent years. Things were getting ugly.

He was getting ready to sue them to get out of his contract to try and recoup lost money he thinks he should have earned that he never saw. So, to answer your question: his record company gets most of it, but he was talking to his attorney, preparing a lawsuit."

Fallon tapped her pen on her knee. "He didn't tell me anything about that. I mean, he said he was unhappy with them, but he didn't go into it."

"He didn't like to talk about it; the situation made him angry. He was pretty confident he could handle it. You have enough going on; I can see where he wouldn't have wanted to even mention it to you."

Fallon was annoyed by the idea she had too much going on to be bothered.

"I only know about it," Lisbeth added quickly, "because he had some massively explosive phone calls with Rylan for several months. I just happened to be in the house somewhere, usually, and I asked him about it later."

When Lisbeth had departed, Fallon was thoughtful. A contract-breaking lawsuit would be unpleasant for sure, but it wasn't something that justified elaborate kidnappings and murder. Not for artists of Jack's and Bret's caliber, anyway. Jack and Bret were popular mostly among their old, die-hard fans who had loved them for years. Though she supposed they picked up their fair share of new fans just through media exposure and concert appearances, as evidenced by the younger people in the crowds at Bret's shows. The two men were both still moneymakers, yes, but their days of blazing glory were past. They were not huge cash cows for their label.

Until now, she thought, eyeing the headlines. And especially if the label had them under contracts that were unfairly weighted in the label's favor. Still, she hesitated. They were not enormous superstars. Their story would likely fade in the next few days, replaced with whatever trending topics next captured public fascination. The problem was that she had no other ideas to explain what was going on.

She sent a text to Simon: "Investigate Red Racer Records. Who they're owned by, what else the owners own, what they're involved in."

He returned a text: "I'm on it."

* * * * * * * *

The next morning Fallon took Tayce and Bergen into Dutton with her, in part so that she could use her own money to purchase groceries to replenish Selah's supplies, and also to get Bergen out of the house. Lisbeth was spending hours on her phone, trying to run Daisy long-distance as well as continuing to keep her ear to the ground in L.A. for any potential gossip regarding Bret and Jack that might be important.

As soon as they got to the larger town, Bergen spotted the brightly-colored Sunny Girl Bakery. "That place looks fun. Can we go there?"

Tayce was surprised to see Fallon actually clench her jaw, though she quickly released it. "Sure, honey. It will be our last stop."

Doing something as normal as grocery shopping put Bergen in better spirits, and Tayce and Fallon were content to let the girl take the list and lead the way. When they were done, they loaded their purchases into Fallon's Dart and then headed across town to the bakery.

In the parking lot, Fallon hesitated. "Tayce, why don't you and she go in? I'll just wait out here."

Tayce paused to frown at her. "What's wrong?"

Fallon was rubbing her fingers together nervously. She didn't know what Sunny would say, if she would blurt out something awful in front of Bergen or keep her mouth shut.

Bergen stood beside Tayce and stared longingly at Fallon, who soon caved and got out of the car. "Alright, but let's make this quick. There's cold stuff in the trunk."

Inside, Bergen ran enthusiastically from case to case, surveying the wares, while Tayce held back by Fallon, his attention to her bordering on protective. Bluesy seventies rock played through the speakers, and the bakery smelled heavenly.

Sunny was the only one behind the counter. Her long shiny black hair was down, and she was wearing jeans and a dark blue tank top. She looked up and smiled when she saw Fallon, but then the smile faded a little. She looked over at Bergen, and Sunny's bright eyes grew less bright, and what remained of her smile all but disappeared.

"Hello, my Fallon friend," she greeted gently. "What can I get for you today?"

Fallon approached the counter. "Two loaves of honey-wheat bread." She nodded at Bergen. "And whatever she wants. That's Bergen, and this is Tayce. Guys, this is Sunny."

Sunny nodded briefly at Tayce, and then slid down to where Bergen was staring hard at a case of cupcakes. "You look like a girl who loves strawberries, am I right?" she asked.

Bergen looked interested. "I love strawberries."

Sunny nodded and pointed heavenward with her index finger. "I knew this. Wait right there." She headed around a corner out of sight, then returned with a silver pan of puffy-looking pastries. "Filled with fresh strawberries and sweet cream. I guarantee you'll love these. Would you like some?"

Bergen's face was alight. "I'd love some. But..." She looked over at Fallon.

"Get whatever you want," Fallon instructed.

Sunny set down the tray and retrieved an empty box. "A dozen, on the house, because you are without a doubt my sweetest customer of the entire week."

Bergen's eyes widened. "Wow! Thank you so much."

Fallon smiled faintly as the proprietress returned to her at the counter, and she paid for the two loaves of bread. "Thank you, Sunshine," she murmured.

Sunny held out her hand, and Fallon took it. "Be well, my felicitous friend," she said softly, and Fallon nodded.

"And goodbye, Miss Bergen," Sunny sang out. "I hope you come back to my shop one day soon!"

"Me, too!" Bergen waved goodbye as Tayce held the door for her.

"She was really cool," observed Bergen in the car.

"I didn't know you had any other friends," mentioned Tayce, and Fallon threw a glance at him. "Never mind."

"She's an acquaintance. We don't hang out."

"So, you can't get me her number?" He faked disappointment.

She waved him off. "You've got enough to juggle," she observed, and he laughed.

Sunny's special strawberry puffs were a hit back at Command Central, and even Lisbeth consumed an entire pastry—she normally shunned sweets in an effort to maintain her lithe figure.

"Mom's so boring about things like that," Bergen quietly told Fallon with a roll of her eyes, and Fallon smiled.

It was just after lunch when Diego called Fallon's cell. "FBI is here to talk to you, *mija*. Tracked you as far as Solu and hit a wall." He sounded mildly amused.

"Send them over to Selah's house," she directed him. "I'm sorry they bothered you."

"It's a 'him,' not a 'them,' Not a problem at all, Fallon. I will send him."

When she hung up, she looked around at everyone—they all appeared to be in a slight stupor of confectionary happiness after the strawberry puffs. She reluctantly threw a dark cloud upon them. "An FBI agent is on his way over to talk to me."

Selah stood. "Talk to him in the living room. The rest of us will be out on the back patio coming down off our sugar high."

A panicked Bergen ran to Fallon's side and hugged her tightly. "You aren't going to leave with him, are you?"

"No, sweetie, no. He just wants to talk. I'll be here." She placed her hands on each side of Bergen's face and gazed at her. Everyone watched as, under Fallon's touch, Bergen's pinched, frightened features relaxed into a face of complete calm. Without another word the child took her mother's hand and led her cheerfully towards the backdoor to head outside. Fallon turned from everyone else's stares and headed to the front porch to wait.

A few minutes later she rose from the swing and met the agent at the front steps. He flashed his ID. "Detective Josh Ashton. I'm looking for Fallon Quinn."

"That's me."

He looked younger than she had expected, though she supposed he was in his mid-thirties, and his dark hair was cut short. He was serious and alert, with a professional air. "You weren't easy to find. I have some questions for you."

"Let's sit in here." She led him inside to the living room, where he sat on the couch and she curled up in a chair. They dealt with some initial small talk about the investigation and his need to ask her some questions, and then he began.

"You were with Mr. James when he went missing?"

"You have the police report, surely, which tells you otherwise."

"I do have it; I'm just double-checking facts and following up."

"Then you know that Bret and his daughter were staying at my house in Austin with me for a few days before we went back to Bret's tour. I had left them alone at the house to run errands. When I got back, I found the house empty, or so I thought. But then my dog and I found Bergen hiding in the fireplace."

"Bergen is here with you now, is that correct?"

"It is."

"Before I talk to her, I wanted to go over some of the things she said. She said she heard something that scared her, and so she hid in the fireplace. Is that what she told you?"

Fallon nodded. "Yes. When we first got to the house, I showed her the fireplace, how there are metal rungs in the wall and that you can literally climb up inside it. She thought that was cool."

"Did she say what she heard that made her hide?"

"No." Fallon shook her head. "She doesn't know. And the trauma, I think, of losing her father, is making it hard for her to really think about. She just knows that she heard something that scared her, and she hid. Shortly after that she heard at least two men going through the house calling for her."

"They knew her name?"

"Yes. They were calling specifically for her."

"Did she recognize their voices?"

"No. They were strangers to her as far as she could tell."

"She saw nothing?"

"Absolutely nothing. She was up the chimney and couldn't see any of the room."

He rustled his notes. "She remained hidden until you arrived?"

"She said they left just before I got home, but she wasn't going to leave the fireplace till she heard either Bret's or my voice. When she heard me calling her, she came out immediately. She was terrified."

"I imagine so. Miss Quinn, how long have you known Mr. James?"

"Call me Fallon. Less than a year. We met at the restaurant you were just at, when I was at work one night, and he was there with friends."

"Local friends?"

"Paul and Katrine Crist; they live just outside of town at Star Fall Farm. Also, Tayce Williams was there. Bret has known Paul and Tayce for twenty or thirty years."

Detective Ashton looked up. "Paul and Tayce, you mean from Dangerous Eye?"

She smiled faintly at his musical knowledge. "That's them. Tayce is on the back patio, incidentally. In case you're interested."

"I'll talk to him, yes. You and Mr. James are romantically involved?"

"Yes."

"His ex-wife is currently in Italy?"

"Not his ex-wife, they were never married. She's Bergen's mother. She was on her honeymoon in Italy, yes, but right now she's also on the back patio. She came back as soon as she could when she heard."

He nodded. "Actually, our records show she is his ex-wife." He glanced at her. "Maybe you can get to the bottom of that later on your own."

Fallon's expression didn't change.

Detective Ashton continued. "While you've been involved with Mr. James, have you witnessed any drug use?"

"None."

"Alcohol?"

"Social drinking, nothing extreme."

"Had Mr. James received any threatening correspondence or interactions on social media, anything of that nature that you know of?"

"Nothing. And he would have told me." She decided to gamble. "Have you ever worked with people who claim to be psychics?"

His forehead wrinkled. "A few times. Reluctantly. And not with any success. Why do you ask?" He was looking at her curiously.

She shook her head and looked away. "No reason."

CHAPTER FORTY-THREE

He pressed on. "How many days had the three of you been in Austin?"

"Three or four, I'd have to look at a calendar."

"Who did you interact with while you were there?"

"We went out to eat a few times, saw a few sights. There was nothing out of the ordinary. I wouldn't think it was anyone specific to Austin, with the way Jack Lane was taken, too."

"Taken?"

"Jack must have been taken. If only because I know Bret was taken. Bret would never have left his daughter of his own accord; I promise you."

"I learned you have a rather interesting history associated with Austin."

She clenched and unclenched her fists. "You don't have to tell me that. I already know."

He was looking at his notes. "Your parents, murdered in an alleged carjacking when you were..."

"Seven."

"Seven, yes. An uncommon crime for the area at the time, I might add. Then nine years later your brother committed suicide along the greenbelt."

She pressed her lips together. He was watching her closely.

"Then less than three years later you disappear without a trace for seven weeks, only to reappear unharmed and with no apparent memory as to where you were."

She leaned back. "You've got it."

He fiddled with his pen, looking out a window. "You still have no memory of that time, no idea as to where you were?"

"I do not."

317

"At the time of your brother's death, you insisted rather vehemently that he had actually been murdered."

"Yes."

"Do you still feel that way?"

"I do."

"Since then," he eyed his notes again, "you seem to have lived far below the radar. I don't even have a legitimate physical address for you besides the house in Austin."

She could not read him. When she tried, it was a blur... static on the line. Like something was blocking her. She'd never experienced it before, though it reminded her strongly of her inability to read Katrine Crist. All she could gather was that she was not what he had expected, after reading the file. She continued to clench and unclench her fists. She was not used to the disadvantage of being unable to read someone, and it filled her with mistrust.

Nevertheless, she had to try, because she could see they were getting nowhere. "Detective, let me tell you something. I would go about this in a different way, give you more time to get to know me, except that four days have already passed, and I fear for Bret and Jack's lives. Every day that goes by, I feel there's a greater likelihood of them ending up like Peter Stillson."

"And why would you feel that their disappearances are connected to Mr. Stillson's?"

She leaned forward. "This is where you have to trust me."

He watched her.

"The night that Peter and Cyn disappeared, Bret, Jack and Tayce were also out there on the sidewalk, all of them together, as you must know if you've looked at the report. What it does not mention is that I was there, too, but at a distance. That night I was seen only by Bret and, later in the club, by Jack. I had never met any of them before. I've gotten premonitions my entire life. That night I had a premonition of Bret's death, that's what led me to that side street. When I saw them all there, and I realized it had something to do with the blue van I'd seen parked around the corner. I convinced Bret to take Jack and Tayce back in the club immediately. They went in. I followed them to make sure they didn't get curious and try to come back out. I didn't know what was going to happen; I just knew they needed to stay inside. When they finally went back out, Peter and Cyn were gone. I was gone, too. My job was done. There was no more danger in my mind. I went home.

"Eighteen months later, Bret was in Solu the night I was working. It was an astounding coincidence. We recognized each other; we fell for each other. I soon started having horrible visions of his demise, but I couldn't tell what, when, or where. The visions continued—we knew something was wrong. My last vision happened that evening when I was on my way home to them. When I got there, I was too late." She looked away, forcing back tears. When she looked back at Detective Ashton, he was frowning at her. She shrugged. "I know it sounds like fiction. But I wanted you to know. I wanted that information to at least be in your subconscious as you pursue this case. My feeling is it was the same as the night in Vegas. Bret and Jack were meant to be taken that night. The same people who took Peter have now taken them."

"And your prime suspect in this complicated crime-without-any-obvious-motive would be?"

"I'm working on it."

Josh got to his feet. "Well, Fallon, keep working on it if you'd like, and if you learn anything, here's my cell number. Call me any time." His tone of voice did not suggest anything.

She accepted his card. "I think they're going to die."

He considered her a moment. "We're on it; all my available men are on it."

"They're together. They're not well, but they're alive."

He paused, hooked by her non-hysterical voice. "If you think of anything, call me. Day or night. Now I'd like to speak with Mr. Williams."

"I'll get him for you."

Composing herself, she went out to the patio where everyone was pretending to seem at ease for the sake of Bergen, whose calm was beginning to wear away. "Tayce, he wants to talk to you. I told him everything about Vegas." As he passed by her, she added, "Minus the telepathy."

"Gotcha."

She sat down in a chair and Bergen immediately crawled onto her lap.

After a moment, Lisbeth realized Fallon was staring hard at her. Her eyes widened. "What is it? Fallon?"

"How long were you guys married?" Fallon asked.

Across the patio, Selah pursed her lips and looked away.

Lisbeth frowned. "Leo and I just..." A light went on in her head. "Ohhh. He never mentioned it." She shook her head. "Fallon, it was nothing. Years before we had Bergen, we got married one night in Vegas after a wild night. It was meaningless. He and I were never going to get married. We had it annulled two or three weeks later, basically as soon as we could find the time. If he never told you, it's because it was nothing. Just part of the craziness of the night."

"Any more surprises waiting for me?"

Lisbeth smiled. "None that I know of. There may well be some, but they'll likely be as innocuous as this one. Bret doesn't have a lot of skeletons in the closet these days."

After interviewing Tayce, Detective Ashton also spoke to Bergen and Lisbeth briefly before bidding them all good afternoon and leaving. Everyone was moody after he was gone. Selah went into the kitchen and began making chicken salad, and Lisbeth joined her. Bergen, as she had done since they'd arrived days ago, followed Fallon around like a shadow.

Tayce was especially subdued for the rest of the afternoon. When it was time for everyone to leave for the evening, he paused on the front porch with Fallon as Lisbeth and Bergen went out to Fallon's car. She looked up at him intently, waiting.

"I'm the last one left," he said. "It occurred to me today, when that detective was talking to me, of the people on the sidewalk that night in Vegas, everyone is gone now but me. And you. What a weird thing that is." He shook his head. "I can't even make sense of it."

She touched his hand. "Don't feel guilty because you're still here. Don't do that. Think about your daughters and be glad."

He rubbed his goatee. "I hate that I can't hide anything from you and your spooky mind. But sometimes, it's just the right thing."

She squeezed his hand and then turned and went out to her car.

As Lisbeth and Bergen were in the bathroom that night, bathing and getting ready for bed, Fallon's phone rang.

"What have you got, Simon?"

"Looks like Red Racer Records was started about twelve years ago. They've remained fairly small, handling mostly indie artists and the like, though they have a few hard rockers, like Bret and Jack. Bret's got five albums out on their label, all of which are seeing a serious spike in sales. The CEO of Racer is one Rylan Thomas. He also seems to handle a lot of the dealings with artists; you said he was Bret's rep there, right? The owner of Racer is a company named Maelstrom Black LLC. President of Maelstrom Black LLC would be, again, one Rylan Thomas. Maelstrom Black owns a number of small companies in various industries, none of them doing remarkably well financially. Looks like most of them were purchased in a downturn with hopes of the market turning around, but no such luck. A few of the companies are badly in debt. I even checked some underground rumblings for you. Rylan has a bit of a gambling habit, and may or may not be in debt to some unpleasant people overseas because of said habit. Does any of this help?"

"With my motive, yes. Thank you, Simon, for doing this."

"I've always been Research Guy. For better or worse."

"Dig up anything else you can, focusing on Rylan."

"You got it."

"As far as locations where Bret and Jack might be held...I guess there are quite a lot?"

"Yes, Lucky, quite. We're talking in the hundreds of actual property sites in the U.S. and overseas. If Rylan is your guy and had the nerve to hide them at a place he owns—which, judging by his ego, he probably has—there's not a lot of ways to narrow it down. And, incidentally, he owns nothing in Texas."

Simon emailed her everything he'd found, and early the next morning she called Detective Ashton and told him her theory about Rylan Thomas.

"I'll buy it as interesting," he admitted. "Doesn't seem like a situation that would escalate to murder."

"I agree with you on that. I'm going to send you everything I've got, anyway. The email's going right now."

"Everything you've 'got?'"

"I have a specialized researcher on retainer."

Silence.

"Let me know if you need anything else, Detective."

He called her back at the end of the day. "The information you've got here is without a doubt good information, and I'm curious as to how you got your hands on most of it, but we have no reason to arrest Mr. Thomas at this point. It's only speculation. We've interviewed him three times, but his answers are flawless. He has an airtight alibi for last Friday night as well as for the night in Las Vegas. We have no evidence that would justify going any further. It's all speculation."

Fallon rubbed her forehead, frustrated.

"Call me if you find anything out," he added, acknowledging her disappointment.

CHAPTER FORTY-FOUR

LUCA

When Luca came to his favorite place along the greenbelt, he slowed from his run and stood a while looking down at the creek, catching his breath. Fallon usually ran with him—it was so odd to be running without her—but she'd been acting strangely that evening after finding something in one of her old books. She hadn't told him what it was, and she'd blocked him from her mind, but he'd seen her clutching *To Kill a Mockingbird*, her gaze a million miles away. He knew her well enough to know it had something to do with Jacob, for whom she still silently grieved.

When he'd come into the kitchen carrying his running shoes, she'd looked up from where she sat at the table with Selah and shaken her head.

"I don't feel good," she murmured. She got up to hug him and he kissed her forehead, their usual ritual whenever they parted.

He met Selah's glance, and she nodded slightly, letting him know she would stay with Fallon till he got back.

Now as he stared at the water, the pale moon rising in the

darkening sky, he felt overwhelmingly the jitters of anticipation. What was coming? Never had his vision been so cloudy. He sank down to sit a while, wondering if the feelings would ebb away.

It was a few minutes later that he heard a noise behind him, at the same time sensing that someone was approaching. Someone familiar. He turned his head in surprise, a smile coming to his lips. But then there was an explosion of noise and light, and his thoughts slipped away into nothingness.

CHAPTER FORTY-FIVE

J ack's hands were shaking and sweat was beading on his
forehead and upper lip, even though the room they were in
was probably underground and relatively cool.

"Hey, man, are you okay?" Bret asked.

"Yeah." Jack nodded. Then he laughed cruelly. "I need a
drink. That's all. Don't think that's going to happen."

Bret realized then that Jack, always a borderline alcoholic,
was suffering withdrawal as well as missing nicotine. He needed
to stay hydrated, but that was not so easily done. Someone in
a mask had brought them water the day before—had it been
a full day? Bret had no idea—in a semi-clean jug, and they'd
thirstily finished it off. But he was fairly certain no one was
going to open the door and toss Jack a bottle of whiskey to
calm his tremors.

They'd had nothing to eat since they'd arrived. Weak from
hunger, Bret's head was pounding and his stomach cramping,
and he knew Jack felt far worse. Sometimes he thought his
vision was blurring a little, and he no longer felt like standing

up. How long could a person go without eating? He'd read it once, but he couldn't remember. Wasn't it a month? Well, he was going to go as long as it took. The water was the more critical issue. They had been careless with it at first, guzzling it to try to ease their hunger pangs, both of them physically sick afterwards. He had to remember that the next time they brought water—and please, God, there had to be a next time—he would have to ration it out.

"How do you know for sure?"

With a confused frown Bret looked over at Jack, who was lying on his back staring at him. They had been having a hard time following each other's trains of thought, their minds muddled with the stress of confinement, thirst and feared starvation. "How do I know what?"

"That they didn't get Bergen."

A wall of ice rose up inside Bret, then shattered into diamond shards that drove painfully into his heart, his veins. He looked away from Jack. He thought that if he looked at him, he might kill him. Because Jack was right. He'd been unconscious when they took him. How did he know what had happened in that house after that? Just because she hadn't been in the van and wasn't sitting here in this godforsaken room with them didn't mean anything.

"Because that's what I have to believe," he snapped coldly. "If you had a child, you would understand what I mean."

After a moment, Jack turned away.

CHAPTER FORTY-SIX

FALLON

Fallon lay in the backyard under the oak trees and stared at the stars. She was sure she cut a tragic figure there on the lawn, and she laughed bitterly. Four months had passed since Luca's murder. She had not paid attention to a single premonition in that time. She had let go of everything Jacob had taught her. She didn't care about any of it.

Selah still showed up loyally and showed her love, but Fallon didn't want it, didn't want her. Jacob had been right about one thing: love was weakness. Well, no more worries there, because there was no love left in her. Jacob was gone, and no one cared that someone had shot her brother in the head. As much as she hated the idea that it looked like she was letting the loss of the men in her life define her, such seemed to be the case.

A whining nearby startled her, and she turned over onto her stomach to look around. Azul was laying on his belly, watching her sadly.

"Leave me alone," Fallon hissed cruelly. "Go wherever they went; it seems popular."

Azul rested his chin between his paws and continued to stare.

"Go!" she ordered him fiercely, even as tears streamed down her cheeks. "Go away from me; I don't want to see you!" She rested her face on her arm as sobs wracked her body. She did not know how to be alone. They had always been there, Jacob and Luca. Her lessons with Jacob had been so invaluable—he'd been gone three years, and she still couldn't understand why. And Luca—sometimes she imagined, darkly, that maybe he had put a bullet in his own brain. To escape her.

A rough tongue was licking her face, licking away the tears. She buried her face in his black fur and wished for death.

CHAPTER FORTY-SEVEN

As the days passed, the shadows in Fallon's mind grew darker every time she tried to sense Bret. He was slipping away. He was dying somewhere. Her helplessness was agony.

"I feel like I'm being punished," she told only Azul, "though I don't know why or by whom."

Every day she sat among the roses in Selah's backyard with the bee necklace and concentrated with all her might. Sometimes she experimentally touched one of the colored lines in her mind that she'd never used before. Just this act of touching the lines sent little shocks of power through her, leaving her weak and shaky. Mentally she was exhausted, pushing herself too hard, her mind unused to this continuous assault, but she couldn't let herself stop. Frequently she'd concentrate on "seeing" where the guys were, hoping one of the lines in her head would give her the ability to see their location and status, but nothing ever came of it.

Then Friday after lunch, she finally saw them, Jack and Bret, laying on the floor in a room lit with a single dusty bulb. The image flickered briefly like a candle, then went out. Devastated, she tried for the rest of the afternoon to get the image back, like an addict desperate for another hit, but it never returned.

Tayce finally went out to her, when she had stayed longer than usual, and sat with her, not saying a word. After a long while, she turned her head in his direction, though she kept her eyes averted. She looked so tortured, so tired, he touched her arm in concern.

"Help me up, Tayce. Let's go upstairs; I think if I do something, some stretching, I'll feel better. I'll be able to face everyone else."

He took both her arms as she crawled weakly to her feet, supporting her as she swayed and closed her eyes against a wave of dizziness. "Are you okay?" he asked, and she laughed softly and didn't answer.

In the kitchen, he made her drink a glass of water, for the temperatures outside were high, and she complied. Then they headed upstairs together. Entering the guest room, they shut the door and Tayce sprawled on the bed while Fallon sank to the floor and began forcing herself into various yoga positions, hoping to revive her weakened body. Through the room's two large windows, they could see lightning streak across a newly darkening sky, and Fallon was reminded of Jack asking if her other tattoo could bring rain. *Maybe so, Jack*, she mused. *Maybe so.*

"Are you trying just as hard to find Jack?" Tayce asked, as if he'd known she was thinking about him. She was contorting her limber body in ways that were causing him to not look at her too carefully.

"They're together, so, yes," she confirmed. She had needed the water. She felt revived.

"You're sure?"

"I just saw them today in my head. They're with each other. I still don't know where."

He pondered this a moment. "What if they weren't together? Would you still be trying as hard to find Jack?"

She gave him a funny look over her shoulder. "Why wouldn't I?"

"Because he's an arrogant asshole who attacked you in the pool?"

She twisted, stretching the muscles around her spine. "Ahh, he told you that, did he?"

"Bret told me, yes."

"Obviously Jack didn't tell you." She sighed. "It wasn't as big a deal as it sounds, only because I could read him, his true feelings, at that moment. He's a jerk, for sure. You've known him far longer than me; I imagine he's been a jerk for years and years, however charming. But you know, he's human, like you and me. He makes mistakes. He has a soul. He's never actually killed or abused anyone. At the risk of sounding painfully sentimental, he was someone's little boy once. He giggled and played and made someone smile."

Tayce nodded thoughtfully. "His parents are both still alive, you know. Both in poor health. He's got them set up in a nice assisted-living facility. He visits them frequently. He always had a weird softness in his heart for old people, even back in the day. Half the reason he tours so much, I think, is to pay for their care." He rubbed his goatee and glanced at her. "So that's why you're also saving Jack?" he asked. "Because you saw that in him? That propensity for having a heart?"

"People have many facets, Tayce. The ones they show off the most, aren't necessarily the ones that make up the most of their hearts. None of us," she leveled her gaze at him, "are without sin. And far be it from me to make that judgement." She lay back on the floor. "I admit, Bret is my number one goal. Of course he is. I love him, and I'm staring daily into his daughter's sad eyes. I will fight for him before Jack. But my entire goal is to save them both." She glanced at him. "Now go get your guitar. You're just lying there doing nothing, when you could be playing for me. Have you lost your mind?"

He sat up. "Long ago. Be right back."

CHAPTER FORTY-EIGHT

FALLON

Fallon slouched down into the cushioned red velvet seat and kept her eyes on the stage. Her heart felt unusually light—Selah was phenomenal. Fallon didn't get out much these days, and it seemed as if in the months since Luca's murder she had been blind to so much around her. Selah's dancing had continued on in a blur; Fallon had paid little attention to it. Her eyes were opened now, and the graceful eighteen-year-old on the stage held her in rapture. Selah's technique was flawless, her passion extreme. She was a star.

Selah's body type she'd inherited from her mother, and her two sisters did not share it, but it had always been perfect for that of a ballerina. Though her height was average, her bone structure was small, her body lean, and strong, and full of grace. She'd begun lessons when she was three years old, and by the time she was twelve, she had her sights set firmly on becoming the greatest ballerina the world had ever known.

She had recently landed the coveted lead in an original production by a renowned choreographer. Titled "Fire/Wings/

Water," it was being debuted in Austin, and Selah was excited because "very important people" would be coming from all over to see it— "this could mean scholarships, the Julliard, anything!"

She'd been urging Fallon to come to a rehearsal, and finally Fallon had been worn down. And so here she sat, dressed in ragged jeans and a black hoodie, not remembering when she'd last washed her hair, but sober and fully in tune to her friend's performance.

But then somewhere in the middle of the show, Fallon closed her eyes and took a slow breath. When she finally opened her eyes again, they were bright with tears. Sadly, she shook her head.

Late that night, they returned together to Fallon's house. Since Luca had died and Fallon dropped out of school, Selah had been so busy with school and dancing that they had at first rarely seen each other. To correct this, Selah had negotiated with her parents to be able to spend at least three nights a week at Fallon's house, so they could at least be together for a while.

Fallon had spent the months since Luca's death drinking too much and letting Simon do what he wanted with her, and all Selah could do was try and try to bring her back to life. After seven long months, it was still a work in progress.

The dancer went immediately to take a shower, and when she came back out, she noted that Simon was gone, as were his things.

"I sent him away. I was getting tired of him always hanging around," Fallon remarked. "You know I made him move out a few weeks ago. This isn't his home."

Selah nodded without reply. She was quietly relieved, and thought that removing Fallon from Simon would be good. It had not, in her opinion, been a healthy direction for their friendship to take, embarking on a physical relationship born solely of their grief from losing Luca. She sat on the couch and accepted the cup of hot peach-ginger tea Fallon handed her.

Fallon sat beside her, and after a while, Selah noticed that her friend's gaze was on her with intensity. She set the cup on the coffee table, and Fallon seized both of Selah's hands and closed her eyes. Selah recognized that Fallon was trying to get a clearer view of her, and she knew this had to be because she'd had a troubling vision. A tremor of unease ran through her. She did not want Fallon getting a vision about her now, during what was about to be a penultimate time of her life.

When Fallon opened her eyes, they were even sadder than usual.

Selah jerked her hands away. "What is it?" Her tone was sharp. She was scared.

"You have to quit this show."

Selah's whole face darkened. "Fallon. You know better than anyone that that is the last thing I can do. I cannot quit this show. This is the chance of my life."

"You will be injured."

Selah cocked her head slightly. "How badly?"

Fallon breathed in, breathed out. "It will end your dance career."

For several minutes, Selah was silent and still. Then she shook her head. "No."

"Yes."

"I'll be careful, more than ever. It's carelessness that gets you into trouble."

Fallon shook her head. "It's your partner, Todd. A mistake on his part. He is not as talented as you."

Selah was drumming her fingers on her thigh. She leaned forward urgently. "I cannot quit this piece."

Tears streaked down Fallon's cheeks. "I know. But it will be your last."

At her words, Selah's stoicism crumbled, and she also began to cry. "What can I do, Fallon? If I quit, it will be career suicide. But if I go on, you say it will be the same. Either way, it is over for me, if what you see is true." She considered Fallon's lightly disheveled look, the scent of alcohol on her breath. How accurate were Fallon's visions these days, anyway?

"I love you, Selah. If I had the power to change the course of events, I would."

"I know." Selah took a deep, shuddering breath. "Do you know when?"

"No. Soon, I would assume."

Selah covered her face with her hands.

Less than a week later, during a performance in front of hundreds, Todd slipped during a complicated move while lifting Selah. He dropped her and then landed on her, wrenching her knee and tearing several tendons. She underwent two surgeries and was then in physical therapy for nearly a year afterwards, just to be able to walk and run well again.

She faced it with the quiet strength with which she faced everything. And she did not hold it against Fallon, who in turn was brought fully out of her intense mourning and isolation as she cared for and supported Selah in her recovery.

For Selah's injury had shown Fallon something horrible about herself. Within twenty-four hours of the incident, Fallon had sat cross-legged on Selah's bed and placed her hands on her friend's swollen, ruined knee, fully intending to heal it completely, thereby saving the day and her best friend's future. Closing her eyes, she waited for the power to flow through her, for her magic touch to heal what had been damaged. But nothing happened.

Selah saw Fallon's eyes fly open, a look of muted horror on her pretty face.

"No," Fallon whispered. She had squandered her abilities. Abandoned them. Turned her back on them. And they had faded back into obscurity. She remembered how painstakingly she'd worked on the ability to heal. Gone. Her self-centered months of grief had stolen away the one thing that could have fixed Selah. *You were wrong, Jacob. Love is powerful and fierce.*

Selah looked confused. She had never known about Fallon's power to heal, and so she didn't know anything had been lost. "What are you trying to do?" she asked.

Fallon hesitantly took her hands away from Selah's knee and shook her head. "Nothing. Just an idea."

Immediately Fallon began training; for hours every day she practiced. Because of her new laser focus she was able to regain everything she had lost, though in the end Selah's injuries were too complex for Fallon to heal completely.

"I want to get into physical therapy," Selah told her one day, "I want to move, but they want the swelling to go down more first, and it just won't."

Fallon knelt and placed her hands on Selah's knee and felt the power respond immediately. Within a minute the swelling had vanished completely.

Selah's eyes widened as she sat up straighter. "Did you just heal me?" She studied her friend. Fallon appeared strong, healthy, clean, and sharp. A change had been wrought in her. A sudden one.

Fallon held a finger to her lips and winked. "Shhh."

Selah began physical therapy the next day, her doctors baffled.

Purposeful vision-seeking was the one thing Fallon did not relearn. The visions had betrayed her. She would deal with the ones that came to her, like a good citizen of the universe, but she didn't want any more than that.

CHAPTER FORTY-NINE

In the mornings, when her brain seemed sharpest, Fallon tried the most dangerous of mental stunts. She focused inward, disappearing inside her own head, past the colored lines—she likened it to swimming blindly in night-dark water. Often, the raven came at her when she first entered, but now instead of cutting her with its beak, it bumped her with a powerful wing. This hurt far more than any real-world raven wing would hurt. Deep purple bruises appeared on her shoulders and arms. Her weary body did not heal. Azul never left Fallon's side when she was in the backyard.

Everyone noticed the bruises. No one said anything, though they wanted to. The tension in the house was approaching an overwhelming level.

The early morning exercises weren't showing her anything about Bret that she could tell, but she thought that if she went deeper and deeper, they might. Sometimes it felt like she was flying, and she wondered if she had become the raven. She was soaring over forests and prairies, scanning the ground. Every image was tinted with red as though with blood—she thought frequently of Jacob's silver dagger, the bright red blood dripping down his strong arm, that crystalline moment when her fingers touched his blood just before she began to heal him. That moment returned to her again and again, and she wondered what had passed between them, binding them.

She felt power all around her, pressing in on her, sometimes enough to make her feel as if she were suffocating. On Saturday morning, the power pressed on her so hard that she began to lose consciousness while she was still deep inside her head. The raven darted in and wickedly slashed her upper arm with one of its claws. The intense pain slammed her back into awareness long enough for her to crawl back out of her mind before everything went black again.

Inside the house, everyone heard Azul begin barking fiercely. Selah ran to the door, pausing to glance at Lisbeth and Bergen. "Keep that child inside," Selah instructed, as she hurried out into the yard. She fell to her knees beside an unconscious Fallon, took one look at the blood seeping out of her arm, and called to her husband.

Tayce, who had followed her, headed back towards the house, but then he saw that Michael was already on his way. From inside he could hear Bergen protesting loudly, and Lisbeth's quieter voice, pleading, yet firm.

Selah watched as Fallon's blood painted the green blades of grass, and inexplicably her head was suddenly full of a song—it took her a moment to place it, but then she remembered the piece: the last song she'd ever danced to on a stage. The song that had ended it all. She wondered at the bittersweet memory, her eyes going to Fallon's serenely unconscious face. She wondered, for the briefest of moments, if her friend was dying.

Then Michael and Tayce were there. Tayce held a towel to her wound as Michael scooped her up in his arms. As they headed back to the house there was chaos as Tayce yelled at and even tried to kick Azul.

Selah seized his arm. "That dog did not harm her. Let him alone."

"Do you see her bleeding?" he protested. "No one else was out here! You heard the barking!"

Her eyes burned into his. "Let him alone."

Tayce turned away and followed them into the house.

They ferried her quickly past Bergen's wide eyes and into the privacy of the master bathroom, where Michael laid her out inelegantly on the cold tile floor. As Selah fetched a pillow to place under Fallon's head, she knew with some amusement that her husband was keeping his mind right enough to know she wouldn't appreciate blood all over her house, and the bathroom would be the easiest to clean. She also knew Fallon knew the same thing, and wouldn't care where they placed her. Possibly Fallon wouldn't have minded being left in the yard to bleed to death, but Selah knew those feelings came and went.

The cold tile was enough to wake Fallon up. Azul, who was not normally allowed in at Selah's, quickly licked her face and then backed away to give Michael room, keeping a wary dark doggie eye on Tayce.

Selah lay a hand on the dog's soft head. "Go to Bergen. We've got her. Go on."

Azul gazed at Selah and then dutifully left the room.

Michael was cleaning up Fallon's arm, which was still bleeding freely. "It's deep, it needs stitches," he determined, and Fallon glared at him.

Selah leaned in close to her friend. "Can you heal it?" she asked, but Fallon shook her head.

"Too weak," she whispered.

Nodding, Selah went and retrieved a locked metal case from the closet and opened it up. Tayce watched as Michael removed a glass vial, filled a needle and gave her a shot in the arm. Then, after a little more preparation, he proceeded to stitch up the slash.

"Was that shot for the pain?" Tayce asked uncertainly, as he saw Fallon gritting her teeth and tensing her entire body.

"No." Michael shook his head. "That was an antibiotic, not knowing the cleanliness of whatever the hell sliced her. There was nothing for the pain. I want her to feel these stitches, to remind her that what she's playing with is bigger than her."

Fallon spat at him, and though Michael kept his cool, Selah furiously slapped her friend's thigh with stinging force. "Stop it! You're going to kill yourself! Whatever you're doing, Fallon, stop it! You're playing with fire. You don't know what you're doing well enough."

A single tear streaked down Fallon's cheek. "What am I supposed to do, Selah?" she asked in a hoarse whisper. "He's dying. He's dying because I can't find him. What am I supposed to do?"

Selah bent her head and held Fallon's hand. "I don't know, love." Her voice was trembling. "Dear Father in heaven, I don't know."

Tayce looked away, feeling emotion welling up inside him at the exchange. What had cut her arm? There was so much going on here that he didn't understand. He'd been surprised to find there were people who accepted and fully believed in Fallon's unusual abilities. Who were completely at ease talking about them openly as if they were only talking about a trip to the grocery store. Selah Lowe seemed like a sensible, intelligent, no-nonsense Christian woman, yet out of everyone she was closest to and most supportive of Fallon.

Bergen also seemed to be taking everything she heard and saw in stride, though she was so sad and withdrawn that it was difficult to tell what she thought about it all. Tayce didn't know who Simon was, and he refrained from asking, but he was dying of curiosity. He could tell that Lisbeth was in the same boat as him. During these past strange days, they often found themselves hanging out together, feeling uninitiated and uninformed, talking about the good old days to pass the time. They could see clearly that no one in the house seemed to have any faith whatsoever in the police or FBI.

Lisbeth had confronted Fallon just the night before at the apartment, while Bergen was languishing in a long, lonely bath. She had joined Fallon in the kitchen, leaned against the counter, and stared at her. "I think I might want to take Bergen home."

Fallon contemplated this a moment, rolled the use of "think" and "might" around briefly in her head, and then met Lisbeth's stare. "If that's what you feel is best." Her voice was neutral and easy.

Lisbeth had to look away, chastened by the compelling green gaze being leveled at her. "I don't know what's best. But we just don't know, do we? If he's dead, or alive... if this will go on for weeks, months, years..." Her voice shook with emotion. "How can I know how long to stay here with you? Every day that we remain here with you gives everyone..."

"False hope?" Fallon's face did not change, but her voice had taken on a dangerous edge.

Lisbeth bent her head as tears streamed down her cheeks. "I know you love him, Fallon, but he... he's been my best friend for so long..."

"And I haven't known him long at all, in comparison, and he's not the father of my child?"

Lisbeth cast a quick glance at Fallon, and was further shaken by the dark fury she glimpsed in those eyes. "I'm sorry, I," she covered her face with her hands, "I'm not saying things well."

"Maybe you should go home, to your husband," Fallon allowed, the hardness slipping away from her words. She turned away from Lisbeth. She took a long drink from her wineglass, warning off the ready armada of catty, cruel remarks that were waiting to be lobbed at the statuesque beauty quivering beside her. "I don't know how long this will last, Lisbeth" she said finally. "I don't know how long Bret will last. But he is alive at this very moment. And I will not rest until he is found. And every piece of my being believes we will find him alive, and soon. But those feelings are probably largely a self-preservation tactic of my already-shattered mind and heart." She downed the rest of the wine and immediately poured herself some more. "So do what you will. But I'd like to keep her with me. Because I am going to find him." She turned away and went to sit on the couch with her phone.

For the rest of that day, after the mysterious slashing of Fallon's arm—it was a testament to the high level of quiet tension in the house that no one asked her how it had happened—the presiding mood was dark.

When Bergen first glimpsed Fallon's bandage, she asked immediately, "Does it hurt really bad? Like last time?"

"Worse, actually," Fallon told her quietly. "This one is much deeper."

Tayce and Lisbeth exchanged a glance.

When he heard her answer, Michael felt guilty about stitching her up without using a numbing agent, and a moment later he offered Fallon something for the pain. She declined, and went upstairs to lie on the bed in the guest room. Azul followed her, curling up with her.

Outside rain began to fall heavily, lightning flashed and thunder rumbled. Lisbeth, ever the organizer, took a break from the endless and somewhat difficult task of running Daisy by phone in order to engage Bergen and Selah in a game of Scrabble. Michael departed, as planned, to go collect Indio from Dallas.

A subdued, distracted Tayce watched the Scrabble game without interest. When Lisbeth tried to draw him into the conversation, he mumbled something unintelligible and left the room to go sit on the swing on the front porch alone, watching the rain. He was hollow inside. He replayed in his mind the sight of Fallon's mysteriously bleeding arm, her fury at Michael, the doctor's seeming heartlessness that was apparently born of his affection for her... Tayce was lost. He had now seen sides of Selah, Michael, and Fallon that he had either never seen before or expected, and it left him feeling strange and out of control. And according to Fallon, one of his best friends in the world was dying—*dying*—somewhere unknown.

That evening when he left the house, instead of heading straight back to the farm, he drove across town to Madrigal, where he sat at one end of the bar and ordered a strong drink. His shoulders hunched, his eyes faraway, he invited no company.

He'd been there about half an hour when he felt light fingers on his arm, and he turned his head and found Fallon standing close beside him. The colored lights that were strung a little excessively in the bar area reflected against her gold hair with rainbow effect. He felt better immediately in spite of himself, and wondered what kind of witchcraft she was working. Her face and eyes radiated calm, though he knew a storm raged inside her mind and heart.

She reached out and tucked his hair behind his ear. "I'm going to sit and have a drink with you. Would that be alright?"

He tore his eyes from hers. "Stop trying to bewitch me," he scolded her dryly.

She reached out and stole his drink, downing what remained in one swallow. "If I was going to bewitch you," she warned, "there'd be no 'try' about it. You'd be done for." Then she leaned in swiftly and kissed his cheek, very near his lips, and his entire body felt like it was bursting into flames.

He looked at her sharply, clinging with great effort to his usually unreliable self-control. "You've been drinking already," he accused her.

She sat down on the stool beside him. "You would've started early, too, with this kind of pain going on."

He looked at the bandage around her left bicep. "Bad?"

"Bad," she confirmed. "Burning. Excruciating. I feel like I've been poisoned."

The bartender, a cousin of Mariana's who knew Fallon well, set glasses of whiskey before them, and then left them alone. They sat silently for a while, concentrating on their drinks.

"I tried to warn you," Fallon said softly.

"About what? About getting involved with all this? I was involved the moment you encouraged Bret to get me off that sidewalk in Vegas. You turned me into a fixture in your life the second my name left your lips, instructing Bret to try to take me inside with him. You will not easily get rid of me now."

Her elbow on the bar, she rested her head in her hand and gazed at him.

He turned his body towards her. "You're concerned because I had a weak moment? Because I was disturbed by an up-close view of something that is your lifelong reality?" He shook his head. "Don't waste any energy worrying about me." He lifted one shoulder. "Though I enjoyed the kiss."

She smiled down at her glass.

He looked around. "Can't believe you were able to slip away without Bergen."

"I was cruel. I left while she was in her bath. Lisbeth will have to deal with it. Seeing her sad face is just draining me."

"Poor thing. She has definitely always been daddy's girl. Just like Annie was with me." He looked at his watch.

"You have somewhere you need to be?" she asked, raising an eyebrow.

"I was planning on closing the place down with you."

She raised her drink. "Cheers."

After nearly two hours, quite drunk and now overly brave, Tayce leaned in close to her. "So, what really happened to your arm?"

Chapter Forty-Nine

"I heard you tried to kick Azul."

"Answer my question, woman."

She held his gaze. "Raven talon."

He paused a beat, then squinted at her.

She squeezed his wrist. "You asked."

He turned her hand over and rubbed her wrist with his thumb, the tattoo of the bird. "Is this the raven?"

She watched, unsteady in her own intoxication, as the raven disappeared and reappeared with each pass of his thumb. As if she were watching a super-eight movie. Her heart began to beat faster, and she felt fear for him. Jerking her wrist away, she looked up. "Yes, it is. Be careful."

He sat back and wrapped his hand around his glass, eyeing her thoughtfully. She looked away, and he took a deep breath. "I'll probably regret telling you this, but you know what? Sometimes when I'm with you, I feel dangerous. And I have determined that I am jealous of Jack Lane."

She looked up, surprised. "Of Jack? No. Why?"

He was laughing quietly at himself. "This is the part where I regret telling you, after I've sobered up. Some dark part of me wants a scar like his. A scar that you caused. Something visceral and permanent all at once that comes from this elemental thing within you."

It took her a few seconds to process this thought. "So, Bret can communicate telepathically with me, and I burned Jack with my tattoo, and now you're feeling all left out in the cold?"

He shrugged. "I didn't say it made sense."

Her eyes were drawn to the silver crescent moon he always wore on a long chain around his neck, and she leaned in close to him. "Be careful what you wish for, my friend. Because there are all kinds of strange things all around us in this world, things that can harm and kill. And you and I, we have miles to go together..."

Her voice had an odd tone to it, and he frowned. "Miles to go. You mean before we find Bret?"

She hesitated. "No." And then she looked away from the crescent moon, a puzzled expression on her face, as if she wasn't entirely sure of what she'd just said.

After all of that, they needed a break, so Tayce headed to the men's room and Fallon checked her phone. There was a text from Tessa warning her that Casi was livid after hearing that Fallon was making out with Tayce at Madrigal. "She has ideas, that one," Tessa added sagely. "Ideas I'm sure Tayce is blind to."

Fallon shook her head. Of all the staff at Solu, twenty-four-year-old Tessa had always been the most like a friend to her, and she was Diego's second-in-command after Fallon. A single mother raising a little girl, Tessa was tough, loyal, and mostly mature, though she had a tendency towards pouting when she didn't get her way.

Twenty-two-year-old Casi, on the other hand, was flighty, immature, and madly jealous of Fallon simply for being Fallon. She had only been working at Solu for about a year. From hints Casi had been dropping lately at work—and which Tessa had relayed to her—Fallon had figured out that Casi seemed to want everyone to think that Tayce was going to leave his wife for her and take her back to L.A. to live fabulously. Fallon didn't have to ask Tayce to know that he had led Casi to believe no such thing. He was careful in his affairs, careful with both secrecy and with the feelings of the women he had affairs with. But his propensity for often pursuing young women, Fallon thought, would surely get him into trouble one day.

"You don't need to see Casi anymore," she mentioned, as he rejoined her at the bar.

"Haven't seen her in over two months," he reported, stretching his arms over his head and yawning. "She was too crazy for me. Why?"

"You've just answered your own question. Stay away from her."

At two in the morning, Fallon trusted neither of them to drive. She had walked the half mile from her apartment, but he had the Range Rover with him and didn't want to leave it in Madrigal's parking lot. Eventually, they maneuvered it to her place— she would not let him drive it all the way back to the farm.

They'd been giggly for the past hour, but the thought of Bergen hearing them come into the apartment drunk and laughing did much to sober them up enough that they were able to enter and set up beds on opposing couches with enough care that they only woke Lisbeth.

CHAPTER FIFTY

On what Bret could see by his watch was the sixth day of their imprisonment, Jack started to seemingly lose his mind. With knife in hand, he started yelling and cursing and pounding on the door, demanding to be let out. Bret remained quiet where he sat on the floor against the wall. He had no idea how Jack had found the strength to stand and jump around like that; he himself had grown so dizzy lately that he tried to stay low to the ground. They were both badly dehydrated.

He assumed Jack's outburst would be ignored, and so was surprised and a little afraid when the door flew open and Jack stumbled out. There was a loud crash—Bret staggered to his feet in alarm—and then Jack fell back in as he was thrown, stumbling to his hands and knees. The door slammed and locked, and Bret feared with a sinking heart that they would not be given water again after this, as punishment. Their jug of water was currently less than half full; Bret had put himself in charge of rationing it out.

Jack was lying on his side on the floor, moaning, face twisted in pain, clutching his left arm.

Bret knelt by him. "Is it broken?" He reached out and tried to touch it, but Jack growled at him like a wounded dog, and Bret sat back on his heels. Then he went and fetched the mason jar. They'd long ago dumped some of Peter's things in a corner, the rest of which Jack now wore in tribute. Bret poured two inches of water in the jar and set it near Jack. Then he resumed his position against the wall, placing himself between Jack and the water jug.

Jack was never able to tell what had actually happened, everything had moved so fast. His left arm—the same arm Fallon had burned—had been seemingly crushed. He hadn't seen their faces—he thought they might have been wearing their masks. The arm was swollen and red and purple in places, hanging limply at his side and causing him excruciating pain. He never really got back up again after that, except to raise up enough to drink the water Bret gave him sparingly.

Hours passed slowly, now tainted with a greater sense of dread and hopelessness. To get Jack's mind off the pain, Bret made him reminisce about the old days when their bands had been on top of the world. Sometimes it seemed to do the trick—they even laughed out loud a few times—but still Jack did not get up. Bret felt his own mind growing foggier and foggier, and he was often so cold. When he and Jack weren't talking, he tried to focus on Bergen and Fallon, thinking of old memories, imagining new memories he'd make with them one day. As time went on and things got even hazier, he had lengthy imaginary conversations with both of them in his head.

At some point—was it the next day? Or the next? —Bret was aware that the jug had gone dry. His mouth and throat were burning with thirst, but he didn't know how long ago it had happened, for he'd lost track of time. He could no longer focus on his watch. Jack was slipping in and out of consciousness, not lifting his head off the floor, eyes staring dully, unable to carry on a conversation.

Bret was lying down as well now, no longer interested in moving much. Bergen and Fallon flashed continuously in front of his eyes like a reel of film. He saw images of Bergen as a little baby, of her riding her first tricycle, and singing into his microphone with him on a stage during sound check when she was about five. He wondered if they'd gotten her after all, if his precious baby girl was dead. He wondered if maybe Fallon was dead, too, and that was why she hadn't found them.

He closed his eyes.

CHAPTER FIFTY-ONE

Fallon was in her kitchen late in the evening, mechanically pouring sugar into a pitcher for iced tea. She could hear Bergen and Lisbeth in the bathroom together, talking a little, but not much. The strain was wearing everyone to the bone.

Azul was lying at Fallon's feet, looking around alertly, ears up. She watched him with a vague frown. Bret had been missing for eight days. Every cell in her body wanted to panic, but she forced herself to remain calm in order for her mind to be still enough to seek him. She'd been having clearer visions in the past twenty-four hours: Jack and Bret in the empty room, both lying on the floor; an empty jug; a pile of silver and leather, jewelry and such; a man with a mask over his face. Visions of amazing detail, turning off and on like flashes in her mind, but none of them helped in determining the location.

As she looked back at the pitcher of tea, she heard Azul growl, and then everything went black.

She awoke to pitch darkness. She was seated in a chair, arms bound tightly at her sides. Her legs were free but she didn't try to stand or flee, feeling the need to assess the situation. The back of her neck ached, as did her head. Somewhere to her left, water was dripping on stones. The air was damp and cool, with an earthy smell.

She'd been taken again, just like at twenty, she recognized the sensation. She struggled furiously a moment against the cord that bound her, but it held her tight. She felt around with her mind, but she kept coming up against a hard coldness, she could sense no living thing. She was also blind. Darkness was normally not a problem for her, but this darkness did not allow her to see into it—she thought there must be magic in it.

A light, several yards in front of her, flickered. First just a pinprick, then it grew, till it was a spotlight shining on her.

"It's been such a long time since you've been with us, my Rose."

Fallon caught her breath. It was the same voice from her memory. Immediately she grew angry, and the voice chuckled, as if it knew. After a quick internal assessment, she reassured herself that her mind was still perfectly closed and guarded, determining that he had seen the anger on her face, not in her head.

"Who are you? Why am I here?" she demanded, wondering for a moment why her arms were bound, but not the rest of her. "Why can't I see you?"

There was an audible sigh. "Ah, yes, that. I maintain a lower profile than even you. Though it does not allow for a reunion that is warm and fuzzy, I continue to feel that it is best if my features were not in your mind."

She reached out to try and read this stranger, to see whether he intended good or evil, but something like an electric shock bit back at her, and she jerked.

He laughed softly. "Child, child. Don't try your tricks on me."

Her confusion about the situation was paralyzing. So many thoughts and feelings were flying around in her head that she couldn't see straight. First and foremost, she feared this was wasting valuable time; she needed to get back to seeking Bret. What if she was gone for weeks again? Bret didn't have that much time left. He would be dead by the time she got back.

"I need to get home. I'm looking for someone. I have to find them."

"'Home'—an interesting choice of words. Will you, my Rose, ever truly be home?"

She hated the smug, possessive way he spoke to her, and why was he not calling her Fallon?

"What am I doing here? What do you want?" She strained hard against the cords again, feeling them burn into her flesh as she twisted and turned.

"You are here to be warned. You delve too deeply into places your mind is not prepared for. You must slow down. It is dangerous for you."

"I'm trying to find Bret James! What do you know about my mind?!"

"We know everything about you. We are devoted to protecting you. For your entire life, we have done so. When they murdered your brother, we doubled our reserves, and they have not been able to touch you since."

She was momentarily still. "You agree that he was murdered? You know why, and by whom?"

"An enemy killed him, to extinguish his powers. They realized too late that *your* powers far surpass anything he ever had. But also, his murder was done to get to you, to affect you, leave you vulnerable. One of the same reasons your adoptive parents were murdered when you were seven. They thought that by murdering them, it would leave the two of you unprotected."

"Adoptive?" She almost came out of her skin.

He sighed again. "There is so much to be learned. I protect you by withholding knowledge; you must believe me."

She did not believe him. "Was Luca even my real brother?" she snapped acidly

"Yes, he was your true brother; you share a father. Sadly, my children have always been vulnerable."

She turned her ear to him, listening. "Your children."

"You and Luca were the last of my line. You are my last surviving blood, ah, I should say, you and one other. More precious to me than jewels. Little Rose, I have loved you and feared for you since the moment of your birth."

She bowed her head, wanting to block out his words, all of them dripping with deceit. This was too much. Too much to take in, her head already full of Bret and Jack.

"I heard that you burned the unfortunate Mr. Lane, scaring yourself as much as it scared him. And Mr. Williams, not unsurprisingly, is drawn to you like a moth to flame. Your mind is powerful, more powerful than you can imagine. Your powers are beyond what any of my children have ever possessed, but they are raw and hidden. You are untrained—Roth had no business attempting it, and I imagine he did a poor job. Your mind is unused to the things you are currently subjecting it to. You must slow down. You are diving into waters too deep. You will come to grave harm if you continue to push yourself like this. You could lose yourself. You could die."

She had raised her head at the mention of Jacob, but she kept her face masked. This mystery man before her was the one who had placed Jacob with them; she was sure of it. The one Jacob had been doing a "favor" for. Her mistrust for him grew.

"It's not my fault if I am poorly trained! You don't understand that I have to find Bret. Alive. I will die trying—I have to find him for his daughter. And if you hold me here until he's dead, hoping to keep me from my task, you will lose me forever; I promise you."

There was a moment of heavy silence. Then, "If you ever choose to cross me, Rose, you will regret it for eternity. Keep that in mind as I release you. And rest assured that I have dealt with those responsible for the targeting of one of my family. They are no longer a threat."

And then everything went dark.

CHAPTER FIFTY-TWO

When Fallon woke up, she was lying on the couch in her apartment. Morning sunlight was pouring in the windows. Her head and neck still hurt, and her arms were sore—when she looked, she saw the skin was burned from the cord that had bound her. Not a dream, then. She sat up, knocking her phone onto the floor with a thud as she did so.

There was a flash of color, and Bergen was kneeling beside her, eyes red with tears. "I thought you were gone!" She buried her face on Fallon's lap. "I thought you were gone like my dad," she sobbed.

Fallon put a gentle hand on her quivering back. "No, sweetness. Here I am. How long has it been?" She bent and picked up her phone, looking at the time.

"Since yesterday evening." Lisbeth was sitting on the bed, pulling back the curtain to watch them. "You vanished. I was in the bathroom with Bergen and when we came out, you were no longer in the kitchen where you'd been making tea."

Fallon glanced out the window behind her, and saw Azul down in the yard, romping around. She looked again at Bergen, who was struggling to gain control of her tears. "I'm here," Fallon whispered. "I'm so sorry."

"It was like a bad dream," the child told her, and Fallon caught her breath as something in her mind clicked.

Lisbeth stood up. "We called Tayce, but you weren't with him. We called Selah and told her. She advised us not to panic quite yet. But some of us did anyway." She glanced pointedly at her daughter. Lisbeth looked tired. It had been a long and sleepless night. "I'm going to take a shower. Then maybe you can tell us where you were. Or not."

After she'd disappeared and closed the bathroom door, Fallon seized Bergen's shoulders and hauled her up onto the couch beside her. She closed her eyes and held the girl's arms tightly, concentrating, reading. Then she opened her eyes wide.

"Dreams, Bee, your bad dreams. You have to tell me what they're about."

Bergen shook her head violently, alarmed.

"Are you still having them?"

The girl nodded.

Fallon sighed. "This is important. More important than anything, maybe."

"No." Bergen was crying again. "If I say it, they might come true."

"They've already partly come true, haven't they?" She was guessing, but she thought she was right.

"Yes."

"And see, that's without telling anyone. Every time you had a dream, afterwards you always called your dad to talk to him. You didn't tell him what it was about, but you had to talk to him. It's because the dream was about him, right? You were calling him to make sure that he was okay?"

Bergen nodded.

"When did you have the first dream?"

"I don't remember."

"Was it about two years ago? When he was in Las Vegas? You called him late at night, and then started talking about a pool party you'd been to that day."

Bergen remembered. "Yes, that was it."

"And since that night you've had them pretty regularly?"

"Not every night. But yes. They won't go away."

"Are they dreams of your dad being hurt?"

"He's scared," Bergen explained. "He's crying." She scrunched up her face in misery. "I don't like it when he cries."

"Come on, Bergen. Please."

"He's on the ground, like he's too tired to get up. He's… dying." Her voice cracked. "I don't know how I know, but I know." She trembled with silent sobs, and Fallon rubbed her arms reassuringly.

"Okay. That's good. Can you tell anything about where he is?"

"No. I've tried. There's someone else on the floor, too. I can't tell who. They have dark hair. They aren't moving at all, but my dad still is."

Fallon nodded. "Have you dreamed of anything else lately? Anything besides your dad?"

CHAPTER FIFTY-TWO

"Nothing important."

"Any recent dreams you can remember, tell me."

Bergen shook her head. "Just stupid stuff. Like, for the past five nights straight, I've dreamed about the Wizard of Oz."

Fallon's phone was to her ear in seconds. "Simon, connect Rylan Thomas to Kansas."

"Already done, Lucky. I mapped out all the properties his company owns, and…. yes, one is the old family farm near Argonia, Kansas."

"Text me the address. You're magic."

"No, that would be you, witch. Done."

She hung up and called Detective Ashton, trembling, clutching Bergen tightly to her side. "I'm texting you an address, Ashton. Please send someone to it. As fast as you can."

"Where did this information come from, Fallon?"

"Tell me you're sending guys out there, and then we'll talk."

He sighed. "Call you right back."

She shoved Bergen away. "Go get your mom, both of you get dressed, grab your bags. We're leaving." She called another number as Bergen scampered off. "Tayce, I need you to pick us up at my apartment. Full tank of gas. And pack a bag. Now."

"On it. Glad you're back."

She got up and threw some things into a backpack as Bergen did the same and begged Lisbeth to hurry. Fallon's phone rang as she was surreptitiously filling a bag of Bret's things as well. "Detective Ashton."

"Our guys will be at the location in fifteen to twenty minutes. I hope to God it's a worthwhile trip."

"So do I. Much more so than you."

"Where did you get Kansas?" he asked.

"It's one of his properties." She was herding Lisbeth and Bergen out the door, pointing them all in the direction of Tayce and the Range Rover that was pulling into the driveway. "I know you don't want to hear that I had a vision. I've got to go. Call me when you know something. It will not be a wasted trip." Hanging up, she bent and rubbed Azul's head. "I've got this one," she told the dog. "You stay here. I'll call Katrine to come get you."

Bergen and Lisbeth sat huddled together in the back of the Range Rover while Tayce drove fast and in the passenger seat Fallon texted back and forth with Selah.

"Are we going to get my dad?" Bergen asked, with a heartbreaking look on her face.

"I hope with all my heart, Bee."

Bergen leaned her head against her mother, whose eyes were shut in silent prayer. Tayce didn't ask any questions; he simply drove, and for this Fallon was grateful. Her head was pounding badly and her neck still ached, but she knew she couldn't take one of her shots right now. She swallowed a couple of Advil with the large coffee Tayce had brought her. It would have to do.

It was forty-five agonizing minutes later that Fallon's phone rang again. Her hand was shaking as she brought it to her ear. "Detective Ashton." There was silent tension in the Range Rover.

"Congratulations, Fallon." His voice was professional and warm.

She closed her eyes and relaxed against the seat.

"They found them locked in the storm cellar, both alive. House was empty, no vehicles present. They're on their way to the hospital. Bret's conscious, but just barely. Only enough to ask about you and his daughter; he wanted to know if you two were alive. He was told that, yes, you both were fine. Jack's condition seems worse, and he is not conscious. They're both badly dehydrated. Jack's arm is broken in multiple places and he's got a black eye, but other than that it seems they weren't harmed. They were suffering from a severe lack of hydration. We're having them transported to a hospital in Wichita."

Fallon swung around, tears in her eyes, and nodded at Lisbeth and Bergen, flashing an unsteady smile.

Bergen was screaming, "Daddy!" and Lisbeth broke down in tears and hugged her daughter fiercely. Tayce let out a long, shaky breath and smiled at Fallon.

"Thank you so much, Detective," she said softly.

"And I thank you, Fallon. Despite the information you gave me a few days ago, we weren't looking seriously at Thomas as a suspect. We likely wouldn't have investigated that farm till it was too late."

She bit her lip, then lowered her voice. "What are you going to say? In your report? When people ask?"

There was a moment of quiet. "I'm assuming you want no part of it," he remarked.

"You assume correctly."

"I received an anonymous tip suggesting I investigate the dealings of Red Racer Records. My suspicions led me to investigate the old family farm, because of its proximity to Texas compared with all the other properties he owns."

When she'd hung up with him, she covered her face with her hands and sat quietly. Everyone refrained from asking her any questions.

With Tayce driving as fast as he dared, it took five and a half hours to reach the hospital in Wichita. At some point, Bret had called Bergen's phone from his hospital bed and spoken to her briefly, just a few words, for his throat was raw, and he was quite weak.

When she hung up, Bergen looked sadly at Fallon. "I'm sorry you didn't get to talk to him."

But Fallon was smiling serenely. As soon as they'd crossed the Kansas state line, she and Bret had begun talking in their heads. Tayce had looked over and seen her smiling, gazing at nothing, tears running down her cheeks, and he'd wondered.

Fallon, my God, I love you. I didn't want to die and leave you and Bee. I just found you, I couldn't leave you!

Shh, it's alright now. The storm is gone. You're safe.

I knew you'd find us. I told Jack that you would.

She glanced back at Bergen. *I had help. In many unusual ways. It definitely wasn't me alone. And I'm now on the FBI's radar, or at least that of one detective in particular.*

Detective Ashton? I met him a few minutes ago. He gave me a brief synopsis of what happened. What a crazy mess this was. Who'd have thought? He laughed a little. *The detective told me that I made a very lucky choice of girlfriend.*

She smiled. *Rest. We'll be there soon.*

CHAPTER FIFTY-THREE

Bret was in the hospital for a week, Jack for a little longer. After the first couple of days, Lisbeth went home to Leo, leaving Bergen in Fallon's care. Bret's two older brothers showed up on the first day and stayed most of the week, and Travis and Seth came and stayed a couple of nights. Calls and texts from friends came streaming in. Kara updated Bret's website and social media accounts with messages of thanks from Bret for everyone's prayers and concern.

Fallon and Bergen were rarely gone from him. They slept in the hospital room with him at night because neither could fathom the idea of going to the hotel and letting him out of their sight. After a few days, Bret began eating plain broth, then, slowly, heartier fare, all of which he had Fallon and his brothers bring in from outside, as he was unable to stomach the hospital food.

Every day Fallon went down to Jack Lane's room for an update, and to bring an update on Bret. The two men maintained no fondness for each other, but they had developed a state of tolerant interest that caused them to be concerned about each other's recovery. On the third day, when a normally lethargic Jack was able to leer at her and look her over from head to toe—in an almost playful manner, as if he and she shared an inside joke—she told Bret that Jack was back.

Tayce left them mid-week, but the night before he was to depart, he invited Fallon out for drinks. For simplicity's sake, they went to the not-very-crowded bar in his hotel, and sat at one end where they were mostly by themselves.

"We often seem to end up in a bar together having drinks," she observed.

Tayce shrugged and raised his glass. "Cheers."

She smiled, then sighed. She was exhausted, but she had a feeling that sleep was going to do nothing to change this condition. She rubbed her still-aching head. At her vehement request, no one had said anything to Bret about her brief disappearance.

"So, you're heading right back into rehearsals," she noted.

He nodded, aware that she remained distracted by things he could not fathom. "Paul is getting antsy, as you know. Granted, we've got venues booked; we need to leave. Tour starts in a week. He's been practicing with the other guys, doing my guitar parts, but he doesn't know them perfectly, and it's not the same. I need to go." His deep brown eyes met hers. "I have a feeling you aren't going to be out of my life anytime soon, though, so this goodbye is only temporary."

"I'll be around." She sat up straighter. "And I want to see you guys do a show at some point. Just have to..." she waved her hand in no particular direction, "...get this all settled first."

"I think I'm kind of indebted to you for life," he admitted softly, looking away. "But I also think you hate it when people say things like that."

"Really, I just never want to speak of it or even think of it again. How easily the three of you could have been lost." She swallowed the whiskey quickly, closing her eyes as she felt the burn slide down her throat and into her belly. "Who would I drink with, then?"

He grinned and nudged her with his elbow. "I'm doing whiskey shots with the coolest girl in the whole world."

A full smile lit her face as she laughed, and she reached over and grabbed his hand for a moment. "I appreciate you, Tayce. I appreciate you with all my heart and soul."

"Likewise." They clinked their empty glasses together in a toast, and the bartender headed over to give them refills.

Fallon returned to the hospital after midnight, warm and vaguely unsteady from the whiskey. In Bret's room, she paused to observe the peaceful scene of Bergen curled up in the bed with him. The girl was sleeping soundly, but as Fallon moved around, Bret woke up.

"Hey," he whispered.

She came immediately to his side and slid her hand in his.

You went out drinking with Tayce?

She nodded. *I needed some Tayce time. The past several days have been intense, to say the least. He's going back to Dallas later this morning. He's been with us every step of the way, as soon as he heard you were missing. He didn't know how to help, but he wanted to, and he refused to leave us, tour be damned. He's as loyal a friend as you could have.* She leaned down and kissed him. *Sleep. I'll be here on the couch.*

She went into the bathroom and brushed her teeth. Then she pulled on a sweatshirt, for it was cold in the room, and lay down, pulling a scratchy blanket up to her chin. Her mind would not be still, and she knew she would not sleep much tonight. Now that Bret was safe, all her thoughts were focused on the unknown man from her vanishing.

Who the hell was he? Her father?! And if by some crazy circumstance this were true, if Faye and Steven Quinn had not, in fact, been her true parents, then who in the world was her real mother, and where was she? Was she dead like all the rest? Why had she and Luca been living with the Quinns in the first place, and what, exactly, was running through her veins—what kind of blood? For the place she'd been in, tied in that chair, had been some otherworld, not this one. She had felt that unquestionably. And had felt her body respond to it.

Why, if she was in danger, was everything still being kept from her? Might knowledge have saved Luca? It was so frustrating that she had no one to ask. She wished for the millionth time she could locate Jacob. Did he not realize she needed him? How was he involved with all of this? He wasn't the invisible man who had spoken to her, laughed at her from the darkness, claimed to be her father, and threatened her even, at the very last. But he was tied to it all somehow. It was not by mere coincidence that her raven tattoo exactly matched Jacob's.

She pondered the idea that Jacob had been defying her father by training her. It wasn't so much Luca they'd been keeping it a secret from, but everyone else. Every lesson had been in Jacob's room, nowhere else in the house. Had his room been somehow protected? More private than the others? If, as her "father" claimed, "they" knew everything about her, could they spy on her, see her whenever they chose? It just didn't make sense to her.

How was she going to figure any of it out, when she'd never been able to before? And what had Luca known? Had he taken secrets to the grave—the same as she'd kept secrets from him?

* * * * * * * *

"Fallon!"

She slowed as she came out of the coffee shop, cautiously sipping her overly-hot chai latte as she glanced up to see the dark-haired federal agent jogging across the street to join her. Casual in jeans and a navy blue shirt, he pushed his sunglasses up on his head and smiled at her in greeting, and as she smiled back, she observed that he looked far more at ease now than at any of their prior meetings. She reached out deftly with her mind, but pulled back quickly when she touched the strong attraction that was coming off of him in heated waves. He was also hiding something, but still she couldn't get a clear read; something was still blocking her.

"Detective Ashton," she returned pleasantly, checking that the cardboard container holding coffee for Bret and his brothers, as well as an icy drink for Bergen, was not tilting.

"Let me get that for you." He took the drinks from her, and she thanked him and took another sip of her chai.

"Are you here to interview Jack and Bret again?" she wondered, as they stood side-by-side and watched for a break in the traffic so they could cross. It was Bret's fourth day in the hospital. The interviews had been extensive, and she had thought they were done.

He shook his head. "No, I'm getting ready to head home, but I wanted to update you guys on what we've learned so far before I head out."

She nodded, drinking more of the chai and thinking that it would be all but gone by the time she returned to Bret's room. She was glad she had gotten a large. She was relieved that her headache was finally fading, and wondered what had brought it on. Something to do with her vanishing act, she supposed. The ache at the back of her neck was fading as well.

Ashton was watching her out of the corner of his eye. In jeans and a black and white striped shirt, Fallon looked pretty but tired. "How did you know?" he asked finally, as they headed across the street.

She took a breath. "About what? About Kansas?"

"You provided me with an exact address. Anyone else would think you'd been somehow involved."

"But you don't think that." She cast a brief glance at him.

"No." He looked thoughtful. "I'd like to know. I would think I had some sort of right to know, since I did pretty much obey you blindly by sending a team to an address that I only had your word about."

"For which I am grateful. You know that the address was among the hundreds I provided to you earlier, as being owned by Rylan Thomas or by his company, right?"

"Yes, I got that far."

She shrugged. "I had a vision involving Kansas. I realized that was the information I needed. The farm was fortunately the only Kansas address. I could only hope it was the right one. And it was."

They headed to the elevators. "Have you ever been involved in something like this before?" he asked. "I mean in giving assistance to the police or FBI?"

"Never." She shook her head as they entered an elevator alone. "And I'm not interested. I run my own show."

"I recall reading that the police wouldn't listen when you said your brother was murdered."

She gave him a dark look. "My entire family and one of my best friends...they've all been murdered. Local authorities solved none of the crimes." She lowered her eyes. "But you listened to me, and you followed my directions, and Bret was saved. So, I don't hold you with the rest of them."

They spoke no more as they stepped off the elevator and headed down the hall to Bret's room, from which there was the sound of talking and laughter, all of which died away at the sight of Fallon with the FBI agent. Ashton greeted them all, and as Fallon handed out the drinks, she asked Bret's brothers if they could take Bergen away so that she and Bret could speak with the detective. Then Fallon sat on the bed with Bret as Ashton pulled up a chair and told them what they knew.

On the day of the rescue at the farm, Rylan Thomas had tried to flee to Mexico, but had been apprehended. The individuals responsible for carrying out the kidnapping and murders of Peter Stillson and Cynthia Woodard, and the kidnappings of Jack Lane and Bret James, were gone without a trace. Rylan Thomas wasn't talking, but he'd left enough evidence in his phone and laptop to prove his own guilt. There was simply no information to identify who he'd been working with. Every trail had gone expertly cold.

"They're professionals that he hired," Ashton told them. "From the burned-out van to the planting of Stillson's corpse nearly two years later to feed the media attention, to the complete lack of evidence at the farm, and the way you and Jack were taken with no witnesses...these guys know what they're doing. But here's the thing." And suddenly Ashton looked uncertain. "Number one: you and Jack were not supposed to be left to die. Your captors were supposed to give you food and water until a set time when you would be 'rescued'. You were both supposed to be healthy enough to tour again soon, to take advantage of the attention. And number two: Rylan Thomas didn't have anything at all to do with Vegas."

Fallon flinched in surprise.

"Absolutely nothing. We have enough information to be sure of it. The disappearance of Peter, the rumblings it created in the music world—that's what put the idea in Rylan's head of staging a kidnapping to draw media attention. He needed some cash flow, and he was desperate. He chose you and Jack as his targets. He lurked on forums, dark web kind of stuff, throwing out vague hints that he was interested in working with whoever was responsible for Peter's disappearance. Eventually, he was contacted, and he was able to set it up. By the time all of this got underway, he knew exactly where you and Jack were at all times because you were coincidentally both on tour. He wanted Bergen taken, too, to create extra drama."

Bret was cursing then, but Fallon was sharply hung on the news that Vegas had not been directly connected to Bret and Jack's kidnappings. Her mind was reeling, looking for an explanation.

"So, whoever did this is still out there." Bret lay propped up in his hospital bed, shirtless and barefoot in a pair of dark blue athletic shorts. His face was losing some of the pallor that had clung to it when he'd first been brought in, the light was returning to his eyes, especially with his anger at Rylan Thomas.

"They don't want you, though," said Fallon soothingly. "They were careful enough that you couldn't ID them, right? With Rylan in jail, their job is over." She looked to Ashton for confirmation.

Ashton nodded. "I agree with Fallon, though that doesn't mean we won't keep an eye on you for a while. But for certain, they were operating under Rylan's orders for the sole purpose of building record and concert ticket sales to earn money to pay off some of his outstanding debts."

"What about Peter and Cyn?" Fallon pressed.

Ashton appeared slightly annoyed that he didn't have an answer for her. "Everything about Vegas goes into a black hole. The trail goes cold, there is no trail. No information. No leads. We know it was the same people only because they had Stillson's remains. But we don't know who they were, who their intended target or targets were in Vegas, their motive...nothing."

Fallon's eyes widened as she remembered something the faceless man had told her. That he had dealt with *the threat to his family.* She blinked, and she knew: Jack and Bret's kidnappers had stopped giving them water because they were *no longer alive.* They had been eliminated. But what family did he mean, that had been targeted? He clearly hadn't cared for Jack and Bret, who would have died without Bergen's intervention. And she herself had not been kidnapped or threatened. Peter? Tayce? Cyn?

Bret and Ashton were both staring at Fallon's internal struggle, and it was the latter who finally spoke. "Obviously you turned out to be invaluable, Fallon. I know you were doing everything you could to find these guys. I still don't know how you were able to get your hands on some of the information you forwarded to me. And I don't tend to put much stock in things like you described to me—visions. I still don't know how I feel about it. But I'm glad I listened to you." He rose and shook her hand, then shook hands with Bret. "Hope you're back on your feet and back on stage soon. I'm heading home to Dallas tonight. Both of you take care. The media are ready to descend upon you."

Bret laughed. "My publicist is texting me every twenty minutes. I know."

When Ashton was gone, Fallon lay down beside Bret, cherishing the moment of quiet, knowing that soon Bergen and her uncles would return.

"Isn't it unbelievable?" Bret asked. "The whole crazy story?"

She nodded. "Crazier is that Simon and I had pretty much nailed the bad guy as being Rylan, and sent all our info to the FBI within the first few days, but it wasn't enough for them to take action. So frustrating. I knew you and Jack were dying somewhere, and I knew who had caused it, but I was so helpless."

He kissed her. "Thank you for taking care of my girl. Thank you for showing her the ladder inside the fireplace that day at your house."

"I'd felt something that day," she admitted, "as soon as we entered the house. I had a sensation that I needed to show Bergen the fireplace in my room. It was the perfect hiding place. Anywhere else and they would have found her."

CHAPTER FIFTY-THREE

He closed his eyes against the thought.

* * * * * * *

It was after midnight in the hospital, the halls mostly empty and haunted. Troubled Fallon was wide awake, unable to find peace, wandering in search of something to drink. She settled reluctantly on a peach-flavored green tea, the only reasonable choice from the vending machine. Then she slowly started making her way back towards Bret's room, where Bergen was sleeping curled up against her father. She paused at a closed door and eyed it thoughtfully a moment before knocking softly and pushing it open a crack. Inside the TV was on, and when she glanced quickly at the bed, she saw Jack watching her. He was alone. A smile spread across his tired face.

"I knew you'd come around eventually."

She toasted him with her tea. "This would have to be filled with something much, much stronger for me to contemplate that."

He motioned for her to come in, his wrist affixed with seemingly more tubes and wires than what Bret was hooked up with. He was pale and haggard-looking, life not returning to him as quickly as it was returning to Bret. She entered the room and shut the door, joining him and even sitting up on the side of the bed with him when he patted the mattress.

"How are you?" she asked, sipping her tea and looking with interest at his bandaged arm.

"I'm fine," he lied, turning down the volume on the TV. "Sick of being in this effing place."

"A step up from the storm cellar, though, right?" she asked, smiling for him.

He cracked a grin. "Yeah, that place got old real quick."

"At least the company was good-looking."

He flipped her off with his good hand. "Should've been you trapped in there with me, darling. Could have passed the time much more pleasantly."

She shivered. "Hey, I'm sorry about Peter."

He nodded soberly. "So am I. He was a good kid. Fun to be around. Having the grandest time. What a fucking waste of a young life." Ashton had filled him in on the entire chain of events, including Fallon's involvement, after Fallon and Bret told him that Jack was somewhat aware of her unusual skills. "You know, Tayce Williams is a lucky son-of-a-bitch," Jack noted. "He owes you till the end of time."

"I don't like to think of it like that. I was just in the right place at the right time and made some lucky judgement calls."

He looked at her. "You saved me and Bret. Twice."

"I had help the second time. Lots of people wanted to get you guys back."

He made a face. "FBI didn't have a clue. Still don't, apparently. If Ashton hadn't listened to you, I'd be dead right now."

She shifted and said nothing, because it was true. He placed a hand on hers, squeezing it clumsily, unused to displays of genuine emotion. She turned her hand over in his and squeezed back, eyes going back to his.

"You're..." he looked down, "...a good friend to have. And I don't have many." His voice was husky and low.

To her surprise, she felt tears pricking her eyes. "Don't go soft on me now, Lane," she murmured.

A sly look crossed his features, and he brought her hand over the sheets, pressing it down against himself. "No worries there, darlin'."

She jerked her hand away, laughing, and got to her feet. "Good night, Jack. I'll see you around."

The volume on the TV went back up as she slipped out the door, not entirely muffling his low laughter.

CHAPTER FIFTY-FOUR

Upon his release from the hospital, Jack ate up the ensuing media attention with gusto, granting every interview and appearing on every talk show that would have him. He still wasn't anywhere close to one hundred percent. He had undergone two surgeries on his arm; his energy level was low, and he looked older. But in the interviews and on camera he was as smugly charming and snarky as ever. To his credit, he never once mentioned Fallon Quinn and even went out of his way to be vague about knowing her at all.

Bret, desiring to leave the memories of their strange abduction behind him, was not as interested in playing to the media. He went on one late night talk show with Jack, and also granted one interview to a magazine, including an artsy photo shoot with himself and Bergen, donating all the money he received to charity. He'd wanted Fallon included, but she cited her below-the-radar status and declined to be featured.

After they were done with the media, Bret, Bergen, and Fallon disappeared to Gray. It was Katrine's idea to have them stay at the farm, reasoning that it gave them more room to be out and about without running into anyone. They all hoped it would prove to be a distraction for the still-shaken Bergen. Paul and Tayce were already out on the road on tour, so there was no one at the farm but Katrine and some local workers.

Bergen immediately fell in love with Katrine and with the entire place, and Bret knew it had been the right decision to bring her there for a while to help her calm down and be reassured that everything in her world was going to be okay.

On the second day, Katrine took the child off for a few hours to watch the shearing of the angora goats, allowing Bret and Fallon some rare time alone.

Fallon gave him back the bee necklace. "It didn't help. I'm sorry. I lost you anyway, I couldn't stop it." Her voice was hard as she acknowledged her failure.

He touched her arm. "Is that how you've felt? That you failed me? I'm alive. Jack's alive. But most importantly, you saved Bergen. You saved her from the trauma of being stolen by strangers, locked away, terrified, starving. You saved her life; I'm sure of it. That means more to me than anything."

She looked at him in misery. "I could have done more."

"How? You told me yourself the visions are an imperfect science. That you can't save everyone. Well, you saved us all." He kissed her, and she clung to him in tears.

At one point that afternoon, while Bergen was still gone, he swept the hair off the back of Fallon's neck and leaned down to kiss her. And stopped.

She sensed the change in him, and turned around. "What?"

He looked funny. "New tattoo?"

Her face went pale. Without another word he led her into the bathroom, turned her around and handed her a mirror. As he held up her hair, she used the mirror to look in the larger mirror. She stared at the quarter-sized star tattooed into the flesh at the back of her neck. A tear burned her eye, but she blinked it away. She thought about the days-long headache she'd had, the aching in her neck. Then she lay the mirror down.

"Come back to bed," he ordered gently.

She pulled on a t-shirt and sat down beside him, looking troubled.

"Fallon, I was only gone for nine days. What in the hell happened?"

She sighed. "The day before we found you, I vanished from the apartment."

He jerked as if someone had struck him. "What do you mean? No one told me this! Like when you were twenty?"

She nodded, and placed a hand on his bare chest, calming him just a bit. "Lisbeth and Bergen were in the bathroom; I was in the kitchen. They came out because Azul was growling and whining. I was gone."

"When did you come back?"

"The next day, the day of the rescue. Suddenly I was on the couch."

He touched her knee. "Do you remember anything this time?"

She hesitated. "I do. I didn't know about the tattoo. But I remember the rest. Or as much of the rest as I'm aware of. I was gone about ten hours." She met his eyes. "I'm not ready to talk about it with anyone yet. Is that okay?"

"You'll tell me eventually? Soon?"

"Yes."

He leaned forward and kissed her. "I can wait. Is it bad?"

She suddenly looked so weary. "I'm not sure what it is. I did find out that the Quinns were not Luca's and my real parents."

* * * * * *

After they had been at the farm a few days, Fallon left to join Selah at her home for lunch. Selah listened intently to how it had all come about, startled to learn of Bergen's involvement. "You and Luca—siblings. Bret and Bergen—father and daughter?"

Fallon shrugged. "Who knows how any of this happens? Bret's only skill seems to be communicating with me telepathically. But Bergen dreaming visions of the future as well as clues? That's intense. This may be the only one she ever has, or it may be just the beginning. I'm pretty sure she can read people, too. I believe she tried to read me the first time she met me. She seems to always be very in tune to how people are feeling. I'm not sure she even knows that she's doing it."

"I knew you and Bret were meant to be in each other's lives. Maybe this is why. So that you can guide his daughter."

Fallon looked away. "I don't think I need to be guiding anyone. Least of all a vulnerable child."

"A child who loves you and trusts you. No one else in her world is going to understand what's going on. She's going to need you." Selah swallowed the last of her iced tea. "Does Bret know about her part in all this yet?"

"No. You're the only one I've told. She and I haven't had time to talk about it, either. I don't know how much she realizes she saved the day. It's a lot for her to process. Right now, all she cares about is being back in his arms. I don't know how he's going to take it. He won't be happy."

"No, I could see that. How long are they going to stay out at the farm?"

"I'm not sure. Since Paul's gone, Katrine is busy spoiling them both with food. Bergen is in love with Katrine and with every animal out there. She's talking about being a vet when she grows up, and about how she wishes she had her dirt bike to ride around the farm."

Selah smiled briefly at the idea. She was distantly studying Fallon. Her friend looked different, but she couldn't put her finger on anything in particular. She thought Fallon looked a little reckless. A little wild. Angry? That was to be expected. Ah, there just weren't enough words in her head to figure out what it was that was changed. But there had been a definite change, no question about that.

"And the tour?" she asked, trying for normal conversation.

Fallon played with the condensation on her glass of tea. "Will resume in January, from what I hear. It will give Bergen more time to get situated with Lisbeth and Leo and back in school, having Bret around during the transition."

"And how is the other one?"

"Jack? He's looking at months of physical therapy to try to regain full use of his arm, they're still not completely sure what happened to it. He had to cancel the rest of his tour. He's having a much harder time bouncing back physically. Not only was he starving and dehydrated, but he was going through full alcohol and nicotine withdrawal. He's pretty hard-headed, though. I think he'll be alright."

Selah crossed her ankles. "And what of the handsome detective? Does he have you on speed dial now to help out on future cases, just like in a storybook?"

Fallon ran her fingers through her hair. "I sincerely hope not. And I doubt it. I don't trust him at all, but we're lucky that we got him on this case—someone who was willing to believe some of the crazy things I say."

"It's because you seem so serene and grounded," Selah explained. "You're stunningly easy to believe. Which helps with your whole task in life, I think."

"That it does."

"So, tell me." Selah was watching her with a strange new look. "How are things between you and Bret? Now that the horrible thing has passed."

Fallon's face turned cautious. "What do you mean?"

"I mean, I truly never imagined you'd be in love one day. Are you?" To be honest, Selah could not tell. She'd been puzzling over it lately, trying to figure out where Fallon's heart lay.

Fallon turned her wrist over and stared at the raven tattoo, which was tingling faintly, as it had been doing for several days, drawing her mind again and again to Jacob. "What is love, though, Selah, but a terrible weakness? 'One weakness is enough,'" she whispered, "'and love is the deadliest.'"

Tears stung Selah's eyes, and she fought with everything she had to hold them back so that Fallon would not see.

Fallon looked up, and Selah thought she looked tired. "He is in love with me."

"Very much so," Selah agreed.

Fallon's eyes went away for a moment, and she was quiet. "If I could walk away from him, from them, I would. I would do it today." She looked back at Selah. "But I can't. He has my heart. And so does she."

Selah turned the words over and over and tried to interpret what Fallon meant. "The loss of control makes you angry?" she guessed. "That they both have your heart, when you are so used to being alone?"

"That's not it. Well, maybe a little. Oh, but Selah, they are in danger being with me," Fallon suddenly snapped, leaning forward, surprising her friend. "There is so much darkness," she hit her fist to her sternum, "here. And all around. There is so much still to happen, so much to overcome, things I have no idea about. Selah, the war, it's only just beginning. I can't protect everyone; my focus has been spread too thin." Her eyes were glittering; Selah was spellbound in spite of herself. "But I will be ready. They will not expect the warrior I can become." She swept her hair away and showed Selah the new tattoo. Then she let her hair drop. "All this time they have believed they owned me. This cannot continue. I will not allow it."

Selah touched her finger to her lips and whispered something Fallon thought sounded like a prayer.

Back at the farm, Fallon parked under the shady oak tree and sat in the car with the radio playing. The top was down, the day blazing hot, and sweat beaded all around her torso and down her neck. A wasp buzzed around her a moment and then moved on.

Bret and Bergen were sitting on the front porch drinking fresh-squeezed lemonade and watching Azul furiously chase a deer fly that was bothering him. The other dogs were all sleeping in various shady spots in the yard.

As Fallon watched the two on the porch, she felt something growing inside. It was like strength, like daring, but also danger. There was a great change being wrought in herself, and also a fierce love for them, a desire to keep them safe and with each other at all costs.

She brought up her left hand and stared hard at the raven tattoo, unblinking, till her vision blurred and the raven's wings looked like they were in motion. She touched the tattoo with her index finger, rubbing a slow circle around the raven, concentrating. Her skin tingled with anticipation, the hairs on the back of her neck stood up.

"I need your help," she whispered, voice hoarse. "There's something I want to do. That I want to be able to guard against. You're the only one who can help me. I want to stop him from taking me against my will. I need you."

Under her touch, the raven began to glow with a phosphorescent light—her eyes widened a little when she saw it—only for a moment, and then all returned to normal. Her hands dropped to her lap, and she leaned her head back against the headrest, staring out through the dusty windshield.

Bret had been watching her, wondering why she didn't get out of the car. It looked as if she was watching them for the last time, as if she were about to drive away and out of their lives. He got to his feet and went over to her, opening the car door and holding out his hand. She hesitated for too long, but finally she took his hand and allowed him to pull her from the car and wrap her up in his arms.

"I love you," he told her. "Please don't leave us."

She shook her head. "I'm not going anywhere."

Later in the day, Fallon went for a walk with Bergen down by the pond, and Bret drove into town, ostensibly for wine. He headed straight to the Lowes' home. Selah was on the porch with Indio, and she waved to him.

He was speaking before he was even all the way up the steps. "The Quinns were not her real parents. Her real father, he's the one who steals her, at twenty, and now, while I was gone. What does this mean?" He stopped before her and narrowed his eyes. "And why are you not at all surprised when I say she was adopted? She didn't know."

Selah stood and beckoned him inside, sending Indio to his room to play. Off the wall, she took down a large framed black and white picture of Fallon holding a laughing ten-month-old Indio. She slid out the back, and removed a folded piece of paper.

"Luca left this for me. He had, at some point, attained an attorney and written a will—we don't know why. Maybe he knew he was going to die. All the money and property were already in Fallon's name alone, so Luca didn't have much to leave, but in his will, he left the Dart to her, and his lawyer sent this letter to me. Fallon doesn't know. I never told her. I didn't read it for a long time, and then when I did read it...I didn't know what to do with it. I knew I needed to keep the information close, that we might need it someday."

She sat down on the edge of the sofa and held the folded paper in her hands. Bret wanted to tear it from her fingers and read it, but he inhaled deeply instead.

"It doesn't say enough, that's the first thing about it, so don't get your hopes up. He could have given me so much more information. But he didn't." She opened it with care, as if afraid of losing what little details it held. "It says he learned some things from Jacob, before Jacob went away, but that he never told any of it to Fallon." She began to read:

To Selah, my second sister: if you are reading this, it means I'm gone from your lives. I ask please that you love Fallon always. She has suffered, and will most likely suffer more, but you have always been part of her strength. I wish I could protect her, but if this is in your hands, it means I can't. So only you remain, lovely one. Be patient with her.

There is something I wanted you to know, so that someone close to Fallon would have this information. When I was sixteen, I learned from Jacob that the Quinns were not mine and Fallon's real parents, and that we share only a father. Jacob refused to identify him (except to confirm that it wasn't Jacob). Fallon's mother's name is Carolina. She is not to be trusted under any circumstance. She wants to steal back the child that was stolen from her. She is a damaged woman and a great danger to my sister.

I also learned that Jacob was in Fallon's life till she was three years old. He was the one who stole her from her mother, to protect her, and brought her to me. Jacob's main purpose in life seems to be to protect my sister, and I can tell, maybe you've noticed, too, that he loves her very much. There is something between them, Jacob and Fallon, that I can't quite figure out. Maybe one day you will.

Selah looked at Bret. "Honestly. He could have written me pages and pages, but this is all I got. To say I was disappointed would be an enormous understatement. Though his assessment of Jacob is interesting."

"So, you've known for a long time that they were not her real parents."

Selah lifted her shoulders. "This letter sounds so unlike the Luca I knew, I've half-disbelieved it all this time. Can you see why I never told Fallon? It opens up so many questions, and answers none. I always told myself that if she ever called and said she'd just met this amazing woman named Carolina and was going to head off on a holiday with her, I would intervene. But what good would it have done, for me to tell her that the Quinns were not really her parents? They were dead and gone. I never felt Fallon needed more mysteries in her life. And the news that Jacob had always been in her life, unbeknownst to her... what good would that do? She was in such terrible pain after Jacob disappeared. Sharing that with her would only have torn her heart open even more. She never understood, I don't think, why he left her, and honestly, neither have I."

Bret felt the jealousy blooming in his chest.

She looked at the paper again, shaking her head. "Luca...he would have written me a novel if given the chance. He was always talking, talking. This is too brief, too concise. Too inadequate.

It begins rather well, and then it just ends. It riles me with its inadequacy, and he would have known that, and laughed himself silly. Then again, maybe this is the only information he ever got. Perhaps he was riled with its inadequacy himself." She refolded the letter and set it aside. "You know who I've needed all this time? Jacob. He was a man of answers."

Bret latched onto this. "I thought you didn't want to talk about him? I want to know more about him. Were you around him a lot?"

Clasping her hands together, Selah focused on some middle-distance between them. "For the first seven years that Fallon and I were friends, I was around Jacob quite a lot. He was more often a ghost in the background; he was never sitting at the dinner table with us sharing wild stories or anything like that. A mysterious figure. It was always so odd to me, so foreign, early on, when I thought about Fallon and Luca living in that house without any sort of loving parent, no mom, no dad. Because Jacob was surely none of those—he was not a parental figure to them, though he did often cook for them and ensure they had everything they needed. For sure, that arrangement instilled a sense of independence in those two.

"Jacob rarely showed emotion; I don't know that I ever saw him laugh or become angry, but he had always seemed to have a soft spot for Fallon. On the occasions he did smile—and it was a glorious smile—it was always because of her. And I could tell, in those final years he was with them, he and she were drawing closer and closer to each other. But I couldn't figure out in what way."

He frowned. "Like what? Romantic love?" His heart began to beat a little harder.

Selah remained thoughtful. "No. I just couldn't tell, and back then, she and I never discussed Jacob, I don't think I even ever tried; it was just a known forbidden topic. She was thirteen, fourteen, and absolutely stunning—no awkward teen years for her, even if she was mostly friendless. Jacob was incredibly handsome and mysteriously interesting. Mind you," she pointed a stern finger at him, "I could never tell which way they were headed, and I was around them a lot. She wasn't lying around in a bikini trying to catch his attention or anything crass like that. I don't think I ever once saw him touch her, not even a hug. Though really..." she seemed to consider something for the first time, "if I had to say...they seemed like...friends. Close, dear friends. Despite the difference in their ages. In that last year especially, Jacob was around the house more and more, and I swore they could communicate with just a glance."

Bret sat back, trying to rein in his emotions, mostly failing. "I wonder if that's why Jacob disappeared. If he and Fallon were becoming too close, either for his liking or for someone else's."

Selah nodded. "Exactly. Someone else's, I would imagine. I didn't get the feeling that he would have wanted to leave her. Towards the very end, I had the idea that he loved her greatly; I could see it in his eyes when he looked at her. But not in an inappropriate way. Just *love*. He cherished her. I don't think Luca realized the depth of it, though apparently, he had noticed something. I was always the quiet observer in that house, taking it all in."

* * * * * * *

Bergen and Fallon were throwing sticks into the pond for Azul. The sun was setting behind the trees, the steady buzz of cicadas rising up in the still warm air. Finally, the dog grew tired of swimming after sticks, and after shaking dramatically, he ran around on his own, chasing dragonflies. Bergen, in a white tank top and denim shorts, sat down by Fallon on the grass and pulled at a tiny purple flower blooming beside her.

"How are you doing?" Fallon asked the girl, who threw a loopy grin at her in response.

"I'm great!" She stuck out her tongue. "But Mom wants me to come home, and school starts soon, and I just want to stay with you and Dad."

"Ah, school." Fallon wriggled her toes in the grass. "Well, you do need to go to that. Get back to your friends. I'd be no good at homeschooling you, on a tour bus or otherwise."

Bergen leaned against her, and Fallon wrapped an arm around her. "Thanks for finding my dad."

Fallon bit her lip and looked up at the sky. "I'm not the one who dreamed about Kansas," she gently pointed out. Then she waited.

Bergen pressed against her a little harder. After a moment, she said, "So, what? It was like when you get a vision? A premonition? That's what I got?"

"I think similar, yes." Fallon leaned her cheek against Bergen's hair. "You were dreaming a premonition of him being held prisoner with Jack—for two years you dreamed this. And then you dreamed the clue we needed to find them."

Bergen sat up and looked at her. "Will I do it again?"

"I don't know." Fallon shrugged. "What if you do? Would that be okay?"

A smile was tugging at Bergen's mouth. "I can't believe that I might be magic like you."

Fallon smiled but held a finger to her lips. "Tell no one. Not even your parents, yet. Okay? It's kind of a big deal."

"No kidding." Bergen giggled self-consciously. "I promise."

"Whatever it is, I'll be here to help you work it out."

Bergen hugged her. "Always."

"Yes, Bee. Always." Fallon frowned briefly at an unsettling feeling that flitted through her heart like a shadow, and then was gone.

CHAPTER FIFTY-FIVE

Detective Josh Ashton saw the figure coming towards him across the empty warehouse and glanced at his watch. Right on time.

When the man was finally standing before him, Ashton tried to make out his features, but in the dim light and with the way the man was standing, he could barely make out even a profile. No matter. Ashton happily accepted the thick envelope of money that was handed to him.

"Well, I did everything just as you asked." Ashton sounded cocky as he sifted through the money in the moonlight that filtered unevenly through filthy panes of glass. "I got myself assigned to the case, I made contact with the girl, and I did everything she wanted me to. Which turned out alright in the end for her. I mean, because of me, she got her boyfriend back."

The warehouse smelled of dampness and rot, and was eerily silent. The faceless man said nothing but lit a cigarette. Ashton could make out dark hair, but little else.

"You, um, you need this back?" Ashton held up a dark crystal, about the size of a half dollar coin, peering at it in the shadowy light. "I guess it did what it was supposed to? She couldn't tell what I was thinking." Not that he believed a crystal was anything more than a crystal, and this one an ugly one at that. But for this amount of money, he'd done what he was told, and that had meant carrying the damn crystal in his pocket whenever he was around Fallon Quinn.

The other man held out his hand, and Ashton dropped the crystal onto his palm.

"So," Ashton continued, enjoying the weight of the envelope in his hand, "you don't have any personal attachment to that girl, right? I mean, you said you were doing this as a middleman for someone else?"

"That's correct," the man finally spoke. "I know nothing of the girl beyond what was relayed in my instructions to you."

Ashton looked smug and dangerous. "Good. Because I've never come across someone like her, and I don't intend to let her get away. I'm going to find out if she really can get 'visions,' and if she can, then I'm going to put her to good use. If it's all true, I could be a very rich man."

"How do you propose to get her to go along with what you want?" the unknown man asked casually, tapping ashes from his cigarette.

Ashton grinned an ugly grin. "Oh, I have a few things in mind. And more than a few uses for her, if you know what I'm saying. That girl is hot, have you seen her? She won't be saying 'no' to me; I can guarantee you that. Or if she does, she won't be saying it for long." He shrugged. "I'm used to getting what I want, you know? And Fallon Quinn is going to be mine in every way you can imagine."

Ashton didn't notice any sudden movement, but he felt the pressure on his chest as the dagger sank into his heart. A moment later, he dropped dead to the warehouse floor, alone, the envelope of cash still gripped in his hand.

EPILOGUE

A few months later, on a crisp November night, Bret and Fallon were sitting in comfortable silence, waiting inside a dimly lit, retro-styled hotel bar for Tayce to join them. Patsy Cline was playing on the jukebox. Bret was texting on his phone. Fallon, in a sweet little black and grey sleeveless vintage dress, sipped a cherry coke through a straw and went worlds away in her mind. They had flown out to Nashville to catch one of Dangerous Eye's shows before the restart of Bret's tour, and Tayce was supposedly heading downstairs to hang out with them in the bar beforehand.

Fallon was running through a number of items in her head. With new energy, she had been spending hours each day meditating to heal her tired mind, and then focusing on fine-tuning old abilities and figuring out new ones. But carefully this time, secure in the knowledge that for now, at least, everyone she loved was safe.

The house in Austin remained off the market. Fallon had thought that Bergen would never want to see it again because of the memory of the terror of the night when her father was taken, but it turned out that wasn't the case.

"We had so much fun in Austin," Bergen told Fallon and her father on the morning they were saying goodbye to her, having ensconced her securely with her mother and stepfather in California. "I can't wait to go back."

"There are some cool hotels in Austin we can stay at instead," Fallon offered.

"But I love that house." Bergen was frowning, a familiar stubborn look on her face. "You can't sell it."

Bret placed a hand on his daughter's shoulder. "It costs money to maintain a house that's not lived in. And having renters isn't always the easiest, either."

Bergen was staring hard at Fallon, who in turn tilted her head slightly, sensing something. "What is it?"

The girl quickly looked down, as if suddenly afraid to speak.

Don't say a word, Fallon warned Bret. She leaned down so that she and Bergen were face to face. "Did you dream about the house?"

Bergen looked at her and nodded.

"A good dream?"

"The three of us were there," Bergen explained. "We were so happy."

"Bee," said Bret, unable to hold back, "you're just dreaming about our visit that just happened."

But Bergen shook her head, eyes not leaving Fallon's. "No, I wasn't. Because in these dreams, you have a tattoo that you don't have yet."

Fallon didn't blink. "Show me where."

Bergen touched the inside of Fallon's right forearm.

Fallon straightened back up. "What's the tattoo of?"

Scrunching up her face, Bergen looked less happy. "A black scorpion."

Fallon ignored Bret as he slammed questions into her mind. Then she reached out and rubbed Bergen's arms. "I'll see about listing it as a short-term vacation rental." She looked at Bret. *You and I need to talk later.*

They had departed for Nashville mid-morning. After the plane was in the air, Fallon took Bret's hand, glad that they were in first class, affording them more privacy. She squeezed his hand tightly. "I need to tell you something about Bergen."

He looked at her soberly. "She loves you. She's fallen in love with you nearly as quickly as I did. Even Lisbeth talks about it."

"And I love her just as much." *I can sense her, like I can sense you.*

His forehead wrinkled a little. "Because you've gotten so close to her?" he asked cautiously.

"I can't sense Selah. Or Indio. The only person I've ever been able to sense, was Luca." Though back in August she'd noticed she could now sense Tayce. But she pushed that aside to deal with later.

Bret licked his lips. "Go on."

"Haven't you wondered how I was able to figure out that you were being held in Kansas?"

"I'm assuming through a vision. Isn't that what you told Ashton?"

"Do you remember when Bergen first began having the bad nightmares that made her need to see or speak to only you?"

He thought a moment. "She's had them for a couple of years, I guess. Lis and I assumed she was just going through a phase of having a hard time dealing with me being away."

"She's not going to have those particular dreams anymore. And her first nightmare was that night when you were in danger in Vegas. She was dreaming that bad dream at about the same time the vision hit me."

He was watching her closely. Tensely.

"She would never tell anyone what it was, but the nightmare was you, locked in a room, lying on the bare floor, crying and scared, dying. Sometimes she could see a dark-haired figure near you, but that person never moved. She's been dreaming this dream for two years."

Bret's stomach dropped.

"When I finally got her to tell me this, on the day of your rescue, I asked if she'd been dreaming anything else lately, anything at all." She touched his knee. "Wizard of Oz, for five straight days."

Bret blinked. "Kansas."

She nodded. "She didn't realize that any of it meant anything. I was immediately on the phone with Simon, who had an address for me in Kansas. I sent it to Ashton and begged him to send someone out there right away. And *voila*. You were saved. By your daughter."

"And by you. And by Simon. And by Ashton." His breathing had quickened. "Tell me what you're saying."

"She repeatedly dreamed a premonition of your fate, and then she dreamed the clue that saved you."

He rubbed his chin. "So, the Austin house, the scorpion tattoo..."

"Another vision. Meaning, I'm going to get taken again." The raven on her wrist flared with pain, then settled as she touched it gently.

Bret let out a long breath. "Does she realize what's going on?"

"She and I talked about it, while we were at the farm. Just a little. I told her not to bring it up to you and Lis quite yet."

"My God." He leaned forward, covering his face with his hands as he tried to take it all in. "Why does this scare me?"

"Because you want her to have a normal life. And you look at me and see how dysfunctional things have been. But that's me. Whatever things are in my life, the history, the people...that's my life. Her life has always been with you, safe, untouched. There's no hint that any of the chaos of my life will mirror hers."

"Hey, beautiful!"

They both glanced up at Tayce's enthusiastic greeting as the guitarist made his way over to them at the bar, smiling his usual smile.

"I was talking to Bret, but you're cute, too, princess," he quipped as he hugged Fallon tightly and kissed her cheek. He gave Bret a one-armed hug before sitting down with them on the other side of Fallon. He picked up her drink and sniffed it suspiciously, tasted it, then narrowed his eyes at her when he'd determined it was free of alcohol. "Honestly, my girl, have I been gone from you that long? It's only been a few months."

She gave him a languid smile. "I needed to slow down. The Tayce Williams Drinking Schedule was killing me."

Bret chuckled at her words, still texting.

Placing his elbows on the bar, Tayce leaned forward and looked back and forth between them. "So, here we all are, together again. Will it freak you out if Jack Lane walks into the bar?"

"That sounds like the beginning of a joke I don't want to hear," observed Bret, putting his phone down and reaching for his beer. "He's not really here, is he?"

Tayce shook his head, laughing. "Keeps talking about trailing around with us on the tour—docs still haven't cleared him to return to his own tour—but he hasn't materialized yet. Has he talked to you any more about his grand idea?"

Bret took a long swallow of his beer. "He has. I've stopped answering my phone."

With time on his hands, and a loathing of inaction, Jack had poured himself into organizing a world tour consisting of his own band, Bret's band, and Dangerous Eye, capitalizing on their recent media attention. Bret and Paul had paid no attention to him until Jack's team started getting immediate shows of interest from potential sponsors and venue locations globally. They already had a tentative line-up of venues that were interested and available. It was no longer something any of them could ignore. A world tour was something none of the guys wanted to pass up.

"Of course," Tayce warned, "I'm not agreeing to go anywhere until I can be sure our prophetic princess is coming along."

She grinned at him. "Like I could be pried away. You saw how starry-eyed I was at the farm when the three of you played for me."

"I wouldn't go without her, either," Bret agreed.

Fallon was smiling slyly. "I'll text Jack and tell him you're both in."

Tayce shook his head in despair. "She and Jack are in collusion. The end is near."

Slipping off the barstool, Fallon threw a kiss over her shoulder at him. "You know you want to go." She headed for the ladies' room as Tayce leaned over to talk with Bret.

The restrooms were located down a long, shadowy hallway papered with vintage posters and newspaper clippings giving a history of the hotel and its past musical glory days. On her way back to the bar area a few minutes later, she paused, glancing with interest at some of the stories. "I Fall to Pieces" was now playing in the main bar area, piped through speakers into the hallway. Her lips moved unconsciously as she softly sang along.

Then she caught a familiar scent in the air, and she felt as if all the blood was suddenly drained from her heart. She couldn't move; everything in her stilled but her breath.

For the first time in fifteen years, she was inhaling the smoke from an early-1900s Ramleh Turkish cigarette.

Acknowledgments

This has been an incredibly long journey, and so many people have supported me along the way. I've had a large and gracious group of readers over the past few years, too many to name, but please know that I am grateful to you all.

Special and fabulous thanks to my soul sister Jenn Mendez, for being right beside me at all times; for consulting, questioning, critiquing, supporting, and other craziness—I love you with all my heart and soul.

Big love and thanks to my husband and son for their unwavering support and willingness to put in as much time as needed to help me get this done. I could not have done this without you both.

Many thanks to Sylvia Bartles for being this story's first reader and first fan of this trilogy.

Thanks to Brandi Hyde for helping me get certain details correct.

Endless thanks to Casey Cease for assisting me in going after my big dreams.

NOTES

1. Bertolt Brecht, *The Good Person of Szechwan (Modern Classics)*, trans. John Willett (Methuen Drama, 2015).

ABOUT THE AUTHOR

Erika Fair was born and raised in Texas, where she lives with her husband and son. She graduated from The University of Texas at Austin, and stayed in Austin as long as she could. When she is not forcing her favorite music upon her family or writing, she can usually be found hiking or planning future travels. *The Secret Girl* is her first novel.